I0561817

A Light Chop in Protected Waters

A Novel

Calvin Jones

Callimachus Press

2023

This is a work of fiction. Any references to historical events, real people, or real places are used fictitiously. Other names, characters, places, and incidents are the product of the author's imagination. Any resemblance in the portrayals to actual persons, living or dead, business establishments, events, or locales is entirely coincidental.

A Light Chop in Protected Waters. Copyright © 2023 by Calvin Jones
All rights reserved.

Published by Callimachus Press, South Orange, NJ
callimachuspress@gmail.com

Printed in the United States of America and Distributed by Lulu Press, Inc., Research Triangle Park, NC

Library of Congress Control Number: 2023906557

ISBN 979-8-218-17167-4 (hardcover)
ISBN 979-8-218-21352-7 (paperback)

Jacket design by Sara Jones
Jacket photograph by Calvin Jones
Interior design by Calvin Jones

For Isabel Clare, who loves life

Contents

α
Prologue

Before there were seas or lands or the sky that covers all
Nature showed its face the same throughout the universe's orb,
That is to say, as chaos: a confused, unfashioned mass,
Nothing but inert weight and the seeds of things, poorly joined,
Warring in discord.
—Ovid, *The Metamorphoses*, Bk. I, 5–9

*U*TTER CALM, NO MOVEMENT BUT THE REGULAR, *rhythmic lapping of the little swells under the tropic sun, unheard because there are no ears for miles; a gradual warming of the waters to approach the temperature of the stifling, humid air, unfelt because the nearest bare skin is many leagues away; increasing evaporation, with moist air soon condensing into clouds above; a slight westerly movement of the winds, a drop in pressure, a practically imperceptible change, affected by and colluding with other alterations to tip the balance just enough; a concatenation of variables too numerous to measure, too seemingly irregular to serve as the basis for precise predictions; a slow but deliberate organizing, the birth of something out of the vast nothing of apparent sameness, a whirl, an eddy, the beginnings of scattered counterclockwise gusts; the gradual organization into a circular shape with silent, spiral feeder bands contracting around a spinning eye; at times fragile, liable to sudden dissipation at the slightest shear or transit over cooler seas, but ripe for development under prime conditions; then strengthening and thereby ascending the categorical scale of arbitrary numbers devised for it, following the laws of geoclimatic physics devised to describe such processes; gaining the specificity of a name; continuing westward on an inexorable and, to myriad distant observers nervously waiting on islands and mainlands, seemingly inevitable path; extracting the heat at its base, gobbling up the moisture into clouds that spin at a dizzying pace and obscure with their greying darkness the serenity of its center; a monstrous* *column growing ever higher as it pulls air and vapor into its feeder bands, which rotate lofty cumulonimbi over distant miles of land- and waterscape; the building force, many times that of the strong- est that humans can produce, carried along through wind and waves; attaining the form encountered by early explorers of "a dreadful storm and hideous, which swelling and roaring as it were by fits, beats all light from heaven, which like an hell of darkness turns black upon us;" rain bands that bring walls of water before the howling vortex, ready to toss large freighters to the highest peaks of waves before hurling them down into the abyss of the deepest troughs as panicked sailors struggle to keep them afloat; pushing on toward shorelines where everyone knows from the past what will happen; roaring up the beachfront in a surge which all hope will remain beneath the floor of the living quarters of flimsy cabins perched on stilts, but if hopes prove vain will slap them off and drive them inland to the spot where the waves at last lose force and spread out thinly, leaving piles of rubble in a cruel mockery of the plans of men and women and even of the extreme order of the laws of nature that brought this force to pass; the howling winds of the eyewall, shattering the glass of unboarded windows and exploding the house from within, "like matchsticks," in the oft- repeated parlance that attempts to convey the helplessness in the face of devastation; the hours of pounding force, broken only temporarily by the cruel, deceptive lull at the center of the eye, followed by the snap of gales from the opposite direction; and finally, much later, a weary winding down: the softer nervous swaying of remaining branches and the uncertain breezy rustlings that accompany the cautious outings to survey the damage from something that has happened before and will at some point occur again. . . .*

6

Then Odysseus awoke from sleep,
lying on the native soil from which he'd been away so long,
though he failed to recognize it, for round about him
the goddess Athena had cast a mist. . . .
Thus to him all things seemed strange. . .
*   "Tell me truly, so that I may know,*
what earth is this, what land, what manner of men
that in these parts do dwell?"
*   And then with gleaming eyes the goddess Athena answered:*
"Stranger, you must be a foolish child or come from far away,
if indeed you need to ask what land this is.
Truly, it is by no means nameless: many are the ones who
*   know it,*
both those in the east who face the rising sun at dawn,
and those who live in the west toward gloomy darkness."
*   —Homer,* The Odyssey, *Bk. 13, 187-90, 194, 231-41*

IT WAS SUPPOSED TO BE A HOMECOMING, a return to the familiar, a chance to reestablish what he had lost, to straighten out what had gone wrong or been put awry. But since his coming back, everything somehow seemed strange: it was as though his exile were taking a new turn in this place where he had once started out. He had rarely felt nostalgia during his many years away, so why should he long to feel any now? He had never been homesick (or so he told himself): whenever he had perceived in his mind the overpowering, ambrosial scent of sweet olive, or recalled the ocher-vermilion of the native red clay, or heard the deep, resonating horns of steamships pulling into port, he had never felt them as a clarion calling him to return. Unlike some others he was aware of, he had never carried around a vial of his native soil, so why should he long to dig his toes into it again? He shoved aside for the moment those doubts that he knew would have to be eventually resolved.

He paused a while in the seat of the rental car before making the effort to get out and enter the realtor's office, wedged into a row of businesses with plate-glass windows and nondescript stucco facades of indeterminate age in a part of town he didn't recall—it could be anywhere, he felt. But had he recognized anything at all since his return—what was there to discover?

Once inside the building, he was greeted by the friendly, extended hand of the garrulous agent.

"Well, if this isn't a surprise! I never expected to meet you in person after all these years of corresponding by snail mail—or is it decades already? Did some kind of magic bring you here? It seems like most people retire to Florida, or the excitement of the Big Easy, or maybe some exotic island. But why not come back home, I suppose?"

J.P. was again confronted with the question of whether he was indeed returning home or simply starting over in a new place, as he had done repeatedly during the long years of his career. Not only would he need to tell himself what he was doing, he would have to come up with answers to offer the persistently curious, to the extent that they deserved to know. He clasped and unclasped his fingers to gain time as he began putting something together that avoided the temptation to indulge in sarcasm, yet somehow his reply spilled over into verbosity instead.

"I never really expected to return either. But an unanticipated constellation aligned itself. Most notably, I managed to reconnect with my daughter, who as fate would have it, has ended up nearby. It is indeed almost magical, how all that came together. Then, there are a lot of conflicts from the past and worries about how to arrange the future that are mixed in as well. I suppose I didn't explain in my last letter—in any event, we needn't go into all that now."

But was this the right way to phrase it? Was his language too grandiloquent? he asked himself. He realized that he had talked to fewer and fewer people in recent years and wondered if he was beginning to sound like the books in which his nose was inveterately buried, or even to speak in a voice from another time.

"No, it doesn't matter. After all, I inherited your account when Jim Thigpen retired, and somehow you and I always managed to stay focused on cut-and-dried details—income and expenses, tax statements, repairs, information about new renters on the few occasions when that became necessary. Your last occupants were there for almost ten years—you're lucky they told me they wanted to move out shortly before you asked about returning."

"Yes, that was a stroke of fortune. Is the house in good shape?"

"I was there just yesterday. The old girl is showing the signs of age, but also the added grace. She lends dignity to the neighborhood, if I might throw in some realtor-speak. Fortunately, she hasn't yet reached the point of becoming a handy-man's delight. Everything seems to be working fine, no imminent repairs in sight. I guess all I need to do now is hand over the key."

J.P. looked more carefully at the middle-aged agent, who leaned back in his squeaky swivel chair, allowing his cautious burgundy tie and pin-striped shirt to sweep across the expanse of his belly. The chair, his clothing, his posture show that he has reached the status to which he has aspired. But can he be so easily summed up at a glance? Perhaps he's actually an enigma. J.P. supposed he should probably avoid easy typecasting, especially in this setting to which he had returned and which he was so quick to criticize. He noted that he himself had put on a tie that morning, along with a wrinkled, linen sport coat. There was really no reason to get dressed up for the simple task of picking up the key—just his old fastidiousness manifesting itself again. The realtor reached down to give his calf a leisurely rub, and J.P. wondered if that was an indication of the simplicity of life here: if you have an itch, you scratch it, problem solved. Perhaps in worrying about his own situation and how to resolve his conflicts he was creating a tempest in a teapot. The realtor certainly seems satisfied and at ease, he thought, and without any sign of malice toward anyone: people here don't seem to suffer in any big way, unlike in many of the places to which I was posted in my career; they can just complacently make their way through life, while all the time ignoring their petty self-indulgences, outright greed, exploitation of others, and virulent racism. Maybe that's how things will now proceed for me. J.P. realized, however, that the image of his hometown which he had been carrying around was a self-constructed agglomeration based largely on what he had suffered personally, along with what he had read in newspapers over the years. But wasn't a place always a blank to be filled in, a combination of ingredients that are constantly being assembled: geographical setting, numerically precise coordinates of longitude and latitude, delineation on a map, arbitrary name, acquired nicknames, climate, both meteorological and sociological, distinguishing landmarks, prominent events in history, symbolic depictions, personal experiences, and shared sentiments, all of which vary from person to person? His own image of the place had been formulated in part to counter the self-promoting myths of the local boosters: it would take him a while to get re-acclimated and find his footing. And, moreover, the formation of the community was ongoing: it needed to be improved, certainly, but what could he give back, contribute? Was it possible to orchestrate it?

"I'm looking forward to moving in and getting settled yet again. Have any boxes arrived?"

"A few. I put them inside the front door."

"Thanks. And I would also be much obliged if you don't mention to anyone that I'm back. You're too young to know anything of my history with my family, but I would prefer to ease back in slowly if possible. Just say there's another tenant, if anyone asks." He felt his irascibility once again coming to the fore, but was determined to keep it in check, at least in front of this man who had only been of service to him.

"Will do. Sounds like you plan to live as an ex-pat in your home town for a while. In limbo you might say. In any case, feel free to call me if there's anything I can do to help."

"I'm sure I can count on you. You've been of tremendous assistance, as were your predecessors over the years. By the way, has my brother Anthony ever inquired about the house?"

"Not to my knowledge. He has probably either forgotten about it or doesn't care. Our agency doesn't have much interaction with his firm anyway. We're rivals of a sort, but we're a rather small fish in the pond compared to them. At the Chamber of Commerce banquet he's usually up on the dais, while I'm at one of the tables in the rear."

"I plan to keep to the back row myself for a while. At any rate, I doubt that there are very few around who actually remember to whom the house belongs."

"Probably not. You'd be a stranger to most."

J.P. hoped to maintain that status, at least until he had hatched the plans he had yet to devise. His closest relatives had not seen him in almost forty years, and others in nearly half a century. His hair had in the meantime turned silver-white, and he had recently grown a full beard, which he tried to keep neatly trimmed, on those occasions when he remembered to take the time. He no longer wore the owlish eyeglasses of his youth, but had traded them for ones with thinner, more stylish frames. He doubted that Anthony would recognize him at first glance, not expecting him in this locality, though he realized he should be careful about the places he haunted if he wished to lie low: he still had his slender frame and his characteristic hurried, forward-leaning gait, always in eager pursuit of new knowledge.

• • •

He pocketed the house key and climbed back into the rental car, which he resolved to get rid of as soon as possible because of the expense. Searching for a practical, affordable vehicle would bring another time-consuming annoyance to the process of getting settled, although he told himself he should accept and master what came his way, rather than chafe at it. He would delay returning the rental car until after he had looked up his daughter, however. This event, which was foremost in his mind, he looked forward to with hopeful excitement, but also with trepidation: what would she think of him, and would she harbor any recriminations? How hard would it be to reforge the bonds that had been broken?

He followed Old Shell Road to the west, first passing under the dirty, dreary concrete swath of interstate that had not existed when he was last in town. He then headed up the hill amid a greener stretch of live oaks, whose ponderous, serpentine branches provided a welcome respite of shade for the asphalt underneath. The older frame houses on either side brought a sense of familiarity: many were painted in the traditional white with shutters the deep color of magnolia leaves, though a few were decorated with brighter, pastel shades or sported doors of bold crimson. Nearing the crest he turned right and began looking for the old house that was to become his new home, but the steady growth of some of the trees and the loss of others to hurricanes and age, as well as the presence of new constructions among the old on what had formerly been vacant lots contributed to a sense of confusion. He soon realized he had pulled off too soon and began looking for an opportunity to turn around. But when in his life had he ever taken the right path the first time? He began to read the street signs more carefully and, after some driving and backtracking, eventually made it to his destination on Bienville Lane. A good city, he freely translated: if only it were.

The handsome, 1½-story Creole cottage, with its high-gabled roof extending over the full front porch, sat farther back from the street than the others on the block, and its irregular lot was larger than most. A row of azalea bushes, eight feet tall and prolifically extending their foliage in broad circumference, lined the yard next to the street, partially blocking the view of the residence while offering tantalizing gaps. A southern Indian hybrid, *rhododendron indica, elegans superba, 'Pride of Mobile'*: the favored cultivar of stately mansions, suburban ranch houses, and mobile homes throughout the South, the bushes were overflowing with buds that were just beginning to open into luminescent, rose-pink flowers. A slight breeze kicked in, and the blooms began to move as if autonomously animate, in a graceful, elegantly choreographed dance.

The tires crunched on the bleached, crushed oyster shells as J.P. pulled into the driveway and stopped at the front steps. A wrought-iron chair which had been set out in the front yard appeared to be waiting for him. How comfortable can that be? he wondered. Along the side of the yard stood the evergreen camellia bushes, flowerless at the moment and awaiting their turn in the next winter, when they would silently burst into blossoms of ivory, ruby, and blush pink. Soon the magnolia tree by the driveway would be adding its overwhelming redolence to the profusion of the garden, a fragrance that one might employ unadulterated as a perfume fit for the most beautiful and alluring of women. Now he remembered why people lulled themselves into staying here, sinking into the subtropical luxuriance, deadened by the stifling humidity. He knew he would have to exercise caution lest he himself fall into the arms of the cliché: if he wasn't careful, he'd soon be longing to gaze at the blossoms in the moonlight. Home? He would have to be the one to make it that.

When he entered the house, he was greeted by the stale, musty odor of emptiness and mildew; light streamed through the windows and hit the hardwood floors in rectangular, mullion-shadowed patterns. He wandered through the vacated rooms and thought: it's more than I need, but it will certainly do. But how should I furnish it? With what I've collected and made of my life so far, or should I try to complete it with something new? First, though, I'll need a bed, and a desk, and a chair—I'll bet Aunt Clotilde has some she could part with. And bookcases, lots of bookcases—that's what's most important of all.

But then his thoughts moved in other directions, and he wondered if it would have been more fitting if he had returned a month sooner and made a dramatic entrance on Shrove Tuesday to reclaim what had been taken away from him. Or a day later, on Ash Wednesday, when all the foolishness was over and everyone was supposed to be focused on atonement. But what did he have to repent? His long-held conviction whispered that it was someone else who should make amends. In any event, he decided that rather than participating in misrule and chaos, it would be more suitable to devise more careful plans. Now that he had a daughter again, he felt an additional compulsion to regain his rightful place for her sake, so that she could have what she deserved. Or should he give up those notions altogether, and simply cultivate his classical garden?

Y

Quis hic locus, quae regio, quae mundi plaga?
[What place is this, what region, what shore of the world?]
—Seneca, *Hercules Furens*, Act V, l. 113

THE TWO OF THEM STOOD IN THE SAND behind the jumbled, granite boulders that formed a breakwater along the island's southern coast; they looked out across the expanse of greenish grey to the carmine sun, setting on their right. Did it betoken sailor's delight, he wondered, in contrast to the red sky of morning, which would augur *"Wreck to the seaman, tempest to the field?"* They could just glimpse the old brick lighthouse three miles out from shore and wonder when it might once again start sending out its recurring, guiding beacon. Occasional breezy gusts of salt air made them grateful for their light jackets. *Ubi sum?* he wondered, trying to situate himself.

"We could be tourists in this picture-postcard setting," J.P. said. "Just passing through."

"Maybe," replied Miranda. After a pause, she continued, "Does it really matter where you happen to be at a given moment? Isn't there always something new to discover and appreciate?"

The wiry, older man looked at his daughter in renewed esteem for what she was, and what he was confident she would continue to become. She still had the same driving curiosity that she had displayed in her earliest days: her vibrant blue eyes were taking it all in. She had her mother's high cheekbones, chestnut curls, and long legs: it was fortunate that she inherited her looks from the maternal side, thought J.P. Above all, as with her mother, her inner beauty shone through in the spark of her eyes. He noticed in the illumination of sunlight hitting her face that she still had a soft down on her cheeks, a remnant of what he had known so briefly when she was an infant. But of course it was no longer exactly the same: she had changed in ways he had yet to learn about. He resolved to be careful in this first, tentative opportunity for re-acquaintance: he did not want to spoil the relationship at the outset.

She must be cool in those shorts, he surmised, but maybe not, given her adventuresome spirit that seems to know how to adapt to any condition. Not yet a quarter of a century old, she looked the picture of youth, whereas he, he felt, must seem like a doddering old man with his silvery, thinning hair and increasingly hunched back, looking like some grizzled, bearded sage of the seashore. But how wise was he, as opposed to senile: he saw that his beige, twill trousers had a smear of dirt on the shins that he had not noticed when he put them on. The century was nearing its close, and he had already passed his three score years and ten: about the same span of time that Xenophanes, one of his beloved classic poets, had spent in exile, *"tossing my fidgety mind hither and yon in the land of Greece . . .if my calculations are correct."* J.P., shivering slightly, was again glad he had brought his navy-blue windbreaker, which had served him so well in so many countries.

The sound of little waves, lightly splashing against the rocks of the breakwater, lent a peaceful rhythm to their musings and filled the gaps in their conversation, which they were not always sure they knew how to advance. The incessant murmuring of the water was punctuated from time to time by the raucous cries of gulls, which, because of the direction of the wind, seemed farther away than they actually were, while scintillating droplets of sunlight turned the quivering plane of the Gulf into dappled velvet. A red sign with a dire depiction of a swimmer in distress warned of dangerous currents; a lone angler ignored them as he balanced precariously on the slanting surfaces of the boulders and even stepped at times into the water to pursue his prey. J.P.'s darting brown eyes took in all the details of the sights along the shore with the same perceptiveness and attention that he devoted to texts; he glanced over at his daughter and noticed that she seemed equally observant.

"I feel like Pericles, in the famous drama, separated from his infant daughter Marina, who was born at sea in a storm, where her mother was also thought to have died. He gave the baby into the care of others, but in the end was reunited with her as a young woman. I can't imagine a more dramatic event than the almost identical one that has now occurred in my own life. Do you know the play?"

"I know Eliot's poem," she replied. "In one of my college English classes the professor made us all memorize at least one piece of poetry to help us really get to know it. After quoting a Latin line from Seneca's *Hercules* the poem begins:"

> *What seas what shores what grey rocks and what islands*
> *What water lapping the bow*
> *And scent of pine and the woodthrush singing through the fog*
> *What images return*
> *O my daughter.*

"Amazing! It's like where we are now. You seem to know a lot about a lot of things. What more could a father want? I'm eager to hear all about your work. What you have chosen to do is fascinating to me—such an unusual combination of fields," said J.P.

She hesitated a moment, as if trying to fathom this older man and his remarks. "Unusual, maybe, but to me it's the only one that makes sense. Do you know how totally different chemical elements can hold a natural attraction for each other and combine to form an entirely new compound? Elective affinities they used to call it."

The old man smiled in recognition and fond recollection. "Yes, I know. Science and art, art and political action, matter and spirit, fact and fiction, or poetry: they have more in common than most realize. As do seemingly different people as well. If they are able to realize it." He wondered whether the two of them would make the proper connection.

"I'll enjoy showing you around. But you've certainly got a lot to tell me too. The couple of letters we've exchanged have only scratched the surface. It's all been so unexpected: it's stunning. I can't wait to hear everything. I have so many unanswered questions."

She looked down a moment at the rising and retreating water.

What is she thinking? he wondered. Does she find this sudden new acquaintance disquieting, or a blessing? Her words sound positive, but is there some underlying accusation? She certainly has a lot she could blame me for. Do her eyes display openness, or harbor a lingering skepticism?

A slight wrinkling in her brow conveyed a determined seriousness as she continued. "I need to find out more about who I am, about my parentage—how and why exactly we became separated in the first place. You've been so reticent about your background, but now that I'm here of all places, I'm especially curious. And my mother—you need to really tell me about her. I feel like I don't know her at all. I always found that the rosy picture her parents painted was incomplete. And you of course: they somehow always avoided mentioning you. Was there a reason?"

They walked slowly back to the barracks of the sea lab where Miranda lived and worked. On the way they passed the weathered brick walls of the old fort that guarded the entrance to the bay: a large black cannon pointed silently from the ramparts at a nonexistent enemy. A similar nineteenth-century fortification, its counterpart, stood watch at the tip of land on the other side. Admiral Farragut had once stormed his way through there to the roar of guns and torpedoes in the midst of a fratricidal struggle. Although it was quite peaceful at the moment, J.P. was apprehensive that another big blow could be coming. No storm appeared to be brewing at the moment, however; no dark clouds had of yet breached the horizon.

At the door to her building Miranda paused to remove her sandals and shake them out before placing them on two short, upward-pointing branches of the posts installed on either side of the entrance. Shoes of every type and color that were already hanging there gave them the appearance of bottle trees.

"To keep out the evil spirits as well as the sand?" asked J.P.

"It's only partially successful," she replied.

They walked down the hall and entered her room.

"Well, here's where I live," she said. It was a fairly large but simple affair showing the wear and age of what had originally been an Air Force radar installation decades before. Numerous drawings and photographs were pinned to the walls, and though the desk was covered with all sorts of materials, the room had a neat and cozy feel. "I think I'll change into long pants before we go eat," she said. "But before we go to the restaurant I want to show you my lab-slash-studio."

"I'll wait outside," said her father.

The lab/studio was in another building: large and well-lit with north-facing windows, latticed shutters, and a functional concrete floor. A tall counter with a sink at one end and a massive microscope at the other extended the length of one wall. Before another was a drafting table containing a sketch in progress. On a table next to it were jars of brushes, tubes of paint, palettes, and boxes of pencils. Taped to the wall were several large, bright watercolor drawings of magnified plankton, diatoms, radiolarians, algae, and fish: in one a swerving shark seemed almost capable of actually biting with its sharp teeth.

"This is what I do. I couldn't have asked for a better job."

She let him look through the microscope at slides of creatures she had collected, and pointed out that she had noticed differences in what had previously been believed to be one species. "It may get incorporated into an article," she said proudly.

Her close observations of various flora and fauna also led to the drawings that she was making: as she explained, cameras and digital technology had not yet advanced to the point of being able to surpass artistic renderings in conveying certain features, nor in her opinion, expressing the full beauty of these living beings.

"They're not just collections of data, although we have to accurately observe and understand every fact about them and render them to scale. But they also exist in how we comprehend and appreciate them. In any event, everything's connected. I discover new relationships all the time: I've even started trying to use materials from nature to make my own colors."

J.P. gave a contented smile, pleased that his daughter already knew what had taken him so long to learn and displayed an inventiveness that he still had to bring to fruition. And in delight at her articulate speech, that came out so naturally in contrast to his ofttimes belabored attempts, even when she got more technical in talking about her work.

Miranda had talked her oceanography professors at Scripps into letting her incorporate her other true love, painting, into her master's degree, and she had just recently found a first job down on the nation's third coast in which she could use them both.

"You seem to gain great satisfaction from your artwork," said her father, peering more closely at a lacy, radially symmetrical orb with projecting spiny rhizopodia in vibrant cadmium yellow and alabaster—a mandala, a geometrical perfection with just enough irregularity to characterize it as a unique individual. The picture radiated harmony and exactitude. "The paintings don't just give these phenomena their due, they are creations themselves, which, starting from the world, throw something new back into the world and challenge the observer."

"Wow. You seem to notice more than most people, who don't pay much attention to the visual art around them and take it for granted as just another wall decoration. I get lost in the process of painting. It's like paying me for doing what I would do anyway. But the other stuff I like too. I get to take part in research trips and explore new things. In late summer I'll be going on the lab's research vessel, the *Cosmos,* all the way to Belize and back. We'll be comparing different ecosystems at different depths from around the Gulf and Caribbean."

"Any chance they'd like to take on an old man as crew?"

"I'll check," she smiled. "Maybe you could clean my brushes or prepare my slides."

"It's amazing what you do—almost as though you invented it."

"Hardly," she said, waving the palm of her left hand down dismissively. "There've been lots of others—Maria Sybilla Merian, Georg Forster, Frederick Pursh, Martin Johnson Heade, Ernst Haeckel, Dorothy Sturm, to name a few. Maybe you've heard of them."

Some of the names rang a bell with her father, but he realized there were whole new realms he still had to explore in more detail. He had spent a lifetime studying, but was now discovering that he could learn from his child.

"What do they do with your pictures?" he asked, gazing up at her inquisitively.

"All sorts of things. Put them in scientific publications, since you can provide more contrast, resolution, and detail than in photographs, and we also use them in the educational programs for people of all ages. That's an important part of our mission here: summer camps, school field trips, lectures. And they've already put some on display in the museum-aquarium across the street that opened just last year. Come back tomorrow when it's open. You can tour it on your own if I'm working. I love watching the excitement of school-children when they see it for the first time."

Or of an old man, he thought. "Thanks, I can't wait."

The restaurant was farther down the island, near the public beach; as they drove west, J.P. kept his eyes open to see if he could spot any sights he might recognize after forty-some lapsed years. He remembered the dense forest of the bird sanctuary, bounded on the east side by Audubon Street (another artist-naturalist, he noted); the names of subsequent cross streets continued in ascending alphabetical order. Most of the houses were typical island or beach homes—little cottages of wood or cinder blocks with screened-in porches which had presumably survived the many hurricanes that periodically crossed or grazed the barrier island. No doubt many others that he had seen in his earlier lifetime had meanwhile been destroyed or unrecognizably renovated. A few larger, gleaming structures on massive creosoted piles with hipped roofs and wrap-around porches were recent products of the wealth that the upper classes had seized by storm. The median of the road was dotted with palms, showy crepe myrtles, and pines; nearer the intersection with the road that led to the bridge to the mainland small pink and aqua shops on stilts had air mattresses and beach towels waving from their porch railings. The little frame schoolhouse, painted a dark, brick red, provided a connection to his past memory, but who knows how many times it might have been rebuilt in the intervening years. Would that make it the same or different? He recalled from his student days the paradox of the ship of Theseus, which had been restored a plank at a time until it no longer had any of the original wood.

They pulled into the parking lot of the restaurant on the sound side of the road and went inside: it was an older concrete-block structure with small windows and dark paneling.

"There's a newer one with big glass windows, a deck, and a carpet that doesn't smell dank, but they try too hard to be trendy with their menus. This place has been here for a long time, and I like the food better. Not that I get over here that much. Usually I make myself a sandwich or eat in the cafeteria."

There was a step up to the front door which he hadn't seen, and he stumbled slightly. Miranda reached over and grabbed his arm, and he felt a sudden thrill through the surface of the skin that separated him from, and connected him to, the world around him. Aside from routine handshakes or an occasional slap on the back, he had rarely felt the touch of another human being over the last couple of decades. He hoped that this was a harbinger of a deeper, more spiritual bond.

After looking over the menu, J.P. ordered the fried shrimp and oyster platter and wasn't disappointed. The seafood was fresh, caught just that day, and J.P. realized he had not had shrimp like that since his trips home from college. He savored every bit of the evanescent flavor, the delicate texture, and the maze of scarlet lines across the snow-white flesh. He relished the hush puppies too, which he had not encountered anywhere else in the world. He realized that the Tabasco sauce with which he spiced his dish was now to be found on the restaurant tables of almost every country, but he couldn't decide if that was good or bad. As he enjoyed the food, his mind wandered to other things.

"What are you thinking about?" Miranda wondered, as she set down her glass of iced tea.

"The name of the island. It was named for the heir to the throne, Louis Quatorze's successor. How appropriate that is. I guess I am in fact right at home here."

"Appropriate? You certainly are enigmatic. I've started showing you what I do, but you still haven't answered my questions." Her voice took on a more impatient tone. "I still want to know: Who am I? Who are you? What was my mother really like? Why don't you get along with your family? Can you tell me?"

"I will. It's high time. I guess I should start at the beginning. But I'm not sure what that is. My own birth? Or my father's or grandfather's, or other ancestors', since they are also who I am. Or the city's and the country's birth in the eighteenth century, since the whole society makes us who we are as well. And what they claimed to be or actually were? And if I told you everything about my life, wouldn't that take another lifetime? Going back in time can seem like stepping into a dark abyss. In any event, for it to make sense, the whole context needs to be considered. It takes time to tell the truth, and it's not the truth if it's shortchanged. It'll certainly take longer than a single sitting. Let me ponder it and put it together, and I'll try to relate it to you in coherent fashion next time we meet. I promise. You'll have to promise me though, you won't let on yet who I am or that I'm back in town."

She looked at him quizzically for a moment before responding. "Sounds like you're making excuses. But okay. It's a deal. I won't let on to anyone for now."

Was he delaying his narrative because of the reasons he stated, or because it was hard for him to confront and justify the decisions he had made in his life? In any case he knew that he must tell her the truth, but whatever he told her, she would eventually have to piece her lineage together for herself. Though the earlier poet she quoted had put into words an inkling of a similar situation, he would have to express theirs in his own way.

> *This form, this face, this life*
> *Living to live in a world of time beyond me; let me*
> *Resign my life for this life, my speech for that unspoken,*
> *The awakened, lips parted, the hope, the new ships.*

δ

Sails flashing to the wind like weapons,
sharks following the moans the fever and the dying;
horror the corposant and compass rose.

Middle Passage:
voyage through death
to life upon these shores. . . .
—Robert Hayden, "Middle Passage"

I SPENT MY EARLIEST CHILDHOOD, he would tell Miranda, *in the old family home in the Garden District and later in the one my parents built in the 1940s in the new suburbs to the west. The old place seemed pleasant, even idyllic, both at the time and in retrospect, although I was aware back then, as well as now, when I examine it more closely, that there were certain, mmm, insufficiencies, certain frictions or hindrances, stemming perhaps from the way I was, but more likely from the way the family was, not to mention the whole world they lived in.*

The house, set back far from the street, stood half hidden in the shade of massive live oaks, whose meandering limbs scrawled arbitrary patterns according to their own unfathomed logic. Large and rambling and built in the 1850s, it had two stories, with tall windows and dark-green shutters which actually functioned, if anyone ever bothered to operate them. No doubt they had held off many a wind in their day. After his long absence, J.P. found that the old homestead looked much as it always had. Despite a scarcely perceptible settling of the structure on its piers, or the chalking and flaking of the brittle lead paint that became more evident as he approached up the walk, it was the same place where he had happily spent many days and where his father had lived as a child before him.

Back then little metal automobiles with solid rubber tires would race across the boards of the broad verandah extending the length of the house and sometimes crash over the edge into the ivy below, providing a further delight to the excited children, who could play for hours and ignore the sweat of humid summer days until called inside for a glass of iced lemonade.

The commodious wicker chairs, sagging asymmetrically on their own beneath years of the weight of countless loungers, sat poised in a semi-circle to accommodate yet more reminiscing.

"Did you see the iris in Delilah's garden? I believe she outdid herself this year. I swear, mine look like pitiful weeds in comparison. If anybody has a green thumb, she does."

"That may be, but her cheese straws don't hold a candle to yours. She may have a way with plants, but she's helpless in the kitchen."

The grey, uneven flooring creaked underfoot, and nailheads stuck out at random intervals. Were these boards, which had been joined to form a venerable house in the pleasant Garden District, what made a home? Although he had once shared in place and time within those walls a life with immediate family, somehow the connections that should have bound them in affection were never fully cultivated; most of his relatives were now long dead, and the closest to him by blood who still remained was in his mind in the camp of the enemy. In the meantime of his years he had tried instead to make his home in numerous places throughout the world: running away, or deepening his knowledge and experience? In any event, he had not returned to this house to indulge pleasant memories, real or imagined, but to see the one relative who had remained steadfast and to whom he still felt closest: to find his place, to pick up and start anew.

J.P. pushed the black button next to the screen door and listened to the insistent, high-pitched ringing of the old electric bell that he had not thought about in years. After waiting a considerable amount of time, he was about to press it again when he heard slow footsteps coming from the back of the entrance hall. Through the sidelights he saw the outline of an approaching figure in a long dress, and the door was thrown open to reveal his Aunt Clotilde, who greeted him with a wide smile and open arms.

"John Prosper! I can't believe you're finally back! Come in and give me a hug! Step back and let me look at you," she called out in contradictory imperatives. After the embrace, she kept one arm at the small of his back, ushering him into the high-ceilinged parlor. "Just sit down and make yourself at home. It is your home too, you know. My, my! It was a shock to see an old man standing at my door just now, but you know, I would have recognized you anywhere—same old expression, same bearing despite the beard. It makes you look like an ancestor, though I'll bet you haven't changed a bit otherwise. What can I offer you? Coffee? Tea? I suppose it's too early in the day for something stronger, though I doubt your father would have refused, bless his soul."

"I'm up to here in coffee. I drank several cups while trying to wake up and get used to the idea that I'm actually back. If that's the right word. I might have a cup of your tea, though. That always tasted so good, as I recall."

"Mary Merritt! Come on down and look who's here," Clotilde yelled up the stairs as she headed back to the kitchen to fetch the tea.

Mary Merritt Hollinger, neé Devaux, a widow, had moved in with her older, unmarried cousin when her husband had died some fifteen years earlier.

"What? Who?" came the reply, but it wasn't until much later that J.P. would hear a slow shuffling on the stairs.

J.P. reflected on his renewed impression of Aunt Clotilde, whom he would have also recognized in a heartbeat. Still standing erect despite her advanced age, she retained her fine features and piercing, sparkling eyes. Her silver hair endowed her with nobility, although the brittle skin stretching over her diminutive frame now looked like parchment on which one could record the trials and triumphs of the century. The thinness of her arms made them appear as fragile as wishbones, though J.P. knew she possessed a wiry strength that enabled her to withstand almost anything, just as her eyes, somewhat clouded now with cataracts, discerned practically all that passed before them. She was wearing earrings and a handsome, indigo dress of fine fabric with lace collar. Anyone else might have wondered why she was so dressed up at home of a morning, but J.P. knew she was not trying to impress or put on airs, since she could give a damn about what others thought: she was merely wearing what she found fitting.

While he was waiting, J.P. stood up and looked around the room at the Victorian furniture and various objects set out for display on the tables, shelves, and ornate mantelpiece. Perched atop the latter was the brass tray he had bought for his aunt years ago in Beirut. He walked across the worn, intertwining flora of the deep red Tabriz toward the bookcases in order to peer at the titles behind the glass. He recognized many familiar volumes over which he had spent hours, some of which had belonged to his father and grandfather and even more distant ancestors: Grimshawe's *England,* Humboldt's *New Spain,* Murphy's *Tacitus,* Kenneth's *Roman Antiquities,* Homer's *Odyssey, Beauties of Shakespeare, Joseph Andrews, Peregrine Pickle, Ivanhoe,* Wordsworth's *Lyrical Ballads, Great Expectations, Tom Swift, The Grapes of Wrath.* These pages did indeed exist, he assured himself, and were somehow part of his makeup, even though many of his relatives seemed to have let them pass by unnoticed. He hoped that his own books, the boxes that he had left here long ago, were still stored upstairs in the large attic, along with many that he had shipped back in the intervening years. He wondered whether his father's illustrated editions with lithographs of duck hunting were still around. Interspersed on the shelves were glass figurines purchased on long-ago trips and a number of war relics—leaden Minié balls and rusting cannon shells dug up by some ancestor not long after the Battle of Blakeley.

How often had he as a child sat in one of those wicker chairs on the porch, eagerly reading one of the big books he had grabbed from the shelves in the living room—exploring the world through Richard Halliburton's *Book of Marvels,* for example. But when others would sit in nearby chairs or approach the house in avid conversation, he would closely observe and listen to what they said and did. They, however, usually had other ideas about how he should be spending his time.

"John Prosper! Stop reading those novels. Go work on your math. You'll need it later."

"John Prosper! Get out here! We need a right fielder."

He recalled that at the time he felt that the knowledge he had acquired entitled him to correct even adults:

"John Prosper! Don't forget to put up your wheel before you come into supper."

"Grandmother, we call them 'bicycles' now!"

Sometimes voices from outside found their way into the family's little world. Men walking down the street in the summertime with baskets on their heads would cry out an invitation to buy in a low-pitched, lilting *"Cante-loooooooooupe!"* A pleasant image, but what had that man been forced to endure in his life?

He recalled not only the voices, but the perceptions from the other senses as well: that certain light, unique to the time and place, which he had observed nowhere else; the all-surrounding warmth and humidity; the sweet smell of snuff that the maid dipped and the fresh smell of her starched apron; the sound of the wooden beater hitting against the sides of a stoneware bowl; and the sweetness of the lucid globe of nectar, withdrawn on its stamen from a pale-yellow honeysuckle flower and savored on the tongue.

Even then, however, J.P. had a vague notion that he wanted to pull away from the familiar, the secure, because he could feel its constraints, its limitations.

With both arms Clotilde carried in a silver tray loaded down with a dainty Limoges teapot, matching creamer and sugar bowl, cups and saucers, and a plate with slices of her famous pound cake.

"I always loved spending time in this house, and I'm so glad you're still here," J.P. said as she handed him a cup. "The house our family moved into when I was young was fine, but it always seemed there was something lacking."

"Yes, your father took a notion in the late '30s already to build a 'modern' brick house in the newest subdivision. He never wanted to be left behind the times. Always active, dabbling, developing, constructing—that was his way. You know he was planning to build an even bigger house farther out before he died. Which Anthony eventually did. And young Anthony—it wouldn't surprise me if he built out near the Mississippi line before long. Speaking of family—let me show you something I'll bet you've never seen before. Bertha found it recently when taking all the books from the shelves

to dust behind them. It was in a box along with some other things
that had been stuck in the back."

She stood up to fetch a small journal with a worn, marbled cover,
which she held out to him. "Your great-great aunt Volumnia made
this book with plants she collected on her travels."

J.P. opened it to read the word "Relics" inscribed in brown ink in
a neat, nineteenth-century hand on the first page. Small globs of
shiny red wax held pressed flowers and leaves affixed to subsequent
pages and the same brown ink noted where they had been collected:
faded yellow blossoms from the Luxembourg Gardens in Paris, a bit
of cedar from the tomb of Molière in Père Lachaise, heather from the
Highlands, a sprig from a small shrub at the grave of Robert Burns
along with a quote, a leaf from a tree along Queen Victoria's coronation route, some foliage from beside the cathedral of Charlemagne in
Aachen, ivy from Jefferson's chamber window at Monticello, a pansy
from the grave of her infant brother. Once living plants, now faded
but springing from the page while maintaining their link to the past:
unmediated instances of botany, with links to history, current events,
literature, and family. The connections to all were revealed to J.P.
through his eyes and fingers. It was a book of a kind he rarely
encountered: "This is truly remarkable," he said.

They continued their conversations as they sipped their tea and
simply enjoyed being in each other's company.

"I was so glad when you wrote me that you were coming back.
Even though you've been away for—what is it, forty, fifty years? I
never could get used to your being gone. I still can't believe you could
spend all that time overseas and not even pop in here once, not even
when you were assigned to Washington. I want to hear all about it
though. The one time I saw you on my trip to Europe was too brief
and too long ago. Tell me, what ever made you finally decide to
return?"

He was still wrestling with the answer to that question himself
and began putting together a response, more precise than the one
given to the rental agent, which he would also be able to pull out for
subsequent queries: the opportunity to retire, having done all one
could over there, and Miranda's decision to pursue her career here,
at least for now. He didn't know whether he should mention the

gnawing urge to attempt to set things right with Anthony, which formed a principal motivation. He added, however, that he appreciated his aunt's not telling his brother about his return just yet—he would do it himself eventually, when the time was right.

"Don't you worry, I won't breathe a word. I don't expect I'll see him before Christmas anyway. I'm not high on his list of priorities."

J.P. then asked how she thought Anthony might take the news if he did hear.

"He would probably just shrug his shoulders and say, 'I reckon he can do what he wants.' I doubt that he will bother you if you don't bother him."

"You're probably optimistic, but we'll see. There are so many unresolved issues."

The sun had risen above the trees on the eastern side of the house, illuminating the designs in the carpet at his feet and heightening the vermilion and peacock blue. Encircling colors were what he remembered from his childhood, and he wondered whether their fervor or patterns could be brought back with the same intensity.

In the pause Clotilde asked, "What are your plans?"

"I haven't really made any yet. Get my things in order. See what the possibilities are."

"John Prosper, you don't have to be vague with me. If you had plans, I certainly wouldn't tell Anthony. Don't you think I can see what he's about? Always have seen through him. It's no different now: he's got some scheme going that he didn't think up himself that he claims will double his share in the market. Him and that boy of his—a chip off the old block if ever I saw one. Not quite as bright though. Ten percent is the most they're likely to get out of their conniving if you ask me."

"Do you still attend board meetings?"

"Ha! Lot of good it does. I go occasionally, but I mostly let Thomas Gonzalez keep me informed. At least you can still trust him. Be glad you're not into any of that. It's a good thing your talents and interests lie elsewhere and that you got out of here when you could."

"It wasn't entirely my choice, if you recall."

"Maybe not, but I think you had a great deal to do with it, and little sense of regret."

"Maybe so. In all the years, you're the only one who understood, and the only one I felt I could keep contact with." He knew, however, that she didn't realize how strongly his anger still festered beneath the surface, though it had never erupted full force.

At length Mary Merritt trudged in in her slippers, looking around the room to get her bearings.

"Mary Merritt, you remember your cousin, John Prosper."

"Who?" she asked with a blank look.

"John Prosper, my brother's son."

"I used to push little Johnny on the swing," she replied as it gradually seemed to dawn on her.

"She probably thinks the little boy will pull her out to the swing to play now, poor thing," Clotilde whispered softly. "Sit down, Mary Merritt, and have a cup of tea with us."

J.P. in many ways still felt no different from that same little boy, though he had come quite a ways, and doubtless still had a ways to go.

As they gazed at Mary Merritt, who was absently staring at an indeterminate something in the distance, Clotilde said, "Mary Merritt usually has a hard time remembering things. We used to refer to people like that as 'blessed.' I guess in some way that is the proper designation. She mostly just lives in the present moment. Maybe that's what we all should do. After all, the past is long gone."

"Are you sure? Some people say it never left, that we are our history, and carry it within us. But you're probably right. The present is underappreciated. Most people rush through it without even knowing where they're headed next."

Changing the subject, his aunt asked, "Tell me about Miranda. I had no idea she was here."

"I suppose I failed to explain everything in my letter. She took a job at the Sea Lab last fall and really enjoys it. I went down there on Saturday: it was exciting to see her again after all the years. It was a shock though, encountering a young woman instead of a toddler. I guess I wanted to bring her up here and introduce her myself, which I promise to do. She'll be delighted to meet you, and you her. You know, from your letters I could tell your mind is still as sharp as a tack, but seeing you—it's amazing. That you can still live on your own and do practically anything you want at 98."

"We don't name numbers around here," she scolded in mock anger. "But yes, the Lord has been good to me. Some are not so fortunate," she said looking over at her cousin. "A dozen years younger, and her mind is about gone. But there I go! I said we didn't mention numbers. You mustn't think I can do everything though—I gave up driving a long time ago, and I have help. I don't expect you remember Bertha Pettway. She's worked for me a long time and lives here in the house in the room next to the kitchen. She does my cooking, shopping, and laundry. In fact she's out buying groceries right now. And of course, she helps with Mary Merritt. That way she has a job and a place to live, and I have the assistance I need to allow me to live on my own. I can't imagine going into one of those homes. Nothing but old people!"

He was aware that since he had been gone African Americans now voted, held seats on the city council, served on the police force, presented the news on television, attended and taught in integrated schools: progress, certainly, but was it enough? How broadly did it extend, and how much of the old still lingered? Was progress permanent, or might the old racism reemerge in a virulent form? He had never in his life heard his aunt utter a racial slur, though he could not say the same of his father or the other members of his family. But was conversational respect sufficient, or was some other action required? Racial harmony was at present tantalizingly visible, but at the same time frustratingly remote. It would be a mistake to assume that just because things are rocking along all right we don't need to do anything, while millions are meanwhile being worn down outside our field of vision. How to oppose the coercion of those in power, or the subtle methods they employ to obtain the willing consent of the dominated? Diana would certainly have held all their feet to the fire.

And then there was his aunt's name: why had his grandfather called her that? He knew that his great-grandfather had been somehow involved with a man who had emigrated from Maine and later initiated and carried out the last importation of slaves into the United States, defying the ban on the international slave trade that had been in place since 1808. To win a bet and to make money with his act of bravado, and firmly believing in the rightness of owning people as property, that man conspired with a shipbuilder and sea captain to outfit the latter's recently constructed schooner *Clotilda* as a slaver for a run to Africa in early 1860. Even in the slave-holding South they could not pursue their plans openly, but had to camouflage the many barrels for holding water and the supplies of flour, rice, pork, and other foodstuffs that would feed their "cargo" on the return voyage. They could not even construct the cots for sleeping in advance, but had to stack the lumber as a screen for the other items in order to assemble it later. These modifications were made not at the foot of St. Anthony Street, where the ship had originally been built, but hidden upstream within the confines of the Chickasabogue. Despite storms, pursuits by patrolling men-of-war of various nations, and a mutiny of the crew when they discovered what type of ship they were working on, the captain of the *Clotilda* made it to Ouidah in the Bight of Benin, where he purchased 125 men, women, and children from an African prince who had seized them in a war with another tribe. The skipper returned with his captives to their home port in July, waiting in the Mississippi Sound until they could link up with his patron and be towed under cover of darkness up the river, past the city to Twelve Mile Island. Even then they had to transfer the Africans, already humiliated by having to give up their clothing for the voyage and heartbroken by the sudden, cruel separation from family and home, to canebrakes in the swamp, where they were forced to sleep without shelter and endure the swarms of mosquitoes until the ringleaders thought they could safely transfer the newly enslaved to their promised owners. Not wanting to risk that the *Clotilda* be revealed as a slaver, they burned it in Bayou Canot, according to various legends. The ship thus ended not by sinking into the water, but in fire: living in lies and exploiting others resulted in self-inflicted immolation. But despite the attempted cover-up, the deed was an open secret which was quickly reported in newspapers throughout the country. Some of the men, including his great-grandfather, who had contracted for a share of the shipment, pulled out, no doubt more from cold feet than moral scruples. The ringleader continued to deny any involvement and attempted to dispel the stories as rumors or the work of someone else, yet he could smirk with pride concerning the accomplishment, which he knew that everyone was aware of. Though indicted, most of those involved got off lightly because of their connections to lenient judges, and in any case the state's secession from the Union in December soon made the issue a moot point. Like the ruined hull of the *Clotilda*, which was occasionally still visible in the mud years later, the whole affair could simultaneously be observed and denied.

In similar fashion, thought J.P., too many people can even today admit that slavery existed while maintaining that it was not really all that bad, or at the least, that since it is over and done with it's best forgotten about. And he also noticed how whites in this decade could compartmentalize their feelings about and responses to race: embracing the avuncular Black TV newscaster while fearing the Black youth approaching on the street and resenting the "welfare queen." But why did his aunt have to wear this heritage in her name? Did his grandfather christen her that way on purpose, or was he stupidly blind to the implications? In her case, *nomen* was not *omen*, since she had lived her life differently—yet neither she nor I can escape, nor should we deny, what went on before, he thought. The name she bore constantly was a reminder of the repeated lashes bestowed upon those who had endured the Middle Passage and whom his ancestors had violently enslaved, though it could not remotely approach the pain that they suffered. Instead of punishment, perhaps it was the gift of truth. We just need to get it right from now on, thought J.P. No doubt his aunt could tell stories about that, and lots of other things as well. Her narratives were what had always sustained him in his youth.

Those Africans, exiles as he had been most of his life, with the striking exception that they had physically and violently been uprooted and coerced into servitude against their will, gained their emancipation five years later and managed to set up their own African Town community on the northern edge of the city where they spoke their native language and attempted to farm and live in their old ways, saving up money from their meager post-war wages to buy land and build up a community, persisting in the midst of a society that provided them no help. J.P. had even gone there once as a very young child, when his mother had taken him to deliver a basket of Christmas food to the grandfather of their family's housemaid. He remembered the grey-haired old man with a pipe in his mouth, who, he was told, had been born in Africa, and who spoke with a funny accent, one of the last remaining vestiges of the homeland from which he had been untimely ripped. Was this man's name Cudjo? Or Kossola? Or was this a designation later placed by a trick of his memory, based on what he had subsequently read? Why are the names of the perpetrators still so evident on public parks and institutions, while the names of those they snatched away remain ignored? Why hadn't he talked about this more with his relatives? Or is that just the way it is in old families—certain things remain unspoken? How blind we often are to the threads of intertwined lives. His long-ago visit to Africatown, the even longer-ago passage from Africa itself: so far and yet so near. J.P. wondered how free the descendants of the unwilling immigrants were today.

"What are you thinking about?" asked Clotilde, interrupting his reveries.

"Lost in history, as usual."

"Well, you've got plenty in the present to keep you occupied. A lot of your boxes have begun to trickle in. Bertha's been stacking them up in the dining room, which we never use, since it's easier than carrying them up to the attic."

"I'm sorry," said J.P. "I hated to burden you, but I really appreciate your storing my things and accepting shipments over the years. I can start taking them back to my house in the car today."

"It's no trouble. I'm glad the room can be used for something, and we rarely go to the attic anyway. And you've started getting a lot of mail too. I've been collecting it in a box on the dining room table."

Looking through the pile while Clotilde got up to answer the phone, he wondered if the world would have ended if he hadn't gotten back to deal with it. Back out in the hall he gazed up the stairs and spotted a door he could not recall. Closing off a room whose memory he wanted to repress? An opening to a threat or a promise?

"That was your cousin Louise," Clotilde said when she returned. "She's going to stop by in a few minutes, so you'd best leave unless you want your presence blabbed about all over town. She's like her mother was—far too interested in the goings-on of other people, especially if there's a secret or hint of scandal, or something that might affect their status. And she's far too eager to disclose anything she might learn. I'm sure she thinks information isn't worth very much if you can't pass it along. Sorry to kick you out like this, but we'll have plenty of time to catch up."

"I haven't seen Louise since I was last here. Somehow, I'm not surprised she hasn't changed. But you're right—we'll get together again soon."

As he was getting into the car, J.P. felt the muggy air already beginning to settle down upon him, bringing with it a whiff of the familiar, sulphurous paper-mill smell: the air was not as pure as the cerulean sky made it appear. Neither was he: his family had accumulated a large share of its wealth selling timber for pulp, he recalled, and he was quite a consumer of paper himself through his incessant purchases of books.

On the drive home he realized he had forgotten to inquire whether his aunt had a bed or other furniture he might borrow, but decided he could sleep on his pallet for another night at least. His lodging was for now even more Spartan than in his graduate school days or his first posting to Africa, but he could endure it. He would soon enough be able to start undertaking what needed to be done.

It's how I began, how I grew up, he would tell Miranda. *It's all changed, it's all the same. Do you see why it's not easy to relate? But there's more, that's perhaps even harder to tell.*

Someone told me you were dead, Herakleitos,
and brought me to bitter tears.
I remembered how many times that while we talked
we caused the sun to sink.
Now you, my dear old friend and guest,
have been ashes for a long, long time.
Yet your poems, the "Nightingales," still live:
Death, who seizes all, cannot take them away.
—Callimachus, Epigram

J.P. PULLED BACK THE CURTAINS OF THE ROOM he had designated as his study, threw up the sash, and leaned out to open the shutters and let the morning light stream in. Surveying his arboreal domain before replacing the screen, he watched the squirrels running along the limbs and cavorting from tree to tree. We're bound to the two-dimensional plane of the earth, he thought, but they can navigate in 3-D. A hawk circled leisurely above, perhaps waiting to seize one of the lively grey creatures. J.P.'s house was near the top of the highest hill in town, just over 200 feet in elevation, and he wondered if he now stood above everyone else in the city. Across the vacant wooded lot behind his home he spied some shotgun houses and little sided-over cabins on the next street, which was now paved but which for years had suffered the municipal inattention that resulted in the nickname "Sandtown" for this poor community on the edge of the wealthier white neighborhood. Though the residents there were by no means responsible for the lack of asphalt on their rutted streets, they were forced to suffer the pejorative designation as if they were: yet another case of assigning blame to those who had played no role in their own victimization.

Now that he had prepared the basics of his existence, J.P. could finally set to work arranging all his books. From the realtor he had obtained the name of a carpenter to build bookcases in the study, the living room, the bedrooms, along hallways, and anywhere else acceptable space could be found. He realized that there was no point in designating a single room as the "library": the whole house was becoming one. The man, who in his overalls, demeanor, and thick local accent seemed to be a simple country fellow, turned out to have an acute native intelligence with skills in visualizing space and wood-working that made quick and elegant work of the job. He somehow fit with grace and ease the bookcases within the walls of the old house that had settled irregularly with age. J.P. wished that they could have used walnut, but since the cost was prohibitive, he settled for yellow pine. The carpenter was not a talkative man, but his occasional sly observations delivered with a twinkle in the eyes set deep in his wrinkled face delighted J.P., who hoped he might have an excuse to call this man back sometime to take on another job.

"This here wall's further off o' plumb than I would-a thought. I kin angle the back edges o' the casings so that it looks right while keepin' the shelves level. It'll take a little longer, but I'll be glad to do it if you want. Course, as far as them books is concerned, I cain't do nothin' about whether their contents is on the level."

J.P. agreed to the suggested adjustment, though he was less concerned with the appearance than with allowing the carpenter the opportunity to practice his craft to a degree that would bring him pride. He must think I'm strange to be putting up so many book-cases, thought J.P., but except for occasional teasing, he never judges me and instead accepts me for who I am.

When this work was near completion he began hauling the remaining boxes from his Aunt Clotilde's. The ones stacked in the dining room were the easiest to take, but he then had to tackle the ones in the attic. This meant climbing two staircases, not to mention the steps leading up to the front porch, before entering the swelter-ing 110° Fahrenheit space where the long array of stacks of boxes was stored. He was greeted by the stale smell of cardboard which had spent countless summers in the baking heat and the frigid cold snaps of winter, absorbed the moisture of periodic roof leaks, served as food for various insects and even rodents who had left their drop-pings, and which had stood motionless as repositories for the hard black dust that inevitably settles from the undersides of aging rafters oozing pine resin. J.P. pulled out a volume from the top box of books which he had purchased in his student days and found to his dismay that the years and climate had caused the pulpy, acid pages to yellow and become brittle, as well as bring on the stray, discoloring stains of foxing; the faint, dusty, sweetish smell of decay made him aware that he was outliving those storehouses of truth and expression in which he had invested to take him through life, and that their plots and characters, thoughts and ideas, metaphors and rhymes might live on longer, though imperfectly, in the unreliable synapses of his brain than they would in the deteriorating pages on his shelves. He rummaged further and hoped to discover no silverfish scurrying to find nourishment in the pages or cockroach egg cases on the point of hatching. During his time abroad he had been able to avoid those thumb-sized, sickly brown, disgusting creatures which were the bane of the Gulf Coast, and he did not look forward to facing them again or having to squish their stinking masses underfoot.

He hefted a box, marked "History" in fading black marker, and, straining under its load, wished he had packed his prized possessions in smaller cartons. Craning his head to see the steps beneath his feet and trying not to bang his elbows against the walls, he slowly descended to the yard, taking only one pause to rest. Subsequent trips required more stops as he grew tireder, and, because the used Toyota Corolla that he had bought was not very large, he had to repeat the route between his house and Clotilde's many times before the job was done. During one of his gasping pauses for rest he remarked on how he was being physically linked with his treasures: corporeal effort was being required to pursue his intellectual work. He was glad that his aging body had not completely given out yet.

History, the first box retrieved from the attic, he had placed in the study, thinking he would begin with that topic. But maybe he should start with some other category, since he couldn't remember exactly how many history books he had and how much space they would take up on the shelves, possibly requiring a fresh start to the ordering to allow more room for another group. But wouldn't that be the same for any category? If he paused to think it all out before placing actual books onto the shelves, he would never get around to starting. He saw that he couldn't begin at the top of the bookcase, since many of the history books were rather tall and the uppermost shelf did not allow enough vertical space to accommodate them.

Author or period? How did the Library of Congress arrange them exactly? What about the *Pinakes*, the system devised by Callimachus for the ancient library at Alexandria—was it still valid? But whether he followed or violated a pre-established organization, what chance would there be of a random visitor to his study becoming confused by his eccentricities? He decided a chronological order made sense for this topic and began lining them up one by one. He was up to the Renaissance when he pulled out a tome on the Peloponnesian War and had to shove the bunch aside to fit it in near the beginning. As he stooped to pull out another, they all fell sideways with a thwack on the unfilled portion of the shelf. So far the books took up five and a half shelves, and J.P. wondered if he should leave gaps in case more scattered volumes of history emerged later from other boxes. And what should follow history? Politics, religion, art? Or whatever was in the next box he put his hand on? Somehow he eventually made his decisions, pleased at his progress in setting his volumes out in an orderly display. Nature, mathematics, music, literary criticism, and a vast amount of poetry and fiction: he took satisfaction at the array of his interests. And what about those scattered samples of rare old periodicals—*The Spectator*, *Harper's Weekly*, *New Directions*, the German Expressionist journal *Der Sturm*?

The process took several days: running into space problems, he would not infrequently have to shift whole categories up or down a shelf to allow room for other groupings, but he didn't mind, since the occupation was all for a good cause. He had wanted to leave a few gaps here and there for future acquisitions or boxes that were still to arrive, but his present collection took up every bit of available space: it had even grown larger in the process, since Clotilde had culled many items from her shelves to bequeath to him as well. He was forced to array rows along the tops of the bookcases, anchoring them at the ends with stacks of volumes laid on their sides; boxed sets could stand on their own on the window sills. And there were even extra books for which there was no room at all. Were they doomed to be relegated to his own attic, or stacked up in piles on the floor, or given away to some charitable book sale? He began perusing the shelves for items that he could dispense with: certainly not the signed copies or first editions, or the antiquarian tomes whose rich, brown leather covers, embossed with gold lettering, had taken on a velvety feel from years of use and weathering. Had their content matured over time as well? Nor the books authored by friends or acquaintances, or heirlooms handed down through generations of family. Not the ones that brought back memories from his own life because of where he had acquired them—from *bouquinistes* along the Seine or ill-lit, dusty shops down the winding side streets of Prague. Not the ones that he had once read with great pleasure and might someday read again. Not the reference works that were so frequently consulted. Not those acclaimed authors for whom he had not yet had time, but which he had added to his mental list for future reading. Not the ones for which he had paid a pretty penny, but also not the ones that he had gotten for a steal at yard sales and therefore just as valuable for the amount that he had not paid. Duplicates? But didn't different editions of the same text have different introductions or annotations, not to mention his own inked-in observations? Perhaps the books that he had not looked at in years and that dealt with topics of only peripheral interest to him—but who could tell? He just might need them at some point. What if some issue arose during an upcoming political campaign, and he found it handy to grab *Common Sense* off the shelf to see what Tom Paine had said about a similar concern? Or if the current world situation piqued his interest enough to cause him to delve more deeply into the nature of Islam? Would he really have time to read *Adam Bede* again? Or desire? Maybe a friend would want to borrow it sometime. You just never know. And what good does all this reading do anyway? He pondered the etymology of the German equivalent *lesen*, which also means to gather, collect, glean, or select and that of the English *to read*, which comes from a Middle English verb that also means to explain. It's an active process then, not a passive one, and something new must be consciously assembled. He hoped he could arrange it all, on the shelves and in his mind, before entropy caused all the assembled knowledge to deteriorate into chaotic fragments. Maybe he should begin to piece together a commonplace book, or *Kollektaneenbuch*, to collect and distill all that is crucial.

He repacked the remaining volumes and shoved them out into the hall, postponing the decision for another day. He had done his job:

the books were on the shelves; order had been achieved. They were now at last available for him to peruse. He gazed contentedly at his library, comforted in being surrounded by his books, which stood around him like sentinels. Containing, guarding knowledge, wisdom in its manifold forms, all enhancing one another. Would one ever receive the same assurance from the sight of a single computer at a work station, a device which seemed to be gaining ever increasing prominence as a principal source of information?

He sat down at his desk and eagerly anticipated the next stage: actually starting his explorations. He leaned back and breathed with great relief; he was inspired by the realization that he was now at the age at which he could devote himself to his books and take each one for what it was: he was no longer compelled to feel the need to finish one in a certain amount of time, or like a student, to account for it on an exam or regard it as an important piece that he must retain as part of the sum of his knowledge; or like a teacher, to prepare a presentation and discussion for instructional purposes; or like a reviewer, to provide an evaluation for a journal; or like a member of a book club, to come up with comments that did not sound stupid; or like an employee in his earlier profession, to synthesize its contents in order to provide a summary for his superiors. His search was open-ended: his collection could lead in so many directions, and he was not restricted to any of the areas that centuries of pursuit had fixed into discrete disciplines. But would all the effort be in one direction alone, and would any linkages or new intuition remain forever locked within his own mind? Did he first need a method and a goal before he even began? Looking back across the span of his life, he thought he should have learned by this point. One's first pursuits were easier and undertaken without question. The purpose was clearer back then: to attain a college degree or follow what everyone else said should be followed. Then as now the drive of curiosity played a role as well, but was that sufficient? And besides, what good is knowledge when it's hidden between book covers stuck away on the shelves? Don't you have to engage with it and relate it to the world? His brother had never wrestled with such problems and had quickly gone on to amass his wealth in seemingly effortless fashion.

J.P. stared at the small bronze statue in its place of pride at the upper-left corner of his desk: a Greek youth reaching for the laurel wreath atop his head. It was a talisman which had accompanied him in his odysseys around the world.

In one of the boxes he had sent back he discovered a hand-crafted journal, which he had once purchased in Italy: its handsome cover of distressed brown leather with a raised spine bound a hundred or more handsewn sheets of rich, cream-colored paper with deckled edges. He thumbed through it indulgently, enjoying the pleasant mixture of scents borne on the breeze created by rippling the pages, all blank. He could fill them now himself: they invited inscription.

But what was his agenda—that which is to be done, should be done, must be done? The future necessity conveyed by gerundives: *delenda est Carthago*—Carthage must be destroyed. Was his own purpose *delendus est Antonius*? That would still have to be considered, and the plans mapped out. More important to him at the moment was Miranda.

• • •

Miranda! He had told her he would meet her at 4, and it was practically that time already. She had informed him that she had to come into town to talk with some professors at the university, and he had agreed to meet her afterwards at a coffee house near the campus.

He pulled into the gravel drive of the little tin-roofed blue house and parked in front of the fan-like spikes of a saw palmetto growing in the sandy soil by the establishment's red sign. Miranda was already sitting at a table on the porch with a steaming cup.

"You'll have to go inside to order. I splurged on a cappuccino," she said. Wrinkling her nose, she picked up an overflowing ashtray from the table where she was sitting and moved it as far away as possible. J.P. was glad he had given up smoking long ago: too late, but as a token tribute to her mother. His restlessness had in the meantime found other outlets.

Inside, he paused to inhale the rich aroma of coffee, which, with his increasing age, he was coming to find more appealing than the taste. When he returned with his dark roast, he asked his daughter how her meeting had gone.

"Really well. A couple of professors in marine and earth sciences have come up with a long-term project to more precisely catalogue the various ecosystems between here and the coast of Colombia—in estuaries, coral reefs, and at greater depths—so that baselines can be set and comparisons can be made in the future to measure the effects of climate change."

"Climate change? I think I may have heard about that."

"I hope so," she said, creasing her forehead slightly in serious concentration. "It's been getting more publicity over the last couple of decades. Even farther back scientists began noting that the earth has been warming at an ever-increasing rate, and in fact last year was the warmest year since people started collecting such widespread data in 1880. If this continues, it will have effects in so many areas, including the very way we live. Everything's connected. We have to know what's going on so we can be prepared for the future. And more important, change our ways, I mean like, stop burning so much coal and oil. It may be the most crucial issue we face: we gladly ignore it to maintain our comfort, but at our peril."

"There's so much to keep up with. I suppose I should turn my thermostat down, or up in the summer. For all the good one person can do." Had she inherited a didactic streak from him?

"It's something everyone has to get together on. We're less than a year away from the 21st century: what's going to happen then?"

"Yes, the future, that's what we have to concentrate on." J.P. took a careful sip of the still-hot brew and wondered to himself whether he had always been too preoccupied with the past. Perhaps that attention also intensified his focus on revenge: maybe he should focus on justice in the here-and-now, but then it would have to be about people and things beyond himself.

Miranda continued, waving the long fingers of her graceful hand lightly back and forth in tandem with the recounted facts. "In any event, they wanted me to help with the research, since I'll actually be going out on the ship this summer. Some of the faculty members are involved with other things in addition and can't spare the time for the voyage. The data are what they need. I'm not sure, though, how seriously they take me since I'm still so new and art makes up such a large part of what I do. But I'm part of a larger team, and it'll give me the chance to focus on finding an area of concentration."

"I've seen what you do, and know that it's all very accomplished. They'll see it too, don't worry. Don't sell yourself short."

J.P. noticed that she drank her coffee slowly, savoring it thoughtfully in the way her mother used to do. She was wearing attractive silver earrings, shaped in interesting abstract curls —no doubt the work of some local artisan.

"But we need to pick up where we left off," Miranda went on, impatient to get to the point and staring at him with a penetrating gaze. "I know about your childhood now, but what came after that? And I still can't wait to hear in more detail about how you met my mother, and what she was like."

"She was all that anyone could hope for. But one thing at a time," her father said. "I suppose I'm clarifying it for myself as well." Or was he mainly trying to postpone what might turn out to be the trauma of a sudden revelation, one so profound that it could even cause a new separation between them?

He looked up into the crown of the live oak, whose massive limbs spread wide enough to shelter in its shade both the coffee house and the little dwelling next door that now housed a barbecue restaurant. Its branches were rife with epiphytic resurrection fern, forming a crinkly, pale-lime band beneath the forest-green leaves of the venerable tree on which it made its home. Beards of Spanish moss hung from the limbs, grayer even than the undersides of the leathery leaves. He knew that invisible under the grass and little houses was a network of roots as massive as the canopy, connected by networks of mycorrhizal fungi to the roots of the neighboring trees all around it: communicating, nourishing, supporting, healing. And that the tree as a whole formed a living community with species living in mutual benefit, a home to creatures from the microbes in the crannies of the furrowed bark to the squirrels that gathered the acorns and the birds that perched and nested in its branches. He admired how those winding limbs with their numerous divisions and sturdy but flexible wood enabled them to withstand the high winds which they were frequently forced to bear in their life span of centuries. Live, because they were seemingly evergreen, unobtrusively dropping the previous year's leaves as the new ones emerged. Always living, he pondered, and part of a community: I must remind myself that I should be too. The fact that so few species of tree in the area showed a change of color in the fall gave the appearance that there is no change. He wondered whether this led to a tendency on the part of people to stagnate, to bask in the chiaroscuro of amber light and emerald green surrounding them and resign themselves to the status quo. He remembered how much he had loved the native vegetation that he could not only see, but also feel and smell in the fecund air, and how as a teenager he would head out on his bicycle through the Garden District and the Negro neighborhoods closer to the waterfront to reach the edge of the bay where he searched the shoreline and bordering woods and shrub lands for glimpses of snakes and insects, sea creatures and shore birds.

"See, I might have become a scientist myself," he said.

But he had also biked down Government Street to the library, a white, two-story, Classical Revival structure that he was gratified to learn was still in use. Though its holdings could not compare to those of the impressive institutions he encountered in his later travels and studies, in his youth they had represented a treasure trove, as opposed to the meager collection of the private school he had attended. In the public library he had discovered the worlds of art and literature, history and human civilization that would continue to compete for his attention as his life progressed.

Sometimes he would continue all the way down Government Street to the banana docks, where he would watch the unloading of the tropical fruit from countries that bordered the same Gulf, smell the salt air, and follow with his eye the freighters plying intently down the bay toward more distant ports as he tried to keep up with them in his imagination. Now, he reconstituted the visions from his memory.

"On the far side of the river were still a few ships with tall masts, and trains that carried freight along the waterfront were pulled by steam locomotives. All that must seem like a different world."

"Ships with masts? That does seem like a different era, a lifetime before my birth."

"Yes, but there are overlaps in the human experience that aren't always perceived as such."

"I'm sure an awful lot continues, the bad as well as the good. What about athletics and girls?" Miranda prodded, seeking to gain a complete picture.

"I tried my hand at each," chuckled J.P., "but never became a star at either. I had dates with a few girls to the movies or the dances. But remember, teenagers didn't have their own cars back then. We were still slow to recover from the Depression, and during the war, gas was rationed. And despite my parents' best efforts, I was slow to master the social skills."

During the back and forth the tale spun forward, and the portraits gained in depth. Family members were introduced in greater detail, and the subject of sibling rivalry was broached.

"But that's a big subject, to be covered in detail next time. I was wondering though. What are your earliest memories? Do you recall anything at all about the time before you were taken off to Iowa?"

"There's one image that recurs, but I don't know whether it's memory or imagination. It's very sunny, and the walls are all white and bright. There's a palm tree, and I'm playing on a blanket, with another child. A woman is sitting nearby and singing in the soft, wavering tones of Arab music. I am very happy. A man and woman walk out, arm in arm, and smile at us. Everyone seems very content."

"It's real," said her father softly. "It's where we last lived together. You had just begun to toddle and we had an Arab maid who brought her little girl with her to work. We were indeed, for a brief time, content. Hold on to it."

After a while the friendly young man with short dark hair who ran the place came out to collect cups and trash from neighboring tables and to ask if they would like anything else.

"I didn't realize it had gotten so late," J.P. said to Miranda. "We didn't get as far as I thought we might. I hope I'm not boring you."

"I could sit rapt for hours. I don't want to leave, but I unfortunately have to get back to the island. I'm impatient to hear the continuation though. Let's make it soon."

"Let's do," he agreed.

When he reached the crest of the hill on the way back to his house he noticed a vast thunderhead grasping up into the stratosphere above the bay. He recalled that when he was a child, thunderstorms would form every summer afternoon around three o'clock and enthrall the area with deafening cracks and deep rumbles. The rain would start with heavy bulbous drops that splattered as they hit, and the thunder would roar in mighty claps, the wind would come up in fitful gusts before the regular pounding rain began in earnest. All it took was a single glance at the looming cloud to bring back that recollection, and he almost longed to wrap himself in the storm.

Clutching the wheel nervously though, he asked himself if that had really happened so regularly, or whether it was a trick of memory. He had often caught himself examining his recollections and noting how much they diverged from what had actually occurred in life: when seemingly objective opportunities presented themselves for comparing his mind's picture with that of "reality," for example through actual visits to places experienced in the past or through photographs or home movies, he was appalled at the discrepancies between his own remembrances, which he had always taken for gospel, and what the counter-presentation threw up as if in mockery. But even photographs—those supposedly accurate documenters of the way things were—could play tricks. They were products of the technology at the time they were made and themselves subject to the ravages of the aging process: many of the old ones take on a yellow-brown tone with faded colors and present a different way of conveying what is portrayed from that of newer prints. This can transfigure the event with a nostalgia for what has been lost, even as the photo preserves details that otherwise would have been forgotten. But does memory itself do both of these? In his or her own present, the observer/participant may be aware of the significance of an ongoing event such as the march from Selma to Montgomery, or on the other hand may unthinkingly participate in the everyday activity of sitting on a segregated bus. But looking back on either may add or detract from the significance by providing a historical context of the development, or a glorification, or even a nostalgia for an unconscionable situation, merely because it is gone. But isn't there a third perspective that could arise from an observer's awareness of the

present and past: a future in which things are different—the
nostalgia of hope.

And in addition to the visual images: what of the auditory
impressions, the feelings, the judgments that took place at the time
of the actual experience? Even with much shorter time spans, the
same phenomenon occurred: in transcribing a passage, J.P. often
found that when he looked back from the notebook or keyboard to
the original text, he saw that he had written a synonym, or ended a
sentence too early, or expanded a contraction into the full set of
words, assuming that the phrase's importance must have called for
a more formal style. And if memory was not to be trusted at all, what
was this phantasm of a world through which we moved? Are the very
identities of our own selves that we construct in our brains a fiction?
Was Mnemosyne really the mother of the muses?

He wondered if this present storm was now heading their way,
and, if so, he hoped that Miranda would escape it. But then he
remembered the astounding remark she had made as a toddler: "It's
so magical that things so fluffy like clouds can make so much water
and noise." Maybe things needed to be shaken up from time to time
in order to clear the air. Was Miranda currently shaking him up?
Would their relationship culminate in a blow-up or a contented
resolution?

• • •

Back at home a few days later J.P. stood before the massive bookcases in his study and skimmed the titles, looking for the volume on
place names in the state that he knew he once had owned and most
certainly had seen fairly recently. Since his return his mind had been
reintroduced to appellations that he hadn't thought about in years,
and the sounds of those toponyms and hydronyms churned around
in his head in stormy but enchanting patterns: Mauvilla, Satsuma,
Saraland, Citronelle, Semmes, Prichard, Plateau, Magazine Point,
Africatown, Kushla, Creola, Chunchula, St. Elmo, Grand Bay, Bayou
la Batre, Coden (with accent on the second syllable, a corruption of
Coq d'Inde, he knew), Fowl River, Isle aux Herbes, Mon Louis,
Apalachee River, Chocolatta Bay, Polecat Bay, Little Lizard Creek,

Blakeley, Crichton, Wheelerville, Whistler, Bayou Canot, Vinegar Bend, Bon Secour. . . . This was the milieu from which he had somehow evolved, and he wondered if discovering the diverse etymologies of the names could help him determine not only their roots but also his own. Or how about the fiction in his section of local authors—Augusta Evans Wilson, Marie Sheips Stanley, Herbert Lyons, Frances Gaither, Eugene Walter, Julian Rayford, Albert Murray, and many others, including those who had published more recently? He was not sure whether his search was linguistic or geographical, ethnographic or poetic, aesthetic or personal, or which of those would be the most revealing. Perhaps these were not discrete categories, however, but somehow all connected.

The book was not among the ones he had recently culled from various spots and gathered together for imminent consultation on the one shelf that still had a few inches of free space, where in bindings of assorted color and thickness the volumes to be perused were propped up against one another at varying degrees of departure from the vertical. "Imminent" meant some time over the next few months, or whenever he would have an opportunity to pursue the spark of curiosity that had set his mind on wanting to learn more about whatever topic it was that they covered. He tried to think where the book he now sought might be filed: most logically among the lexicons or reference works, or perhaps with the volumes on local history and lore? Onomastics was too narrow a topic to warrant its own section. He failed to spot it in any of those areas and glanced over the economic and political texts on the top shelf to see whether it had perhaps been misplaced. Later acquisitions or finds often got squeezed in as best they could, stuck sideways across the tops of other books or placed in nearby groupings that had more room. Older, less important books were relegated to a spot behind the first row with the hope that he would remember to look for them there. Ones that seemed even less crucial were banished to a spot under the bed in the guestroom. Gadamer, Hegel, Heidegger, Horkheimer, Hume, Kant—it wasn't among philosophy either. But now that he found himself here: shouldn't he look up what Hegel said about the master-servant relationship in *Phänomenologie des Geistes*? He moved that volume down to his shelf of books to look into and continued his searching. Since he couldn't remember who had written or edited the book on names, the alphabetization by authors wouldn't help him in this case. Institutional libraries have call numbers, catalogues, and systems of cross-referencing, but his own collection had few of these aids: only the system based on his own mental constructs, modified by the physical limitations of space and the current collection. Many years ago he had begun listing his books on index cards which he kept in an olive-drab tin box as a means of imposing order, but which he had soon given up, since the cards gave little clue to the location and merely added another physical presence to that of the books: it was as easy to examine the shelves as to shuffle the cards. He had learned to use computers in his last years at his job and even planned to buy one now; he again considered cataloguing his entire collection electronically but dismissed the thought when he realized it would take almost as much time to create an inventory as to read the texts themselves. He thought he remembered that the book had a brown binding, but he wasn't sure.

Maybe he should skim again on the basis of color. That reminded him of his perplexity at a party he once attended when he couldn't figure out the order of books on the hostess's shelves. In response to his inquiry, she informed him that she had paid a decorator to do the room, and the "expert" had arranged all the books on the basis of color and size. Starting again at the top left and methodically raking his eyes over the shelves again, he was struck when he noticed that the movement was identical to that used in reading the text within a book: left to right, top to bottom. He wondered if Arabs or Chinese would have looked over their shelves in a different direction. When he reached the bottom he still hadn't found it.

J.P.'s bookcases were also taken up with binders and files of business papers, as well as photo albums and boxes of his own correspondence and that of family members going back to the eighteenth century. More family papers and photographs, collected by himself and older relatives, filled box after box in the attic, and the genealogical explorations that he undertook from time to time were consumed by similar hit-and-miss inquiries. Newspaper clippings, pamphlets, old issues of journals, certificates of award, medallions, photocopied articles on items of interest to his life and pursuits, Indian arrowheads, and artifacts from the Civil War or other noteworthy events made up another substantial portion of the collection, making it as much a museum as a library. He was just one person, born of one family, and he wondered if everyone held on to as much: at what point would these ever-expanding accumulations run out of room? And what should Miranda do with all of this? Move into his house when he died, buy another larger abode for herself to take it all in, rent storage space, donate it, or throw most of it away? Even now boxes had begun to appear on the floor of his study, a repository for items that he had no other place for. But until the mass of items went so far as to block his path to the door, he considered it best just to leave it all as it was. On a lectern beside his desk, altar-like, was the massive, comprehensive Webster's New International Dictionary which he was delighted to have in his possession again. He always wished he could have taken it with him during all those years, but it would have consumed a whole suitcase in itself, and it weighed almost as much as his entire wardrobe. What more could he want than the 550,000 words it contained? He could stay up all night reading it alone. The expressions that had come into existence since the dictionary's publication three-quarters of a century before would probably be of little consequence. Or would they?

The sight of the dictionary prompted a consideration of the letters of which its words were composed. The order of the alphabet is seemingly inviolable: *a* is followed by *b*, which in turn precedes *c*. But isn't the imposition of an alphabetical order arbitrary, and therefore artificial? Is *aardvark* more important than *abacus*, or anterior to it in either time or space? And anyway, when the letters are actually used to form words, rather than merely recited, they are arranged in the order necessary to provide meaning and not bound by their sequence in the list. Similarly, the ordered chronology of the time through which we move, Monday following Sunday, January following December, 1901 following 1900, is hardly an accurate account of the chronology of our lives, which consist of numerous interweaving strands of momentary experience, memories, new recognitions, polychonicities, and simultaneities. He had attempted to arrange the books in his library in juxtapositions that seemed to provide sense.

So far he had only examined the shelves in his study: in the living room were floor-to-ceiling cases filled with fiction, poetry, and books on nature, travel, and art. And of course his beloved classics of antiquity, which held the place of honor: he always enjoyed letting his eyes graze over the red and green dust jackets of the Loeb Library volumes, as well as the numerous other books by Greek and Roman authors, many purchased at antiquarian booksellers throughout Europe, texts that he tended to think more accurately represented his true origins.

> *Thy Naiad airs have brought me home*
> *To the glory that was Greece,*
> *And the grandeur that was Rome.*

The ancient books contained that glory, he thought, and where they were, was home. Or was it?

Carefully grasping the banister, he descended the stairs on his thin legs in order to continue his search in the other parts of his domain.

Finding, comprehending, telling, acting: there was still much to be done. Realizing he might not otherwise begin, J.P. reached out and grabbed a volume. Since the loss of his wife—wife? Soulmate? Yes, that's what she had been—books had been his closest companions, even at nighttime, when he snuggled under the covers. But then he remembered that she was the one who had really brought him home.

And over the next few weeks and months he and Miranda continued to meet as frequently as they could at his house, on the island, or at those restaurants where he thought he would be unlikely to encounter Anthony or any of his cohorts, to talk and to continue the process of learning from each other what they had missed during the intervening years.

If one were to win a victory by swiftness of foot
at Olympia, by the river where stands the grove of Zeus,
or to win at wrestling, or in the painful sport of boxing. . .
he would appear more glorious in citizens' eyes
and gain a front-row seat at public occasions. . .
yet he would not deserve it as much as I.
For better than the strength of men and horses is our wisdom.
Custom is in error: it is not right to place strength
above the excellence of wisdom.

—Xenophanes, Fragment 19

But after childhood and adolescence, which had been spent under the shadow of my parents, I thought I would finally be able to pursue my own path in college, though I didn't always know the way ahead or the extent to which my family could still influence it.

J.P. had picked up his mail after class and was heading back across campus toward his room in "the barracks." The air had become warm enough to release the rich odor of the soil, along with the resinous scent of the fallen pine needles which covered it and of sweet-smelling blossoms that were beginning to open all around. He was in his final year at the only university anyone from his position and background ever considered attending, and where his father and grandfather had gone before him: the state's flagship institution in the little college town a couple of hundred miles to the north. That morning he added a loop to his route to pass the Little Round House, that strange, crenellated structure that had somehow been spared by Federal troops when they sacked the campus in 1865, and the large white president's mansion with its wide portico and Ionic columns. The antebellum structures gave him a sense of pleasing continuity with the past: he felt immersed in tradition, as did many of his fellow students, who tended to venerate it long after they had returned home. But a tradition of what? Was it just the idea and feeling of veneration without any content, which gave them the license to keep things as they were and not have to think very deeply about them?

Even at the time J.P. was too discerning to long with false nostalgia for times that could not be brought back, even if for any reason that would be desirable. He was glad that the Round House, originally a guard post when the university was militarized before the Civil War, was no longer used for martial purposes, pleased that it could serve as a reminder of what should be avoided, if anyone ever noticed. But unfortunately, too few did: lulled into complacency, they fail to realize we might still be living "ante bellum."

He was entering the final stretch: he would soon graduate, but first he had to complete, among other assignments, his paper on the poet Anacreon.

> *Ashen grey are now my temples,*
> *Snowy white my hair. Youth's grace is*
> *gone away; my teeth are ancient.*
> *Sweet life's remaining span is brief:*
> *for this I have much cause to grieve.*

These lines were hardly applicable to him, he thought: how could he, in the bloom of youth, possibly understand them? Or did the situation in fact apply in ways that were only intermittently but deeply apparent, and do we not all inevitably imitate those who have gone before? At times he felt one with older members of his family, or even ancestors whom he never knew, or aged poets like this ancient Greek or the medieval troubadour Walther von der Vogelweide who conveyed the winding down of life in their verse. Was his own life a pale repetition of Anacreon's poem? Could it possibly be, on the other hand, a more animate version? Why was he, or anyone else, studying the classical world at all? Because the western world had somehow declared it to be the pristine origin for all that we are today? If it provides a mirror, what do we see? And why do we think it is a mirror at all? He pushed aside these vague inklings, as he often later would, and instead paused to consider that perhaps the end of his collegiate idyll was indeed a variation on the same condition that Anacreon expressed. Everything was on track at the moment for him where he was, however; all was proceeding smoothly: he had learned to navigate the university structures and requirements and felt comfortably in control, but soon he would be thrust over into the uncertain turbulence of the afterlife.

He wrinkled his brow as he walked on, wrestling with his old problem of knowing what to do. What he did know was that he wanted to continue his studies: he was most at home among books and the lives and ideas that they contained. He had already been accepted at an Ivy League university, but though he had been promised a fellowship, he still needed to convince his parents to finance the rest of the expenses that the pursuit of a graduate degree would require. His father was determined that he come home to enter the family business, to be groomed to head it at some point down the road. He was smarter and more organized than most of the men who worked for the firm, but his complete lack of interest in such matters forestalled any ability that he might have had in that regard. His father had never expressed a lot of faith in what he did, however: his many strikeouts and fumbled grounders when playing on the baseball team; his clumsiness on the summer job at the company's sawmill that led to a seriously injured hand; his seeming indifference to the family business; and perhaps worst of all, his pursuit of a worthless subject like classics at the university. Maybe if he had simultaneously played quarterback and garnered victories for the football team he could have pulled it off. But he was the oldest son, to the manor born, destined for the position, and it was unimaginable that he would not fill it, and fill it nobly. He could imagine, however, what daily life in the firm would be like, given his experience with the incessant carping on his trips home. How much more suited his brother Anthony would be: even though he was only a senior in high school, his unflagging determination to take advantage of the main chance, which substituted for sensitivity or intelligence, made him a better candidate.

J.P. entered his room, simply furnished and decorated only with a picture of Socrates at the banquet; books were piled high on the desk, barely able to be contained by its narrow surface. The room was cool compared to the warmth of the sunlit air of the quad; the radiator was cold to the touch. He looked at the letter, the one piece of mail that he had received. It was from home, but instead of bearing the usual handwriting of his mother, it was inscribed with his father's large, forceful scrawl. He hardly expected a concession at this point on the matter of graduate school financing, and he nervously tore open the envelope to see what it contained.

"Dear Son," the letter began, before going straight to the point. "At the last meeting of the Carnival Association I placed your name in nomination to be King of Mardi Gras next year. There is no doubt, given my position in the community and my influence with the Association, that you will be selected—you remember, I was King just before the Depression and you would in fact be the third generation to wear the crown. Not to forget that your cousin Louise was destined to be Queen in 1942, until the war interfered and needlessly cancelled the whole celebration. Hierarchy and precedent would demand that you, as my son, be in line for this honor." J.P. noted that his father's sense of self-importance remained strong, and that his identity was predicated on his paternity. But why did his own talents not make him eligible for elevation to such a position? Does not the ability to recite lines from "The Works and Days" count for anything, he thought sarcastically.

The letter continued in its pompous way: "Since the carnival season kicks off with balls in November, and you would have to be involved with preparations long before that, it would require your presence in the city for the entire fall and much of the winter: Mardi Gras day is in late February next year. This would, of course, make study up north impossible during that period. You could consider postponing things a year, assuming you still wished to at that point. We can discuss the subject of your further studies at a later date." He is presuming, thought J.P., that I would be so taken in by the grandeur of the role I would be performing that I would never wish to leave again.

"Needless to say, it would behoove you to consider this matter seriously, and I have no doubt that when you do, you will accept the mantle for which you are destined."

J.P. wadded up the letter and threw it across the room in disgust, not sure whether the principal source of his anger was a further attempt to thwart his timetable for graduate study, the implied blackmail of withholding funds that would make that possible, the arrogant presumption that his father knew what was best for him and that he would automatically accede to it, or the aristocratic sense of entitlement that pervaded it all. King Felix indeed! Why wasn't he happy?

He sat down at his desk and opened his notebook to continue work on his paper, but his head felt as though it were about to explode: he could hardly concentrate his thoughts on anything. Why had he ever thought he was walking in his father's footsteps as he strolled across the university campus: what had his father ever learned there except to express himself in florid, empty platitudes? His business sense and ability to make the family firm succeed had come from somewhere besides books and the classroom.

That evening J.P. went out to seek his friend Franco Minetti, a student from up north whom he had befriended his freshman year, to gain some insight and calm himself down.

"The problems you people have! If New Jersey had more colleges and I didn't have to come down here to get a degree, I never would have learned how different things are here. Man, what an education!"

A knock on Franco's door announced the arrival of Billy McCall, who was from J.P.'s hometown, but whom he had not met before coming to the university because Billy had gone to the big public high school, while he had attended the private boys' academy. Billy had moved with his family from upstate to the port city during the war, when his father, like scores of other hardscrabble farmers, had taken a welding job in the shipbuilding industry.

"I'm not from up north, but all this royalty stuff is a mystery to me too," said Billy, plopping his lanky frame down on the bed.

"I think they want to keep it that way," said J.P.

"I just want to finish and get a job when I get out. I'll guaran-damntee you you won't catch me in some king's costume."

J.P. had come to appreciate Billy's intelligence and ability to zero in on how to accomplish things, not caring whether he was pursuing or altering established ways.

They didn't solve any problems, but the general chatter until late in the night over bottles of Miller High Life that Franco had smuggled into his room helped to put things on an even keel. It had taken

J.P. a while to appreciate how legendary bull sessions in the dorm added to his perspective.

"Hey, you guys, listen to this," said Franco when he detected a new song on the radio that had been playing quietly in the background.

"That's *y'all*," said Billy. "You at least gotta learn that before you graduate."

"Y'ALL," screamed Franco, unconvinced. "I mean it," he said, turning up the music's volume. "I heard this song when I went home with Tommy Ellis. It was taking Memphis by storm, and now it's about to flood the country. We're going to be hearing a lot more from this singer, who's even younger than we are. It sure ain't our fathers' music. Our lives won't be the same, I tell you."

> *I'm leaving town, baby, I'm leaving town for sure*
> *Then you won't be bothered with me hanging 'round your door*
> *That's all right, that's all right*
> *That's all right now, mama, anyway you do*

The beat somehow got under his skin, but J.P., who was not known for keeping up with the latest, couldn't make much of it, and couldn't even tell if the music was Black or white. But maybe they were indeed on the verge of a new era when new kings would replace the old, and he resolved to keep an open mind.

● ● ●

He delayed a decision about his father's request, or more precisely demand, as long as he could: he was of age and could do what he wished, but the problem of financing was one he couldn't immediately solve. And furthermore, he feverishly conjured up worse scenarios, such as a complete disinheritance. This was part of a long pattern of his father's attempts to chart his course in life. He had joined his father's fraternity his freshman year, his father's mystic society not long after that, and he was certain his father was behind the mysterious delivery of an invitation the previous year to join the "Corporation," that secret organization without an official name to which a select group belonged and which for years had controlled the student government behind the scenes and provided grooming for later positions of power within the state, when graduates went on to serve in business, law, and government and to use their network to continue exerting influence and advancing their own aims. He knew his father had been in the Corporation in his student days, though no one had ever said that: like the Mardi Gras societies, it was "secret." He accepted that invitation, even though he was not an especially eager participant. Their activities failed to interest him very much, and he found their sense of self-importance at times ridiculous. He skipped many of the meetings and had the feeling he was purposefully excluded from others, probably as a result of his offhand comment before the initiation, which was offered in a spirit of self-effacing camaraderie but which was no doubt taken as an insult: "I find it a great honor to join you as a cog in the machine."

He had assented then as he had many other times, but he was not sure how long this pattern could continue. He wondered when he would finally acquire the courage to stick to his convictions. This time the decision posed more of a dilemma: he could not just tacitly accept and then sit idly on the sidelines, as he had done with the Corporation. At length he gave in and told his father he would play the role for a year (though he didn't use those exact words), but that he was determined to study after that. He tried to present it as a compromise, in which each side had to make concessions. Another flowery letter followed, expressing "delight at the rational decision I knew would prevail."

Graduation took place on schedule a few months later; he was happy that a Latin phrase was appended to his diploma in classics to indicate the highest honor with which he had achieved his degree. His father pleaded business matters as an excuse to stay at home, but his mother was driven up in the Cadillac by Leon, the family's loyal retainer, who maintained the various functions of the house along with his wife Lucille. His mother had reserved a room in the downtown hotel; Leon was staying with a relative of the pastor of his church, since there were no hotels that would have put him up. When they arrived, J.P. felt a certain unease: the lugubriousness of the black vehicle reminded him of a hearse; its oversized, pointed grill ornaments projected like threatening fangs; and the small fins housing the taillights looked like a pretentious afterthought. Leon sprang out and promptly adjusted his chauffeur's cap, before opening the rear door for his mother. She came forward to give her son a respectable hug and turned her cheek so that he could plant a light kiss.

"How is everyone?" he asked dutifully.

"Your father's busy, as always. I never have any idea what he does all day down at the office. We're trying to get Anthony to study more for his exams. At least you'll be able to go to his graduation. Aunt Clotilde sends her best: she also sent a little something, which I have in my suitcase and will give to you later." His mother tried as usual to make up for the slightness of her frame and personality with a dignified reserve.

"And how is Lucille?" he asked Leon with more interest.

"She's fine. She sends her regards too. She sure is proud of you."

He appreciated the warmth of the reply, but wished the sentiments could have been conveyed with a bit less obsequiousness. But perhaps Leon was maintaining his integrity behind the facade he had adapted to negotiate the constraints of reality. J.P. wondered when things would ever change, and people could come into their own. If he paid more attention to such things, he might have surmised that the recent decision of the Supreme Court in the matter of Brown v. the Board of Education would mark the start of a new period for his native region as much as his own graduation would for his life. Perhaps the nation was beginning to grow up—or was it? He was not aware that a Black woman had applied for admission to the university and been accepted at first, before being rejected later "on a technicality" when it was discovered she was not white.

"Should we go ahead and put my things in the trunk now, or wait until we leave tomorrow?" he asked, eager to move the conversation on to other matters. "I don't have very much really. Mainly a few boxes of books—you know I'm not much of a clothes horse."

"Let's do it tomorrow," replied his mother with deliberation. "We'll have plenty of time."

The outstanding feature of the graduation was not the ceremony, which seemed interminable and contained a tedious speech filled with advice that somehow everyone already knew but would never follow. The highlight for him was opening Aunt Clotilde's gift and note in his room the night before. It was an eight-inch replica from the Metropolitan Museum of an ancient Greek sculpture, a victorious youth raising his hand toward the laurel wreath on his head. A body of ideal perfection, yet completely real at the same time: somewhere, there had been an actual youth who had served as model. The writing in Aunt Clotilde's careful penmanship on the ivory vellum stated, "He's no doubt an athlete, but I thought of you, since there are many ways to achieve victory. Your scholarship is no less deserving, and I know you'll take it to even loftier heights." The sculpture was something J.P. would end up carrying with him wherever he went. At least someone understands, he thought, even if she's never read Xenophanes.

On the four-hour drive home through the Black Belt, largely uneventful except for the sight of a couple of men in a field, beating or trying to revive a dead mule, he managed to broach the subject of graduate studies, but his mother only raised her fragile hand half-heartedly and said, deferring, he was sure, to her absent husband, "We'll have all the time in the world to talk about that later."

Time was one thing J.P. felt he didn't have when they returned home. As the summer sped by, the upcoming carnival season seemed to be the only thing that anyone ever talked about. They arranged to meet with the family of the young woman who was to be his queen in order to plan further events. He noted that the queens were always referred to by all three of their names, since it was important to put their bloodlines on display. He also realized to his annoyance that the decisions to be made regarding the design of the costume and the elaborate, jewel-studded train took up much more of his attention than he had anticipated. His mother engaged him in long conversations about the exact shade of velvet to be chosen, and whether ermine or some other fur should be used as a lining. He realized this was a task in which she could feel useful, and he knew that in addition she wished to do it for him. She was such a dear, and he couldn't fault her, though the whole endeavor made him even more resentful of the social order that relegated her to this position and in which she so readily consented to be imprisoned.

More disturbing to him was the realization of how much of the family's wealth the whole undertaking was consuming: he had no idea it would cost so much to outfit himself, host events, and take care of other unanticipated sundry matters. He began to convince himself that his parents would consider this outlay to be their investment in his future, instead of contributing to his studies.

When the topic came up once again at supper, he launched a feeble protest, speaking at first in general terms because he thought that raising his personal objections would seem too self-interested. He argued that the whole celebration was an incredible waste of money, which could be better spent feeding the poor.

"It is feeding the goddam poor!" screamed his father. "Who do you think lines up to watch the parades? It's the grandest entertainment they have all year, and it's all for free. Who do you think pays for the candy? Hell, some of the members even want to start throwing moon pies."

"It looks like the future is bringing bigger and better things."

"The future doesn't bring anything. You have to make it yourself. And if our putting on this whole spectacle for the public at large isn't charity, I don't know what is."

"*Noblesse oblige*: that it pat itself on the back," muttered J.P.

His father, who was practically screaming at this point, pounded his fist so hard that the plates clattered. "We can't help it if we're the ones in a position to do it. Besides, all the money stays in the local economy. The float builders are given jobs and can feed their families with their paychecks. Think of all the money spent on throws! And street vendors come in and profit as well."

"Not to mention the liquor distributors," chimed in Anthony.

"Tell Lucille her shrimp creole was delightful as usual," said J.P. in an attempt to calm things down when he realized how livid his father was becoming and fearing that he might pop a blood vessel.

The contentiousness seemed to have become a regular feature of their dinnertime gatherings, and J.P. did not see how it would ever disappear.

One evening when he was writing Princeton to inform them of his dilemma, his father came into his room to discuss the design of the crown and scepter, which he thought should echo the past glory of his own reign and contain additional elements symbolizing their family's history.

"And the future?" asked J.P. "Shouldn't that be recognized as well?"

"What do you have in mind?"

"Frankly, I hadn't thought about it yet. Maybe different figures clasping hands in unity, maybe a dove of peace." A white yin, intertwining with a black yang, or vice versa, he thought but didn't say.

His father wrinkled his brow, saying skeptically, "Certainly, we can think about it."

• • •

But his time was also taken by his summer employment, "another form of learning" as his father put it, no doubt repressing an urge to say "a more sensible and profitable form of learning." J.P. was working in the office this time, instead of in the sawmill or out in the bottomlands north of the Chickasabogue feeding logs down the chute. This year it would be Anthony's turn in the sawmill, and he would no doubt be able to use his fullback's arms and hands to safely guide the big boards past the deafening, screeching rotation of the giant blade, which moved so swiftly that its dangerous teeth were just a blur. The office work was certainly calmer, though the boredom seemed almost as deadly to him. Filing the papers, answering correspondence, sitting in at occasional meetings all bore a superficial resemblance to classroom work, but there was little to inspire his mind or engage his talents. At slack times, of which there were many, he would gaze out from the eighth-floor windows across the mouth of the bay and up toward the river delta, relishing the expanse of unspoiled nature and its possibilities, so different from the monetary possibilities that the family business saw in the land along its edges. Finding out about the firm's concept of opportunities and how they came to be realized formed the bulk of his learning in the time spent in the office: scouting out available acreage, buying it up at an advantageous price, cultivating some lots for timber to be processed at the family mill, razing others for development as subdivisions or shopping centers, all in a multitude of interconnections. It was extremely complex, but his father had an eye for it, and changes to the landscape and the community came about as a result, as well as a fattening of the family bank account. J.P. found many of the intricacies of the transactions arcane, and although he was capable of understanding them by dint of forced concentration, he was less eager to parse them than he would have been to analyze a line of Attic verse. He was not certain that everything was always legal, but the distinctions between the questionable, the ethical, and the lawful were at times so minute that he could not make them out. The firm, however, had attorneys to work through it all.

J.P. considered his employment, like that of previous years, as merely a summer job, though he was sure that his father regarded it as a transition that would proceed without interruption to the real thing. He closely observed his father's behavior with various people: his hearty laugh and slap on the back with friends and trusted business associates; the immovable expression with which he greeted those whom he hoped to best in a business deal; his friendly flirtatiousness with Mrs. Lillian Padgett, the secretary, who, J.P. was sure, could see right through him but nonetheless respected him; and his general ignoring of the cleaning help. "Always look a man in the eye—show him you're not afraid," his father would often say to him when he caught his son glancing down at his shoes in uncertainty. He realized there was a lot of knowledge to acquire in various respects, and he was still trying to figure out what to emulate and what to ignore. The firm, after all, actually did things, and what did his own studies ever accomplish?

He was reminded of another type of learning when he noticed his father's frequent absences in the afternoon, with only vague references to "business." Although his mother couldn't always figure out what her husband did down at the office, J.P. thought he was beginning to get a clue. He recalled one of his father's few visits to him at the university, when they had walked around the campus as the older man pointed out buildings where he had taken classes ("I don't remember a word of the German I was taught or any of the dates from history," he recounted with a sort of pride) or engaged in various sorts of mischief. J.P., on the other hand, proudly pointed out the Gorgas Library, where he spent much of his time.

"When I was a student, it was in Carmichael. One or two floors was all we needed for books back then."

J.P. thought about how the sites for repositories of knowledge changed, even though the words that were contained in the older volumes didn't. Knowledge merely expanded, and he wondered when Gorgas would become too small. But then he recalled with horror the burning of thousands of papyrus rolls in the library at Alexandria, and how much was lost to humanity through the flames. He wondered if it could happen again.

Of greater interest to his father was the stadium, which could now seat twice as many spectators as in his own student days. And more important than that was the postwar renewal of the football competition with the cross-state Polytechnic Institute, which had been suspended for forty-one years after 1907, but in which the old man could now finally participate as a spectator in annual trips to Legion Field in the state's largest city. Which side one took in this athletic rivalry, J.P. came to realize, was the defining factor of one's identity in the state.

After dinner in the dining room of the hotel, his father had driven with him out of town to a two-story frame house in need of paint, set back from the road and marked with an ivory-rose porch light and dim illumination from the curtained windows.

"What is this place?" asked J.P.

"I see you don't know. It's time you found out."

As they got closer he could hear the tinkle of a piano and the sound of jazz. A man sitting in a metal lawn chair beside the front door rose as they approached, and after his father whispered something in his ear, he opened the door to admit them. The muffled conversations became louder as they entered, and when J.P. observed a man on a sagging couch grinning to the attention of two heavily-made-up females on either side of him with their arms around his neck, he began to get an idea of the type of establishment in which they found themselves. Bright light bulbs were shielded by

tasseled shades, and spots of illumination were overshadowed by
corners of darkness; there was a lot of purple, and J.P. could not
decide if the atmosphere was garish or exotic. An older woman in a
decent dress and a hairdo that had obviously taken hours under
curlers to create came over to meet them; her neutral face quickly
broke into a smile of recognition.

"Why, if it isn't John P. Devaux! I haven't seen you in ages," she
said.

"You've got a good memory, Miss Rosa," his father replied.

"How could I forget?" she asked, wagging a finger in his face. "And
who have we here?"

"Another John P. Devaux. We'll see how much alike he is."

"Well, if he's anything at all alike, he'll be well taken care of. As
you will too, of course."

"Well, this is another day. I think I'll just start off with a glass of
Jim Beam."

They were soon sitting at the bar in the next room gripping their
glasses and listening to the comments of a rowdy group of Kappa
Sigs, who, although they seemed to consider their off-color remarks
oh-so clever, nevertheless gave their insecurity away with their
smirks. After a few moments J.P. was aware of a young woman with
bleach-blond hair in a short dress and fishnet stockings standing by
his side. She had a blank, though slightly anticipatory expression on
her face.

"Well go on," said his father, nudging his arm with his elbow.
"She's got something she wants to show you."

J.P. slid off his stool and followed her as she turned to walk down
the hall and up the stairs to a little room at the back, furnished only
with a chair, a narrow bed, and a little table on which stood a clock
and a lamp with a violet shade. He had obliged because he sometimes did not know how not to obey his father, but also out of
curiosity and the urges that he naturally felt as a young man who had
often thought about such things. He didn't know, however, whether
his father was trying to initiate him into the real world or into the
means of escaping the real world's unyielding demands.

They stared at each other for a moment, until she removed her
shift with one swift cross-armed motion and laid it across the back

of the chair. A patch of pale skin shone through the tear in her stockings below the garter; he could not take his eyes off the thick tangle of black hair above it. Although she must be experienced, he thought, she somehow seems equally shy: does either of us know what we're doing here? He looked to his Ovid for answers:

> *I myself was lazy, born ungirt for leisure;*
> > *A couch for reading in the shade had made my spirit soft.*
> *But attention from a comely girl forced up idle me*
> > *And impelled me into service.*
> *Hence you see me now, lively and engaged in nightly combat.*
> > *Let anyone who doesn't wish to stay inactive seek out love!*

She wasn't exactly pretty—more of a thin country girl of a type he wouldn't have normally considered. The application of paint to her face was designed to create an attraction that should have been in the essence, rather than on the surface. But when her eyes darted with an inquiring, almost vulnerable look, he threw his arms around her and buried his face in her small breasts. They tumbled to the bed and did what they were supposed to do. For the moment, he thought, I will call it life.

When he returned to the bar, his father was nowhere to be seen, but soon reappeared with a drink and a look that seemed to ask, "Well, how was it?" J.P. merely looked at the floor of the dreary establishment, covered with dust and stained with beer. Inwardly, however, he felt a sort of glow that he couldn't explain. Father and son then made their way back to town.

Now standing at the eighth-floor window, he wondered what he might accomplish if he were indeed to take over operations here one day. His father's immediate plans were to move out of the Van Leyden Building, where they occupied half a floor, and into their own structure, which would be designed by the architect of the Waterman Building and the Grand Hotel at Point Clear. "Why not something grand for ourselves?" his father had said. "I mean, this building may have been quite the thing fifty years ago when it was one of the first skyscrapers in town, but it's only got one tiny stairwell and two old Otis elevators. I mean, what the hell?!" They would hardly need a whole building, but the rest could be rented out for a profit in their burgeoning real estate empire. J.P. lacked such imperial dreams, but was not sure what the most desirable way of structuring things would be.

> *Hearken well when you hear the voice of the crane,*
> *crying each year from the clouds on high*
> *To mark the rainy winter and the time for plowing*
> *so that you can make plans.*

Beyond the windows a freighter steamed slowly upriver to the port. A distant bird—a heron? an eagle?—soared languidly above the Delta.

A couple of weeks later, in reply to his letter, Princeton responded by saying that they had decided to award him a more generous fellowship, and in addition, that he could take a job in the library, which should cover any other expenses he would incur. No doubt the *summa cum laude* had played a greater role in their decision than the title of *rex carnevalarii*. After he had let the information sink in, he realized he could swing it. He would have to move quickly, however, since classes started soon. But he didn't relish the inevitable confrontation that would occur when he announced his decision; he therefore put off acting as long as he could.

There appeared to be no right moment, so he finally dived right in. Before he had even finished with what he had to say, his father's face had turned a frightful scarlet, and J.P. feared he was being confronted with a case of apoplexy.

"How in hell's name could you possibly imagine you can back out? It's all settled—it can't be undone."

In his father's mind the course was set in stone, but to J.P. the outcome was hardly inevitable, or even serious.

"You know there are plenty of young men eager to leap at the chance. Besides, the king is always called Felix III, so what difference does it make?" He realized almost too late that the last remark was the wrong way to address his choleric parent, adding gratuitous insult to injury and compounding personal disloyalty with a questioning of the validity of the whole enterprise.

"How little you know, you little shit! They wouldn't have time to prepare. Work has already begun on the costume!" His father slammed his fist into his open palm.

"Let Anthony wear it. We're the same height."

"He's too young," sputtered his father. "Nobody has ever been king at that age."

"It'll make a man of him. Besides, as you previously argued, with his lineage, how could they reject him?"

But attempts at rational arguments were futile. His father, unaccustomed to being contradicted, was only able to fume. The tempest in his mind was so strong it was palpable, and it rendered him temporarily speechless. But before he stomped out and slammed the door behind him, he managed to spit out, "What kind of son have I raised? Filial ingratitude!"

This too, J.P. tried to convince himself, will blow over: it's not the tragedy we make it out to be.

η

Most beautiful of all the things I've left is the light of the sun;
second the sparkling stars and then the face of the moon,
as well as ripe cucumbers, and apples, and pears.
— Praxilla, fragment from "Hymn to Adonis"

J.P. SAT IN HIS FAVORITE HIGH-BACKED CHAIR, the nap of its roseate upholstery worn smooth in places from a previous generation's years of talking and contemplating. He settled down into the cushion and let his relaxed hands flop over the ends of the extended arms. He closed his eyes and regarded across from him on the harder seat of an ancient Windsor chair his favorite conversation partner, his friend in dialogue, his companion in dialectics, the adversary off whom he could bounce ideas and who would, on occasion, hold his feet to the fire. Books stood heavy on the shelves surrounding them.

"You know, things haven't really changed around here much, have they?"

"What do you mean?"

"For example, I was amused when I noticed that people still describe the location of establishments through their spatial relation to places that no longer exist: 'That store is across from where Constantine's Restaurant used to be.' That designation would be meaningless to anyone who had not been present at the earlier time and place."

"You're right. I'd never noticed that. I probably do it myself."

"And Miranda. Has she come back to circle through it all again? I sometimes despair of her situation now, and her future." J.P. seemed to sigh after a long lull.

The other, puzzled, looked at him a while before replying.

"How can you say that? She's smart, beautiful, has an advanced degree and a secure job that she likes—it even has benefits. It has the variety and opportunity for creativity that make it interesting. She's capable, and knows how to deal with people and situations. What more could she want, or you for her?"

"I know, I know."

"What then?"

"It's just that, like everyone, she's thrown out into the world. The waves are not always placid or predictable. Despite her character, accomplishments, and what she's discovered and has experienced, she's still learning. There's always a chance. . . ."

"Yes, yes, but as you say, that's true for all of us. And it's the feeling of almost everyone who has children. They won't know how to deal with the hard knocks, however, unless they actually experience them. What more can you do? You seem to have done wonderfully as it is."

"You're exaggerating. How much was actually my doing? Even genetically: she's her mother's child too. She was more or less taken away at an early age, and I was absent for so much of the time. What control do we have over offspring, even if we've been there all along to raise them? What determines that they carry over some of us nonetheless, or what makes them veer off in their own direction? How well do I really know her? In any case, it still cannot mitigate the feeling of despair."

"Can bourbon?"

"No, no, that can't either," said J.P., pouring himself another inch and opening his eyes and raising them, as if searching among the titles of his books.

"She'll turn out. After all, didn't you?"

"I was turned out, but I don't know if I *have* turned out. I feel as though I've turned too much inward. In any case, I've resolved never to turn *her* out again. At least she has that assurance."

"I don't know if I really know you. Sometimes you seem as ancient as those classics you love so much, filled with all the wisdom you have absorbed from them, and sometimes your remarks strike with the spontaneous force of youth. Are you a chip off the old Devaux block, or a rebellious changeling?"

J.P. sighed and looked around. "That's what I've been wondering my whole life. It seems like all of the above. Don't we all maintain numerous identities within our persons, ones that we can't fathom ourselves, and which others have no chance of comprehending?"

"I'm sure you're right. But doesn't that seem kind of obvious? I'm apparently a simple sort, however, not plagued with such worries."

"You're perhaps lucky in that regard. It's hard for me to imagine that Anthony is concerned with such matters either. He just charges along, carrying out his plans for conquest and empire. But does he really move things, or is it the need to develop things, whatever the course, that moves him?"

"He's certainly been successful."

"And highly thought of—which is sometimes hard to grasp considering the ruthlessness he so blatantly displays and the number of people he's trampled in the process. But the public admires wealth and assumes that those to whom it has accrued deserve it and have achieved it through their own merits. They're all too eager to subordinate themselves to those who seem to be able, and from whom they might someday gather some crumbs."

"I couldn't have put it better myself. He probably has had lots of help from the mayor. Aren't they pretty close?"

"Alphonse Rapier? They conspired against me at one time as you know, and there's certainly no love lost between us. But Alphonse is getting on in years, and besides, my brother's occasional reliance on Thomas Gonzalez might keep him in check."

"You mean that nice old man?"

"Nice old man, decent human being, magnanimous spirit, great-hearted soul: what you will. He has certainly aided me from time to time. But in any case I'm more concerned with the rest of Alphonse's family: his much younger half-brother Sebastian, for example. He's more Anthony's age. And I've heard Alphonse has a very young son from a late second marriage. Who knows what he's like? A chip off the old block, the spit and image?"

"Like you in respect to your father, you mean?"

"Touché."

"Tell me, when do you intend to make yourself known to Anthony, and how? And what do you intend to do about him, and your own situation? What are your plans?"

J.P. waved his hand back and forth in indecision. "All I can say is, my plan for today was to procrastinate, but I decided to put that off until tomorrow."

"Ha, ha, clever. Could you repeat that? I would like to be able to use it."

"Sorry, it would be something different the second time. The words will have become reified and seemingly exalted, but actually diminished as a result of being frozen. Like bumper stickers: I mean, how many times can you read 'Be the truth you would like others to be' without becoming stupefied or nauseated?"

"Does that mean there is no such thing as truth?"

"Of course not. We would not know how to live otherwise. It's just almost impossible to encapsulate without running the danger of becoming empty, or employed as ideology or morality to beat others over the head with. But to answer your original question about my plans for Anthony: I don't know yet exactly, though I'm working on it. I've got a book, a journal, on my desk, where I propose to lay out what I have in mind, adding ideas from other sources that I run across. Justice must be done, and not for my sake alone."

"Miranda's?"

J.P. stood up and began pacing in circles, as if to gather his thoughts. "Yes, but not necessarily in terms of money. Her focus is elsewhere now, and I wouldn't want that ever to change. I'm thinking about those people who, among other things, are having to decide every day between food, rent, and medicine."

"What do you mean?"

"Where have you been? Who do you think owns that great swath of apartments along the interstate and little ranch houses in subdivisions scattered here and there? Who built them with inferior materials that will give out in the next decade or two and which no doubt are filled with chemicals that will destroy the health of the people crammed inside them? And charging exorbitant rents, because he's bought up or forced out any meaningful competition. Have you ever looked at any of those houses? The windows are barely half as big as they should be, ruining the proportions and making the entire facade look ridiculous, not to mention denying light to the interior. He probably installed them because that's what he had an oversupply of, not because he had any architectural sense. And the D'Iberville projects: he got that contract more by crook than by hook, and you can be sure he skimped on the construction there too."

"You've picked up a lot since you've been back."

"Not only since then. I have my sources, who kept me informed over the years, and you can gather a lot by reading the newspaper, both between the lines and even in the lines themselves."

"Maybe your younger brother is the true scion, carrying out what your ancestors have always done. Isn't that the true history of this country—being enterprising and knowing how to build things? Or, if you want to be cynical, how to exploit the labor and possessions of others for your own benefit? Isn't that what really made this nation, rather than the ideals of liberty. justice, and equal opportunity for all? Those things are intangibles—words and ideas, just like you."

"You may be right. Free enterprise. Free for those who know how to take advantage and game the system. But that's another example of things not changing. Back when I was in college I had a friend who worked summers in his uncle's country store in a little crossroads community somewhere in the Black Belt. He manned the cash register, and his uncle instructed him to place his thumb on the scale unobtrusively when Black customers made purchases. Back then there was segregation in the schools, suppression of voting rights, and outright violence and lynching, but it is also astounding that the greed for wealth and power, the prejudice, the willingness to take advantage of the ones least able to resist extended even to such forms of petty meanness. Like the bus drivers who drove right past Blacks waiting at bus stops. You can't tell me those subtle and not-so-subtle injustices have completely disappeared."

"No, I'll have to admit you're right."

"But the question is, what do I do next?"

"I'm afraid I can't help you there. You'll have to answer that yourself, if those books can't," he said, giving the shelves a glance with a roll of his eyes. "In fact, I wonder sometimes why you don't talk more to other people."

"Other people are all too often satisfied that a sentence or two is sufficient to cover a topic, and it's hard to probe deeper with them. Or they think the purpose of a conversation is to give them the opportunity to spout off their opinion. For me, the purpose of a discussion is to engage in exploration, in ways that are both wide-ranging and deep, and, I hope, to arrive at a new place, instead of merely seeking confirmation of what I already know."

J.P. let out an audible breath as he sat back down. "Forgive me for lapsing into sadness. I wonder though: does sadness come from being abandoned, ignored by other people, or from an abandonment of one's own ability to reach out to others? I am indeed isolated, and no doubt I'm responsible for that myself. Do you know etymology? *Isolate*, from the Italian *isola*, from the Latin *insula*, meaning island. I feel as though I'm stranded on an island. I'm king in my own little world, but humanity continues all around, elsewhere."

He took another swig of bourbon and looked dolefully about him, before continuing: "It's funny, Miranda's on an island too. Maybe we do have a lot in common."

"Yes, but isn't her island on the forefront and she on the cutting edge, working to make new discoveries and launch us into something better?"

"You're right. Thanks for keeping my perspective in line."

"But I hear you have another protegé. Tell me about that one."

J.P. looked up quizzically. "You mean Ariel?"

"Yes, that's right."

"Ariel's the only child of my old friend Billy McCall, who died not so long ago. Ariel was at loose ends, had problems with finding a direction, especially in the teenage years, and was sent by Billy to Lisbon when I was posted there to see if I could help. A bright wisp of a thing, a lively sprite, but with inner demons I was unaware of at first and which Billy probably did not fully understand either. Ariel was supposed to be enrolled in a total-immersion language camp, but I was unable to do much. I wasn't really able to act *in loco parentis*: in fact, to my regret I had little knowledge or experience of being a parent at all. A glimpse of a figure in a knit stocking cap and a shapeless jacket disappearing around the corner of a narrow street in the old quarter, usually humming some mournful *fado* picked up in one of the taverns, was sometimes the only sign I encountered for days. I could tell the child was not happy: it was not the difference in culture, however, but other differences that made it hard for someone like that to fit in. Observing things, I experienced disquiet myself. Eventually Billy summoned Ariel home again. My old friend was by then a widower, in between jobs and without health insurance when his cancer was discovered. The treatments took most of his money, and the rapid progress of his disease made him anxious about Ariel's future."

"Is this a great country, or what?

"To be honest, much of the time I would have to answer with 'what.' But I suppose I should try to do what I can about it. Around that time Ariel suddenly seemed to find a focus in computers and began studying at the junior college. I sent tuition money to make sure that a lack of funds didn't foil this newfound purpose and, even after Billy died I continued paying for studies when his penniless heir went on to the university. Ariel had decided meanwhile to undergo a series of expensive medical treatments, an undertaking to which I readily consented. I mean, can you imagine being imprisoned by physical limitations that prevent you from becoming who you really are? This of course required even more financial aid from me. I felt as though I owed it to Billy, and I wanted to do right by Ariel, who finally graduates this spring. I wrote to Thomas Gonzalez to see if he could work behind the scenes to get Ariel a position in Anthony's firm, which he was able to do. Although I don't stress the issue, Ariel has a strong, inherent decency and feels a great sense of obligation to pay me back, but, knowing that it would take forever to accumulate the money that is owed, I suggested that as a substitute, access to the firm's computers might provide me with valuable information or the ability to carry out other tasks that I might find useful."

"I see. You've done more thinking than I realized. I'm curious as to how things will turn out."

There was a pause, when nothing could be heard but the ticking of the antique ogee clock on the mantel that had been in the family for years; the steady tick-tock did not signal to him the passage of a time that would never be regained: it provided instead a reassuring presence, a constancy, like the gentle rocking of a boat on a voyage across a sea of limitless horizon.

"Enough talk about your whiskey and your bygone days. It's time for me to go, I think."

"And time I should get moving."

He drained his glass and rubbed his eyes. Their conversation had unfolded at a pace that wasn't hurried, appropriate to the elapsing of time. A moth fluttered upward in nervous, erratic circles—a pathetic embodiment of what was going on in his mind?

He blew out the candle, because sometimes he saw more through the smoke than from the light of the flame as the ashen vapor rose in a thin, brilliantly pale line of orderly exactitude to a certain point high above the wick, where it dissipated, curling out and spiraling back in unpredictable directions, then continuing upward in its tumultuous path, mapping out the way things really were.

θ

CREON: *Am I to rule this land by others' judgment or my own?*
HAEMON: *A city for one man alone is truly not a city.*
CREON: *The city is the ruler's, so it is held.*
HAEMON: *On a desert isle you'd rule beautifully alone.*
CREON: *This boy, it seems, is taking up the woman's cause.*
　　　　　　　　　　　　　　　　—Sophocles, *Antigone*

AFTER THE ERUPTION OF THAT LAST SUMMER at home things did somehow resolve themselves, or rather the various players took steps to enable their lives to go on. J.P. boarded a train for New Jersey in time to catch the start of classes, and his father delayed announcement of the abdication long enough to make it difficult for the Association to consider someone other than his own choice of his younger son Anthony to be king of carnival. His mother could continue with her part in family preparations for the big event, and Anthony could proudly strut among his friends.

The initial adjustment into graduate courses soon settled itself into a familiar rhythm; J.P. felt comfortable in the old Gothic classroom building, erected in the 19th century just across from the university's oldest hall, which had been built in the century before that. The authors in the books on the desk in front of him went back much further still, and he pondered the sweep of history as he tried to decide if he wanted to concentrate eventually on the Archaic, the Classical, or the Hellenistic period. His job in the library gave him time to read, despite the frequent interruptions as he examined books to see if they had been properly checked out before patrons left the building. It paid enough to enable him to barely get by and to afford meager, shared lodgings a mile from campus. The Spartan existence hardly bothered him, however, since he was following his aspirations.

Letters from home were infrequent: his mother was the only one in his immediate family who wrote, since his father was no doubt still too pissed off and Anthony had never been much of a letter writer to begin with. Yet the correspondence occasionally contained feelers about his ultimate intentions—apparently there was still a possibility in their minds of his heading the family firm at some point. To these he responded with vague comments of his own. He exchanged letters from time to time with Aunt Clotilde, whose remarks were usually trenchant: "I hope Anthony doesn't peak too soon: I don't see how he can pass his freshman year, given his poor high school record, the amount of time he has to spend down here with the Mardi Gras doings, and his general attitude that a college education is superfluous for a career in the family firm." She also indicated her approval of the course of his own life: "I'm glad you're where you are: it's where I thought you should have gone in the first place."

Billy McCall, who had gotten a job with the Merchants Bank, also informed him about various goings-on around town: "I overheard some fellows in the loan department chuckling because your father has been buying up a lot of the swamp between downtown and the foot of Spring Hill. 'I wish I had some swampland I could sell him,' one of them said. I myself can't believe your old man's that stupid, but I don't have any idea what's going on." J.P. didn't either, but he had to agree that it was likely his father saw something they didn't.

J.P. stayed up north for the holidays, spending some time with Franco Minetti's family and going into the city with him to catch "Show Boat" on Broadway and watch the ball drop at New Year's. As February approached, however, J.P.'s curiosity got the better of him, and he even wished he could return home to see how things went at Mardi Gras. But he couldn't take time off from his classes, and there was no way he could have been a fly on the wall, even though as a member of the society he would have been entitled to wear a mask. Who we are is always a secret, he thought, although obviously someone there would certainly be able to pin a name on him if he were spotted. He did, however, write to Thomas Gonzalez, the lawyer who was an acquaintance of his father's and a member of the same mystic society, to see if he couldn't wangle an invitation for Billy to attend the ball and coronation so that he could provide a first-hand report. Gonzalez, despite his surname, was no recent immigrant: his ancestors had arrived from Malaga to work in the administration when the area was under Spanish rule before 1819. A thoughtful, kindly man, he had always had a fondness for J.P., and J.P. knew he could entrust him with any confidences despite his closeness to the power structure and occasional advice on legal matters to the family firm. The invitation was forthcoming, but Billy was unable to provide him with eyewitness accounts for pecuniary reasons: he could not afford to rent tails, the *costume de rigueur* for such festivities, and J.P. had no way to provide him with his own formalwear which hung in his old bedroom closet. Billy was able, however, to watch the arrival of the king and queen on their barge at the foot of Government Street and view the royal coach wending its way down Dauphin Street on Fat Tuesday; he also sent clippings from the *Press-Register*. As usual, Black society had its own king and queen and separate Mammoth Parade. Two groups of people, side by side but in parallel universes, doing the same thing at the same time but not together. The newspaper accounts painted a rosy picture of everything, but Billy enjoyed portraying how a red-faced and grinning Anthony, who had obviously had plenty to drink, almost fell from the float as he twirled himself around one of the pole supports while hurling doubloons. In his letter Thomas Gonzalez asked whether J.P. had any regrets and wondered whether things might have played out for the better if he had performed the role expected of him both at the festivities and in the firm. He also described the celebrations, giving particular attention to the ball's *tableau vivant* of *A Midsummer Night's Dream*. Is everything a fanciful vision, a case of mistaken identity, to be corrected through magic, thought J.P.? But there is no magic anymore—or is there? And in any case life doesn't usually have the satisfying conclusions of comedy, although it does somehow manage to go on nonetheless.

And it did, though not, as you will see, Miranda, in a straightforward fashion.

Newspapers from the area in which he was now living had no interest in reporting on the Mardi Gras in his home town: the closest they came was giving brief mention to the celebration in New Orleans. Of more concern to them were events which were occurring farther north in his home state, where Negroes had been boycotting busses in the capital city since December. Initially they merely sought to be treated with respect, but soon sued to overturn segregation in the transportation system altogether. Although Blacks made up the vast majority of the bus ridership, they had second-class status in the treatment they received. The existing "order" was one J.P. had grown up with, and it was so ingrained into his being that he only slowly came round to siding with the protestors. And that African American woman who had been denied admission to his university: after several years of litigation, she was finally able to start classes. But this simple, lawful act provoked violent riots on the part of whites, and she was expelled, this time on the pretext of protecting her own safety. When J.P. became aware of the remark-able tenacity and ingenuity the wrongly excluded showed in their resistance, and their refusal to sink to the level of their opponents, his sense of justice began to win out. He could recognize nobility when he saw it. Things in the wider world were changing in various ways and making themselves felt far beyond. If he had still been at the university, however, would he have been courageous enough to take the proper stand?

J.P.'s principal concentration remained nevertheless on his studies, and both at the time and years later in retrospect he would regard these days as among his happiest, when nothing was required of him but to read his beloved texts. When summers rolled around he managed to find fellowships to take him to Greece and Rome, mainly to improve his language skills and engage in research, but also, for his purposes, to provide an excuse not to go home. In contrast, Anthony spent his summers closely tied to positions of increasing responsibility within the family firm. In his second and third years J.P. was awarded teaching assistantships, and despite some trepidation and rough starts in the classroom, he realized that he did not mind teaching and could perhaps pursue it as a career after all. He received a Fulbright grant to work on his dissertation in Athens for a whole year, and after that he returned to Princeton to continue writing it. His meticulousness and compulsion to track down all leads and cover all bases drew the process out, though he did not really mind, since the pursuit was so satisfying to him.

But the calm flow of his life was interrupted one Saturday after Thanksgiving when he was working late in the library. An assistant came to his carrel to tell him just before closing time that he had received an urgent phone message and was to call home immediately. His heart began pounding rapidly, since he knew that unexpected telephone calls, especially those introduced in this fashion, could bode nothing but ill. He found a pay phone, and after several rings, his cousin Louise picked up.

"Louise? What are you doing there?"

"John Prosper? I came over here to see if I could find Anthony. I'm afraid I have some tragic news to report. I don't know how to say this."

Just get over your damned Southern sense of not wanting to talk about unpleasant things and say it, was what he wanted to blurt out. "Just go on," he said instead. "You can tell me. I need to know."

"Your parents—both of them—were killed in an automobile accident late this afternoon. They were driving back from the Iron Bowl when an oncoming 18-wheeler skidded in the rainy weather and crossed into their lane. I'm sorry. I just can't believe it."

She seemed to be stifling sobs; he was too stunned to say anything. He had never thought that things would not simply continue as they had been, and he felt pangs of regret at having returned home so infrequently since he started graduate school. He and his parents had had their serious disagreements, but he did not hate them. He had no idea how a resolution might have been effected, but now it was too late to even try. In any case, the shock of the news was keeping feelings of profound grief at bay for the moment: as he would often do throughout his life, he pushed stronger emotions aside.

"At least the Tide won after five straight losses to the Tigers, your father must have been happy to go out on that note. Maybe this means a streak has started," said Louise, grasping for anything positive she could find and coming up with a non-sequitur whose connection was dubious.

"What about Anthony?"

"I don't know if he knows. My parents wanted me to come over here and wait. We weren't sure if Anthony was planning to come back tonight or spend the night with friends up there. I hope he doesn't drink too much before he starts home. It's agonizing to wait for him here all alone, and then to have to break that news."

He silently criticized Louise for thinking first about the effect on herself, but maybe he was doing the same thing. It was slowly beginning to sink in that he might be expected to return to fill the vacuum left by his father and to give up his hopes of a career in the classics.

"It must be hard. I can't believe it either, but I appreciate your telling me. Make sure you or someone else calls to inform me about funeral arrangements and to let me know what I can do. I'll be there as soon as I can."

He did return for the funeral, which was held a week later in the old Gothic Episcopal church downtown. Without too much urging from J.P.'s mother, who had grown up in that denomination, his father had early on switched from Catholicism, less from doctrinal reasons than for ones of social standing. As if it mattered a great deal to his father, who rarely sat in a pew and was now lying in a coffin at the front in his last visit to the sanctuary. After all, J.P. had come to observe, churches and religion for most people had less to do with faith, the metaphysical, and the ethical than with a tribal need to belong and shore up one's own sense of security amidst those considered to be like oneself.

J.P. simply let the ritual of sight and sound take place around him and paid little attention to the words. He knew the eulogy would paint a one-sided picture different from the man he knew and scrape for words to form the character of a woman who was not allowed to do it herself. But the reasoned reservations nonetheless made way for the affectionate feelings which he did maintain for his parents: despite his father's authoritarian attempts to dictate his son's course and his insensitivity to learning and society's downtrodden, or his mother's meek acquiescence and superficiality, they were the ones who had raised him and with whom he had also shared so many pleasing and intimate moments. Family, he reminded himself, was a blessing, and not just the restricting curse he sometimes thought it was: his parents had, in their own way, done what they thought was best for their children. Grief was beginning to take hold amidst the confused pain—he felt at the moment like an orphan, but reminded himself he had become used to making his own way and would be able to survive. But for the moment he pushed aside his conflicting feelings—affection, sense of loss, resentment, anger, regret—to mull over later.

Anthony, sitting beside him in the same pew, succeeded in displaying the requisite gravity and slightly moist eye. Next to him was his new bride Susu, a thin, attractive, bird-like young thing chosen from an acceptable family; J.P. wondered whether his brother truly loved her, though he himself did not know what that would entail. To people expressing their condolences afterwards in the reception line in the church parlor he uttered his appreciation, not insincere, though soon turned into clichés through the repetition of phrases. When he was able to break away, he spent most of his time talking to Billy McCall. Aunt Clotilde stayed by the side of her remaining sibling Helen, Louise's mother. The later lowering of the coffin in the cold drizzle at the cemetery remained a blur in his memory. On the walk back to the black limousine Anthony grabbed his upper arm and announced that a meeting was planned for Monday at ten in the firm's office; he said that he hoped J.P. would be there. Or does he hope that I won't, thought J.P. He told Anthony he would, though the idea disgusted him, a too-hurried pushing aside of respect for the dead in pursuit of personal advantage.

• • •

The meeting began promptly with a half dozen men sitting around the large table in the board room, together with the two aunts, Clotilde and Helen. His father's younger friend and ally, the banker and city commissioner Alphonse Rapier along with Alphonse's much younger brother Sebastian, both of whom were also members of the board; his father's attorney and the firm's sometime legal advisor Thomas Gonzalez; and a few others whom J.P. vaguely recognized were all waiting patiently. Lillian Padgett, the middle-aged secretary who had served the company loyally for a couple of decades, expressed her deepest sympathies to J.P., though she seemed more solicitous of Anthony, into whose coffee she poured the right amount of cream and sugar, which she then stirred for him. Attired in a sober business suit that somehow didn't sit quite right, despite being of the proper style, fabric, and price—J.P. assumed that it was the wife's duty to take care of these things—Anthony pulled uncomfortably at the tight collar of his shirt. J.P. found it easier to imagine him in a polo shirt and boat shoes, sitting on the deck of his yacht or at a table overlooking the country club golf course, domains that he was sure made up Anthony's "real" life. He felt fortunate that his own real life consisted of following his chosen calling; his worn navy blazer and grey slacks fit both there and here in the board room.

"It's a sad occasion," Anthony eventually began, "and I know some might find it a bit rushed. But as you know, we were basically shut down for all of last week, Christmas is coming up, and there are tax advantages to getting things nailed down before the start of the new year. We also need to get matters settled while John Prosper is still in town."

As if I'm responsible for the haste, thought J.P.

"The will has been probated, and we'll read that first."

Thomas Gonzalez leaned over and whispered in J.P.'s ear, "I don't like rushing things either, but it had to be done some time." He then proceeded to read the document in his measured, dignified voice with the local accent and cadence of the older generation that J.P. hadn't realized he had missed. He had not thought a great deal about the matter of inheritance before and was not sure what to expect. He assumed that he and Anthony should share equally, though he was unsure what his father might have been thinking in the years immediately preceding his death. In fact the bulk of all cash and shares of stock in ventures outside the firm was split evenly between the two, with smaller bequests to his father's sisters and nominal amounts going to the church and to the Turkey Shoals Hunting Lodge. Is that the extent of his eleemosynary contributions, wondered J.P.? Anthony was given their parents' home, and J.P. a house in Spring Hill that had once belonged to his father's uncle. Clotilde already owned the large family house in the Garden District where she had lived since his parents had moved out of it. A codicil directed that any tangible property within their parents' house could be divided by Anthony and J.P. according to their own discretion. In addition, to J.P.'s surprise, the will suspended the mortgage payments which the family servants Leon and Lucille had been paying and granted them their little home outright. Quite generous and deserved, thought J.P., or is it like slaveholders waiting until after their own death to grant manumission? Perhaps he should not be so hard-hearted: his father's grave was not even cold yet. A bigger surprise came with the disposition of the firm: Anthony got 51% of the shares owned by their parents to J.P.'s 49%. In addition, Anthony was named executor of the estate. Not exactly a disinheritance of the eldest son, thought J.P., but neither was it an unqualified expression of faith in Anthony's abilities.

Another cause for annoyance was that it was his father's will which was determining things, even though the marriage to his mother with her holdings in upstate timberlands had provided her husband with much of the financial footing to make the firm successful in the first place. Why is everything perceived as a patriarchy? he wondered. For her part, his mother had tried to increase the value of what she had acquired, a new family name, by searching genealogies, and came up with the claim that the Devaux ancestors were Norman transplants who had arrived with the English rather than the original French colonists of the Gulf Coast. In making her husband's forefathers more waspish, she would also be slightly elevating her own Scotch-Irish predecessors. As if that mattered, thought J.P., even if it were true.

"The next order of business is electing a new director of the firm. Do I hear any nominations?"

"I nominate Anthony Devaux," proposed Alphonse Rapier without delay.

He must think he can gain some sort of advantage by installing someone whom he can more easily influence, noted J.P. He also observed that Sebastian was studiously trying to maintain a serious composure, despite being unable to completely conceal the hint of his trademark shit-eating grin, the expression of an attitude that would enable him to go far by signaling to confederates that he was one of them. The two were good old boys, who were throwing in their lot with Anthony, because they perceived that their own power might be enhanced by such an alliance. Gonzalez would later inform him that having developed a close relationship with Anthony, Alphonse was angling to have the firm retain his bank to handle its extensive investments and thus gain more control: one hand washes the other. Maybe Alphonse will see the light one day, thought J.P.; I wonder if Anthony ever will.

Clotilde immediately exchanged looks across the table with J.P. Her nephew, who had continually shoved aside any thought of running the firm, didn't know what to think. Clotilde made up his mind for him.

"I nominate John Prosper Devaux," she said decisively.

Anthony smiled insouciantly, as though he had expected this development. "Do I hear any other nominations?" he asked.

There were none of course, and he asked whether anyone had anything to say.

Alphonse spoke up and said that John P. Devaux, Jr., had been blessed with two capable sons, both of whom would have important roles to play. But since Anthony had been taking an active hand in the actual working of the company for a number of years and was most familiar with its operations, and since the testament and recent practice indicate the deceased director's views, he endorsed putting Anthony in charge. Anthony next looked at Clotilde, who didn't say anything. He then proceeded to pass out slips of paper.

"The votes will count proportionately according to the number of shares. That number has been indicated on your ballot. Write in the name of the person for whom you are voting, and Thomas will count them."

Gonzalez owned no shares and was mainly retained when needed as the firm's attorney; the investors Alphonse and Sebastian each owned a small number, Clotilde and Helen somewhat larger amounts, and Anthony and J.P. the most, with Anthony now holding slightly more. J.P. noted that his proportion had already been written on his ballot: somehow Anthony had known in advance about the terms of the will. The outcome would depend on Helen, with whom Clotilde was whispering furiously in the meantime. Helen only shook her head, as she whispered something back. And on me, thought J.P.: what do I want? He stared at the table for a moment before writing in his own name, a furious reaction to the railroading. He had not thought to question at the outset why Anthony was running the meeting: even though both he and his brother already held identical titles of Vice President on paper, he was forced to admit that, being more wrapped up in his studies, he had not been involved in any way in the last few years, and that his father had assigned Anthony the role of "Acting Director" on those occasions when he was absent.

The slips of paper were passed to Gonzalez, who jotted down the numbers, added them up, rechecked them, and announced that the new chief executive was Anthony, by a margin of 53% to 47%. Clotilde looked in sympathy at J.P., who merely shrugged his shoulders.

"I think congratulations are in order," said Alphonse. "And to honor the late John P., how about a toast to his memory and to the future of the firm, which I know will continue to enjoy the climb to even brighter days. I know he would have approved of our taking a swig."

And our mixing of metaphors, thought J.P. Lillian Padgett must have been clued into this beforehand, since she was quick to fetch a silver tray of tumblers and a crystal decanter of bourbon, which she began pouring. Since no one, including J.P., could show disrespect, all joined in raising a glass. He wondered briefly, as the burning descended his throat, what Anthony might have promised Helen, but then tried almost immediately to suppress the turn to cynicism.

On the way out, J.P. offered his congratulations to Anthony and told him to enjoy himself. He added that if it was all right, he would take all the books from the house and the mantel clock, and Anthony could keep all the knickknacks and furniture.

"That's more than fair," beamed Anthony in a generous mood. "Should I send checks for your share of profits up north along with any proxies for board meetings? As executor, I'll also take care of the division of stock and all other financial matters."

J.P. noted that Anthony assumed he would not be coming back. "I'll let you know. I've got several irons in the fire," he replied.

At least clarity has been achieved, he thought—a *modus vivendi*? Maybe he was reluctant to admit to himself what perhaps the others perceived: that he really wasn't suited to running the business and had little desire to devote his efforts to it, having in fact already abandoned it. Nonetheless, his composure had been completely unsettled, and he felt himself the victim of a vicious usurpation. Pacing alone outside the building he grabbed his pack of Camels and puffed furiously on a cigarette until he could no longer hold the nub between thumb and forefinger.

• • •

Before leaving town—to Clotilde's disappointment, he did not even stick around until Christmas—J.P. kept the appointment he had made with Father Clement at the Jesuit college on the hill. In the fall he had begun sending out letters of application for teaching positions to various universities; he was not sure whether the institution in his home town had an opening, but thought he would put out feelers, and in case something should develop, he would be able to pursue his own ambitions and yet not be too far removed from family and firm. But his father's unexpected death had catapulted the question of eventual succession to the forefront, and Anthony's quick maneuvering had almost as immediately removed it.

The department chairman received him warmly and praised his credentials, but told him that all the fathers had been trained in Latin and the offerings in that subject as well as their one course in beginning Greek had been adequately covered for the last thirty years by one of his colleagues. Should that venerable teacher decide to retire in the near future, they would certainly keep J.P. in mind. J.P. was in a sense relieved that this decision too had been taken from him, for his feelings about moving back had changed considerably since writing the letter some weeks earlier. Yet as he left the century-old building of amber stucco and strolled down the crenellated arcade which lined the cloistered yard and provided protection from the elements, he felt that he might have found a comfortable shelter there for pursuing what he loved.

His last task was to box up the books in his parents' house: Thomas Gonzalez kindly agreed to see that the bulk would be delivered to Clotilde's attic with a smaller, selected set to be sent up to him later, and he promised to keep J.P. informed of what was going on in town.

Back at the university J.P. continued work on his dissertation and sent off more letters: replies were slow to come, and the ones that did were mostly negative, even when they were polite. He was getting the impression that his chosen discipline was not expanding, and those who still held existing positions seemed to be staying put to prevent the field from shrinking further. He was convinced that these branches of knowledge were of utmost importance to human-ity: why didn't the nation think likewise? By late spring he had had a few interviews, though none resulted in an offer. A number of fellow students managed to find jobs, while others were in the same boat as himself. Faculty advisors tried to encourage them by saying that a few things pop up unexpectedly in the summer, but that did not seem to be the case this time around. After receiving his first disappointingly small quarterly check from Anthony, or more precisely from Lillian Padgett, he realized that although he could hold on for a few months, he was hardly independently wealthy and would not be able to sustain himself when his student status and assistantship ran out. He thus took a friend's advice to talk with visiting recruiters on campus in order to look for something in the State Department or one of the forty-some other government agencies that had branches overseas, where he could get far away from it all.

You should wait for the right season to take a sailing
voyage,
then haul your swift ship down to the sea and load
a fitting cargo
so that you might bring home profit,
just as our father, foolish Perses, used to sail the sea
because he lacked an adequate livelihood.
                                        —Hesiod, *The Works and Days*

S*O THAT'S THE REASON I ENDED UP SPENDING* most of my time
abroad."

J.P.'s searches for various employment possibilities, which proved
to be almost as exhausting as the research on his dissertation,
eventually resulted in his applying to the United States Information
Agency, then sitting for their version of the Foreign Service Exam,
undergoing a subsequent oral interview, submitting himself to a
security clearance, learning eventually of his acceptance, receiving a
brief orientation in Washington, and flying off to his first assignment
at a lower-level position in a medium-sized, newly independent
African nation. He had decided against the Peace Corps: that
organization had been called into being only recently, and the duties
seemed too untested and primitive for his tastes. Something within
the foreign policy branch of the State Department might have offered
a securer and more permanent position, but he was not sure whether
diplomacy was something he wanted to pursue; the USIA appeared
to offer a closer match to his interests in its dissemination of
knowledge and culture. Besides, the independent agency seemed,
from what he could tell, to be on an upswing, with more impetus to
modernize and expand into former colonies that were developing as
fledgling nations and with the widely-respected correspondent
Edward R. Murrow as its new director. So, upon receiving his orders,
he packed his bags and headed to his new post with the United States
Information Service, as it was known abroad. He had originally

requested Rome, where the office was housed in an ancient palace on the embassy grounds, but that post was a plum more readily delegated to "hands" who had already put in more time. He hoped, however, to gain enough experience to get there eventually. Besides, they already had a seasoned academic classicist there and doubtless wanted to avoid concentration in one area. His year of French for reading knowledge in a secondary language course in grad school no doubt led to his being picked for his new post, and Africa would provide a new field of interest, a new challenge, and a chance to get his mind off the things back home that continued to gnaw away at him. That he would also be doing his brother a favor by removing himself farther from the picture was the last thing on his mind.

As the plane landed, J.P. peered out the window, trying to assemble the visual impressions before him into a coherent image of what would be his new home. All he could spy at first was a single runway in a dusty field beside a tin-roofed building and small control tower. At the gate, the post's affable public affairs officer Frank Dalton was waiting to shake his hand and expedite him through customs. The PAO (J.P. was rapidly becoming proficient in government acronyms) then escorted him to his waiting Citroën, and, on the drive into town, began outlining the duties in the first part of the on-the-job education that J.P. realized would form his real training. With one hand on the wheel, and the other waving in various directions as if pointing to the different tasks he was naming, Dalton ticked off acquisition of books for the new library; organizing lectures, films, and musical programs for the public; setting up exhibits; helping devise a "country plan;" compiling and mimeographing a local news bulletin from the daily wireless file from Washington; training local educators in the teaching of English; making drives by jeep to outlying towns to present programs there; and so on; and so on. The post hoped eventually to have information and cultural officers as well as branch public affairs officers in other towns, and it had already hired a number of host-country employees ("We don't call them natives," Dalton reminded him). The list of tasks facing him seemed overwhelming: J.P. realized he would be a jack-of-all-trades helping out in any way that was needed at a given moment, a juggler of a great many balls.

Near the center of the city they pulled up to a former store with large plate-glass windows which was being refurbished as the USIS post. "We recently acquired this and have been able to move out of the embassy, which is also in temporary quarters. We're hoping the big windows will indicate our openness to the world, not just provide targets for the unrest that occasionally sweeps through," explained Dalton.

Just inside the entrance a middle-aged African woman with her hair wrapped in a bright canary-yellow scarf was sitting at a desk with a telephone and unruly piles of papers; she looked up as they walked in.

"Mathilde Oyono, this is John Devaux, our new employee."

When the secretary responded with a big, toothy smile and a "Welcome" pronounced in a thick French accent, J.P. stumbled to make use of his orientation language training. "*Enchanté.*" he managed to get out, determined to work on the local language in addition as soon as he could determine what the principal one might be.

Men in shorts and T-shirts were busily constructing shelves in the next large room; the whine of hand-held circular saws and the smell of sawdust filled the air, and boxes of books that had already arrived were scattered about. Dalton showed J.P. the small space that would serve as the "office" that he would share with the other junior officer trainee, who had arrived a few weeks earlier. They then drove to the lodgings the agency had found for him not far away: relatively clean, but even sparer than what he had inhabited in graduate school. Paint was peeling on the window sill, and the room had not been swept in quite some time.

"You'll have to get used to the fact that things are simpler here than what you may be accustomed to," explained Dalton. "But you can of course move later if you are able to find something more to your liking. That might be a while though—things are a bit cramped in the new country."

"It's fine," said J.P., who felt that he had all that he needed. He had shipped a foot locker, which would probably arrive in another month or so, and he had stuffed his large suitcase with clothes and a few books, including an anthology of classical poetry into which he could dip on long evenings. The heat and humidity reminded him of his home town, and he realized he had probably packed too many of his warmer New Jersey clothes.

In the coming weeks he threw himself into his assignments, eagerly trying out new ways to reach his audience while enduring frustrations with local customs and attempting to understand the intricacies of the Muslim/Christian and intertribal relationships. Gradually, however, he learned to appreciate the myriad aspects of the local culture. After all, he was now not all that far from the spot where he had heard that *homo sapiens* had first emerged. He realized that his job was something more than introducing the people to the works of the dead, white, European classics, and he had no great desire merely to present his own country as the pristine exemplar that all should follow. He knew the task would not be as easy as simply telling the Africans about the American way of life, expecting them to see the advantages and adopt them. He was aware that in addition to the informational function, the agency was assigned the political task of waging a "war of words." He was not sure how he felt about this second role of disseminating propaganda, but knew he would have to feel his way as he got used to his new job. Along with the people who came into the library, he too was learning—most importantly perhaps, that he needed to listen. The process involved friction at times, not only with the citizens of the host country but also with his own colleagues; he tried, however, to negotiate it in what he hoped was a profitable way. Despite the differences to which he had to adapt, the stresses of the job at times, and the minor hardships that he was forced to endure, he was glad to be away from home: as he would continue to experience throughout his career, he felt more comfortable and at ease in his life abroad.

He had kept his bank account in New Jersey and instructed Anthony to send checks in care of Mabel Harper, the departmental secretary there, for deposit, but to direct any other communications to his current USIA address abroad. He figured it would be simpler to keep a permanent U.S. account and pay Mabel, over her protestations, a small fee to carry out this task. The only drawback was a slight delay in knowing when and for what amount deposits were made, but since he was drawing a salary, this inconvenience was not crucial. He came to find out, however, that the amounts and timing of distributions varied, and, at first swallowing his increasing annoyance, he finally wrote to Anthony to inquire about the reason. After much delay, he got the reply that funds were tied up in a new project that prevented more money from being devoted to profits or dividends. Increasingly riled by his brother's lack of precise information, he wrote back to ask what the hell kind of project was being worked on and reminding him that he was due reports as well as checks. After another lapse of time a financial statement with a minimum of itemization arrived, along with a letter explaining that Devaux Brothers was planning to build a new shopping complex in the currently fashionable style of an enclosed mall across the busy boulevard from Spring Valley Shopping Center, which their father had opened shortly before his death on the site of the recently drained swamp.

"But don't worry," wrote Anthony, "it's a sure thing and will pay off big in the long run. It'll be well worth it. People have money to spend and will love passing time in the new shopping environment. And in the meantime, I've had the property surrounding the mall site reclassified as timberland to delay the paying of property taxes until the trees are harvested. So you can rest assured that I'm looking out for the bottom line. We're thinking of calling it 'Mall DeVille.' What do you think? It would echo our name, and sound classy, like the Cadillac."

Ah, Anthony, he thought, whenever he comes up with something he considers halfway clever, he has to over-explain it, rather than letting it hit the listener on its own. Instead of putting J.P.'s mind at ease, the forced, upbeat tone only galled him all the more. But what upset him most were the business decisions: although he admitted that he had little interest or talent in that area, he questioned the wisdom of the plan to locate two shopping centers across the street from each other, not to mention the original decision to drain the wetlands. And timberland, in the middle of the city? The real harvest wasn't the timber, he was sure, but the tax money Anthony was conning the public out of. What a clever scoundrel his brother was! His anger subsided somewhat as he turned his attention back to his job assignments, which were proving to be even more hectic than

Dalton had indicated at the outset: acquainting a roomful of chattering teachers with the new English-language materials, being bumped by jeep over rutted roads to show a film on cotton harvests in the American South to farmers in an outlying village, or working with host-country employees to train them in using duplicating equipment and film projectors. He often returned to his lodging quite late in the evening, with hardly any time left for reading. The PAO's coordination with a man whom he suspected of being connected with the CIA and who set up student exchanges, some of which had a suspicious cast, bothered J.P. a little, though he convinced himself that it made sense for everyone to be on the same page and not be working at cross purposes. But he wondered how much information the CIA was providing to USIA about what it was doing. Its main task was keeping Moscow's influence at bay; his own agency's was presumably to help develop the new nation.

Walking home late one afternoon and crossing the street to his quarters, he was almost hit by one of the city's numerous whining, exhaust-spewing motorbikes. Cursing, he went upstairs, poured himself a warm gin and tonic, and opened his Hesiod.

The oppressive heat, the town's decrepit buildings, and the petty corruption all reminded J.P. of home. But even more than those things, or the film on cotton, or the increasingly difficult attempts to describe, let alone defend, the civil rights situation in the United States, there was another event that made it seem to him that he could not escape his native environment altogether. When the political counselor at the embassy came down with a fever, J.P., as a Southerner, was assigned as a substitute to escort a visiting senator from Louisiana to some of the rural areas. The politician was making a tour through Africa in hopes of finding evidence that recognizing the new countries was a mistake. He had already gotten into hot water by telling a white audience in still-colonial Rhodesia that Blacks were not capable of governing themselves, and though he had begun to exercise more caution in his public utterances, he continued his racist remarks around J.P., who he assumed would be in sympathy. J.P. agreed with little he said in this regard, but kept his counsel to himself, not wishing to jeopardize the post's chances to gain more resources. When the senator, who was also on a crusade to ferret out wasteful government spending, criticized as excessive the cost of the post's subscription to *The New York Times*, J.P. lost his patience altogether and returned him as quickly and politely as possible to the embassy. Though previously aware of the meanness of which elected officials could be capable, he had until that point held a vague notion in the back of his head that people who achieved the rank of U.S. Senator would possess a certain minimum of intelligence and character. Fortunately, a visit from the Assistant Secretary in charge of the Africa desk at the State Department proved to be more satisfactory and indicated that there was quite a range of understanding and sensitivity among governmental representatives, of which, he reminded himself, he was also one.

When communications with Anthony remained minimal over the next few months, J.P. considered writing Thomas Gonzalez for more information, until he reminded himself that Gonzalez had taken a judgeship and was no longer actively working as the firm's attorney. And even though he was both discreet and forthcoming in his dealings with J.P., he was equally so with the firm and would not have wanted to act as a mole. J.P. still corresponded with Billy McCall, but the information he provided was more indirect. From driving by the mall and reading the newspaper, Billy was able to report that construction was continuing apace, and that the firm in general seemed to be flourishing. This news of course did nothing to assuage J.P.'s suspicion that he was being taken advantage of.

At times he realized he also had himself to blame: he hadn't wanted to deal with the affairs of the business personally and had not strongly protested Anthony's accession to its chief position because his desire to pursue his own interests was stronger. Nonetheless he could not refrain from occasional, aggressively cantankerous inquiries, until, well into his second year in Africa, Anthony wrote to suggest a deal: since the company's funds were tied up in so many projects, which J.P. apparently opposed and lacked the insight to see the wisdom of, he was writing to propose buying his brother out so that he could get his 'fair share' now and not have to worry about the firm's ventures in the future. At first holding the letter at arm's length in a fit of furious rage, J.P. eventually began to imagine the peace of mind that would result from this course and finally acquiesced, even though it would also mean that he would be totally divorced from the firm and no longer able to cast a dissenting, if meaningless, vote against potential shady dealings. When the detailed proposal arrived, however, it did not offer a payout in cash, but in shares of stock in various secondary corporations, bonds, and pieces of scattered property. Although the values of all these were listed, J.P. had no way of determining their accuracy or ascertaining their future prospects, since he had no broker locally or in Princeton, and all the items were too minor to be listed in the daily market reports of the *International Herald Tribune*. He felt that Anthony's valuations were manipulating the fake as only financiers can: imputing a mythical "marketplace" value, instead of assigning to real things the real value that only real humans can place. Certain that Anthony was attempting to unload junk on him, he wrote back to say he would agree only if Anthony would sell the land first and add a significant chunk of cash to the total value that had been proposed in the first place. He convinced himself that he at least knew enough about business not to accept the first offer, but to demand instead even more. Anthony's reply stated that the firm would not be able to reap future gains as planned if the land were sold now, and he would have to recalculate in terms of potential loss to the firm. J.P. responded by asking sarcastically whether the firm's total value and his share had also been calculated in terms of future expectations in the first offer. Moreover, he suspected that many of the expenses deducted from the assets resulted from inflated salaries and overblown consulting fees to insiders. After much haggling, a deal was eventually reached, and J.P. was able to extricate himself from the situation that had burdened him long enough, though he now had quite a number of questionable corporate certificates that he would have to figure out what to do with and whose value turned out to be even less than he anticipated. But he was unable to extricate himself from the lingering feelings of resentment and anger.

He pushed away further thoughts about such matters, even when, ironically, he himself got some practice in business when he had to use surplus PL-480 funds in local currency from the Food for Peace program to purchase books for the library. Like his colleagues, he worked overtime, occupying himself with meetings with local businesses and youth groups, fielding inquiries that came on the telephone or from walk-in visitors, helping Fulbright grantees from the U.S. get situated, aiding local students in their search for study opportunities abroad, and, particularly enjoyable, organizing a concert for a touring jazz group. He wondered how much effect all this was having, but he came to the conclusion that it was probably impossible to measure precisely: there was no objective grading system at his disposal to evaluate it. Instead, he concentrated on individual moments, like the one in which he tried to answer satisfactorily the questions on the poets of the Harlem Renaissance from the polite young man with the precisely articulated English: contacts like that might end up providing the most value.

κ

When, in mingling, moisture joins with heat,
they conceive: from these all life originates.
Though fire oft fights with water,
the two in concert create all things:
Their discordant harmony bears abundant fruit.
—Ovid, *The Metamorphoses*, Bk. I, 630–34

*W*HEN ARE YOU FINALLY GOING TO TELL ME *who you are really, and inform me fully about my mother? You can't just keep putting it off!"*

"I will, I am. I needed to start at the beginning, whatever that is. It's the only way to tell it. To rush things, to oversimplify, wouldn't do it justice. I have to say, however, with your mother, it was also a process of discovery."

J.P. was taking his afternoon coffee in the outdoor café beside the Hofgarten. The Dallmayr blend was a little too acid to his liking, but otherwise everything brought contentment: the sun that warmed his back as it illuminated the pavilion devoted to the Roman goddess of the hunt, the moon, and childbirth; the simple tables and chairs beneath the orderly rows of small trees that were just breaking out in lime-green foliage; the soft crunch of gravel beneath his feet, and a momentary lack of any pressing tasks, other than to peruse the *International Herald Tribune* and the *Süddeutsche Zeitung* laid out on the table before him. Murals on the outer walls of the palace which bordered the garden depicted events from the house of Wittelsbach, which J.P. was certain had been less glorious in reality, yet he was content for the moment to let himself be surrounded by a general "history" rather than to concentrate too closely on its details. He had turned his back on the Feldherrnhalle, where the Nazis had once erected a memorial to party members killed there during the Beer Hall Putsch of 1923: their commemorative installation had in turn been smashed at the end of the Second World War. History had moved on, but who moved it? And can one really turn one's back on it? Why had the local people waited until the war destroyed their city and revealed the full extent of the horrors of the Holocaust to rid themselves of the plaque? Why had not more spoken up in outrage at the first enactment of racial laws or vandalizing of Jewish businesses? How was the spurious notion of anti-Semitism able to gain such traction and spawn the crime of the century, and how could one explain the outbreak of the very worst in human behavior in a country that had produced some of the very best? This was not such distant history for him, but something that had occurred in his lifetime. Was the veneer of civilization really that thin? Could it happen anywhere, at any time? He decided that for the moment he found the garden with its temple more alluring. Following his initial three-year posting in central Africa, and additional assignments in Tunisia and Malaysia, he had finally been promoted to cultural affairs officer and made it to *Mitteleuropa*, where he had become comfortably settled in.

Others were out enjoying the pleasant weather, almost 20° Celsius on the last weekend in March. The winter had been long and dreary; the view from his apartment window had revealed only the black silhouettes of bare limbs against the leaden clouds of a silent grey sky. Though cold in the building, it was colder outside, and he had cozied up under a blanket on the couch with his cherished books and a comforting pot of warm tea. But now spring was arriving: mothers were pushing their children in carriages in the sunshine; elderly couples who had still not abandoned their forest-green Loden overcoats walked side by side; and students taking a break from their endeavors strolled leisurely among the first flowers. The conversations of people at neighboring tables rose in a gentle hum; not far away a pretty girl with curly brown hair was sipping her glass of hot tea and staring at a large volume in a puzzled fashion. He wondered whether it was a tourist guide, or if she was a student. In most cases clothing signaled nationality, but in her case the wool skirt, red sweater, and leather boots lent her an appealing look without giving her away. He thought he caught her looking at him at one point but convinced himself that he had only imagined it, and that her eyes were instead darting in all directions around the café. He was, after all, much older than she was and had never considered himself

particularly noticeable to members of the opposite sex. He had
begun reading a news story on the upcoming Olympics, when he
heard a female voice say, "*Entschuldigen Sie, braucken Sie den
sooker? Der Kellner hat vergessen.*" The young woman had appeared
by his table, and her accent and grammatical slips revealed what her
appearance hadn't: she was an American too. He looked up at her in
surprise and smiled, answering, not altogether consistently, "*aber
natürlich*", responding with "but of course" not so much to her stated
inquiry of whether he needed the sugar as to her implied one of
whether she could borrow it. He handed over his unused package of
two sugar cubes, wrapped in white paper inscribed with the name of
the establishment. "*Danke,*" she replied, and paused, as though
searching for further words.

"Are you a student?" he asked in English, filling the gap.

Not missing a beat she answered, "Supposedly. Junior year
abroad. But I don't know if I want to finish. There are so many other
things that interest me at the moment."

"You looked like you were studying that book pretty hard."

She stared at him intently and asked, "You noticed me?"

He blushed and hurriedly said, "I wasn't gawking. It's just that
you were in my line of sight toward the garden." Trying to get the
conversation back on its original track, he continued, "What are you
reading—Goethe's *Die Wahlverwandtschaften*? It looks pretty thick."

"*Die Grundrisse*. It is."

"Are you taking a course on Marx?"

"No, just reading it on my own."

"Perhaps you'd be interested in coming to the program tonight at
the Amerika-Haus. A professor from Wisconsin is giving a reading
from his new book on development in the Third World."

J.P. almost surprised himself with his spontaneous invitation.

"Amerika-Haus," she repeated, with that tone of skepticism he
recognized as greeting most things connected with official
Americadom in the Vietnam era. She nodded her head slowly, less
from assent than to gain time to ponder.

"Yes. You might like it," he went on. "The author is actually quite
critical of much foreign intervention and sympathetic to local efforts.
I'm in charge of programming there and have to pick him up in a

little while at the *Hauptbahnhof*. The program begins at 7:30, if you're interested."

"I'll think about it," she said slowly, and, switching back to German as if to distance herself while thanking him again and supplying the excuse that her tea was getting cold: "*Nochmals danke schön, aber mein Tee wird kalt.*"

As seven-thirty approached, J.P. looked nervously around the large room where programs were held; he observed that the majority of the chairs remained empty. Twenty years earlier Thornton Wilder and William Faulkner had been able to draw large, enthusiastic crowds to this venue, and even he himself had had success with writers and musicians, but a lecture in English on a specialized economic topic on a Saturday evening was a lesser attraction. He had had to scramble at the last minute to find a replacement for the German-speaking professor who was supposed to talk on the limits of growth. The current speaker, sitting beside him, was reviewing his notes. As he surveyed the room again, J.P. realized that he was curious as to whether one face in particular would show up. A face, since it occurred to him that he had not even learned her name. At five minutes past the half hour, when a few members of the audience began impatiently glancing at their watches, J.P. stepped up to the podium, tapped on the microphone, and announced, "*Herzlich willkommen, meine Damen und Herren.* Welcome, ladies and gentlemen. Tonight we are fortunate to have. . .", pausing briefly as he noticed a certain latecomer entering to take a chair near the front. He did not exchange eye contact with her, but continued with his introduction. The speaker then stood to polite applause, gave a brief overview of the topic of his book, and followed with a thirty-minute reading from a chapter on setting up cooperatives. During the question-and-answer session that followed, the first to raise his hand was an earnest young man in black-rimmed glasses who posed an overly long query, the gist of which was to solicit confirmation of his own assumption that large corporations were unfairly appropriating the resources of developing nations. The speaker agreed that that was often the case and was a matter which was addressed in Chapter Three of his book. An older, grey-haired man in a suit next began by apologizing for the aggressive tone of his countryman's previous question and saying that since more advanced nations have the know-how, wasn't it only logical that they be the ones to develop the resources? The speaker agreed that they had a role to play, but stated that the outsiders and the locals needed to work in tandem. Several other questions, pertinent and not, followed, and near the end the student with the curly brown hair raised her hand.

"But the examples of the cooperatives that you mentioned only involve monoculture cash crops. Aren't the native people being poorly served if they turn away from their own food production and a diversity of economic efforts?"

J.P., somewhat taken aback at first by the assertiveness of her question, was nonetheless surprisingly impressed by the knowledge and thought behind it. For the first time, the professor seemed somewhat flustered, and danced around an answer that acknowledged the basis of the assumption without providing an indication of how his analysis might point toward a solution. After a few more questions the evening was wrapped up, and the crowd began to disperse. A few people paused to thank the speaker on the way out, and the young woman stepped up to say she was curious to learn what his students did upon graduation.

"Some of the undergraduates pursue further studies in political science or economics, or go on to law school. The graduate students usually look for jobs in foreign service or one of those organizations that does work in developing countries," he replied with a general answer that seemed to indicate to her that he was little involved in their actual paths. As the three stood around for a few moments not saying anything, J.P. finally asked if anyone was interested in going out for a glass of wine to cap the evening off, looking at the young woman as he made his proposal.

"Sounds good to me," said the professor.

"Where were you thinking of going?" the student asked.

"I thought maybe the Pfälzer Weinstuben. We could walk there."

"Isn't that a little stuffy and elegant—you know, the moldy smell of long-departed royalty? One would think you had spent enough time today in the shadow of palaces."

"You've got a way with words." The surprise was evident in J.P.'s face, though he was not offended by her perceptive jab. He reminded himself, after all, that he was supposed to be done with kings, carnival or otherwise. "What do you suggest?"

"We could walk the same distance in another direction to a place in Schwabing, say the Türkeneck, and see how some of the indigenous survive."

"Let's let our guest decide. What'll it be, wine with the ghosts of kings, or beer with the counterculture?"

Since the guest chose the "more daring option," as he put it, they headed out to the Karolinenplatz, its black obelisk barely visible in the night, and followed the woman up the Barerstraße. "By the way, I'm John Prosper Devaux," the cultural officer at the Amerika-Haus said in order to learn her name and perhaps, somewhat self-consciously, to indicate to the professor that she was not a previous acquaintance of his. "I assume you caught our speaker's name."

"Yes, I'm Diana Williams," she said, shaking hands with each in the German fashion and striding forward to indicate the way toward the Türkenstraße.

After they had seated themselves at a corner table surrounded by dark paneling, they looked in search of a server through the thick curls of cigarette smoke illuminated by the green-shaded bulbs hanging on long wires from the ceiling.

"You know you can order wine here too," said Diana. "You're perfectly free."

J.P. in fact chose a Müller-Thurgau and she a Riesling, while the professor from Wisconsin opted for a mug of Spaten. The men had eaten a hearty dinner before the talk, but their young companion looked over that day's mimeographed menu, which filled a whole page, before settling on *Tiroler Gröstl mit Salat*, a local one-dish meal of fried-up potatoes, bits of pork, and an egg for four marks.

"A dollar," said the professor. "Things are such a bargain here."

"Depends on your situation," said Diana. J.P. wondered if price was her principal reason for rejecting the wine tavern, and gazed at her sweater, somewhat worn but nonetheless fashionable in the way she wore it, and expanding and subsiding with the rise and fall of her comely breasts as she breathed.

The conversation did not stick to the evening's formal topic, but centered more around impressions of Germany from the different perspectives of visitor, resident, and student. J.P. tried to keep it balanced and not reveal his main interest in letting the conversation disclose more about Diana. He had been somewhat successful in this latter regard by the time the speaker announced his desire to head back to his hotel, saying he still had not overcome jet lag with his subsequent travel and lectures in Frankfurt and Berlin. J.P. summoned the waiter, who asked if everything was on one check. Diana was getting out her money when J.P. answered, *"Ja, alles zusammen."*

"Wait a minute—I don't expect you to buy me supper."

"But I insist."

"We're living in different times now."

"I see. At least let me get the wine."

"OK. It's a deal."

J.P. offered to accompany the professor to his hotel, but he protested, saying that his brief time in the two previous cities had given him enough experience to find his way around in this country. J.P. then chivalrously offered to walk Diana home, having found out that she lived in Schwabing, but she merely said, "Don't you think I walk home by myself every night?"

"Of course, I didn't mean it like that. I'm sure you can. But I hope you'll walk back down to the Amerika-Haus again some time. I didn't have a chance to show you the library. It's quite extensive and might prove helpful for your studies. For me, it's probably the greatest perk of my job. It's open every day from noon to 19:30."

"Thanks, I'll check it out." She shook his hand and turned to walk away, before turning again. "It was nice to meet you," she said as she looked up at him.

• • •

She did return to the Amerika-Haus a few days later near closing time and appeared to enjoy her tour of the library with its array of current periodicals and extensive collection of books. J.P. was not surprised that her seeming admiration was punctuated by questions about the possible propagandistic nature of some of the offerings and why the holdings seemed to lack certain magazines and coverage of the issues stressed by recent protesters at home and abroad. A skeptic himself, he preferred her questioning to the blindly acquiescing. "We'll look into it." A promise or an avoidance?

He overcame another hesitation and asked if she would like to join him for supper.

"As long as join doesn't mean *einladen*," she replied, making the German distinction between invitation to accompany and offer to treat.

"Of course not," he said, playing it by ear. Why was he so awkward, he wondered, and why had he gained so little experience before now? He even retained some of the clumsiness for which his mother had chastised him so often, when he bumped into tables or inadvertently knocked over water glasses. Was it him or the females? The debutantes he had been matched with at the Camellia Ball in his younger years seemed so superficial as they giggled with one another in their floor-length, pink satin dresses while clutching their matching bouquets of the eponymous flower. The coterie of correct families maintained their position by creating traditions to keep the circle intact. The first dance of those events was always a relief for him, since he could avoid displaying his lack of terpsichorean talent while the fathers whirled their daughters around the floor in front of backdrops suggesting the gardens of Versailles in pastel-tinted *papier-mâché* before handing them off, enacting the ritual which society prescribes as proper. The girls themselves seemed to be fungible placeholders, a role in which they acquiesced because they knew no other. Perhaps he was unfair—surely they would have been able to reveal a different inner substance if he had taken the initiative to scratch the surface. Maybe he would view it differently in his old age and recall fondly the halcyon times of his youth: but no, his friend Billy had not long ago sent him a clipping from their hometown newspaper, and on the back was a report of the most recent Camellia Ball, a description that could have perfectly matched the ones he had attended years before. He did not doubt that almost identical accounts would be appearing in the next century. How can nostalgia be conjured up in memory if it is being repeatedly enacted in reality?

The variation on the debutante theme that he found among coeds at the university, to marry an eligible bachelor and gain themselves security for life, appeared little different to him. Initially his gangliness attracted scant attention on their part, but when they found out he was the scion of a wealthy "old" family, matters changed, though he never let things go very far. Getting away from that whole faux-aristocratic order had been paramount in his mind. There must have been other girls there with whom he could have made a connection, but he had been too shy to devote a lot of effort to the pursuit. In graduate school there were fewer female students, and the ones in his class appeared, like him, to be so absorbed in the pursuit of knowledge that they had little time for other matters, or at least that's what he told himself. Although he became friends with some with whom he later maintained a correspondence, he never seemed to meet anyone toward whom he was romantically inclined. Sometimes when he found himself with a possible companion he would notice that her eyes were darting elsewhere, as though she were merely tolerating him as the next-best thing for the moment, and, not wishing to remain in that status, he would cease his efforts. And the trip that time with his father to that "house": that was something different. True, he conjured it up at times in his lonely room in his mind and with his hand, but he knew it lacked completeness. In his career, the ratio of eligible females declined even further, and in his first overseas posts he had found the culture gap with foreign women too daunting to know how to overcome it. Reading Ovid failed to help him find someone, or know what to say when he did. Did his lack of close relationships to this point result from a congenital inability to form them, or a calculated defense put into place to simplify his life and keep things under control?

"What are you thinking about?" Diana asked, interrupting his musings.

"Which place we might end up at," he replied.

"Have you ever been to the Indonesian restaurant in the Heß-straße? If not, it might be time to try something new."

It was tasty, filling, and cheap, as she promised, and he enjoyed the evening. He was pleased to note that his attraction to her did not rest solely on her clear complexion or her alluring figure: she could hold her own in conversation and frequently contributed quite unexpected observations. He was hesitant to repeat his misguided request to walk her home, but he did get her tentative agreement to accompany him to the exhibit of contemporary German painters in the Haus der Kunst. Since neither had a telephone, they exchanged addresses. Leaving notes in mailboxes or under doors if one missed the other at home was to prove an occasional, frustrating experience, though she could always contact him at work, and they learned to be more specific when arranging subsequent meetings. This tactic did not always work either, however, as her spontaneity often proved unpredictable. Nonetheless at intervals he considered decent, they took in concerts in the baroque hall of Schloß Schleißheim, went for walks along the Isar, and visited the beer garden surrounding the Chinese Tower in the English Garden. She introduced him to the museum dedicated to Karl Valentin, the comedian whose zany, anarchist humor often took on an edge that subverted authority. J.P. was touched when he observed her tickled reaction to the silliness in some of the old black-and-white film clips. But they made a certain sense: *"I'm not an impudent lout, but a stinging nettle among the flowers of love."* Or: *"Did that happen yesterday, or on the third floor?"* Or: *"The future used to be better."* He had to admit, intellectually, that humor was perhaps the best means of dealing with the situation in which one found oneself: maybe someday he would be able to laugh wholeheartedly.

Each time he got together with Diana, it seemed to him that he had never looked at her before: whereas he would have said after their first meeting that her hair was "brown" and "curly," now he would describe it as chestnut, with a multitude of little ringlets that made an irregular but fascinating pattern as they cascaded in waves to her shoulders, the strands reflecting bright gleams in the highlights. And although she was fortunate to possess attractive features overall, he realized where her true beauty lay: in her eyes, which were thoroughly alive and revealed with their piercing, scimitar flashes the beauty within her. He had sometimes noticed previously how girls or women who were not otherwise particularly striking clearly stood out in a group because of what was displayed through their eyes—how often the judges at pageants overlooked this, and got it wrong. And hadn't he read in a play just a few nights before the wise words of a counselor to the king who decried the foolishness of restricting oneself to books *"without the beauty of a woman's face"*? It was from women's eyes that the counselor derived his doctrine: *"For where is any author in the world/ Teaches such beauty as a woman's eye?. . . Then when ourselves we see in ladies' eyes,/ Do we not likewise see our learning there?"*

A day trip to Brannenburg with a hike up the Wendelstein proved relaxing, and he was happy not to be tramping alone as he often did, yet J.P. could not help noticing that there was always a certain restlessness to Diana: she was looking for something more than nature could provide. Even the summit with its panoramic view could only point out a direction rather than provide a goal. He was hesitant to push things too rapidly: he was not sure whether it was proper to consider a closer relationship, given the twenty-year difference in their ages, or whether that supposed concern was just a cover-up for his fear of rejection or reluctance to take on an encumbrance. He was aware that she had other friends and involvements, about which he knew little, except that some had to do with political matters. Once, when he was walking down the Leopold-straße, he passed a café where she was sitting with a group of young people; he paused to speak, and though she was friendly, she did not invite him to take a seat. But then why should she have? He wondered if his work attire of suit and tie marked him as too different from her group.

He enjoyed his work: it provided a regular structure that lacked crises, even though it was often hectic, and it gave him the autonomy to exercise a certain amount of control over his activities, as well as providing precise but interesting assignments and enough free time to occupy himself with books and ideas. He could rise early in the morning and prepare his coffee at leisure, partaking of the Kaiser roll that he had bought the evening before, or, if he felt particularly enterprising, obtained fresh that very morning on a walk to the bakery in the next block. Work was a short bus ride or a somewhat longer but pleasant stroll down the Nymphenburger Straße. The sights and sounds along the route kept him interested, since there was always something to observe: Munich was a big improvement over his previous post, and at least as varied in its offerings as those he had experienced on visits to London. It seemed as though there were hundreds of opportunities for attending the theatre, concerts, or museums, either alone or with colleagues, or recently, on occasion with Diana. Entering the Amerika-Haus, he would exchange pleasantries with Frau Huber, the receptionist, before heading across the atrium and up to his office with its window overlooking the lawn and trees. He would glance at his calendar for the day's agenda and begin organizing. When the secretary brought him the mail he delighted in opening packages of recently arrived books or new issues of magazines, cataloguing and assigning them to their proper spots. What a thrill he got from the chance to build up the collection. He would take regular strolls through the reading room, not to check on the assistant who supervised it, but to cast admiring glances at the shelves or pull out a volume for perusal. If a university or school class had scheduled an orientation session to the library, he would conduct that: he had brushed up enough on the German he had learned in graduate school to speak on familiar topics. Or if a workshop for teachers or some other group had been planned he would check to see that the room was in order and the person conducting it had everything he or she needed. Working with the planning for visiting speakers or art exhibitions provided pleasant variations that kept things from getting stale. He was glad he didn't have to deal with the tasks of the information affairs officer, who was responsible for briefing local journalists and putting out "our" story more effectively by getting it transmitted through regional news media and even submitting editorials to local papers. For J.P., there were also frequent meetings with other individuals or organizations throughout the city, and of course regular discussions with the public affairs officer who headed the post and with other colleagues within the Amerika-Haus who dealt with educational and economic exchanges. Even when the tasks sometimes crowded in on one another, or when he and other colleagues had to spend extra hours laboring over the right wording for a cable or figuring out a way to avoid stepping on the toes of a political counselor, he was able to get things accomplished.

One meeting, after he had been there for a few months, involved a request from his boss which seemed innocuous enough at first but later began to trouble him.

"J.P.," his director addressed him with his poker face and generic brown suit, "there's another assignment I'm going to have to ask you to take on, namely providing brief summaries of any articles appearing in major Bavarian newspapers on anything dealing with U.S. policy, attitudes toward the U.S., or evolving trends in German politics. As I said, brief: you've got a lot on your plate, and the people who read them have a lot to cover too. A few sentences will do in most cases, enough to keep us accurately informed."

"You mean this sort of thing hasn't been done before now?"

"It is an ongoing task that was being done, but the person left."

"Who was that? I don't remember anyone mentioning it and wasn't aware of any personnel changes here."

"My, but you've got a lot of questions," he said impatiently as he looked down at some papers on his desk which he rapidly pushed around with his left hand. "They didn't work here; they worked for Radio Free Europe in their offices over by the English Garden. RFE doesn't have anyone at the moment to continue it."

"One more question: where does this information go?"

"Washington, of course. It helps us formulate our policy if we know what's going on around the world. But of course, it helps us here as well to carry out our work in a more informed way."

J.P. detected an annoyed, somewhat authoritarian tone but said he would comply. He sometimes had as much difficulty dealing with his superior's demands as he once had with those of his father. He read the papers anyway, and composing summaries would help him organize his own thoughts. And supplying factual knowledge could only be of general benefit. He wondered though why the PAO hadn't asked the information officer to carry out this task since it was more in line with what he did anyway, preparing reports for the local journalists: or perhaps he had, and was doubling up on the task to compare the reliability of the two.

But several weeks later, during another meeting in the PAO's office he could not help noticing an open manila envelope on the desk next to the diplomatic pouch and a stack of his summaries, which were no doubt destined for it. What bothered him was that the address was Langley, rather than Foggy Bottom. He didn't say anything then, but the unintended revelation gnawed at him. If his director played his cards close to the chest, he could too, and he would wait to decide what to say and when to say it. Was his job as benign and beneficial as he liked to believe? Or would he soon be asked to expand his attention to other areas? But even so, wasn't it preferable that information go to Langley as opposed to Moscow? He certainly wasn't a double agent.

He thought about what he was finding in his research and passing on to others: facts, information, knowledge, intelligence, analysis, opinion, data, hunches, persuasion, truth, or some warped version of those? What is the difference among these, where is the overlap? At what point does any of this become wisdom? And in presenting it to others: when is it propaganda, when is it brainwashing, when does it support valid arguments that are there to be countered in order to find a satisfactory position? And what was it that he was conveying in this case? Wasn't it just material he found in the newspapers, available for anyone to read? Wasn't his boss correct in saying that accurate information provided the basis for a better-informed policy? He pondered the alphabet soup of agencies and the fact that the one his paycheck came from and the one his reports were presumably going to both ended in *IA*. But in one the *I* meant information and in the other it meant intelligence. Was his job to provide information to the host country or collect intelligence for his own government? And if the latter, which part? Or do the two go hand in hand? Was it a matter of the purpose to which it was put? He tried to convince himself that everything he did was fully in the "white" area of openness, rather than the "black" area of propaganda, covert actions, or psy-ops, or even some fuzzy "grey" area in between. After the *Ramparts* exposé a few years back of the spy agency's support for the National Student Association, weren't the two radio stations which sent broadcasts behind the Iron Curtain forced to come clean with their funding? Or did they? How could one know? And if the spy agencies weren't accountable or transparent with information about how they themselves collected and used information, could the public trust them? Or did the public prefer not to, wishing to believe that the secret knowledge gave the government an edge that enabled them to protect "us"? He reminded himself that the overt assistance he would be providing was going to that "other agency" that started with C and that often conducted its operations covertly. Or was he merely imagining that was where it was headed? But if so, how were they going to use it? If any of his colleagues actually worked for the CIA, they would have kept that under wraps and not wanted it to get out. Maybe he was letting himself be influenced too much by those students and others who demonized that agency because of its tendency to overstep the bounds between collecting information and actively interfering in the affairs of foreign governments, even to the point, as everyone knew, of committing murder and overthrowing regimes, working behind the scenes to foment a *coup d'état*: Syria 1949, Iran 1953, Guatemala 1954, the Congo 1960, South Vietnam 1963, and so on. He decided he would pass on only what he considered proper, difficult as that was to determine.

• • •

His recent acquaintance with Diana added a new dimension to his life, even if he was not sure what their roles were or should be. She seemed to enjoy their times together, however, and although she was not nosy or prying, she expressed interest in his background and who he was. Though he had few secrets other than the one that had begun gnawing at him, he was hesitant with regard to his personal background as well: she was hardly the husband-seeking coed of the type he had once encountered, but he thought that she might have the opposite reaction to the revelation of a privileged pedigree. Or perhaps she might criticize his failure to live up to expectations, or more likely, his inability to find a way to oppose them more force-fully, given his alienation. He neither wanted to impress nor to put off with those aspects of his heritage. He managed to get past the name of his native state without difficulty, and was almost surprised that she didn't pose the question, as many Northerners often did, "But how can you stand to live there?" He had never known how to begin answering this line of inquiry, not simply because he no longer lived there in fact (though he could not get away from it in spirit), but because, knowing that such queries grew from an assumption rather than from actual knowledge, he could neither give blanket approval to the implied criticism he knew to be deserved nor offer an unqualified defense of his native region on the basis of the good points with which he was acquainted firsthand. It would require a lengthy treatise, which he was not sure that even he knew how to compose. He realized he couldn't impress her with his family, nor would he want to, so he spoke at first in general terms. It was as though he wanted to establish something new, with no ties to the old. He imagined someday telling her everything, but first he would have to figure out for himself how to put all that together.

"I'll whale the tar out of you, boy, if you don't listen to me." Taken aback at first, the little boy, who had engaged in some act of minor misbehavior, realized that she wouldn't and ran toward her to bury his face in the starchy white of her uniform. She stroked his head with her big, brown hand and said, "Chile, I hardly know what to do with you." But she did know, and took his little hand in hers, proceeding on to the park, where she sat on the bench as he swayed contentedly on the swing. She was his friend, and until the baby was old enough to come along with them and spoil their outings with his caterwauling, they had a bond whose link would eventually be weakened by forces of which he was not then aware, and later would never fully comprehend, but which took hold and muddled his outlook in ways he wished had never occurred.

He recalled how he had not too long before taken an extended weekend trip to Paris, and while riding the Métro there, experienced a feeling of comforting familiarity that he could not place at first. Then it suddenly hit him: the crowd around him contained so many black faces, of which he had seen so few in Germany. Not Black himself, not close to that culture, he had no right to claim it as his own, yet throughout his upbringing and much of his later life its proximity had been a presence that made up a part of him. The awareness forced him to accept despite himself the immense variety of reality, and his place in it. He had observed that outsiders, when imagining his home state, think only of racist whites and not the many others who live there too. But he also knew that whites at home work just as hard to keep Blacks under the radar, and he realized he had incorporated this outlook to a certain extent as well, though it hadn't taken complete hold and was gradually wearing off.

In July, toward the semester's close and the end of summer when she was supposed to return to the United States, J.P. noticed that Diana was increasingly distracted. He finally asked her what was wrong, whether she was having trouble deciding what to do about her studies.

"Not just that, everything," she confessed, nervously darting her eyes in various directions.

"Do you want to tell me about it?" he asked, not knowing whether he was performing the role of paternal advisor or would-be lover.

"No, I'll work it out."

Later, she apparently had worked it out, or at least had come to a decision. She told him she had informed her parents that she would not be returning for her senior year, but would stay on in Munich. Her father had wanted to fly over and talk some sense into her, "rescue" her, as he put it, but she would have none of it and somehow managed to convince her parents that it would be no use. She was not eager to return to the Midwest and "that little house with a fence around it," as she always described it. J.P.'s initial reaction was one of delight that she would be there a while longer, though he thought this might be selfish on his part and still did not know what his best advice for her might be.

"What will you do?" he asked instead.

"Some friends offered me a job working in a bookstore. I'll at least be able to support myself, and I can stay in my room until September, when a new student arrives."

"Well, I hope our little outing at the end of the month is still on. Celebrating your staying is as good a reason as having a final spree to say our farewells."

"Yes, of course," she replied, looking up at him with widening, expressive eyes.

They had planned to travel by light rail to Feldafing and swim in the Starnberger See before hiking to Kloster Andechs, where they could drink as many liters of the monk-brewed beer as they wished and eat fish, bratwurst, or the mammoth, spiral-cut white radishes. When they'd had their fill they could take another S-Bahn back from Herrsching.

He found, however, that plans could easily go awry for one who has everything so well regulated and ordered like the contents of a book. As he was walking out the front door of the Amerika-Haus late on Friday afternoon J.P. was accosted by a nearly breathless Diana, who said, "Thank God I caught you."

After a few heavy inhalations, she continued, "I'm sorry, I can't make it tomorrow. 'Students against Imperialism' is having a meeting to plan protests at the Olympic Games. People will be here from Berlin and all over to coordinate. It's really important that I be there."

Observing the sudden falling of his face, as though he had received an actual physical blow, she added, "But we can still do it, I'll be around for a while. Just set a date. And you can come tomorrow too—if it doesn't jeopardize your job, of course."

Fuming, he asked, "But weren't our plans important too?" in a tone that failed to reveal the full extent of the anger that he felt.

"Yes, of course. Why don't we go next weekend? It'll still be fun. But meanwhile I have to run. I have to meet some students who are arriving from Aachen and take them to their rooms. We're assembling tomorrow at 9 in the Mensa to find out where we're actually meeting, if you're interested." She ran the back of her hand gently down his cheek and smiled.

A sign of the soft spot she held for him, or a calculated manipulation? Still hurt and disappointed, he contemplated the matter. It was the first time she had invited him to her political dealings: if they wanted to get to know each other better, shouldn't he make an effort to find out what she was involved in? Even though he had the impression that her enthusiasms tended toward extremes that in his opinion were not well thought out, he told himself that simply appearing and listening did not necessarily mean supporting the same positions. But on the other hand, he did not want simply to be a voyeur, or worse, a cynic. However, he also recalled the director's most recent request, not just to summarize articles, but to report on meetings and comments made by individuals that he might run across.

"Wouldn't that be spying?" J.P. had asked him bluntly.

"It would be reporting." The director didn't miss a beat.

"You mean I wouldn't be an agent?"

"Agent, ha," he scoffed. "You'd be an asset at most. For the really serious stuff they make you sign a contract swearing to a lifetime of secrecy."

J.P. didn't ask him how he knew.

"Listen," the director continued. "We're living at a tricky moment in crucial times. The Olympic Games are coming up, and they managed to dodge the bullet of the threat of an African boycott because of Rhodesia's inclusion. That was a diplomatic problem that could have had a serious effect on the image of the games, on our ally West Germany, or even the entire Free World. But it could get worse: things could get violent, and that would be a disaster. All kinds of leftist groups, and even a few right-wing parties, not to mention various cuckoos from other countries are planning to protest anything they can—Rhodesia, Israel, the Vietnam War, civil rights in America, you name it. And you know what the Black athletes did at Mexico City four years ago: we've heard rumors that colored GI's stationed here may be planning something, so we've got our people at McGraw Kaserne looking into it."

J.P. wondered if his use of the first-person plural pronouns was meant to include him and rope him securely to the proper side.

"And don't forget—Baader-Meinhof's been active around the country and blew up 60 cars right here in Munich at the Bundeskriminalamt in May. Even though the ringleaders were captured earlier this month, there are plenty of others ready to spring into their place. Anything's possible. You wouldn't want violence, would you?"

"Of course not."

"So just keep your ear to the ground. The more people we have paying attention, the better off we'll be. Listen to what people say around here, and go to any meetings you hear about. It would help everyone to head off any violent storms in advance. That student you know—she must have some connections."

"Maybe. I'll see. I'll do what I can."

The bind seemed to become more constricting. It was the first time his boss had mentioned Diana—were they shadowing her, or perhaps even him? No, of course not, the director had seen her at an event at the Amerika-Haus and the party at Fräulein Eberlein's. That party had been an informal, internal gathering where everyone was more relaxed, unlike those ghastly diplomatic events to which he was pressured to go and put on a friendly face in order to gather information from the foreigners present. He tried to avoid those when he could, and would never have forced one on Diana.

Political groups had indeed become more radical in recent years and prone to adopting tactics that mimicked those of the forces they opposed. It would admittedly be a service to head off violence: although J.P. had been slow to pay much attention to the first efforts of Martin Luther King, Jr., and slower than he later thought he should have been to endorse his teachings, he was now fully convinced and determined to apply them across the board. But did he want to become part of an ever-growing machine that collected information to keep itself in power, employing excessive force itself at times? The satellite dishes at the listening post in Bad Aibling were sweeping up signals twenty-four hours a day. He decided he would go to the meeting and form his own opinion, deciding for himself what to pass on, on the basis of its ability to contribute to the common good.

The organizers had managed to find a meeting room in the Mensa itself: they hadn't reserved it, but in merely occupying it they confirmed to themselves their sense of rebellious seriousness. J.P. and Diana exchanged brief, friendly greetings when he arrived, but she hurried off to carry out various tasks, talking to people and placing flyers on chairs. He sat near the back; the meeting seemed interminable to him with a lot of arguing over minutiae: he was glad he didn't have to take written minutes. They discussed the best venues for demonstrations, and whether or not including pranks would discredit their cause or underscore the ridiculous claims of those in power. On the whole it seemed innocuous enough: although some of the rhetoric was belligerent, the canned quality of some of the phrases blunted their edge, and spokesmen for the various groups tended to emphasize the need to keep the planned demonstrations peaceful despite sarcastic remarks from some of the participants and arguments about whether they should respect the ban on assemblies within 500 meters of the Olympic grounds. Spokes*men*, noted J.P., since few women seemed to have an important say, and most of the coffee that was consumed was fetched by the females present. Although most in attendance were young, there were people of various ages, and J.P. felt only a little out of place: the flannel shirt and corduroy pants which he had chosen to wear, more for Diana's sake than as some sort of spook's disguise, fit in with the gathering, although not with the summer temperature. And despite his skeptical outlook toward these activists, he was also pleased to have the opportunity to become more closely acquainted with their viewpoints and be part of this milieu.

For J.P., the meeting was less noteworthy for itself, however, than for its impetus to engage in the dialectic with those closest to him: Diana and his director. Diana remained occupied with the visiting organizers throughout the weekend, but when they next had a chance to meet over *ćevapčići* at a Balkan restaurant, he asked her pointedly, "What do the Olympic Games have to do with the Vietnam War?"

She gazed at him with a long look that said, "How can you not see the obvious?"

He continued, "After all, it's Germany who's hosting the games, not the United States, and their purpose is to bring the whole world together peacefully for a good purpose."

"It's a mammoth event, funded by the wealthy nations and their wealthy corporations, an opportunity to pat themselves on the back and exploit the athletes for their own purposes. The true meaning gets lost in all the hoopla. It's the same imperialistic forces at work that are attempting to dominate through war. Don't you see the hypocrisy of releasing doves of peace in the stadium while bombs are being dropped in Southeast Asia? Can you believe that misguided war is still going on after all these years? Think about it."

"I assume you don't like Waldi either," he jabbed, referring to the Games' cute dachshund mascot.

Though he never would have condescended to say, "I love it when you get angry," he did appreciate how her heartfelt emotion modified the slogans in general circulation when she expressed things she had thought about herself. Ignoring his last comment she added, "Besides, we will have an audience of thousands who are forced to think about their involvement in the war itself. If no one speaks up against it, will it ever end?"

He himself considered his own involvement rather distant: far too old to be drafted, he mainly kept up with it through news reports. Since he could see through the specious claims used to defend the involvement, he was hardly a supporter, but neither was he in sympathy with the Viet Cong and never summoned up the thought or energy to strongly protest. His frequent playing of the role of devil's advocate infuriated Diana: however, he took that stance not to annoy her, but to clarify matters both to himself and to her. He was gratified that she took him seriously and didn't reject him on that account.

Once he had asked her, "Why do you put up with me?"

"You take me seriously."

"You give me reason to," he replied.

With the public affairs officer he sometimes argued on behalf of the other devil. He decided to report his presence at the meeting in order to placate his boss and, he hoped, keep the pressure off. He did not reveal that it was Diana who had informed him about the gathering, however, but said that he had seen it announced on a flyer.

"I don't think there's anything to worry about. There'll be demonstrations, but there doesn't seem to be any intention of letting things get out of hand. They're as worried as the city council and the IOC that excessive force could backfire and harm what they plan. We've had big demonstrations in Washington, after all, and everything turned out OK."

"If you say so. But remember, there are always other K-groups that have their own ideas and probably didn't show up at that gathering."

"K-groups?"

"You know, communist groups."

"Tarring the opposition with one brush?"

"There are too many factions and sub-factions to keep track of. By the way, did you note which organizations were there?"

"I didn't want to be spotted as a stranger taking notes. But this handout probably lists the important ones," said J.P. passing over the leaflet he had picked up.

"Well, that's okay for now. It would be a good idea, however, to go to any subsequent meetings to see if anything changes."

"You mean you want me to become more involved?"

"You academics," complained the director, who had come from a journalistic background. "You never want to get involved. I some-times wonder why the USIA let so many of you in in the first place."

"I'll see what I can do," said J.P.

• • •

But he and Diana talked of other matters as well. One day she surprised him when she asked, "You remember when you mentioned Goethe?"

"No," he said with a puzzled look on his face, "I don't recall."

"The day we first met. You asked me if I was reading *Elective Affinities*."

"You remember that?"

She dropped her eyes, and he tried to determine if a blush appeared in her complexion as well, as though she were revealing something she didn't want to admit to.

"Yes, now I recall. Why do you ask? Are you planning to take up literature?

"Not exactly. But I was curious about him. Did he ever write anything political?"

"I'm no expert—it's other literature I've concentrated on. I've mainly read his poems, plays, and novels. But he was employed in the political realm."

"What did he do?"

"He worked as a privy counselor to the grand duke of Sachsen-Weimar."

"A member of the establishment, carrying out the bidding of the ones in power."

"Well, yes, in a sense. He was conservative, and not one to rebel. There is the anecdote, for example, that while walking with Beethoven down a street in a Bohemian spa and encountering by chance a royal party, Goethe bowed and tipped his hat, while Beethoven strode through their midst without stopping, forcing them to step aside. But Goethe probably needed income at the beginning of his career, and the position provided a place from which he could pursue his many interests. And it was a tiny backwater state—hardly a militaristic, imperialist power. He was mainly an advisor, not simply a lackey. He had the freedom in a sense to create his own dukedom of another sort: he could do his writing, organize a theatre and put on productions, follow his scientific interests, and meet with all the notable people who came to the little town to see him—not just statesmen, but poets, philosophers, musicians, scientists. For example, he got the idea for *Die Wahlverwandtschaften* from an allegory Alexander von Humboldt contributed to Schiller's literary magazine, in which he speculated how the elective affinities observed in chemical elements might behave if they took human form."

"You mean Goethe tended to abdicate from political affairs."

"No, not exactly. He did engage in bureaucratic tasks and diplomatic missions, but what I'm talking about are activities that create an alternative to politics, or a politics of their own. How can you take part in politics without understanding the human whose purpose it is to serve?"

She gazed into the distance, thinking about what he said, and although he suspected she was not entirely convinced, he realized that she was searching for the proper path. Had he found it himself, or should he keep searching as well? They were so different, yet something in common in their beings had brought them together.

Immediately preceding the start of the games on the 26th of August
J.P. saw little of Diana, since she was so busy with her political
activities, including active involvement in the anti-Vietnam-War
demonstrations at the Olympic grounds. J.P. read in the newspaper
the next day that a militant communist splinter group had prolonged
the demonstration by taking the U-Bahn to the center of town where
they unfurled banners on the Marienplatz, dispersing before the
police arrived. There was no real trouble, but J.P. never got around
to asking her if she had been part of that. Any large gathering made
the authorities nervous, and they took numerous steps to limit
events that they feared might get out of hand, though a concert
performed by The Who at the Deutsches Museum four days later also
went off without any violence or signs of extensive drug use. The
Munich police also tried to defuse potential problems by using soft
tactics, which incorporated humor and friendly attitudes instead of
aggressive stances. Things seemed to be going well, and J.P. had
little to tell his boss, other than what was reported in the papers.

But a development in his personal life occurred a few days later
when Diana came to him to say that her plans to move in with a
friend had fallen through because the friend's landlady had forbid-
den her to take in a roommate. J.P. saw that she was at a loss as to
what to do and said spontaneously, "Why don't you come stay with
me? I have a two-room apartment, so there's no problem."

"Really? You mean that?" she said, looking up at him with grateful
eyes. "Just for a while. Until I find something permanent. I wouldn't
want to impose."

"It would be my pleasure," he replied, realizing as he said it that
the standard cliché actually expressed his feelings.

He helped her carry her things over that very evening, hiring a taxi
since her foot locker was too bulky to schlep on the subway. He
offered her his bedroom, saying he could sleep on the couch.

"You're a dear," she said, giving him a hug.

Her job in the bookstore began on Friday the first, though she
started going in before that to get the hang of it: it was at the
Linksabbieger, or "the one turning left," which he soon discovered
was a hole-in-the-wall alternative shop with mostly political books
and magazines, posters, and postcards picturing figures from Che

Guevara to Rudi Dutschke or bearing clever slogans such as *Macht kaputt, was euch kaputt macht*—Destroy what destroys you; *Du hast keine Chance, darum nutze sie!*—You don't have a chance, therefore use it!; *Wer kämpft, kann verlieren; wer nicht kämpft, hat schon verloren*—Those who struggle can lose; those who don't struggle have already lost. Diana worked at the cash register or stocked the shelves for a few hours each day. Since it was only part-time, he wondered if she was able to support herself and whether she was working under-the-table. He knew that she was spending additional time volunteering for political groups. After all, the Olympics were still going on.

"This is it," she indicated with a sweep of her hand when he showed up on Saturday, her second day. "I hope your employers won't mind when they find out where your girlfriend works."

J.P. felt a sudden, pleasant thrill at her use of a word to describe their relationship that he had been reluctant to utter even to himself.

"I don't care if they do," he smiled. "The important thing is, it's all right with me." He extended his arms and gave her a long hug.

At home, they had yet to settle in to a routine: sometimes they would share meals together, such as the typical German *Abendbrot* of bread, cheese, and cold cuts with a glass of beer or tea or even the egg-and-potato dish of *Bauernfrühstück* that he fried up. Since he slept on the couch he usually arose and left for work before she got up. But sometimes they shared a sleepy cup of coffee, and he even worked up the courage to kiss her before he left.

On Monday night of her first full week, she came in late.

"It's Labor Day in the U.S.," said J.P. "You would have gotten a holiday back home. Here you'll have to wait till May 1st."

"Home," she repeated softly, as though wondering where that really was.

"I know what you mean," he replied, reading her thoughts. "I feel the same way."

"Home is family, but apparently neither of us really has that."

This exchange reminded him of how she had recently astonished him with one of her unexpected remarks: when he suggested, for example, that they should make their apartment a little more homey, she said, "To lead a moral life, it is important not to be at home in one's own home." Later, when thumbing through one of her books by the philosopher Adorno, he came across that remark, which she had underlined, in a passage entitled "Asylum for the Homeless." The realization that the observation was not original with her did not detract from his opinion of her, since it indicated that she could incorporate what she encountered into her own life. And into his: it challenged him, and he thought anew about where his home was, and why.

The next morning he had put on his suit, which he had retrieved from the wardrobe the previous evening, and was about to go out the door when Diana emerged from the bedroom, wearing only a T-shirt of a light, clingy cotton that flowed softly over the curves of her wonderful figure and barely reached past her hips, which peeked out underneath. She strode toward him on her long, bare legs.

"Leaving already?" she asked, first massaging his neck and reaching with one hand down his back while loosening his tie with the other.

"Yes, I've got to get to work."

"Good, then you can get to work right now," she said, unzipping his fly and feeling that he was not averse. They two-stepped, lips joined to lips and arms embracing around the waist, back into the bedroom, where they collapsed onto the single bed.

J.P. entered the Amerika-Haus uncharacteristically late, to the surprised and serious look of Frau Huber. He didn't care in the least, however: somehow, he felt that he was right in sync with time.

But somehow the times had their own ideas about the direction in which they were headed. Perhaps Frau Huber's expression had a different source: his secretary soon came into his office with an equally grave look, asking, "I guess you must have been listening to the news."

When he replied with a puzzled glance, she explained. "Terrorists sneaked into the Israeli compound at the Olympics and seized nine athletes, whom they are holding hostage. They've killed two already. Some of us are listening to it on the radio in the conference room."

J.P. attached himself to the small, grim-faced group glued to the seemingly interminable patter that was unable to report anything new, much less anything positive.

"What are they asking for?" he inquired.

"Release of 234 Palestinian prisoners in Israeli and German jails, as well as Andreas Baader and Ulrike Meinhof."

His colleagues walked away from time to time, unable to bear the anguish and uncertainty following one missed deadline after another, and returned to their daily tasks, as he himself eventually did. In the afternoon he joined the public affairs officer in the library where a television displayed images of the balcony and windows of the dorm where the hostages were being held.

"Fucking sons of bitches," muttered the director. "They need to shoot every last one of them, no questions asked." J.P. knew he meant the gunmen and didn't say anything. "If anyone needs the illusions cleared from their eyes about why we do what we do, they just need to look at this."

J.P. had a feeling that the PAO was speaking mainly to him in the voice of one who felt that his was the obviously correct view of the situation, but he refrained from asking, "What is it that we are doing?"

A while later the director screamed "Idiots! Shit-for brains!", but this time J.P. didn't know to whom he was referring and, puzzled, stared at the screen where nothing seemed to be going on.

"The god-damn media. It's unfuckingbelievable. They don't know when to limit their information. You see that sniper setting up on the opposite rooftop? Well, if we can see it, don't you think the terrorists can? They're not about to be ambushed. We might as well hand them our ammunition on a platter!"

He was right: for that very reason the planned "Operation Sunshine" was unable to be pulled off at the end of the day.

Just before J.P. left work to go home, it was revealed that the gunmen and negotiators had agreed to a plan to transport the terrorists and their hostages on a plane to Cairo, where further negotiations would take place.

Diana got back to the apartment sometime after he did; she gave him a stern stare, each apparently trying to judge the other's reactions. He wondered whether her friends at the bookstore agreed with the taking of hostages—he knew they sympathized with the Palestinian cause.

"It's terrible," he began. "There's no good outcome that can result."

She maintained her serious look, and he could tell she was not happy about anything concerning the situation, but was still trying to sort it out.

"If the powerful would just treat people justly, it would never come to this," she said.

"True enough. But the end can never justify such means. If people seize power and slaughter innocents with automatic weapons, are they creating a better situation, or simply substituting one set of tyrants for another?"

"But the aggressors claim the end justifies the means when they use violence to wipe out opposition groups. What can be done to make them see? They don't even have the right end in sight and need to wake up. It'll take something dramatic."

"Maybe so, but not this." He gave her a hug and said, "Come, let's eat some supper."

They listened to the radio, commenting little themselves. They learned that the hostages and their captors were taken to the airport at Fürstenfeldbruck, but for another long period nothing happened, and they finally turned the radio off sometime before midnight.

"Come," said Diana, taking his hand, and they squeezed into the single bed, simply holding each other tightly, as if seeking some stability in the crazy storming world.

The next morning they learned that the second ambush attempt at Fürstenfeldbruck had failed as well, this time with more tragic results: all the remaining hostages and all but three of the terrorists were dead. A pall had been cast over the city and the world, but the day turned warm and sunny. That didn't mean, however, that reason had been restored out of the dark night. Olympic officialdom decided that the games would go on: at a morning memorial service in the stadium the Philharmonic played Beethoven's *Eroica* and the overture to *Fidelio* in tribute. In the afternoon the competitions continued. People sat outdoors at tables in the Marienplatz and quietly drank their coffee.

Life went on for J.P. and Diana as well. They grew closer, though the recent events had cast a shadow that was not always acknowledged. They bought an identical second bed to place next to the first one in German double-bed style, with a two-inch *Besuchsritze*, or visitor's crevice, separating the two mattresses. An American-style double bed, or *französisches Bett*, as the Germans called it, would have been too expensive and bulky. J.P. continued his daily duties at the Amerika-Haus and Diana hers at the *Linksabbieger* and elsewhere, and when they had free time together they went to plays or concerts or for walks in parks or the countryside. Often they spent evenings at home, snuggled up with books—J.P. with classics of German, French, or American literature or his favorites from the ancients. Diana usually read something she had borrowed from the bookstore: although he was impressed with her curiosity and how much, how rapidly, and how eagerly she read, he wished her choice of material did not remain so limited. Perhaps they should trade selections sometime. Diana had her wishes as well: she would frequently get restless and impatient and reprimand him for sitting with his nose stuck into books all the time, reminding him of Marx's eleventh thesis on Feuerbach: instead of simply interpreting the world, what really matters depends on changing it. Even when J.P. replied to an everyday suggestion or request about some minor activity with the non-committal German phrase for "it depends" (*es kommt darauf an*), she would complete it with the full Marx quotation, "*Es kommt darauf an, sie zu verändern.*"

"Rosa Parks sat," she reminded him, "but she took a stand and brought about change through her determined action of sitting. And the scores of unnamed domestic workers along with her: the movement was after all carried out by ordinary people—how many of them do you know? And would you do what they did? Do you realize how much courage it took for them? The fear of losing jobs or homes, the threat of bombings? Just because we don't commit sins by actively hating or wronging others doesn't mean we don't promote through our indifference the harm inflicted by the unjust status quo. Does it take being locked up in a Birmingham jail to make a person see that the real problem lies with moderates who preserve a negative peace, who want to avoid tension and maintain order instead of seeking a positive peace characterized by justice? And don't forget that other heroine from your home state: Helen Keller may not have been able to see and hear, but that doesn't mean she was deaf and blind in the deeper sense. She quite perceptively knew which way the wind was blowing. People trumpet the heart-warming story of her overcoming her personal adversity while conveniently forgetting her socialism. In abandoning violence, don't abandon the struggle. The time is now—it's never too late."

Once when running an errand on a side street in Schwabing J.P. saw Diana at a café table with a shaggy-haired man in a scruffy jacket, who stared intently as he approached; J.P. tried to figure out whether his eyes indicated determination or harriedness.

"*Ich muss gehen,*" the man said abruptly, standing up and leaving without waiting for an introduction.

"Who was that?"

"Someone I knew at the university—just ran into him by chance."

J.P. wondered who else she hung out with. He realized she had things she didn't tell him, and he didn't pry. He didn't want to restrict her liberation, a word that was in everyone's mouth those days. He had things he didn't tell her either, like gathering reports for his boss, because he knew she would be furious, thinking that he had sold out to the dark side. The irony, he thought, of a person who gathers information withholding it. But should he be concerned about that man who just left? And if so, for political reasons or ones of personal jealousy? Or was he being overly paranoid about the groups she was possibly connected with and the depth to which she might be involved?

But there were many occasions that were free of such concerns. On one of the last warm days of the fall, a lazy, sunny Sunday afternoon, the two of them enjoyed what the locals called a "*Schäferstündchen,*" or 'shepherds' hour,' a term that J.P. loved because of its appeal to pastoral poetry. He recalled his Ovid:

> *Hot it was, the day had slipped into the afternoon;*
>   *I eased my weary limbs down to the bed. . . .*
> *As she stood before my eyes, her clothing cast aside,*
>   *in all her body there was not a blemish to be found.*
> *What arms, what shoulders, I saw and touched!*
>   *How aptly did her breasts long for caress! . . .*
> *Why list each lovely feature separately? I saw nothing not to*
>   *praise and pressed her naked body close to mine.*
> *Who doesn't know the rest? Exhausted, we then fell into repose.*
>   *O, that such afternoons might often come to me!*

The past became present, poetry became experience, they became one. While Diana dozed, J.P. recalled their recent conversation about Goethe, who, involved and interested in so many things, had reached a dead-end in his work in the little duchy and talked his noble employer into granting him an open-ended sabbatical that would take him to Italy for almost two years and give him first-hand acquaintance with the ancient world. He wanted every part of the place to inform him of its culture, as he immediately put to paper in his *Roman Elegies*:

> *Address me, stones, directly, O speak, ye mighty palaces!*
>   *Streets, say a single word! Genius, are you not moved?*
> *Yes, all is alive in your holy walls, Eternal*
>   *Rome; only in me is all so silently still.*

And Goethe finds a unity joining the ancients, art, and love: he reads the classics and visits the museums by day, but by night Amor keeps him otherwise engaged. When he observes the lovely breast and lets his hand glide down the hips of his companion, he truly understands the marble statues for the first time, seeing with a feeling eye, feeling with a seeing hand.

> *If she's overcome with sleep, I lie and reflect at length.*
> *Often have I composed within her resting arms*
>   *And lightly, with fingering hand counted on her back*
> *The hexameter's rhythmic beat. She breathes in lovely slumber. . .*

J.P. wondered whether he was learning this through the old poet, or through his experience with the woman now lying warmly beside him: a happy convergence in any case. He thought also about the music of their own day that he was getting to know better through Diana, and realized that the process was ongoing: for example, the song she played for him just the day before, in which the singer sang that the streets of that same city where Goethe had written his *Roman Elegies* "are filled with rubble: ancient footprints are everywhere," before concluding the stanza with "You can almost think that you're seein' double/On a cold, dark night on the Spanish Stairs."

Were ruins, rubble, the only thing around him, the only thing that was left? Or on the other hand, were those classic remnants what we need to embrace and preserve as they once were? Goethe and Dylan knew that wasn't enough, and they kept the process going. Shouldn't we always be seeing double? The past is something that is contained in the present, but the experience is not just a cloned repetition. As Heraclitus said about stepping into the same river again, different and different waters flow. The past remains, but change is constant, and we're part of the process: it's also a different person that steps again into the river. Would J.P. ever create a masterpiece himself, as the singer of the current song hoped to do, or just partake of those of others? As if a perfected "masterpiece" were even possible, rather than one stage in the ongoing assembling of fragments. And if he did create something approaching that, would Diana still "be right there with him?" His thoughts stormed in a whirl. And where does politics fit into the mix? He remembered the slogan on the postcard in the political bookstore: "Make love not war." Lying there, with his own knees snuggled in the hollows of Diana's and her back close to his chest, J.P. marveled at his good fortune, and wondered how their relationship could have come about, when it did not seem to make any sense at all because they were so different. Yet maybe that in itself was the reason. He placed his arm around her and gave a gentle squeeze that was strong enough to express his contentment but not forceful enough to wake her. He fell asleep, dreaming in his happiness. But would they find lasting happiness, and would it coincide with a general *eudaimionia* for humankind? Or *tikkun olam*?

• • •

His connection to his hometown seemed to grow ever more remote, although he truly enjoyed the intermittent letters from Billy and Clotilde, along with clippings from the *Press-Register*. No further talk had arisen of Diana's looking for other lodging: J.P. was sure she couldn't afford one anyway, and both seemed content with the way things had fallen into place.

One evening in winter, when he came home from work, he noticed before she quickly turned her head away that her eyes seemed red, as though she had been crying.

"Baby, what's wrong?" he asked.

"Don't call me that!" she snapped.

"Come on, you can tell me."

She paused, looking in vain toward various corners of the apartment without finding anything.

"I'm pregnant!" she finally blurted out before burying her head in his shoulder and sobbing.

He looked past her to the other side of the room, stunned by the surprising news and wondering what that would mean for his regular life, and whether he was prepared to shoulder the responsibility.

"What will we do?" she wept. The plural pronoun reminded him that his first thought had been selfish, and that the situation was theirs to face together.

"What do you want?" he asked.

"I don't know, it's so sudden."

"Whatever you decide, I'll be there for you," he replied, meaning it absolutely while realizing that it sounded like a hollow cliché and wondering at the same time what it really meant.

Paragraph 218 of the German legal code, which made abortion illegal, would have limited their options, but they eventually made up their own minds and decided they wanted to have a child. Despite the morning sickness and occasional changes in mood, Diana embraced her new role, no doubt looking forward, in J.P.'s view, to gaining an ally in her struggle to make the world a better and braver place. The future father wanted that too, though he did not know exactly what path a child might take to bring it about. As in so many things, he was wrapped up in the process of learning, of *anagnorisis*: developing, growing, evolving, on the path toward acquiring knowledge.

Sometime after this new turn of events had sunk in, friends of Diana's from the university invited her to go with them to a student ball at Fasching, or carnival, which was late that year and not until early March. J.P. readily agreed, since, despite his conflicted feelings on the matter, the thrill and fascination of Mardi Gras still ran in his veins, and he hoped to witness a refreshing variation on the theme as it might play out here. He hated the hierarchies he had experienced back home, with their self-congratulatory attitude that resulted in a forced, artificial compulsion to have fun, while he gladly took part in the abandon, the immersion in all the senses, that emerged nonetheless.

The topic of costumes naturally came up, and J.P.'s suggestions, unsurprisingly, came from literature.

"How about Romeo and Juliet?"

"We're not teenagers," Diana scoffed.

"Antony and Cleopatra?"

"You may be royalty, but I'm certainly not."

"Venus and Adonis," he tried, sticking to the same author but switching from plays to poetry. "You are definitely a goddess."

"Why not Troilus and Cressida?" she countered.

"Do you predict a tragic end for us?" he asked with concern.

"No, but maybe they couldn't survive in a world of war, motivated by greed for money, power, and sex and justified with sham heroics. Maybe that's what we'd be exposing."

She understood more of literature and the world than he thought.

"But did they themselves understand what they unwittingly revealed, or merely succumb to it instead? They hardly did right by themselves, or each other."

"Or maybe then, since it's Fasching, we should go as something more fun."

In the end he wore a shabby black suit, porkpie hat, outsized spectacles, and fake long nose, while she found a loose, mid-length flowered dress and small hat of the style women wore in the 1920s.

Both whitened their faces, applied black highlights to their eyes and bright red to their lips, and went as the local comedians Karl Valentin and Liesl Karlstadt, poking at the world in a different way.

The party was an opportunity to forget everything but the moment: the music, the illuminations in the darkened hall, the costumes, and the swirling, dancing figures. Most of the student crowd was much younger than J.P. and he knew few people there, but it didn't matter: the encounter was immediate and not dependent on prior acquaintance. Since most were masked, he could loosen up and, ironically, feel free to be himself. But was that so different from his daily routine, where he sensed that he wore a different type of mask to negotiate his dealings with other people? In the street celebrations that preceded Ash Wednesday people also wore costumes and seemed altogether free and relaxed. Back in his home town, the crazy time was also a marked contrast to the humdrum order of everyday life—even the schools and the U.S. Mail were suspended on Fat Tuesday—but it was nonetheless a strange mixture of giving into madness and remaining within the restraints of strict tradition. The fun the societies engaged in was highly organized. In the iconic annual representation atop the float of the Order of Myths, Folly and Death unceasingly chased each other around the broken column of life, with neither ever attaining victory: yet the dominant social order remained constant, even if temporarily invisible, in firm control in the background.

At midweek, they went back to their accustomed routine; as the weeks proceeded, Diana's condition gradually started to become visible, and both began more and more to look forward to the new arrival. J.P. thought that they should get married, but did not know when nor where a ceremony should take place, nor what kind it should be. He first mentioned the subject more as a hypothetical possibility than an outright proposal. Diana was in no hurry, since she was not sure she wanted to be restricted by that bourgeois institution, as she called it, even though she assured J.P. that she had no intention of leaving him or looking elsewhere for companionship. "It may not make sense, but I love only you," she said. J.P. worried nonetheless about the fact that he was twice as old as she was, even as he questioned whether you can measure such things in those terms.

One day, while they were walking through the Marienplatz, Diana made an abrupt stop in front of a *Litfaßsäule*, one of those squat, cylindrical pillars set up in public places for displaying information and advertisements. Screaming out at them was one of the ubiquitous wanted posters for still uncaptured terrorists of the Red Army Faction, or Baader-Meinhof group, whose already imprisoned members had been waging hunger strikes in jails throughout the country. This placard seemed to be a newer version, but carried the usual warning in large letters at the bottom that the suspects were armed. Diana stared with intense concern. J.P. followed her gaze and immediately fixed his attention on one suspect with a mustache—was that the fellow he had seen with her in the café? Or was he being overly imaginative?

"Recognize anyone?" he asked, trying to give his question the laughing tone of a joke, rather than a feeling of suspicion.

"Why should I?" she replied, her arms stiff and her fists stuffed into the pockets of her coat.

"No reason. Just making conversation."

"I know you hate them, but they have reason to protest."

"Killing people with bombs and bullets isn't protesting, at least not in a valid way. One shouldn't harbor a secret joy when they escape capture or rob a bank."

"What about Heinrich Böll? Would you criticize him too?"

"His letter last year was written before it became clear that they had indeed killed the policeman. But more people have been killed since. Just because the yellow press sensationalizes, it doesn't mean the RAF is innocent. You can't just look at it as a two-sided struggle, even if they have grounds to condemn what's going on. It's simplistic to divide everyone into just two groups: the terrorists and the orderly society. Putting themselves on one side, people overlook the excesses of their own side—the violence of the RAF, the unchecked police actions of the state—for the valid stances they represent—protest against the injustice inherent in the status quo, the ability to live in a peaceful society. And then they demonize the other side, failing to recognize the validity of some of the their viewpoints. It's not a clear-cut Manichean duality: there is a range of possibilities, with a lot of overlap, that we don't make the effort to see. Look at all the nuances."

He realized that in his turn to pedagogy he was becoming uncharacteristically heated and waving his arms in a way he rarely did; she began stomping off down the street with heavy footsteps, though she didn't pause in giving a reply.

"But we didn't choose this limited position: the state with its resources—capital, industry, finance, the media, the church, the army, the police—cut off the possibilities with all its might. And the so-called left party here capitulated, forcing us into an extra-parliamentary opposition, since the forum for democracy was no longer available. And the people in all those countries still struggling to throw off the constraints of colonialism: don't you see how for them violence is the only way, and how they might provide a model for people here? Obfuscating the situation with appeals to nuance isn't going to get us very far either. You nuance yourself to inaction, and the killing goes on, only it's carried out by the corporate henchmen who rule the state. Our own country was founded on an armed revolution, in case you've forgotten. Maybe we need another."

"And who would be in charge without the majority supporting it?" he asked, hurrying to keep up. "Would the revolutionaries force their way in turn on an unwilling populace?"

She paused in her stride to turn toward him with a penetrating look. "You should learn from the mistakes of the majority of burghers in this country who sat back and didn't say anything until things went too far, and then it was too late. Show a little *Zivil-courage*, take an example instead from the few who offered resistance. "

"Like the Scholls or the Red Orchestra?"

"For example."

"But the situation back then was not the same as today. You can't deny that things have progressed. Besides, the ones that resisted Hitler ended up as martyrs." He cleared his throat demonstratively in an effort to sound decisive, though he knew it could be interpreted equally well as a sign of hesitation. People with shopping bags slung over their shoulders were walking busily through the pedestrian zone in a sign of normalcy, though a few gave a passing glance toward the pair's heated discussion.

"There are some today who aren't planning to sit back and become martyrs."

"They'll be martyrs all right: they're no match for the state."

"Compared with your martyrs dying in the rice paddies of Southeast Asia—why don't you oppose them with equal vehemence?"

"You may sympathize with your armed devils because they rightly know what to oppose, but does their type of violence bring anything new? If the PLO, for example, practiced non-violence, they'd have much more support in the world and be farther ahead."

"You embrace the tactic of non-violence as an abstract, but do you deep-down embrace the content of its goal of full civil rights and justice for everyone?"

"Of course I do, it just takes time."

"You incrementalist!" she screamed with the worst insult she knew as she stormed off down the street, stamping the pavement with extra force. As in many of their tiffs, as he called them, he told himself she was not mad at him, but expressing her frustration with the way things were in the world at large. He sympathized, and wished he knew the answer.

One day when he returned from work he found Diana stretched out on the couch with a serene look on her face.

"Come here," she said, taking his hand when he approached her side and placing it on her belly. "Do you feel it?"

He kept his hand motionless on the rounded, warm spot until he felt a fluttering, which brought on an immediate smile.

"Our new little family member."

"That's so exciting." After a pause, in which he soaked in the new development, he continued. "I got some news at the office today, though not as earth-shattering as that."

Her eyes widened inquisitively as she looked up at him.

"I received notification of my transfer to a new post."

"You mean we're not staying here forever?"

"You knew I would get reassigned at some point."

"Where? Not Iowa I hope."

"Yes, the USIA is opening up a special office in your home town just to educate your father and mother."

Although they corresponded, Diana was not on the best of terms with her parents.

"By the way," he asked. "Have you ever gotten around to telling them you're pregnant?"

"I haven't quite figured out how," she answered with frustration. "I'm sure they would insist that I return to the United States for the 'best medical care in the world.' And you can imagine how they would react to unwed motherhood and start putting pressure on me to hurry up and get married. And then I would have to go into more detail about you. They're decent, church-going people," she further explained.

J.P. wondered why the two adjectives were so often placed together: because they were inextricably connected, or because they were often contradictory and therefore combined in specific instances to differentiate between those church-going people who were decent and those who were not? And what did Diana mean: were the terms synonymous with her frequently uttered epithets "narrow-minded" and "bourgeois"?

"Well, I suppose you'll have to tell them at some point. And despite what they think, and social conventions, we need to consider what would be best for us. I'm not being transferred to Iowa, but to Beirut. Quite a change. Should be interesting."

He looked at her intently, not wanting to jinx the possibility of her coming along by directly posing questions about her intention to accompany him there or to marry him.

She answered indirectly by asking, "When will it be? Before or after the baby arrives? Will that make a difference in citizenship?"

"Most likely after, but we'll have to look into all of that I suppose. Think you can settle into a life on the Mediterranean?"

She considered for a while and answered, "Yes, I'm sure I can."

I heard the piercing cry of the bird, O son of Polypas,
who proclaims to all the season when to plow.
And her voice blackened my heart,
for other men now own my flowering fields
and it's not for me that mules now plow the land,
ever since my exile on the restless sea.
—Theognis

A LOUD, INSISTENT KNOCK ON THE FRONT DOOR jolted J.P. out of his concentration on the book in front of him, causing him to frown in annoyance at what sort of emergency might have arisen. He made his way down the stairs, and before reaching the bottom, he spied through the pane two men idling on his porch. The one situated only inches from the glass was tanned and flinty-eyed and had coarse, scraggly hair; when J.P. unlocked the main door, leaving the screen hooked, the man turned to look directly in. The companion behind him, who had a pasty, puffy face and had been gazing absently off to the side, also turned in his direction; both were wearing khaki work clothes.

"Wonderin' if you was wantin' to get your grass mowed?" the spokesman said straight away with an ingratiating smile.

"My grass mowed?" repeated J.P., in order to gain a little time to assess the situation.

"That's right. We noticed it was gettin' kinda long and figured you might not have time to take care of such a big yard."

Parked out on the street was an old, dented car pulling a flatbed trailer with low sides roughly constructed of chain-link fencing and carrying a riding mower and other lawn equipment. J.P. had been out of the country for so long he couldn't tell a Plymouth Valiant from a Ford Pinto, but decided the brand was irrelevant. He had in fact been thinking about how he should take care of his yard while putting off any decision. He hadn't bought a lawn mower, and, since he had never been fond of physical labor, had just about reached the conclusion that the job was more than he wanted to tackle alone, despite the necessity of having to pay someone more than he had paid workers in Malaysia long ago. Besides, there was the sawmill injury to his hand in his youth, which had removed the end of his little finger with one swift, small chop and cut the ring finger through to the bone. The accident had marked him with a deep red scar and a fingernail that had grown back in a curve over the little fingertip, but it had not seriously crippled him. However, it was manifesting itself again with arthritic pains that made many tasks difficult, especially when the weather changed. Though he thought he detected a scent of alcohol on the yard men's breath, he shoved his misgivings about their reliability aside.

"How much do you charge?" he asked.

The speaker turned to survey the property, and, giving an air of careful deliberation, named a sum that seemed rather high to J.P. But since he had no grounds for comparison, he had no way of knowing. He was convinced, however, that these characters were out to overcharge a gullible old man, and wanting to maintain control, he said he would consider it for a sum roughly ten percent lower.

The man thought a moment, nodded once, and said, "Fair enough." After a pause he added, "Edging and blowing? That would be extra."

Since there was no curb along the street or driveway, J.P. declined the edging but agreed to letting them gather up the clippings. "Carry them off. Don't just blow them out into the street." He nodded emphatically to give additional force to his role as overseer of the task.

"I'm Steve, by the way, and my partner is Trick," the head yard man said.

"Nice to meet you," replied J.P., declining to identify himself, not out of rudeness or oversight, but from a reluctance to let his surname escape prematurely into the community and from an unwillingness to offer them the familiarity of only a first name. He watched as they rolled the Toro and smaller gasoline mower down the ramps and got to work. He went back to his reading, but the intrusion into his routine and privacy disturbed his concentration. The loud, whining, machine noises, particularly the blower, grated incessantly at the base of his brain, even when he occasionally succeeded in thinking about something else. The knocking that followed after an hour or two repeated the insistency of the initial rap on the door, but this time it seemed like a relief by signaling a conclusion to the ordeal. J.P. fortunately had enough cash on hand to pay them, and he stuffed the exact amount, no tip included, into his pocket before he stepped out onto the porch to survey the work. They were hardly master gardeners, and certain aspects seemed to have been taken care of rather perfunctorily, but it was satisfactory.

"Looks good," said J.P. tersely, handing them the money.

"It should. I'm plumb wore out. Check back with you next week?" said Steve.

"How about two weeks?" countermanded J.P.

"Fine. Two weeks," replied Steve, tapping two fingers to his forehead.

As they drove off, J.P. noted that the trailer had a bumper sticker, prominently displayed for Bud "Dupe" Duplin for Governor, with the slogan that to J.P.'s mind expressed the coded racism so readily understood in the area: "He's one of us!" Although this candidate had lost the election the first time he ran, he was again set to give it a go and was pulling all the right stops to rouse his base: the Second Amendment, the Ten Commandments, homosexuality, and abortion. Instead of things that really have an effect on people's everyday lives, he scoffed. Politicians like that would rather get people's blood boiling and make them think there are others out to get them. J.P. wanted to feel that things were progressing in a positive way, but reminders such as this made him aware of the ugly undercurrents that he had known throughout his life and that threatened to resurface at any moment. He thought about the recent ethnic fighting in the former Yugoslavia: who would have guessed that warfare would break out again in Europe for such seemingly primitive reasons so soon after the horrors of two world wars and among people who had lived side by side in one country for over 40 years? Is atavism inevitable? he wondered. Can there possibly be a war to end all wars? Ethnicity, race, religion, chauvinism: all pretexts for a tribalistic urge to ward off enemies, real or imagined, through a self-righteous sense of superiority. Following the catchwords of an unprincipled demagogue frees people from the difficult task of actually adhering to the moral tenets they claim to hold. Is history linear or cyclical? Does the past presage the present? If so, in what sense? Do we ever reach a real turning point, when the citizenry becomes aware and embarks on a better path? Or do people merely give a nod to the concept of a better outlook and simply let things rock along comfortably as before? He realized that some even claimed that since the fall of the Soviet Union we had entered a post-historical era. But how could that be? What would Herodotus or Thucydides have said?

He then remembered how that very morning between 8 and 9 he had wound the old clock on the mantel, the same one whose comforting tick-tock his ancestors had experienced: first cranking up the weight on the right that controlled the time and then the one on the left that regulated the striking. Since the chiming weight had run down before completing its strokes at 9 the night before, it now concluded that number. When the time rolled around to 9 am, however, it struck 10. J.P. halted the pendulum to allow the striker to adjust itself to the correct time and an hour later advanced the small hand before starting the clock up again. He felt as though he were tricking time and wondered if one could not do that with history: halt it until humanity had caught up with where it should be. And that Confederate flag decal on the yard workers' rear window: how could four brief years down a mistaken, treasonous path constitute a heritage?

Turning his thoughts back to the yard, he wished he had not committed to rehiring those clowns, but then wondered if rejecting them and not just their views would place him among those who abetted the regressive divisiveness. If he refrained from using the n-word, shouldn't he avoid the r-word as well? In regarding them with haughty disdain, was he employing the classist outlook of the so-called elite? Or was he mainly galled that their clothing and rough-and-tumble ways connected them with the world of real work from which he was so distant? How much easier it would be to adopt a sweeping Manichaean, either-good-or-bad perspective, but honestly negotiating one's way in the real world was much more difficult. And maybe if they were taking advantage of him, it was because they expected him to try to exploit them.

He paused on his path back down the front hall to recall the nightmare from which he had awoken in a sweat: the kudzu he had recently found encroaching on the edge of his property was slithering its tentacles at the rate of a foot a day, an hour, a minute, over all that he owned, and attempts to hack it off only caused it to multiply Hydra-like and continue in greater force—an alien intruder with no natural restraints, which ruined the best-laid plans of inhabitants to order their world in a rational and pleasing fashion. Perhaps it is a good thing I've found somebody for the yard work, he mused. But how should I really deal with them?

Feeling that the morning was shot, J.P. fixed himself a pimento-cheese sandwich from the little plastic container he had bought at Delchamps and poured himself a glass of iced tea, which he spiced up with a mint leaf plucked from the plant by the back door.

"Maybe I'll be able to accomplish something after my nap," he thought.

• • •

Around six that evening he began chopping up the summer squash, zucchini, eggplant, onions, and garlic from the bright orange produce market at the bottom of the hill where he often shopped. Though no great chef, he had found it convenient to cook for himself in many of his postings: in Marseille he had learned to prepare ratatouille, and on this occasion he was giving it a local touch by adding slices of Conecuh County sausage. He had invited Miranda over to supper and was looking forward to another of those meetings that were the highlight of his return.

"This is delicious, Dad," she said when seated at his small dining room table and taking a bite of the dish he had prepared. "What spices are in it?"

He noted that she seemed gradually to be getting more comfortable around him. "Lots of garlic of course, and *herbes de Provence*. I had a devil of a time finding a package and finally had to mix up my own."

"A real chef. You seem to have a lot of talents."

"I have my limits. I don't seem to be able to make a proper gumbo. I'm all thumbs when it comes to preparing a roux. I guess I don't have enough patience. Do you cook?"

"Some. I never felt like learning how to fix the overcooked vegetables my Iowa grandmother used to make, and in college we had the cafeteria. In graduate school I began to try a little, going beyond the boxes of ramen noodles and macaroni and cheese. I'm thinking about moving into another place on the island, and then I would have a kitchen and could branch out even more. My room's been convenient, but those accommodations are mainly for students and short-term visiting researchers. In the meantime, why don't you let me cook for you here sometime? It'll give me an incentive, and besides I should maybe do something for you." She tried to strike a tone that would move the relationship forward to a better footing, though she was still not completely certain what would be possible, giving what had happened, or not happened, in the intervening years.

"It's a deal."

Wanting to learn more, she continued. "I mean, all you're telling me is a help. Whole gaps in my life are being restored—I feel like I know my mother so much better now. Though the information comes so slowly and piecemeal. Your story seems interminable, but still, I hang onto every word."

"As I told you before, there's so much to it. I can't rush it."

She stared down at her hands with a serious expression. "I just wish those gaps hadn't been there in the first place. You're giving me facts, but I would like to know character as well."

"I know," he admitted, sensing a not-so-subtle accusation and feeling a pang of guilt. "I was absent during most of your upbring-ing—I surely could have done more. At the time I thought you no longer had a mother to nurture you, and I wasn't sure I could provide what you needed. Besides, the living situation was becoming increasingly perilous."

Contemplating now in retrospect, he wasn't sure if his conclusion back then had been a realization or a rationalization: still too awed at the time by the responsibility involved in the situation into which he had stumbled, had he correctly faced his lack of what it took to raise a child, or did his decision come from laziness or cowardice? Perhaps his behavior had been a result of his inherent neglect in cultivating and keeping relationships with other people, starting with his own family. Human connections had often proven too abstract for him. His avoidance of forming close bonds might have been a consequence of his extreme sensitivity to the plights of others, or, on the other hand, of his selfish fear of the difficulties inherent in involvement. Maybe these swirling doubts played a role in his reticence to reveal and explain everything at once. At least this time he had reached out and re-established contact.

"Well, as I understand it so far, it wasn't all your fault. My grandparents took me away and didn't want me to have anything to do with you. I didn't even know your name. They told me they didn't know who my father was—that my mother was a wonderful person who made a mistake abroad and ended up dying in an accident. They were bitter about not being able to bring her body back for a proper burial. Since there was no father's name on my passport, and I never could track down a birth certificate, I couldn't locate you that way either. My grandparents didn't want *me* making any mistakes and kept a pretty tight rein on me. The portrait they painted was like, you know, a static icon made up of a set of fixed phrases. I want to hear still more from you about what she was really like."

"They were obviously possessive of their image of her: I'm sure they thought that the 'mistake' that caused her to deviate from what they considered the normal path must have been the fault of someone else. But I wouldn't call anything she did a mistake."

"You really loved my mother, didn't you?"

"Yes, I did. The two saddest days of my life were when she disappeared and when you were taken away."

"And you're absolutely certain she's dead?"

J.P. sighed and thought, as though recapitulating all the possibilities he had contemplated over the many years. "Yes, I'm sure. I already mentioned briefly what happened, but I still need to tell you in detail all I know about that. She never would have abandoned us. She was too devoted. And, believe me, I didn't want to either. I tried as hard as I could at first to get you back, but my job abroad and your grandparents' resistance and outright legal maneuvering made contact difficult. My letters to them mostly went unanswered. After my initial attempts, I did try at least once a few years later to make direct contact, but I have to confess, a single belated attempt is pretty pitiful."

"How and when did you do that?"

"Listen up," he said, attempting to steer the narrative. "You must have been in ninth grade. When I was back in the U.S. on leave, I went to Iowa and parked across the street and down the block from your grandparents' house, the little one with the fence around it, and waited for you to come home from school, but you never did. I sat in the car until almost dark—I'm surprised nobody called the police. I tried it again the next day as well, and then called the high school to see whether you were enrolled. I pretended to be a school-system psychiatrist, since I didn't think they would give the information to just anybody. They said that your parents had sent you to an out-of-town boarding school, but they didn't know which one. I tried to track that down as well, but without any success. I stopped a couple of girls near the school to ask if they knew you, but they got suspicious and clammed up. Maybe I should have hired a private detective, but I didn't know where to start in that regard. I'm sorry, Miranda, I could have done more. The internet wasn't what it is now. No Alta Vista, or what's that new one they've got?"

"Google," she said tersely.

"Won't that be able to put all knowledge at our fingertips?"

"Depends what you mean by knowledge. In any case, those search engines can't do everything. I wish you had tried harder. But at least we finally made contact in the old-fashioned way. Yes, they sent me away to a boarding school in the East. I was somewhat rebellious, and they didn't know how to handle a teenager and were sure I would make a mistake. They were getting older and sicklier by that point, and it was probably getting to be too much for them. I only came back at Christmas and went home with friends for Thanksgiving and spring break. I don't know how they afforded it; they weren't rich."

Not sure whether he should mention it or not, but deciding he did not want her to believe that he had forsaken her more than he actually had, he added, "They had help."

"What do you mean?"

His voice softened. "Even though they denied me contact, they accepted the monthly checks that I sent. I perhaps should have insisted on a fairer exchange for my sending them, but in any case I felt it was my responsibility, and at the least I didn't want you to be denied other things."

Miranda's eyes widened. "So you weren't completely absent, all along?"

"If you can call it that. It didn't feel that way to me. Maybe. . . ."

"Maybe what?"

"I don't know. Maybe sending money and books was taking the easy way out, a means for telling myself I was doing the right thing. Did any of the books I sent make it through?"

"Books?"

"Yes, at first Beatrix Potter and Dr. Seuss, then the Bobbsey Twins and Beverly Cleary—I had to ask younger colleagues what children were reading. Later *Alice in Wonderland* and Jules Verne and Dickens and Harper Lee and Rachel Carson."

"You sent those? I can't believe it. They never told me, and I assumed they had bought them, though at times it did seem strange since they never read themselves. They even mailed them off to me at school. How about *Moby Dick*, Edith Hamilton's *Mythology*, *Paintings in the Louvre*, and the biography of Madame Curie?"

"Yes, yes, those too, that's amazing. I'm so delighted to hear that you got the books. At least they had sense enough to pass them on. I remember when you were a toddler, long before you could read, how you used to enjoy pulling books off the shelf and riffling through the pages, knowing even then that they were a source of discovery. And no doubt enjoying as I still do the physicality of the experience: the light caress of the pages moving across the fingertips, the soft rippling whispers, the gentle breeze created by the interaction."

Other titles were recalled: "What about the *Diary of Anne Frank*, the journals of Lewis and Clark, *Antigone* and *Lysistrata*, *Walden*, Virginia Woolf, the subscription to *National Geographic*. . . ."

They took turns naming titles until J.P. said, "If we named them all we'd be here all night."

Nonetheless he then asked, "How about *The Catcher in the Rye* or *I Know Why the Caged Bird Sings*?"

"I read those at boarding school, but they didn't come from them."

"I guess they didn't give all my educational ideas *carte blanche*."

"Theirs mainly involved dragging me to church, but somehow that didn't have as much effect as what you apparently provided."

J.P. sensed a gradual, though still somewhat grudging, acceptance. "I wasn't sure what kind of education you'd be getting from your grandparents or your schools, so I wanted to do what I could to help you grow up in the right way and fit into society. No, 'fit in' isn't the right word. There's a lot I didn't like about society, and I didn't exactly try to fit in myself. 'Deal with' might be a better term."

Miranda reached over and grabbed his hand. "So you were taking part in my upbringing." It was the first time she had touched him voluntarily. She looked around at the bookcases, which even spilled over into the dining room. "It makes sense now, where all that came from."

"I tried. I knew I could send the books, but I had no idea whether you would get them, or even if you would want to read them if you did. A great deal results from what you were able to accomplish yourself." He realized again that at twenty-four she was not some guileless innocent, and that their newfound relationship was not starting with a blank slate.

"Who knows where such traits or predilections come from?"

Smiling, J.P. poured them each some more of the Malbec he had recently discovered in the supermarket and hadn't tasted since his time in Argentina: clinking glasses, they downed a sip in unison. But had all the divisions really been overcome, or was he still postponing fully coming to grips with them?

μ

*Wars, terrible wars I see
in the time to come, and the Tiber foaming
with violent streams of blood.*
—Virgil, *The Aeneid*, VI, 86–87

*W*AS MY MOM ADVENTUROUS?"
"*She certainly was. More so than me, I suppose, but I don't know whether the ventures that I proposed were always to her liking. But maybe each of us, and both together, are what contributed to your own bold, inquiring spirit.*"

They got up early to catch the bus, wondering whether it would show up on time or at all, and what the ride might be like. The sun was rising in the east, a bloody-red blob that seeped slowly as it tore itself away from the prostrate earth. Diana had not slept well and seemed exhausted from the journey thus far. J.P. regretted having made the decision to pursue a more adventuresome path to Beirut: instead of flying direct, they had taken the train to Athens, where they had spent a few days exploring the sights. He had looked forward to showing to his love the other loves of his life, and though she was duly impressed by the marble columns of the Parthenon, the caryatids of the Erechtheion, and the sweeping vistas from the Acropolis, her advanced pregnancy made the climb up from the old quarter of Plaka more strenuous than either would have liked. From Piraeus a ferry took them to Rhodes, where they spent another couple of days. They slowed down a bit and wandered leisurely through the narrow streets of the medieval walled city, along the moat, and beside the harbor, taking in the ancient stone fortifications, whitewashed houses with blue doors, bending palm trees, and bougainvillea cascading over walls. They even managed to lie for a while on a nearby beach, retreating to the shade of an olive grove when the sun's rays grew too hot. Turkey, their next stop, was just visible on the horizon. On the way back to the little hotel Diana squeezed his hand, and J.P. wondered whether the gesture meant that she was thankful to be able to rely on him or to plead that she'd had enough.

Now they were waiting for the bus in a little café in Fethiye, where they had arrived after a short boat ride and from which point they would travel along the southern Turkish coast to another port, where they would take an overnight ferry to Tripoli, Lebanon. When the old vehicle finally showed up, a crowd suddenly materialized to clamber on board: women bundled up in blue and brown clothing and head scarves, some holding the hands of little children; around them stood lean men with mustaches, prominent ears, and wrinkled, leathery faces. The couple found seats near the front and sat back to endure the extremely bumpy, all-day trip, which seemed to stretch on interminably. J.P. could only imagine Diana's discomfort; he was relieved that they had at least reserved a small cabin with berths to themselves on the next leg of the journey. He tried to distract himself with the views of the shoreline and the grey-blue Mediterranean. Far out on the water a small fishing boat bobbed at the mercy of the waves; he marveled at the tenuous means with which we make our way through life. A small, framed portrait of a stern Mustafa Kemal Atatürk above the driver's seat kept watch over everyone in the bus; the mosques in the villages through which they passed served as reminders of the new culture they were entering. The skies became increasingly overcast, and the wind had picked up considerably by the time they finally reached the harbor in Taşucu: Diana had to hold tightly to the rails as they ascended the gangplank to the rocking ship, and J.P., who was carrying both suitcases, stumbled once or twice.

Diana wanted to lie down immediately: J.P. wondered whether her occasional moans meant that she was feeling contractions, but she was non-committal. She was not hungry; after assuring himself that she was all right, he went to the brasserie to buy himself a pocket sandwich of grilled lamb and a beer, which he took out onto the upper deck. Numerous others were leaning against the railing or seated in the middle, talking, smoking cigarettes of pungent, dark tobacco, and listening to quavering musical tones on tinny radios. Some even began to dance: Arabs or Turks? He couldn't tell. The steamer had departed after dark, and the wake spread out behind them in a widening V in the black water. Large raindrops began to fall and drove everyone inside before he had even had a chance to finish his sandwich. Most went to a large hall with rows of seats like a bus station waiting room, but he descended toward his cabin. As he made his way unsteadily along the railing it was so dark that one couldn't see very far into the distance: only the whitecaps close to the ship, which were growing progressively bigger and whose nearness made it appear that the vessel was racing at full speed. All he could hear was the rushing wind and the thump-thump-thump of the engines.

Diana was sleeping lightly, and he decided it would be best for him to turn in as well. But he had hardly dozed off when he was jolted to alertness by an anguished, piercing cry from the bunk below. He leapt to the floor, and she grabbed his hand tightly in both of hers as she looked up at him in alarm.

"It's started," she said. "What do we do?"

"Aren't you supposed to take deep, slow breaths? Isn't that what we read?" But his face displayed only helplessness.

"I guess," she replied, though she was having a hard time concentrating. Between moans, and bouts of delirium, she focused and asked, "It's way too early. Do you think it will be all right?"

"Somewhat early, but it should be OK," he tried to reassure her, and himself as well, for he was equally worried. "I think we also read that there can be false, preliminary contractions. Maybe they will subside until we get to Lebanon."

After a while she announced, however, that her water had broken, and, though reluctant to leave her, he stepped out to see if the ship had a doctor, eventually locating the officer who was assigned to provide emergency medical service. That man, fortunately, happened to be aware that an actual physician was a passenger on the trip: Dr. Yasmine Khouri, in cabin 4C, who was still up and more than willing to help. "It's not my specialty, but I have done it before," she said in French.

She sent the officer to fetch clean towels and pans of hot water, while she and J.P. devoted their attention to Diana, whose contractions were becoming more frequent. Also more frequent and severe were the rolls of the ship, which was apparently sailing into increasingly foul weather.

"*Une vraie tempête,*" commented Dr. Khouri, as she diligently tried to calm the mother and keep things moving as they should. J.P. attempted to translate to Diana as best he could, though he somehow had the impression that Dr. Khouri's manner alone was sufficient. The process went on and on, and the intermittent screams which came with increasing frequency and intensity gave him sudden jolts, but he had to remind himself that they signaled the excruciating pain that Diana must be enduring: all he was experiencing were the auditory reactions. Helplessly he held her hand and tried to do what he could. The birth appeared incredibly difficult with many hidden dangers lurking, and the admonitions to push seemed to be repeated endlessly: but perhaps people always felt it to be that way. It was as though it were storming inside and out, and he wondered whether all would make it safely to shore.

At last the head emerged, covered in black hair, and then the rest of the pink little body: the baby's cries indicated good health, and it was placed eagerly on its mother's belly. Exhausted, she managed to look at the little girl and smile. J.P. gazed at both in admiration and gratitude.

Assuring herself that all were in good shape, and that the baby would be securely cared for, Dr. Khouri retired and told them she would check in again first thing in the morning. After an initial feeding, they laid their new daughter in a tub lined with a sheet and blanket, which Diana held close to the berth to keep it from sliding back and forth across the floor. J.P. told her to sleep and said he would stay awake during what was left of the night to make sure everything was all right. The howling winds and deepening swells made him uneasy, but the fact that the baby seemed perfectly content relieved him.

"Isn't she precious?"

Diana's observation as she cradled their little daughter in her arms was the first thing J.P. heard the next morning; he realized he must have dozed off after all. He stretched his cramped limbs and embraced them both as well as he could.

"What will we call her?"

"Miranda," he answered immediately. "We admire her now, and will even more so in the days to come, I'm sure."

"I just wish she could have come into a better world. She is the one who deserves it."

"Ours is pretty good at the moment." The ship's movements had calmed down, and the waves through which they were traveling now had only a gentle, rocking rhythm. "The cradle of the sea," he added.

True to her word, Dr. Khouri appeared promptly and gave both mother and daughter a thorough examination in her serious, professional way.

"I'm surprised they let you on board," she said. "They usually don't like to take a chance with pregnant women."

"My raincoat must have made it less obvious. And they were probably distracted by the weather," mumbled Diana.

"Besides, we thought we had another couple of weeks," added J.P.

"Maybe," said Dr. Khouri. "But the initial estimate could have been off, and perhaps the low pressure of the storm brought on the labor. In any case you're fortunate you're strong and in good health. But you need to take it easy for the next several days. Is Tripoli your destination?"

J.P. explained that they had originally planned to take a bus to Beirut, where they were going to live, but now he didn't know what would be best.

"I wouldn't advise it. Too strenuous. How much luggage do you have?"

"Just the two suitcases. We've shipped the rest."

"In that case, maybe you could ride with us. My sister is meeting me in Tripoli with her Mercedes to take me back home to Beirut. The drive should take less than two hours. Besides, I know the doctors better there—you'll probably want to go to the American University Hospital anyway."

Before leaving the cabin she turned and added: "We'll be docking soon, so I'll come fetch you before leaving the boat. But first we need to get some sort of certificate signed by the captain to attest to the birth at sea—we were out of the jurisdiction of any country."

A citizen of the world, mused J.P.

• • •

The fortuitous acquaintance provided them with a favorable start to Miranda's life, as well as to their initiation into the new country. They settled into their apartment on the top floor of a sand-colored, six-story building in a bustling part of the city: the spacious balcony provided them with outdoor living space and a tiny glimpse of the azure expanse of water to the west: "our sea," they often called it. It also gave a view onto the busy street life below, while being situated high enough above to keep the noise from being too disturbing: the sounds were reduced to a pleasant background hum, punctuated by an occasional car horn or chant of a muezzin. J.P. could walk to his work at the library in the John F. Kennedy Cultural Center, though he eventually bought a small Renault for excursions and errands. Although life was cheaper here, he periodically chafed at the thought that if he hadn't been cheated by Anthony, they would have had a somewhat larger cushion of comfort. The staff at the USIS center was larger than in Munich, perhaps because they were now in a capital city and possibly as a result of the agency's shifting more of its resources to parts of the developing world that the government deemed crucial in a changing global situation. The embassy in Beirut served as regional headquarters for a range of U.S. agencies, including the FAA, AID, and DEA, not to mention, as J.P. surmised, the CIA. He had served in enough posts by now to adjust to the new conditions without undue difficulty, though he worked to remain attentive to the differences in the new languages and populations. He began reviving the French he had used in Africa and was determined to learn some Arabic. The best part of his day, however, was returning home in the evening to hold the baby and see how she was developing. The day she first smiled at him in recognition was of particular delight. He tried to help with things as much as he could, but felt awkward and did not always know what to do; he let Diana take care of most of the decisions and tasks. Soon, they hired a Lebanese woman, Jamila, to come in a couple of days a week to clean and babysit so that Diana could get out from time to time. Although he had hesitated at first to take this step, not wanting to replicate the master-servant relationship that he had found problematic in his adolescence back home, he recognized the necessity, and they soon began to treasure Jamila's company and presence.

In their free hours they took sunny drives along the Corniche or sat on the rocks by the shore, feeling the warm sea air and watching the bathers. The specks of sun on the dappled wavelets lulled them into calm, although J.P. noted that the pattern seemed restless nonetheless: so different from the fury that preceded their arrival, while harboring a reminder that something similar could erupt again at any time. Sometimes in the evening they would go to an outdoor café to drink coffee under the palm trees of the public square. Shopping was usually a pleasure as well, and they both enjoyed their turns stepping out to the little stores in their neighborhood, selecting olives and dates, or oranges from the mounds piled high on the tables of a family-owned fruit stand. On one excursion he purchased an exquisite brass tray from a vendor, which he mailed to his Aunt Clotilde as a present. The city provided an excitingly diverse environment, and he took pleasure in observing the intermixture of confessions and cultures: Sunni, Druze, Shiite, Maronite Christian, Armenian, Greek Orthodox, Jewish, Palestinian, and European. He could sit in one café and sense that he was in the company of Parisian intellectuals, or stroll through the souks and be fully absorbed in the Middle East. And never far away were the ruins of antiquity. Diana was fascinated as well, but she told him he was idealizing, or at most, internalizing clichés. She observed underlying tensions, which in her view were being exacerbated by the Great Powers, and which, she feared, might have ominous repercussions.

"The differences between the poorer neighborhoods and the nineteenth-century villas with their Oriental carpets and Venetian marble that we've been to on some of those stuffy official receptions are something other than picturesque. We can enjoy a peaceful stroll in Martyrs' Square and forget that a little over fifty years ago Lebanese were slaughtered there by the Ottomans," she said.

"The Ottoman Empire is long gone," he replied.

"Yes, but warlords still exist, all warily guarding their own hold on power. And what could be more violently tribal than a misguided attachment to a religious creed? Not to mention the ongoing conflict between Israel and its neighbors and former inhabitants, which spills over in lots of ways, and our own government's involvement, which we rarely think about. We're rocking along without any fighting and devastation going on at the moment, but there's a restless uneasiness. Aren't you afraid things could erupt again if underlying problems aren't addressed?"

"Maybe," he said, reluctantly recalling that the histories of Herodotus and Thucydides were full of descriptions of brutal battles, not to mention the *Iliad*, whose war was hardly conducted in the best interests of those involved. Socrates himself was called into service in the army and the *Aeneid* foresees perpetual war for Rome. Conflict was perhaps more normal than peace in the course of human events. As Thucydides put it, "the strong do what they can and the weak suffer what they must." Did all these past accounts portend the present, which is doomed to repeat the same cycles forever? Are we part of a tragedy, or a farce?

Marriage was another topic of contention: they had never gotten around to it in Munich, but now that Miranda was a part of their family, J.P. thought it would be best for all of them if her parents wed. Although Diana did not categorically oppose the idea, she continued to put it off with vague objections that "there's still time." She did, however, finally communicate to her parents the news of Miranda's arrival, painting a rosy picture and sending them a photograph of the baby in her arms. Her own face was barely visible, however, since she was looking down at the child. In the response, recriminations seemed almost to outweigh delight at being grandparents. Concern for the child's well-being, however, framed their arguments that Diana bring the baby "home from that dangerous place" where she was living without a husband. They offered to send her tickets, or even come get her and the baby themselves.

"How little they understand," said Diana, rocking Miranda in her arms.

Despite the postponement of marriage, they went ahead with the paperwork involving their daughter's birth and citizenship. One day when J.P. was at work Diana took the document from the ferry along with her own passport to the Embassy to apply for a Consular Report of Birth. The young employee had never filled one out before, and since Diana was not married, he left the space for paternity blank—perhaps he was aware of the local law giving mothers custody of daughters until they reached the age of seven, but more likely he was just ignorant or careless. Never one to pay attention to details, Diana simply accepted the documents that were given to her. The American address was listed as the one in her passport: that of her parents in Iowa. Once Miranda's birth and citizenship were properly attested ("at sea" being listed as place of birth), Diana applied for a passport for the baby as well. But the shortcomings of bureaucracy would come back to haunt them.

As Miranda grew older they took longer excursions to the hills east of the city, to beaches farther away from town, and once even as far south as the ancient city of Tyre, the home from which both the widowed Dido and Pericles found themselves exiled, where J.P. took pleasure in exploring the Roman ruins. He imagined what might have been had he been born into the ruling family of this place millennia ago: would he have been prepared to assume princely duties then? Probably not, he decided, since the machinations of those who lust for power would have thwarted him then as now. He preferred to take delight in his daughter's development and how alertly and contentedly she observed everything before her with her wide eyes of lapis lazuli. Her constant, joyful curiosity was something he resolved to try to adopt in his own life. On one picnic, as they lay on a blanket in the sun with the baby crawling between them, a shepherd passed by with his sheep. Remaining aloof behind his flock, the herdsman seemed sure of his purpose, knowing what he had to do: that which was necessary, that which had been done for thousands of years. Miranda sat up to watch them attentively and cooed happily in response to the bleating of the lambs. *Grelot* was the word J.P. had recently learned for the little bells that tinkled from the necks of the sheep: but was there a word that could encompass the wonder that was Miranda? By the waters of Lebanon, he thought, there we sat down: but I have no reason for weeping or regret in the marvel of the present here and now.

Although their lives had for the most part settled into a pleasant routine, Diana's restlessness returned, prompted in part by the daily reminders of local tensions that to her reflected a far from adequate world order. She took on a volunteer job at a children's clinic in the Palestinian refugee camp which had been established on the southern edge of the city some twenty-five years before, following the war that had accompanied Israel's independence. Calm had never been completely restored in the region since that event, with the enemies attacking each other on various occasions. The camp was supposed to be temporary, but who could say how long it and the others would continue to exist? The Six-Day War had settled nothing, nor had the massacre that had traumatized them in Munich, nor the swift Israeli raid targeting PLO leaders in apartment buildings in Beirut, nor the Egyptian-Syrian surprise attack on Israeli forces at Yom Kippur that very year. To J.P. it seemed that violence always seemed to be justified by pointing to a prior attack from the other side, as in the playground retort, "But he hit me first!" The events were naturally of concern to his own government and transmitted to Washington through his own superiors, who were eager to have him gather as many observations as he could in addition to his official, daily duties. A further variation on the supplying of information came with the assignment to write position papers for the Arab-language publications that were distributed throughout the Middle East. He tried to keep the facts as accurate as possible and the tone less tendentious than his directors might have liked. What he really preferred was coordinating the English-language classes, ordering books and magazines, and observing the eagerness with which young Lebanese pored over them on their own in the library. He felt that their acquaintance with Melville, Haw-thorne, Wharton, Hemingway, and Faulkner would do more to endear them to America than would the dry pamphlets and not-so-subtle propaganda that he and his colleagues cranked out.

J.P. was shocked to learn in the course of all this that his superiors knew about Diana's visits to Shatila, which they thought might provide some means of infiltrating the groups there. Knowing how she would react to such a request, J.P. responded with a non-committal, "I'll look into it." He remained torn between his own impression that openly furnishing as much information as possible to all sides could lead to greater understanding and a reduction in the potential for conflict, and someone else's demand that its selective use be employed to further the aims of one party.

These worries caused him to treasure more than ever the moments after work on the balcony (especially on those increasingly frequent days that became impossibly hectic with unexpected demands), when he could lean against the rail puffing his Gauloises and contentedly watching Miranda play on the blanket with Nadia, the little daughter Jamila sometimes brought along. Jamila hummed as she sat in a chair in a shady corner and folded the laundry; the large potted palm that Diana had bought displayed its serrated green leaves against the brilliant white wall behind it, blinding in the sunny, crystalline air of the Levant. J.P. greeted Diana warmly when she returned and didn't even mind when she inquired once again with a scolding look on her face when he was going to stop smoking.

One day almost two years into the pleasant routine of their time there she announced to him that some German friends were planning to pass through and wanted her to show them the sights of northern Lebanon, including Baalbek, a place whose name caused J.P. to perk up with interest.

"Heliopolis. It was an important Greek and Roman town, and there are impressive ruins there from many cultures. You remember I went up there on one of my missions soon after we arrived. I'd love to go back, and I could serve as a guide."

"Yes, you're the expert," she teased with a grin. "They'll come by on Thursday of next week and want to spend that night as well as Friday and Saturday up there—they said they could drop me back here on Sunday."

"Oh," he said with disappointment. "I have to conduct seminars on those days for visiting school classes. There's no way I could get away."

"Is it all right if I go and leave you here?"

"Of course—we'll manage. I'll make sure that Jamila can come on those days." He had little desire to restrict her, and knew it would do little good, even if he had tried. He also appreciated how she respected him and what he did: even though they debated political points and she teased him about his awkwardness and many of his quirks, and though they could also have some rather serious squabbles at times, they seemed to have a basic understanding that prevented either his tendency to get irritated at things or her dissatisfactions from ever lasting very long.

"Which friends are those?" he inquired.

"Oh, Sabine and Hans-Ulrich. You remember."

"No, I don't," he said, trying to match the names with some of the many faces he had briefly encountered with her in Munich, wondering if the fellow he suspected of being on the wanted poster might be the one in question. Would confronting her indicate a lack of trust?

"Mama," interrupted Miranda, toddling over and clutching a rag doll in her hands.

"Yes, darling?"

"Fifi hungry."

"Well, we'll have to get her something to eat," obliged Diana, fetching a small bowl and a spoon so that Miranda could contentedly feed her doll at a little table.

Later that night, in the faint light of the moon that seeped into the room from around the curtains, J.P. observed Diana's form next to him and the soft rise and fall of the sheet in rhythm with her breath. Close enough to touch, but at the same time so far away—her sleeping face failed to reveal what was going on inside her dreaming mind. Was there an inevitable distance in the relations with anyone, he wondered. In the lunar glow she was heavenly to him, like the goddess Selene, but in the everyday she ran firm-footed and seeking in a sure direction across the surface of the earth, like Artemis; and at times, he knew, she could display like Hecate demonic outbursts that seemed to come from some nether world: Horace's *diva triformis*, who could not be pinned down.

The next day he learned that he would have to substitute at a meeting with some Lebanese political leaders for another colleague whose remarks he was expected to present.

"Probably Phalangists," was Diana's response when he informed her as she was preparing supper. "When will the U.S. stop thinking that just because someone's anti-communist, it must mean they're good?"

"Nobody's perfect, but we have to deal with the people who are here. Besides, they want to keep the country free of outside influence. Given the number of groups that would like to meddle, that's probably not so bad."

Diana intensified the strokes with which she was chopping the onions. "Nationalism is another thing that can be carried too far. And what do they think of *our* government's attempts at influence?"

J.P. just shrugged his shoulders. Later that evening he donned his suit and drove to the meeting in the Achrafieh neighborhood, where chairs surrounded a set of four tables arranged in a square. Folded cards with the names and affiliations of many of the participants had been placed at pre-arranged spots: he experienced a horrified shock when he located his own and saw that it read "John P. DeVeaux, C.I.A." At least they spelled my name wrong, he thought, though the other error could be quite damaging, if not fatal. He was aware from colleagues of attempts at intimidation practiced at times by agents of various enemies. Furious, he wondered how the mix-up might have occurred—or perhaps the confusion was in his own mind and he did not know himself what he was involved in. He had heard rumors that the current hard-line head of the USIA, appointed by Nixon, was tightening up liaison arrangements between the two agencies despite his testimony before Congress two years earlier that USIS posts were not being used as overseas cover. Was J.P. the one who failed to see, keeping himself in the dark from an unwillingness to face the situation? He wondered whether he should protest, but instead chose to downplay his role when it came his turn to speak by simply naming his actual affiliation and emphasizing that he was merely a substitute presenting the situation update that had been prepared by his colleague. After his dutiful presentation, and the conclusion of the meeting, he chatted over tea and arak with a number of the others. Despite their cordiality, he noted a certain reserve and a steely-eyed sizing up of his intentions, and by synecdoche, those of his government. Before leaving, he pocketed his name card as unobtrusively as possible to keep it from falling into the wrong hands, including ones that might retrieve it from the trash. Such an affiliation could make him a target.

"How quickly she grows," beamed Diana when they had time together on the weekend. "She knows so much already, and takes in everything around her."

"Yes, she admires just as much as she is admired."

"Give her a rose to examine, or put a crayon in her hand and look at what she comes up with!"

J.P. placed his arm around Diana as they watched Miranda's happy scribbling, which juxtaposed the colors in intriguing ways. She looked up at them with a knowing, mischievous grin.

• • •

On Wednesday Diana seemed tense at first and dismissed any attempts he made to discover the cause. A little later, however, they managed to relax over a glass of cabernet sauvignon from Chateau Ksara, in the Beqaa Valley.

"When you get to Baalbek, note the many reliefs of wine and vineyards in the Temple of Bacchus. Wine has been enjoyed here for a long time."

"Always the supplier of intelligent information," said Diana, with an edgy tone to her voice that had not yet completely disappeared, causing him to wonder about her juxtaposition of those last two words. After another few swallows she added more wistfully, "'All that is solid melts into air.'"

She could inexplicably quote Marx at the strangest of times, thought J.P. But was she describing the momentary relationships between the peoples and classes of the world, or their own situation? And was she aware that Marx's translator for his part was quoting as well in his paraphrase of the esteemed English playwright?

"Is it all a vision, formed of clouds, which will disappear in the next wind?" he asked.

"You tell me. Perhaps our dreams are what we really are. Maybe we can face it soberly when I get back." She looked around uncertainly.

"Do you want to go?" he asked.

"I don't know. But I told them I would."

She looked across to him fondly, with a gaze that he would long recall. Later that night they made love with a heat that mixed all the feelings that were harbored within them: desire, closeness, difference, antagonism, but above all, love. It was one of those most precious occasions in their togetherness, when, for a brief moment, they were outside of time.

The next day Jamila and Nadia arrived before he left for work. As he stood at the door, Miranda came toddling toward him excitedly for a hug. He set his briefcase down next to Diana's suitcase and swooped his daughter up into his arms, giving her a whirl before kissing her repeatedly and loudly on both cheeks. He reminded himself that she would still be there in the evening when he returned: she was not the one from whom he was undergoing a separation of several days.

When it came her turn, Diana put her arms around his neck and kissed him, whispering "I love you" into his ear. It was not something she said often, but for that reason he believed it all the more, knowing that it was not a cliché with her. He waved to all as he went out the door. Miranda, clutching her mother's leg, waved back.

"*C'est la guerre*," muttered Diana inscrutably.

Later, as he sat at his desk, he pondered their situation and resolved to face indeed the conditions of their life more soberly and move more resolutely to make their union official. He absently reached into his coat pocket, only to discover a card that he could not recall being there; when he pulled it out he realized with a shock that it was his identifier from the previous week's meeting, which he had forgotten to dispose of. The jacket had been hanging in the wardrobe all these days, and he wondered whether Diana had run across the name tag, and whether it had been the cause of her tenseness the previous evening. But if so, why hadn't she confronted him? If she thought that he had indeed been keeping things from her, did she perhaps want to keep her own counsel? Who in fact was he working for? And who were those people she was traveling with? He wished he had delayed his departure for work in order to meet them, or, preferably, called in sick so that he might accompany and guide them.

That evening, when he asked Jamila about them, she was able to supply little information besides "*des allemands*," some Germans. She had seen a man and a woman only briefly before they all descended the stairs. When she and Nadia went home for the evening, J.P. and his daughter had supper on the balcony from the large bowl of tabbouleh that Jamila had left for them.

He was distracted at work the next day and looked forward to Saturday, when he could spend all day with Miranda, and Sunday, when Diana would return. On the afternoon of her expected arrival they leaned over the rail of the balcony, searching the street for the sight of her popping out of a car. But the afternoon dragged into evening with no sign of her, and he spent a restless night with very little sleep.

The next morning he had to take the car out early to drive to Jamila's and ask her if she could work that day, since it was one of her usual days off. They were fortunate that she could, and when he got them settled back at his apartment, he hurried to work to see whether a telephone message had been left there. None had, and he cursed the fact that they had no telephone at home because of the expense and interminable delays involved in installation. He searched the local paper for reports of traffic accidents or similar occurrences that might account for her continued absence, but he could find none. Much of the news space was devoted to an explosion with multiple fatalities at a bomb-making facility in the Palestinian refugee camp at Beddawi in Tripoli. He told himself that she was less than 24 hours late and had no doubt found it difficult to locate a phone herself. She still failed to show up that evening, however, and even Miranda began asking, "Where's Mama?"

On Tuesday he explained his situation to the public affairs officer and asked him for advice on what he should do.

"Germans you say?" asked the PAO. "Do you know their names?"

"I only know their first names: Sabine and Hans-Ulrich."

"What car were they traveling in? Their own, with German plates, or a rental?"

"I don't even know that. They came by when I was at work."

"Maybe we can find something through the German Embassy. Let me make a few calls and get back with you."

A short time later the officer walked into J.P.'s little office and closed the door behind him. "This is nothing final, mind you, but I'm afraid that what I've found out so far is not good. That explosion at Beddawi—the destruction was too severe to leave many clues. Most of the victims were burned beyond recognition. However, they did find a passport belonging to a certain Hans-Ulrich Fröhlich. Do you think that might have been someone your wife was with? I certainly hope not, for your sake."

A shocking chill fell over J.P. at the news. He did not know whether his boss's expression of concern was aimed more at his personal or professional situation, but he was too stunned to think about that or to take offense at the implication that Diana might be some sort of suspect.

"No, I'm sure she wasn't involved in anything like that."

"I'm not really authorized to say this, but given your possible close personal connection, I should tell you that our contacts in Mossad have for some time suspected cooperation between German RAF terrorists and the PLO at Beddawi, using the camp for training and other operations. Did your wife contact or correspond with Germans often?"

J.P. wished that the PAO's designation for his relationship to Diana was indeed the legally accurate one, but even though the term had not been officially stamped on paper, he considered it correct in reality. Rather than a cause for alienation, the terrible news, which he refused to accept, made him long all the more to embrace her closely.

"She hasn't met with anyone as far as I know since we came here. She does correspond, but not all that frequently, and I'm not sure with whom."

"I'm sorry. Maybe she'll still turn up."

J.P. stopped him as he was about to leave the office. "Two questions: this Fröhlich—was he connected with the RAF?"

"Not that we know of. The Embassy said there were no records on him. But the Bundesnachrichtendienst, the German intelligence service, is looking into it. I wouldn't be surprised if they contacted you at some point. And the other question?"

"I wondered if I might have some time off to go to Tripoli. I need to get to the bottom of this and try to locate my wife."

"Sure, take all the time you need."

That part of the PAO's response was reassuring, but the first part? RAF, PLO, BND, CIA—what was the extent of actual conspiracies, and where did the conspiracy phantasies begin?

"Don't forget to keep your ear to the ground when you're up there," added his superior.

After giving instructions to Jamila and getting her installed for an overnight stay, J.P. made the drive to Tripoli in well under two hours, despite several traffic jams and some road construction. He looked up his colleague Edgar Callahan at the USIS branch there to take him to the site.

It was more horrifying than anything he might have imagined: the wall to the street had been completely blown out, and inside dust still hovered above chaotic piles of rubble. Anything flammable had blackened to a crisp; a few workers were sifting through the remains. They wore masks to ward off the putrid odor, which made J.P. gag. At a safe distance in the street, a small crowd of curious onlookers, including dark-skinned children in shorts and sandals, strained to get a glimpse. Callahan, who could speak Arabic, asked the crew's supervisor what had been learned thus far and was told it was indeed a bomb-making facility whose stockpile had apparently gone off by accident. Seven bodies had been discovered, but only one, a Palestinian found near the doorway, was able to be identified. The others were too severely damaged: one could not even determine their sex.

"Where was Fröhlich's passport located?" asked J.P.

He learned that it had been found in a backpack in an adjoining room, and although badly burned as well, the name was still legible. His inquiries concerning further luggage, or a car, for which he had no description, were able to glean no new information. There was no question of retrieving Diana's passport: despite his repeated advice to her to always carry identification, she had left it at home before departing on this last trip.

As J.P. and Callahan left the neighborhood, he stared at some men of indeterminate age standing on a street corner, holding cigarettes whose smoke lazily wafted upward. They looked as though they had been waiting for a long time, and like him, would continue to wait a further uncertain period for their home to be restored, either in the devastated neighborhood or the land from which they had fled as refugees. Life for many was a constant state of being placed on hold. The adjacent building had been destroyed only recently, but their lives had been disrupted long before. The stark scene before him reminded him that until recently, his life in this same country had been a pleasant, relatively uneventful one. Now the two planes had intersected. A phrase from news reports about various war-torn regions entered his mind: "collateral damage." But the clinical, bureaucratic quality of the term seemed to deny it any application to their current situation and served only as a cruel insult. Devastated, J.P. spent another day and night in Tripoli, hoping in vain that something would turn up. Callahan assured him that he would monitor the situation closely, and J.P. returned to Beirut to be with his little daughter.

The days went by, with no new developments. He finally wrote to Diana's parents to inform them of her disappearance. He omitted the information about the bombs and terrorist connections, merely saying that she had apparently perished in a hotel fire while traveling with some German friends. In their usual contradictory fashion, her parents, who she always said tended to view J.P. as an ominous, older man with some sort of Svengali-like hold on their daughter, now reproached him for not keeping a closer watch over her. In addition to anguished demands that he locate and return their daughter's remains to America for burial, they renewed their pressure to come take the child, but he resisted, not wanting to give up what was dearest to him.

Jamila was able to come every day to take care of Miranda and the household, and, although J.P. could afford the extra expense, he was unable to give her the raise he thought she deserved. This served as new grounds for resentment toward Anthony, with whom he no longer had any contact, getting only second-hand information in letters from his Aunt Clotilde and friend Billy. But his real bitterness resulted from the absence of Diana in his life: her fate and their relationship still hung unresolved. Unable to comprehend the turn of events, for quite some time he seemed to do little else than pace the floor and stare down at his own footsteps, without finding any answers. Occasionally, he thought, he caught a faint scent of jasmine: actual flowers, the fragrance she had bought at the market, or her very essence? Whatever it was, he held on to it with all he could.

And the situation in Lebanon began to worsen. In April, Christian Phalangist gunmen ambushed a bus, killing its Palestinian passengers and claiming that it was justified by a previous Palestinian bombing of a church in their neighborhood. The attacks increased, and the country soon found itself in the midst of a full-scale civil war. Even American diplomats and tourists were caught up in kidnappings and explosions, causing J.P. to become increasingly worried for his child's sake. When the Embassy began gradually reducing its functions and staff and recommending that dependents leave the country, he finally relented in his position toward Miranda's grandparents, feeling now that it would be safer for his daughter to grow up for a time in the American heartland.

Mike and Betty Williams flew in a couple of weeks later and put up at the new, high-rise Holiday Inn on the Corniche, not wanting to stay in any of those cheaper and more picturesque "Arab places" that J.P. had suggested. J.P. took Miranda to the hotel to meet her grandparents, where they assembled in the lobby before moving to the restaurant to talk things over. The Williamses were a plainly-dressed couple in their late fifties: Betty was small and slightly nervous and already wore her hair in a bun, and when opinions were sought, she tended to defer to her husband. She took immediate delight in her little granddaughter, and J.P. was somewhat relieved to see that Miranda quickly warmed to her as well. Mike was a large-framed sort with a thin, grey mustache; his eyes darted around the room regarding everything with suspicion: even though the decor was completely American, most of the serving staff was local. He appeared to be constantly sizing up J.P. as well.

"I never knew that things would be so modern over here," said Betty. "And so much traffic! I thought it would be all clay houses and camels."

"Don't let it fool you," said Mike. "There's a lot more to it when you scratch the surface."

The discussion went more smoothly than J.P. had anticipated, perhaps because all parties had resolved to maintain their self-restraint. He answered Betty's questions about Diana, assuring them that up to the end she had been happy, in a good situation, and a perfect mother. He conveyed his own devotion to Miranda and said that he looked forward to taking her back once he was assigned a safer post or the troubles in Lebanon settled down. It was at that moment that a loud, shrill whine trailed overhead, followed by a distant rumble.

They all ducked reflexively, and Mike said, "We'll see how likely that is."

The next day they filled out paperwork at the embassy to take care of various necessary matters, including giving the Williamses temporary guardianship of Miranda so that they would be able to get her medical treatment when needed and enroll her in daycare.

During their last night together, J.P. sat by Miranda's crib for hours, gazing at her sleeping form in the protective glow of moonlight, trying to hold back the tears from the imminent, second loss. At the airport he hugged her one last time and promised to come see her as soon as he could.

"We better get on board," said Mike. "The plane might leave without us."

In the nights that followed, J.P. would often roam the empty rooms of the little apartment; the light of the waning moon that fell through the windows provided only cold comfort. Not even words from Sappho, one of his beloved classic poets, could help:

> *The moon has set,*
> *likewise the Pleiades. Midnight*
> *is long past. Time slips by.*
> *And I lie here alone.*

V

A beautiful daughter have I
as fair in form as a golden flower:
my beloved Kleis, whom I hold dearer
than all of Lydia or the lovely land of . . .
—Sappho, poem fragment

B UT I DO TEND TO GO ON WHEN I START TALKING about those aspects of our lives that you want to hear about. And that you should hear about."

"You know I'm eager. I just wish it wouldn't take so long to find out everything."

J.P. looked up at the ceiling as he wondered if narratives were inevitably lengthy when they treated their topics adequately, or if his prolonged recitation resulted from his unwillingness to fully confront his own role in his usurpation or, more crucially, in his separation from his daughter: he hoped that what he might say would not drive her away from him again. But he also hoped that the repeated recountings, spiraling around their topic, would eventually reach the desired goal.

They were sitting in a restaurant, a bistro in a nineteenth-century house on Dauphin Street near the cathedral. The location was somewhat risky, thought J.P., since it was the type of place where Anthony might show up. But since he really didn't know Anthony all that well any more, he couldn't say for sure. He was in the mood for spending more time with his daughter over some good food, and he soon gave up casting his eyes over the murmuring diners at the other tables. He tried keeping his voice down, however, to prevent the curious from hearing any details and passing them on. The sounds in the restaurant were harshly echoed by the plastered walls, but simultaneously muffled by the heavy velvet curtains, eventually to be lost in the recesses of the lofty ceilings.

"So there was never any proof of my mother's death?" Miranda asked, staring at him pointedly and bringing up a topic she had inquired about before.

"No absolute proof, although she would never have simply deserted us, of that I am sure. A death certificate was issued after the prescribed time. I sent a copy to your grandparents, but I wish I had paid more attention to documents from the outset. It would have saved me, and all of us a lot of trouble."

"Do you think she was involved?"

J.P. glanced away, not exactly certain how he should answer, or even what he actually believed himself; he wished he could be completely sure, but it had always been somewhat difficult for him to sort out the web of sympathies, convictions, and actions. "I don't think so. She had her ideals and sense of purpose. I think that put her close to some people who went too far, and she didn't always realize what they might have been mixed up in. She was young— naive, the people who always think they know better would say. I wouldn't use that word. But she would never have taken part in anything that would have caused harm to anyone. She was most likely a victim of circumstances, and in the wrong place at the wrong time."

He carved off a piece of his filet to gain time, and Miranda took another bite of her pasta primavera.

"What kept you from taking me back?"

J.P. paused and took a sip of water as he tried to determine whether the sudden, blunt question was an incrimination or merely a further quest for information. He could not read any motive one way or the other from the piercing expression on her face. Even though she had basically stated previously that she realized the decision had not been entirely his fault, Miranda had apparently not completely settled the issue for herself and was certainly justified in launching an accusation, if that's what it was, as she contemplated the matter anew. She was beginning to home in on issues that he had perhaps only hinted at in previous conversations. When goaded to confront his half-hearted attempts over the years to gain her back, he was forced to admit that he had often made things a little too easy on himself. The difficulty of facing his feelings resulted in a reluctance to disclose what he knew along with the simultaneous urge to impart, and, consequently, to the protracted, interrupted, drawn-out revelations. In any event it had haunted him over the years as the grand failing of his life. He tried to shake off the troubled look on his own face.

"A lot during that time is now a blur. Take note: after my losses, I really didn't know which way to go, and even doubted what service I might have been providing to clients in other countries. It may sound like I'm digressing, but don't worry, I'll get to the point. To pick up where we left off: my job continued for almost another year in Beirut, which got more and more dangerous. I managed to get a furlough to return to the states during that time and corresponded with your grandfather about coming for a visit, but when I got there the house was locked up and there was no one around. I stayed a couple of days and even went to the courthouse to see what I could accomplish, but could get nowhere, since I had little proof, and the few documents I brought did little good. I had to return to Beirut, and when I was finally able to contact your grandfather by telephone, he gave some sort of excuse about a medical emergency in your grandmother's family that had called them away. I was transferred to an underdeveloped Asian country, which was even farther away and where bringing up a young child would have been rough as well. I continued my efforts, but eventually learned that they had applied for and received permanent legal custody. I was ignorant and naive: I didn't know about the official processes for acknowledging paternity, and besides, I wouldn't have known in which state to apply. We had planned to get married soon, and I thought it would all be clear after that. I was not notified in advance of your grandparents' attempts to gain custody, which they were able to achieve because my name wasn't listed on your birth certificate and because Mike had connections with the local judge. After the fact I tried to submit an affidavit acknowledging paternity along with witness statements from Beirut, and even returned to Iowa to press my case, but it did little good: the authorities there said too much time had elapsed. I did get to see you briefly, however, and for a fleeting moment that one glimpse made all the effort worth it, though it hardly compensated for the loss. You had turned five by then: I don't know whether you recall it. They didn't exactly say, 'Come kiss your father,' and I didn't want to confuse or scare you by pressing the matter."

"No," she said softly. "Unfortunately I don't remember."

"They promised to write and let me visit, but their terse correspondence became increasingly intermittent, and the few overexposed Instamatic photos hardly did you justice. I had the impression that your grandmother would have been more forthcoming, but she always deferred to her husband. It became practically a total ban: I had the feeling that they wanted to create a substitute for the only child they had lost and maintain the purity of her image by keeping me out of the picture altogether. I was some sort of threat to the ideal vision they had nurtured: an older man who lured their daughter away, who led a sort of vagabond life and was an employee of the federal government to boot. At least they didn't ruin you: I have no complaints about the way you turned out."

"No, Mamaw was sweet, and things were on the whole good. Pawpaw was stern and distant, and tried, sometimes harshly, to prevent my straying from what he thought was the right path. But I learned how to deal with him and get around his restrictions."

"Just like your mother. I'm proud of you. I can't say that I'm proud of myself, however, when I think about the life we could have had together. I told you about the time I went back and you were already gone. Too little too late, unfortunately."

She stared at him intently, curling a lock of her long hair with her index finger, as if trying to decide what to say. The soft clatter of silverware at distant tables was the only sound punctuating the silence. The pause, the things not said, were almost as painful to him as an outright accusation.

"It can't have been easy," she said finally, but he wondered if she might be concealing a resentful, suppressed anger that might eventually explode. Not knowing whether it would be better to try to get it all out in the open, or to maintain the pleasant spirit of the reunion, he decided, somewhat nervously, to continue with his tale.

"No, it wasn't. Neither the efforts to gain custody nor enduring life without you. Time dragged on, however, and I got assigned to a string of posts in various out-of-the-way places, and somehow, I regret to say, I got used to it. I managed to convince myself that a busy, single father leading a peripatetic existence would not be the best thing for you. I thought it would be better to send you far away from the problems of the violent civil war in Lebanon to a place where all is calm, where there are no real problems, only occasional, minor disturbances: but perhaps that was in itself a problem—how can one thrive, grow, be creative in a place like that? How does one learn to confront what needs to be faced when everything seems basically okay? And I reasoned it would be a mistake to quit my job and bring you back to where I was raised, exposing you to the danger of growing up the way most here do and which I tried to escape. But maybe all those explanations were just excuses."

"In other words, did you end up choosing the easy way or the difficult way? Couldn't you somehow have taken more responsibility, become engaged?" A determined wrinkle had appeared above the bridge of her nose.

J.P. looked down at his half-eaten meat, not knowing himself and not knowing either whether he was mainly disappointed in himself or proud that Miranda was so like her mother. And if she thought he should have tried harder, did that mean she admired him and would have preferred a life with him? In addition, he was not sure in which sense she meant the last word.

"I doubt that moving around the world with you would have hurt me," she continued. "As you see, I travel an awful lot now on my research trips."

J.P., discomfited, became aware of a waiter hovering over his shoulder and looked up impatiently.

"Can I get these out of your way?" beamed the server, reaching for the plates.

J.P. glared, but withheld a sarcastic remark, and the young man continued.

"Did you save room for dessert?"

"We know the spiel," said J.P. curtly, and, turning to Miranda, asked if she wanted anything.

"If they've got something light," she said.

"Go ahead then, recite your list," J.P. commanded the waiter.

Somewhat taken aback, the server nonetheless rattled off the choices, starting with a peach sorbet to accommodate Miranda, and continuing with a number of other items including a *crème brûlée* and a chocolate cake that had the word "sinful" as part of its description. "Predictable as they are, you can't make these designations up," J.P. muttered impatiently.

After Miranda had ordered the sorbet and J.P. the bread pudding which rounded out the list, she said to her father, "You shouldn't be so hard on him, he was just doing his job. I've noticed you sometimes get unnecessarily upset: it's a waste of emotional energy and too small a matter to warrant the attention you give it. I can't imagine it's good for you, not to mention other people."

"You're probably right," said J.P., duly chided by his child, before trying to get the conversation back on track.

"But since I wasn't with you during all that time, you'll have to keep filling me in about your own life during the intervening years," he said.

Miranda took a sip of water and continued. "As you know already, I spent my last two years of high school away at boarding school. Confining in many ways, but also with some freedoms I couldn't have had at home. The academics were more interesting than at my old high school, but the snootiness of some of the girls was a real turn-off. A lot of them went on to fancy colleges in the East, but it was back to the state university for me."

"I guessed as much. When it was time for college, I tried to contact your grandparents again to find out where you were studying so that I could send tuition money directly there, but as usual, no luck. I even wrote and told them I was going to withhold my checks, but I relented after a while when I realized that you would be the only one who was hurt by it."

"I managed to get scholarships as well—who knows how much of your support, which I had no idea of at the time, reached its goal? Biology interested me, especially marine biology, although, being in the middle of the country, they didn't have a proper major for that. A summer semester in the Caribbean is what really got me hooked, and that's why I went on to graduate school at Scripps. And you know the rest. Mmmm, this sorbet is good," she said, apparently deciding that a lightening of tone was appropriate. "I wonder if they make it with Chilton County peaches? Have you tried any yet? They've been at the market for a few weeks now. I bought some just the other day from the man who parks his pickup truck at the corner of the Laurendine Road."

"Of course I have—I must have eaten a bushel so far. That's one taste from my youth that I longed for all over the world. The best peaches are always the ones from closest to where you live. And this bread pudding isn't bad either. They sure put a lot of whiskey in the sauce, though—I hope it doesn't make me unfit to drive home. But anyway: I wanted to say I find your choice of career highly appropriate, given where you were born."

"Maybe so, though I didn't know the details of that either. But I like the sea: there are no boundaries there—just horizons." She looked up from her dessert before continuing. "Did boundaries stop you in your career?"

"Oh, there were boundaries of all kinds besides the geographical." He wondered if her question was rhetorical, or if she was alluding to the limits that stopped him in his pursuit of her.

"I want to hear about every place you've been. Where were you last?"

"Well, at the very end in Washington as you know. I retired after I turned 68, even though I didn't have to, but then I continued working for the agency as a consultant. I sublet the apartments of various colleagues while they were off on tours abroad, but I felt like I was just spinning my wheels. I knew I could find plenty to do on my own in retirement, but didn't really feel like I had a home to do it in. The Library of Congress provided a pretty good substitute, but I wondered, wouldn't it be better to have my own place somewhere, surrounded by my own books? Besides, there was all kinds of talk about shutting down the USIA, and last year they finally passed legislation to fold it back into the State Department. That will actually take place in the fall. So I thought it was time for me to move on as well. The century's winding down, and the agency with it: hopefully that doesn't apply to everything else in the country or the rest of us as well. I guess we all change over time though. But the question remains, what is left of what we once were?"

He took another bite of dessert before going on. "I guess I'm rambling. Anyway, as you know, right after I made the decision to return here and contacted the realtor about moving back into my house, I ran across your picture in National Geographic, beside that fish tank on the research vessel. Your professor was the one featured, but the fact that your name was also listed was a godsend: I almost fell over when I read the words 'Miranda Williams'! But the resemblance in the photograph to your mother would have been by itself enough to convince me. And it turned out really to be you, and we got in contact, and I couldn't have been happier when I found out you would actually be here too. How about you? Glad to have a father now?" He was hoping for a positive answer that would grant some sort of absolution for the shortcomings that he was still reluctant to fully face: the thought of them lingered like some beast, ever lurking in the shadows of his consciousness, kept at bay so that it wouldn't spring and force him to confront his failures as a father.

There was a pause before she answered, as if it were her turn to postpone revelations. "Yes, though I must admit, I didn't know what to think at first. I had no idea what you might be like, and getting truly acquainted takes time. At any rate I had become even more of an orphan: just before I went to graduate school Pawpaw had a heart attack and died. I suppose Mamaw didn't know what to do without him and followed not long after. Even before that though I realized I had to figure things out for myself, both how to acquire the skills I needed, but more than that, how to live. There was a big empty gap as far as parents were concerned, but I had somehow gotten used to it. I guess though, to answer your question, I'm hoping, and thinking, that gap can be filled."

"Poor thing, all alone. I should have been there to care for you." He realized that from her perspective closure had not been achieved.

"But you weren't." She stated it calmly, but the fact of the matter was laid bare before them. Her chastening of his treatment of the server was minuscule compared to the lesson she was delivering on the deficiencies of his behavior.

"No," he said sadly; the pain of old losses and guilt at his own inaction came again to the fore. The hurt also forced him to confront the fact that all along he had mainly considered the effects of Diana's and Miranda's absence from his own life, and not so much the effects of the separation on his daughter. At times he had succumbed to what he now realized was one of the most deplorable of human emotions—self-pity. But when he compared himself to Ibn Kaldun, who, on a trip to Cairo in 1380, lost his wife, five daughters, and entire library in a shipwreck off Alexandria, J.P. tried to console himself by saying that he at least had his library, but more importantly, the recovery of his daughter.

"Let's do what we can to make it up, and start again. But how about now? Have you met anyone you like?" he asked, posing a question that would simultaneously change the subject, point toward the future, and provide him with more information about her. But he also realized it was the sort of question that would have been of prime interest to his mother, and he wondered if he was subconsciously incorporating the prying, society-conscious ways of the previous generation that tried to fit people into expected roles.

"Actually, there is someone I've started seeing. He's smart, curious, and gentle, but also quite strong and with a real dedication to what he does."

"All those positive things? Really? You seem to think you know him pretty well. But can you be sure he's the prince he seems to be? Who is this mystery man?"

"His name's Frederic, and he works for the Clean Bay Fund, a non-profit that's trying to clean up local waters and help people who live near sites contaminated with industrial waste. That almost always means low-income people who don't have the resources or background to help themselves. I met him when his group was holding some panel discussions down on the island."

"Why would anyone name their son for one of the most destructive hurricanes ever to hit the city?" wondered J.P. out loud. "But, come to think of it, he must have been born before 1979, unless you're robbing the cradle—that would be a coincidence, I suppose. Who says *nomen est omen*? Instead of names speaking out from within themselves, we most likely impose meanings on them, based on our own knowledge, whims, or misconceptions. Forgive my preaching. At any rate, I'm glad your friend isn't one of the corporate polluters. Unlike your uncle, who's bound to be in cahoots with some of that crowd. You seem to like him, the way you talk about him. I hope I get to meet him sometime."

"Yes, we like being together: it's amazing how we seem to speak the same language. So different from the guys I tended to meet in college. Of course you'll get to meet him. We'll have to arrange to get together."

"Organizing though. It can't be that lucrative, or even lasting. I hope he's thinking about future prospects as well." Now he became annoyed at himself not only for continuing his mother's train of thought by assuming an eventual match from proper circles, but for adopting the 'realistic, practical' financial stances of his father and father-in-law and his desire to head off any 'mistakes' his daughter might make. He begrudgingly admitted to himself that he actually admired the community involvement and the forward-looking perspective of Miranda and her friend. He tried to modify his last remark with a feeble attempt at humor whose irony would no doubt miss its mark. "Not just an outside agitator, I hope."

"Oh, no, he grew up here, though he went off to college at Duke."

"Must be smart then, or come from a family that can afford high tuition."

"Both, though he doesn't always get along with his family. They tend to have different ways of looking at things."

"Oh, yeah? What's his last name?"

"Rapier."

J.P. immediately grabbed his spoon more tightly as he tensed up inside. "Any relation to Alphonse Rapier?"

"The mayor? That's his father."

In stark contrast to the pleasure which accompanied the surprise at discovering Miranda's name in the magazine article, this revelation was followed by a shock of a different kind: the last thing J.P. would have wanted for his daughter was involvement with one of the old families, and in particular one that had been in collusion with his brother in his own usurpation. He had succeeded in not becoming his father, though Anthony hadn't, and neither had Anthony's son. Somehow all that people around here understand, he thought, is the eternal return of the same inadequacy. He didn't reply, but merely fumed inwardly. He could sort out later whether he should try to thwart what he considered a retrograde union, an inbreeding, a future of the type he had tried so hard to escape, or whether he was selfishly trying to prevent his daughter from becoming lost to him a second time. Was he being overprotective like her grandparents? Or was he justified in his apprehension that having lost Diana, and Miranda once already, he did not want to lose her again? Afraid that she might be falling into avoidable familiar patterns, he wondered whether he was in fact the one doing so and in the process putting too little faith in her. Recently Clotilde had observed to him, "You look just like your father, the way you sit in that chair." Resenting the remark, but noticing when catching himself unawares in the mirror or walking along with an ambling lope that he hadn't yet acquired in his younger years, he was forced to note the resemblance. Is the past a progenitor, not just in the course of so-called civilization, but in our very characters? Can we escape what lingers within us of the genes of our ancestors or the influences of our society? It's hard, but it is up to us to make the changes we must, he realized.

Sensing that something was wrong, Miranda asked, "Do you know his father?"

"I know who he is."

To mollify a situation which she realized she didn't fully comprehend, Miranda added, "But as I said, Frederic keeps his distance. He's the child of a late second marriage: his father's so much older, older than you even, and they've apparently never gotten along. He doesn't talk much about it."

J.P. relaxed his grip on his spoon and replied, "He seems to have his wits about him. But we'll see." He presumed, however, that Miranda's head had been turned, that what he assumed was inexperience had allowed her to be led astray and to consider this Frederic to be more noble than could possibly be the case. Engaged in this train of thought, he ignored his own falling for Miranda's mother, or Diana for him, and did not pause to question his own belief in his duty or power to set things straight. He wondered how he might put Frederic to a test to prove his mettle, or whether he should even try something extreme, such as getting Ariel involved to manipulate e-mails in order to sow suspicion.

While he was wrapped up in his thoughts, Miranda decided to examine her father on the point of the fraternal animosity that he had never fully explained.

"I still don't completely understand why you still don't get along with Anthony," she said. "Will I ever get to meet him?"

"In due time. It's complicated. What he did though was inexcusable, and can't be overlooked. Let's just say for now he took over my place, as well as more than his share of the family fortune. He has different values, leads a life completely contrary to mine."

"But what would you do with the money? Buy more books? And somehow, I can't picture you dealing in real estate or whatever it is that he does. I know I don't need oodles of wealth. Can't you just let it go at this point? It's been years since you were last here."

"Of course I don't need the money. What I care about doesn't cost much. But it's the principle of the thing. To ignore it would be to acquiesce in it and somehow imply that it was right or normal. It's a matter of justice, and something I still have to work out." He shoved the remaining crumbs of bread pudding around the dessert plate.

Or did he in fact have a repressed lust for wealth and power, which he was unable to confront? Or a hidden sense of guilt or regret at not following the path that was expected of him, the one that his brother took? Should the choice he made be regarded as a cause for admiration and a mark of heroism, or a sign of weakness at not being able to act in the realm of so-called reality? After all, every man and woman has to succeed in order to survive, and one's business has to thrive in order to provide for others as well as oneself. But when is the proper limit of success reached, and when does necessary striving begin to surpass its proper domain? One can always use an extra $100 a month to keep from cutting the budget so uncomfortably close—no, make that $200 to afford a little extra well-deserved pleasure—no, make that $2000 to afford a vacation home, which is not too much to ask. Anthony had not let it stop, whereas J.P. had never let it begin in the first place. Or was he merely acting from spite, and all of this was just a bunch of defensive rationalizations?

"But maybe your brother's actions," continued Miranda, "instead of having an evil effect on us, in fact worked unknowingly to our good. Maybe we're actually better off."

J.P. didn't know whether to get angry or to admire what he might be forced to admit was insightful on his daughter's part.

As they walked back to the car Miranda said suddenly, "Oh! I've got something for you." She pulled a cardboard tube out of her backpack and, unrolling the paper contained within, displayed a detailed ink drawing tinted with watercolor of a coral reef and its many interrelated inhabitants: the weaving, intersecting lines amidst the patches of aqueous blue resembled a map of the world. He obviously did mean something to her. Like Clotilde's gift from long ago, this present was a talisman he would keep close. But what would its effect be? He was well aware that, like the creatures of the reef, we depend on one another and are all in it together. He realized, however, that he probably remained too much an individual, acting mainly for himself. Miranda was taking halting steps to fill the gap, and he knew he would have to work harder himself. He wondered how he could find the right balance in his life or the proper connection with his daughter. He would have to struggle to come up with the appropriate expression for it in his book.

ξ

*Sell a country!? Why not sell the air, the great sea, as well as the
earth? Did not the Great Spirit make them all for the use of his
children?*
— Tecumseh, from a speech to Gov. Wm. Henry Harrison

J.P. WAS SPENDING HIS MORNING as he usually did, exploring the
endless realm of his bookshelves and picking out texts for the
day's consideration. He ran across a volume he had purchased in his
student days and thumbed through it fondly, even as he noticed the
brittleness which the pages had since acquired, along with a
mustard-brown color that gradually darkened toward umber at the
edges. He then withdrew a book of his father's that could just as well
have been his own, and in fact was his now, and he perceived a
feeling similar to that which he had just experienced with the one
from his own college years. As he leafed through its pages, a set of
folded, yellowing papers fell out and landed at his feet. He strained
to lean over and pick them up and was reminded that his joints were
becoming increasingly arthritic. Examining the papers more closely,
he saw that they consisted of a deed to a property deep in the river
delta at the head of the bay, along with a hand-drawn map and
detailed instructions on how to reach it. Dated long before the war,
the document purported to assign ownership to his father. He knew
that his father often went out on weekends, either alone or with
hunting and fishing buddies, but he had assumed that they always
went to their club's camp farther upriver. He had not been aware of
this particular spot before and decided to investigate and learn what
sort of domain it might encompass. It was strange that this property,
if in fact it was one, had not been mentioned in the will.

A few days later, during one of his meetings with Ariel, he brought
up the subject of a boat, which he remembered that his old friend
Billy, Ariel's father, had once owned.

"When I was abroad he used to write me in his letters about taking
his skiff out for fishing and how much he enjoyed the thrill of
catching a speckled trout or largemouth bass, or even just partaking

of the solitude on those days when he failed to get lucky. I don't suppose you know what happened to that boat?"

"Yeah, he bought it back around 1960, and he took me out in it sometimes. I still own it, though I've never used it. It's stored in a shed belonging to a friend of Dad's who lives over near the hospitals. His property abuts Three Mile Creek, so Dad would just roll it down to the water and put in. Why?"

J.P. explained his plans, and a few days later they went out to Hollis Evans's house to view the craft. Old Mr. Evans greeted Ariel warmly and commented on how long a time it had been.

"Just the other day I was fixin' to call you to see you if you still had any interest in the boat. It ain't botherin' me none though. Just sittin' there in the shed, mindin' its own business."

Built by the Stauter boat works, it was a green-and-white, semi-V-bottom vessel designed to get fishermen into shallow-draft areas. Twelve feet long, it weighed less than 300 pounds and still had its 5-horsepower motor attached. The paint on its sides was flaking and the brass screws showed the patina of age, but the boat was solidly built, its mahogany frame and oak rims still taut.

"The same company has been building these things since right after the war, and I'll bet you 90 percent of 'em are still on the water. They don't leak none, and you don't hardly need to do anything to 'em, long as you keep 'em covered when you're not usin' 'em. I wished I could take it out again, but my arthuritis has gotten so bad I cain't hardly do nothin' no more. But you're welcome to, any time you want. Water seems okay now. Sometimes though, there's hardly enough to float it."

Grateful to Ariel and Evans for their offers, J.P. returned the following weekend to give it a try. With effort, and help from Hollis, he pulled the trailer out of the shed and, backing it around, pushed it down the slope toward the shallow water. He was glad to notice that he would later be able to back his car down to the edge to pull it out again. He hopped aboard, and with a wave to Hollis, paddled out into the languid current before pulling the cord on the motor with a jerk: after numerous attempts it finally caught, emitting a cough and a puff of powder-blue smoke before settling into its low, rhythmic tack-tack-tack as it pushed boat and rider downstream. J.P. wondered how many people realized that the creek was still navigable so far up, since most of those who owned boats had much larger vessels for showing off on broader waterways. But J.P. preferred his low-tech, low-ostentation barque because it would get him closer to where he needed to go with less notice and less outlay. Even fewer would know about the place that he "owned," a cabin on an island in the midst of the wetlands and sluggish, sigmoid twistings of the Delta.

He passed under bridges where the traffic rattled the concrete sections overhead. He was surprised to notice how few drivers looked to the right or left or down into the creek to spot his boat passing underneath: most people apparently had eyes only for their own destination and simply saw what they already expected to see. If somebody did catch a glimpse of him he could have been anyone in his crushed cap, work shirt, and khaki dungarees with a cooler, backpack, and tackle box at his feet. Under St. Stephens Road, Conception Street Road, Telegraph Road, and the railroads leading down to the State Docks: civilization's superficial overlay on the nature beneath, which is too often forgotten. But the overwhelmingly visible hardly seemed superficial at this point: smokestacks, oil tanks, rusting fences, corrugated warehouses, various factories emitting smoke and odors as they produced what we all consume and claim we need in order to go on: asphalt, paper, concrete, metal products, oil. Somewhere just behind it all, J.P. knew, was Africa-town, striving to survive amidst the ongoing encroachments whose masters would just as soon see it forgotten altogether. He continued on through those fetid industrial waters above Magazine Point, where larger craft were tied up at pile-driving operations and loading areas. Or was it called Gasoline Point? He couldn't remember which was the proper name, since he tended to have a way of mixing fiction and reality. But aren't those interrelated anyway? At one bridge an old Black man had leaned against the rail, watching with an enig-matic smile that indicated that he could see not just through him, but the irony of the entire world as well. J.P. proceeded out into the river proper with an eye out for steamers from the port of Chickasaw or strings of barges heading down the Tenn-Tom from points far inland; he then headed upstream past the mouth of the Chickasabogue. Here, away from the activities of the port, he thought that aside from some little houseboats floating on oil drums and moored to the shore, or a few rickety staircases of weathered wood ascending the bluff in switchbacks to older dwellings, which perhaps had been grandfathered in before ownership became more restricted, the landscape must look much as it had to William Bartram, who made a trip up this same river in 1778, closely observing the native flora as well as the remains of what he called "ancient plantations." But how ancient could plantations have been in the eighteenth century? Or was Bartram referring to fields tilled long before the European colonists arrived?

At the tip of Blakeley Island J.P. turned abruptly south again, into the Spanish River. Hushed and lonely now, with only occasional fishermen to interrupt the scenery, silent themselves in order to stalk their prey at the end of a cast line. Out into Grand Bay and across it at a faster pace, startling up a heron at shore's edge, its gangly limbs graceful in flight, expending the precise amount of energy needed to glide it to a safe spot a few yards farther along the bank. On the limbs of fallen trees near the shore anhingas held out their wings to dry, and atop a taller skeleton of a tree he spotted an osprey's nest. He turned off the motor to enjoy the quiet of the expanse of lotus before him and the patient feeding of a pair of snowy egrets on the other side. The silence of the still waterscape was suddenly broken, however, by a loud, motorized whine as two kids on Jet Skis came hurtling up from the lower part of the river and out across the bay at full throttle. Cursing the invasion under his breath, J.P. wondered why some had to seek thrills through substitute mechanical means and feel compelled to make their presence known by disturbing others. It was a rude reminder that the remote paradise was becoming less and less unspoiled; the floating pieces of styrofoam and crushed beer cans contributed in their silent way to this realization as well. He recalled one of the few times when one of his father's fishing buddies had taken them, along with their tackle and Vienna sausages, out onto Polecat Bay in the days before it had become so silted in. With his hand on the tiller of the outboard motor, the friend had given the throttle a twist that kicked up the prow of the boat and knocked them all slightly but suddenly backward. "Damn the mosquitos, full speed ahead," he said, chortling at the effect of his acceleration and the attempt at a joke which he had no doubt repeated hundreds of times before. What satisfaction he must have derived from the shred of power he held, thought J.P. sarcastically.

He entered the sluggish, saddle-brown waters of the Raft River and kept a close watch for the next turn-off on his little map, which would eventually lead to the hidden entrance of the rivulet that would take him back along its serpentine course to his castle, if it should still be standing. He passed an occasional fish camp with a little dock extending out into the water, but most of the shoreline was deserted. Chuckfee, Chocolatta, Nenemoosha, Akka: he was enmeshed in a thicket of names, lost in a maze of meanders, where the streams refused to take the shortest route between two points but doubled back and twisted in on themselves, the curlicues of their oxbows forming a boustrophedon that he continually strove to decipher. How many of the thousands that traveled the causeway on their daily commute were aware of this natural wealth within sight to their north, and even though the rivers they crossed were named by signs, how many would be able to recite them in sequence— Blakeley, Appalachee, Tensaw, Spanish—before they reached the Bankhead Tunnel? Cattails were being crowded out by dense thickets of invasive phragmites and cogon grass; on wet hammocks stood stands of fragrant swamp lilies, exploding in an array of pristine white petals and blazing yellow stamens to provide a pageant of beauty for no one, or for him alone. The annual spring flooding deposited rich sediments, providing fertile ground for them to thrive. Oaks near the water's edge had trunks slender for their age and branches contorted in all directions in response to spells of harsh weather and gusting winds. Mixed through the forest were sweet gum, sycamore, red oak, post oak, water oak, tupelo, yaupon, and cypress, though the largest specimens of the last had been logged out long ago. He searched for and sometimes glimpsed kingfishers, egrets, coots, and red-tailed hawks: the return of birds since the banning of DDT in the 1970s was at least one positive achievement in the march of history. For species that he spotted but couldn't identify he would later consult the guides to local flora and fauna which he had grabbed from his shelves and packed for this trip. He turned off into a smaller tributary and headed along it a while, keeping his eyes peeled for the entrance to his domain through the ubiquitous canebrakes; he wondered if wind and water or fallen timber had altered its configurations in the time since the map had been drawn, or even if the tiny watercourse had disappeared altogether. At last he discerned what must be the route, hiding behind some piled-up brush, around which he had to navigate.

When he reached a place where the water became too shallow to proceed by boat, he pulled on the rubber hip boots he had brought, flipped up the motor, and began tugging the little craft by the painter. He had to duck to avoid the overhanging branches and, now that he no longer enjoyed the forward motion to produce a current of air, was forced repeatedly to slap at flies and wave away the gnats that hove up in swarms. He sloshed loudly on purpose to scare off moccasins and perhaps even one of those black bears that occasionally roam the Delta. At last he arrived at a tying-up spot, where he bound the rope to a root and pushed the boat in behind some reeds to make it less visible, assuming anyone could even see up this hidden creek whose mouth was so obscure. He could hear no sound of motors nor make out any other signs of human presence: hunters might on occasion follow their dogs in pursuit of game, but the watercourse at this point was too narrow for fishermen. More likely to be encountered were woodmen employed by the timber barons, who were harvesting their clear-cuts by helicopter now, he had heard. The devious, too, might wend their way even to these distant recesses; J.P. knew rationally that most of the criminal element rarely had the energy to hold an honest job, much less endure the discomforts of such a strenuous trip, but he considered himself experienced enough to know that the lowest in the human capacity always remains a possibility, as do the deeds of the desperate.

He headed into the forest of willow, wax myrtle, pine, titi, and live oak draped with Spanish moss, and he rattled brittle leaves in the thickets of saw palmetto as he pushed them aside to clear a path in what he figured must be the right direction. The longleaf pine and loblolly shed needles which provided pinestraw carpets, soft underfoot, covering the shaded, canopied floor. Awkwardly holding his cooler in front of him with two hands, he clambered up a little rise, meticulously documented by parallel hachures on his map. The contour lines seemed to denote increments of one foot, rather than the ten-, fifty-, or hundred-foot demarcations more typically found on topographical maps. If this chart had adhered to those standard intervals, no differences in elevation would have been recorded at all. He wished he could transfer landscape to paper this way and had no idea that his father had been able to do it so skillfully, if his father was in fact the cartographer. The site was chosen no doubt to protect the cabin from high water, but more likely from prying eyes: most lodges were built close to the creeks and rivers for easy access. After a few turns through the woods and scratches from scarious shrubs he spotted it: it was still standing, and the roof, though thick with moss, appeared intact. The weathered cypress boards and shingles had preserved the little structure from rot and taken on a grey that made it almost invisible in its surroundings. Despite its location at a distance from the water, it stood on short pilings to protect it from those occasional floods that occurred even here. Approaching in nervous anticipation, J.P. exhaled a sigh of relief when it appeared relatively unscathed by man, beast, or act of God. Above the entrance someone had affixed the state's coat of arms, now long faded: it was surmounted by the image of the ship that had brought the first permanent colonists, and just beneath it the five flags that Europeans and their descendants had flown over the land they claimed. Defiantly displayed across the bottom was the state's motto, "*Audemus jura nostra defendere.*" How inclusive was the first-person plural of the verb "we dare defend" and its object "our rights"? Were the originators of the phrase referring to whites only? If so, the notion had since been superseded *de jure*, though not by any means *de facto.*

The door was closed but unlocked; he opened it as loudly as he could to scare away any vermin that might have been lurking. In the dim light he perceived a lone table in the middle with two wooden chairs whose uneven legs had been gnawed by termites; in the corner stood a single metal cot. There were some cupboards on the wall, along with lots of dust and spider webs and a pervasive musty odor. On the shelves were a few tin cups, eating and cooking utensils, old hunting magazines, and various other odds and ends. He stepped back outside, not wishing to remain any longer in the oppressive, stuffy air, which he hoped to freshen up by opening the shutters on the cabin's one window. Near the door he noticed piles of fresh-water mussel shells, and not far away a ring of rocks surrounding charred sticks and ashes sodden by recent rains. His suspicion that someone had been there not long ago suddenly intensified. After opening the shutter in the back he returned to the inside to pry open the window. In the increased light, he noticed that a tousled blanket covered the bed. Looking more closely, he saw that it was made of a synthetic material and decorated with images of Superman: he realized that it was not something his father had left behind.

A noise different from the rustling of wind—a crack that interrupted the rhythms of nature—made J.P. perk up and move cautiously toward the door. The approach of man or beast? Seeing nothing at first, he soon spied a small, swarthy figure with a limp emerging from behind the curtain of leaves. He immediately found the stranger grotesque and repugnant, but later wondered whether his perspective was colored by his surprise, apprehension, and wish to be alone. And, though reluctant to admit it, by the tendency of his race to immediately regard those of darker skin as threatening. He looked around for something to use as a weapon—he had not brought a gun, for he did not have one to bring. Observing that the other was making for the door, and realizing that he too was unarmed, J.P. stepped out to make himself visible and crossed his arms before him.

"Who are you?" he asked as forcefully as he could, hoping that bravado might save him in this unavoidable encounter.

Startled, this person, who was fearsome in both senses of the term, reared back and dropped what he was carrying. Snarling, and with his fingers tightly clutched in on his palms, he began flailing frantically in J.P.'s direction. J.P. remained where he was, and, noting the other's uncertainty and possible regard of him as the alpha-male, he stated more confidently, "I asked you a question."

When no answer came, he repeated, "Who are you?"

This time he was greeted by a muffled set of syllables he could hardly understand, as though the fellow had some sort of speech impediment.

"Canub, you said? What kind of a name is that? Are you some sort of cannibal?"

Receiving an answer in the negative, he asked, "What then?"

This time the reply sounded more like "Caleb," which was the name he adopted and continued to use. The newcomer, if that's what he was, had calmed down somewhat in the course of the conversation, if one could call it that, and J.P. offered him a water bottle from his backpack.

"What are you doing here, Caleb? Not stealing, I hope?"

Shifting eyes searched the ground between them, and J.P. pointed to what Caleb had dropped: a stick to which was tied a clutch of limp, feathered bodies.

"Poaching, I see. Well, that amounts to about the same thing. Do you know what the penalty for that is? I bet you don't even have a hunting license. Do you think you own this place?" he concluded harshly, his customary impatience coming to the fore.

Caleb nodded furiously, causing J.P. to raise his arm, as if to strike a blow. Caleb shrank back with a cry, perhaps because, having internalized the prevailing views, he resorted to an habitual submissiveness.

"Am I conducting a monologue? This fellow's uttered hardly a word the whole time."

They contemplated each other in silence, and J.P. realized that he had no idea how often Caleb came there and that he could exert little control over what might happen in his absence. He also had no idea how the stranger might have arrived, since he had not seen a boat. He decided to try to figure out how he might best turn the situation to his advantage.

"Look, this property belongs to me," he said, withdrawing a photocopy of the deed from his backpack, which he had brought along in order to counter any claims that might be raised to the contrary, even though he was himself skeptical of its actual validity.

Caleb stared at the paper with intense distrust, and J.P. wondered whether or not he could read.

"How l-l-long you own it?" he stammered, with his first intelligible words.

"Since 1932," said J.P., checking the document.

"Thirty-two. Ha!" came the bitter reply. "And how'd you get it? Who own it before dat?"

"It doesn't say. It doesn't matter."

"Does too matter. I'll show you. You been t' B-b-bottle Creek?"

"Bottle Creek? What's that?"

"See, you don't know shit. You only b'lieve what you read on paper. My people here first. At Bottle Creek you can see wit' ya eyes what my ancestors built—a whole lot b-b-bigger, a hell of a lot more awesome dan dis lousy cabin."

"Your ancestors? Are you some sort of Creek Indian? I thought you were Black."

"Choctaw. But yeah, Bl-Bl-Black too. I has the blood of lotsa people in my veins. Some o' yours too, I bet. My mama—sometimes the light make her eyes look almost blue. I 'speck you got more in you than you think, if you'd admit it." He paused, and then continued deliberately, "I got just as many great-grandfathers as you; you can't say your line goes back farther."

Is he implying we could all be Melungeons, wondered J.P. before replying, "Well, I didn't know who you were."

"Course not. You wouldn't know me from Adam."

Possession is nine-tenths of the law, thought J.P., feeling that once again he was being usurped from what was rightfully his. He was forced to realize, however, that no one from his family had been there in decades, nor had they, to his knowledge, paid taxes during that time, if there were any to be paid. Still, the document provided some sort of simulacrum of legal claim. He was also forced to recall, however, that Bartram had documented those prior inhabitants, both the ones long gone, and the ones still there when he passed through. Like Bienville before him, he had climbed the fifty-foot mounds they had constructed and left behind on the hidden islands of the Delta, though he hadn't recorded their name.

"Listen, Caleb, I'll tell you what I'll do. You can keep your damn birds, hunt all you want, fish for all the clams you can eat. Just recognize that it's my property and don't bother it, and I'll keep the

game warden and the sheriff away. I'll even give you a little money if
you promise to see that no one bothers it, and if you'll gather me up
some firewood."

A faint shadow of relief seemed to pass across Caleb's otherwise
inscrutable face before he picked up his birds with a wary glance.

"How often do you come here, and how do you get here?"

Caleb waited a long time before answering, "Time to time, 'pend
on the weather. An' other things. Like how much grief dey gimme
back in town. Mostly I stays with my mother."

"And your father?"

"He done died."

Having noticed a bulky canvas tent rolled up in a corner of the
cabin, J.P. retrieved it and spread it out on the ground. It appeared
to be in good order; he informed Caleb that his father must have left
it there and that he could use it if he set it up out of sight in the
woods. He tossed out the Superman blanket as well.

"Just remember, the cabin's mine."

Although initially facing the prospect with a bit of trepidation, J.P.
had looked forward to "camping out" in the solitude of the wilderness. If he had roughed it in his Africa days, he could here as well, he
thought, though he could not avoid the realization that in both places
he played more the role of colonizer than discoverer.

"I'm going to get the rest of my stuff out of my boat. I'll be right
back."

As he walked away, Caleb, who had his own life, his own perceptions, and his own way of doing things before the arrival of this
intruder, simply stared at him, lost in thought. J.P. stepped over a
trail of ants scurrying across his path, busier than he could ever be.
With Ariel's help he had bought a compact, lightweight sleeping bag
and other outdoor equipment. And fortunately he had brought lots
of insect repellent, since the rips in the screens and gaps around
window and door would allow multitudes of mosquitos to enter and
disturb his rest. It took a couple of trips to carry these and his cooler
and water jug back to the cabin. By then the day was on the wane:
time for a drink, he thought. The cooler was filled mostly with ice,
which might last a day at most under the current temperatures, but
he had not planned to stay any longer than a couple of days at most.

But if he did, he could drink his liquor warm, and that would be all right too. He had forgotten to bring a glass, but rinsed out one of the tin cups, into which he placed a handful of ice cubes and poured the gin and tonic and squeezed a slice of the lime which he had not forgotten.

He carried his beverage down to a section of tree trunk lying supine at the water's edge, where he could look out at the swamp lilies in the amber light of the setting sun. A soft "plop" drew his attention out to a log he hadn't noticed at first, where turtles had been warming themselves. The endangered red-bellied turtle he had read about, or some other species? He would have to do some more checking. He should also look around for more of the many other plants and animals observed by Bartram or recorded in his own nature guides: white pelicans, otters, tricolored herons, needle palm, white ibis, toothache tree, the fragrant star anise, Indian pipes, Bachman's sparrow—in all more species than in any comparable area in North America, perhaps a greater number than even the books in his library. He imagined taking his little boat sometime to the northeastern side of the Delta to wander among the extensive pitcher plant bogs.

He returned his attention to the prospect before him and scanned the water's surface for alligators, but knew they would be difficult to distinguish from floating logs as they moved at a barely perceptible pace. His beverage did not bring on relaxation by itself, but served as a tangible sign that relaxation was occurring as a matter of choice. It was enjoyable, and J.P. knew how to appreciate that enjoyment as he downed the soothing coolness, which also brought a pleasing warmth. "To the anopheles," he said, raising his drink in defiance, as if he needed another pretext to justify the quinine tonic that he hoped would actually have an effect against an improbable bout of malaria or whatever might be more likely to ail him. The metallic taste of the cup reminded him faintly of blood, but he dismissed the thought to concentrate instead on the palpable chill it imparted. Now that he was here, he could begin—but begin what? It seemed always to be the same. Was this a fertile ground, an Eden ripe for new beginnings, a calm center in the raging storm of the world where he might engage in further pursuits? It would be insane or impossible,

however, to bring his library out here. But would he need it? One of
Bartram's friends claimed that the naturalist had his library in his
head. Or was this place an escape, a frantic, tangential flight from
what he should be resisting and changing back in town? Such choices
had formed the basis of many disagreements with Diana, or even
within himself at the height of segregation. He knew: but what good
was knowledge alone?

Gazing with unfocused eyes up into the treetops, he recalled his
visit to the Pfaueninsel, the "Peacock Island," just outside Berlin,
where Prussian royalty retreated from the bustle of the city and the
intrigues of the court to the funny little wooden castle they had built
there: was that place a quaint counter to the enormous palace at the
urban center of their empire, or was it a mirror image, revealing the
emptiness of the latter and the vanity of the pursuit of power and
wealth? Somehow, he could not believe they had that much insight.
In their island retreat they had constructed a room called "das
Otaheitische Kabinett," its walls covered with exotic scenes of palms
and parrots to express their longing for warmer, paradisiac climes.
Even the ceiling was painted to give the impression of sitting in a
South Sea Island hut, and, in addition to actual windows revealing
the northern German vegetation outside, there were painted murals
of windows with tropical views. What was real, and what was
imaginary? In which direction was he looking from his place in the
Delta?

Ruminating, he walked impatiently back to the cabin to pour
himself another drink. The smell of wood smoke greeted him, along
with the sound of a fire crackling in the pit, which was thankfully far
enough removed from the cabin not to infect the interior with its
heat. But its usefulness provided the means to roast the birds
skewered on a spit above it. Was this an expression of gratitude on
Caleb's part for his largesse in not calling the cops and for the use of
the tent, or was it merely a quid pro quo? Who was giving what to
whom? In any case the place now had more of a homey feel. Clearly
this fellow was better versed in the ways of the wild, more in tune
with the land than he was. But was he an innocent or a ferocious
savage? Or neither? A blank slate to be filled with his inscriptions?

J.P. was just about to go in and get some more ice when Caleb silently appeared in the clearing.

"You gimme a ax, I kin bust up some o' this wood for kindlin'."

J.P. paused to consider whether that would be safe: he had spotted an ax and some other tools in the far corner of the room. At length he decided it would be best to display trust, and he could certainly retrieve the ax before he went to bed. He fetched the tool from its corner, where he also spotted a machete. Maybe it would be better to take that one back to town, he thought. Would Caleb feel that J.P. was usurping his position and resent it, as he did Anthony's deed?

Back outside, he saw Caleb examining the birds.

"They almost ready," he said, reaching for the ax and hobbling off to chop up some of the larger pieces of wood he had gathered. Not knowing what else to do, J.P. collected some plates and utensils, along with a couple of water bottles, thinking that if Caleb was an Indian, it would be best not to offer him any gin. Or was he merely employing a stereotype? In the cabinet he discovered some more aging magazines: brittle skin mags with pictures of naked white women, from which the covers had been torn and through which he thumbed with a certain amount of interest, thinking at the same time that Caleb must be some sort of sex-crazed degenerate who made it a priority to bring such things out to this remote location. He would have to make sure to be careful if he ever brought Miranda out here. He was startled by a shadow at the door, which had caught him examining the photographs.

"J-j-just like your old man. Look like he left all kinds o' things here."

"Who knows?" said J.P., wondering who was sizing up whom and how far Caleb's awareness extended. And who was the real thief?

Supper they shared beside the fire, amiably enough at first, though J.P. could not long refrain from his usual didacticism, proceeding from observations about the history and biology of the place to ethical observations on how others might best behave. He seemed to regard Caleb as a naive child, in need of educating. Caleb said little, which frustrated J.P., who was forced to realize that in saying less he was perhaps saying more. And at times he sat rapt, as if listening, not to J.P., but to sounds that only he could hear, the green melodies of the natural world. From the other's occasional piercing glances, J.P., discomfited, had the feeling he could see right through him.

Just as J.P. was standing up to end the meal, Caleb mumbled in a low voice, "Sittin' out here, I feel so all alone."

"What was that?" asked J.P.

"Sittin' out here, I feel so all alone," Caleb repeated.

"Somehow though, it ought to feel like home," added J.P., supplying some final measures, unknowingly cooperating to complete the last of the twelve bars of the sad refrain. He could not tell in the light of the dying flames whether Caleb's face registered bewilderment, understanding, or longing; he couldn't get a fix on what he was really like. Or if, in prompting his last phrasing, Caleb had somehow brought him closer to his world.

After sharing in the clean-up, they made their way to their separate lodgings. As he lay in his bunk, sweltering in the air that lacked any cross ventilation because he had bolted the door as a precaution, J.P. struggled to get to sleep. He had come out here in an attempt to find solitude, but had instead been confronted with a person whose presence he resented and found unfair. Now he had to deal not only with the intrusion of another, but specifically of an *other* and face up to his own relationship to a significant portion of the populace with whom he usually had at most only superficial contact. In his accustomed distance he tended to pride himself on his self-perceived enlightened attitude, unlike the majority of his class whose stances ran the gamut from persecution to dismissal to paternalism. He had sought freedom, but found himself locked in behind a door that he himself had closed. He had sought a *locus amoenus*, a natural paradise, but realized the social paradise would still have to be created. The order that had been imposed didn't cut it. What he had found out here was not what he had bargained for. But is anything in life? The world consists of more than ourselves. He knew that already from his years with the USIA, but there he had entered other worlds and could keep his distance; here the other was entering what he considered his own realm. He had halfway dreamed in advance that he might receive some sort of mystic epiphany out in the solitude of the wilderness. Was this it?

He sought distraction by listening to the night sounds coming from beyond, trying to hear them as Caleb apparently did, the raucous, unceasing croaking of a thousand tree frogs, and the much deeper and more intermittent rasping from the *basso profundo* grumbles of bullfrogs farther away in the swamp. Occasionally, the laughing, whirring "hooo-hooo–hoo-ha" of a barred owl punctuated the rhythm. At one point he thought he caught a whiff of a sweet scent that had penetrated the window: was he really smelling the night-blooming *oenothera grandiflora* that Bartram had written about, or was it an imagination triggered by his reading? Before turning in he had been able to observe through a gap in the trees more stars than he had ever viewed before in the milky sweep of the *Via Galactica*, which one was scarcely able to see anymore in today's urban world of artificial lights. Everything was almost too much to contain: the beauty was overwhelming. He was gratified by the certainty at least that there's not nothingness out there at the end, but an abundance promising something better, though he did not know what that something was.

O

Know thyself
Seek wisdom
Ground your knowledge in learning
Never tire of learning
Act justly
Take joy in what you have
Accept old age
As an old man, be reasonable
Look toward what is to come
> —Some of the 147 maxims of the Oracle, inscribed on the Temple of Apollo at Delphi

A T TIMES J.P. WONDERED WHAT THE POINT of all his reading was: what was he accomplishing by simply absorbing in his lonely study what others had written? He told himself he was respecting and keeping alive the expression of certain values and ideas and thereby validating the efforts of those who had written them down in the first place. He reminded himself, however, that in his working years he had also found important the time he had spent interacting with others, informing people in different countries about the culture of his native land and bouncing his ideas off theirs in individual conversations and public panel discussions.

He was beginning to grow restless and decided he should look for a further realm for his activity in this place, in addition to his still-to-be-precisely-formulated plans for Anthony, which he gradually realized could not represent his only purpose. Maybe he should try to 'do good.' After all, in addition to her research job and her art his daughter was active in working with young people at the estuarium, and her friend was certainly contributing to the general betterment, so why couldn't he take a cue from the younger generation? And of course, Diana was, behind it all, admonishing him.

On a Monday he drove out to the western edge of town where a new state university had been established in the years following his departure. It had grown immensely in the meantime, and all of it was new to him. Near the entrance, marked by a small, brick police hut where visitors could obtain parking passes, his eye was caught by a structure of gleaming white marble, which he immediately recognized as a reproduction of the ruin of the Tholos at Delphi: three remaining Doric columns out of an original twenty on a raised circular base of darker stone, surmounted by a remnant of the entablature. In the metopes between the triglyphs of the frieze he recognized the image of a rearing centaur, and from the guttering of the cornice at the top emerged two lion-headed spouts. The purpose of the original Tholos still remained in dispute among scholars J.P. knew, and he wondered as well what those who erected this replica might have meant it to signify. Was it just a random reference on the present, cluttered cultural landscape, a trace that few if any could relate to? What is the point of an imitation? When is repetition appropriate? And why copy a ruin? Does that signify the state of our civilization? Ascending the hill toward Delphi from the east in ancient times, the pilgrim approached the Tholos before proceeding on to the Temple of Apollo, which housed the *omphalos*—the navel, or center of the world. In his high school days some of his more irreverent friends had referred to their hometown as the "armpit of the South," but realizing that no place had a monopoly on either wisdom or degeneracy, he tried as best he could to put together a meaning for himself in his current locus through a linkage to origins. Although the Greek original and this more recent structure were both incomplete, the newer version appeared as though it had been constructed only yesterday and showed no signs of wear from the tooth of time. He wondered what question he might pose to the oracle, or what offering he might bring to her. And would she give him the same response that she did in her very last bit of wisdom, which foretold her own end and which she conveyed to the Roman emperor Julian the Apostate, who wanted to revive Greek culture in the fourth century of the common era:

Tell the king the well-constructed hall has fallen to the ground.
Phoebus has a hut no more, no prophesying laurel,
no speaking spring: the water that foretold has now gone dry.

After picking up his parking pass J.P. paced around the monument a while before heading to the building where the language department was located.

He had made no appointment, but had decided to drop in spontaneously to see if the chairman (or -woman: he reminded himself that there was more than one possibility) could tell him whether there were any Latin courses he might teach. The secretary welcomed him with a big smile and offered him a cup of coffee; he took a seat in the outer office to wait. Although the building was little more than thirty years old, the cinder-block walls in the corridor and the cheap carpet of the office were already displaying serious need of repainting and repair. Things were brightened up a bit at least by posters, some picturing places where he had served. At ten minutes before the hour classes let out, and a flurry of students and instructors passed back and forth in front of him. He eyed the former, who seemed so young in their baseball caps and short shorts, and he asked himself how they could possibly know anything or even be prepared to learn. It had been decades since he had actually stood in front of a class as a teaching assistant: he wondered how he should act, and what would be most valuable to the young students in their lives. Should he supervise the memorization of *amo, amas, amat* from Wheelock or whatever text they were using these days, or assume the role of raconteur and keep them enthralled with tales from mythology and his own experiences? He himself had loved Latin already in the 9th grade. But why? Because the teacher was good, or the language and stories fascinating? How many of his classmates had been equally enraptured? It was normative back then, a standard subject taught throughout the country in that grade, but it had largely disappeared from schools since. What would be the interest of current students in taking Latin in college? Was its minimal presence here the remnant of a ruin, like the Tholos at the front of the campus? What would he be able to tell them? Was education a drawing out of inherent capabilities or a filling of empty vessels? Would his words merely fall on deaf ears? He knew he could transmit the rudiments of grammar, or relate tales of the culture, but could he bring the students to see why they should study the classics in the first place, even if they do not represent all there is to know? Can you really 'teach' anyone? Maybe all one can do is lay it out there and the interested will learn it on their own. Perhaps he should just keep it all to himself. He clasped his hands together around his knee as if to grasp an answer.

When the chairman emerged from his class, J.P. was ushered in by the secretary and introduced, and he explained his purpose in being there.

"Devaux? One of the Devaux Brothers?" was the chair's first question.

J.P. had feared that he would at some point be recognized or associated with family members who had never strayed from the city, and, hardly able to use an alias should the university wish to check his credentials, he merely said, "No, no connection. The name's not that uncommon. I just recently retired here."

The remaining conversation was pleasant, but brief. The chair found his *curriculum vitae* quite interesting, even though it contained no publications to indicate that J.P. had contributed to the store of knowledge, unlike Miranda, whose research was already beginning to add to the world's treasury. He said, however, that since the current semester was nearing its end and they taught only a minimum of courses in the three major modern languages during the summer, the earliest opportunity would be in the fall. He was not sure whether a Latin section would be available, but would keep J.P.'s information on file and let him know if something opened up. However, they had been hoping to begin offering courses in Ancient Greek, though their ability to do so depended on internal politics, funding, and enrollments. He promised to keep J.P. informed in that regard as well, and they parted in an agreeable but inconclusive fashion.

On the way out J.P. noticed a student sitting at a table in the hall selling tickets to the department's annual awards picnic along with T-shirts, which bore a black-and-white reproduction of Bruegel's

"Great Tower of Babel," emblazoned across the top with the word HETEROGLOSSIA. That's right, thought J.P.: different languages don't cause chaos so much as enrich our experience, providing more ways to say things and look at the world. And it's the laudable task of the instructors here to introduce us to them. He stopped short: or of the students, like the one at this table bearing the T-shirt with its fateful word from the ancient Greek. He was coming to realize that those classic times in which he had so long immersed himself did not consist only of the statesmen, generals, philosophers, and poets who managed to get their accounts into writing, which had been passed down and which limited the perceptions that we impose upon the era: there were also women, craftspeople, laborers, farmers, and the enslaved, many of whom were as intelligent and capable as the ones we know, but who lacked the voice to reach us, despite their contributions. There's more we need to consider and do, to make our experience truly enriched.

Another idea that had been forming in the back of his mind was to perform some sort of charitable work. Having done little of that in his life, J.P. somewhat begrudgingly tried to convince himself that he should finally contribute something to society in his retirement years instead of simply criticizing the inaction of others. He drove to the volunteer services office to see what they might have to offer and was shown to the desk of a plump, somewhat bored, middle-aged woman, who asked him about his skills before consulting her files. After some discussion they decided he might teach reading through the literacy program. Although the person in charge of orientation was on vacation, he could receive training when she returned, but could go ahead and start that very week. He should report on Thursday afternoon to the community room in the D'Iberville housing project on the north side of town to be matched up with an adult who had never learned to read. J.P. thanked the woman, thinking at the same time that it was ironic that he would be trying to build up the intellectual skills of someone who lived in dreary, mind-numbing, substandard apartments constructed by his brother.

That thought brought him to his third task, which involved a meeting with Ariel to discuss plans about how to finally set things right with Anthony. In addition to the personal wrong to himself, and by extension to Miranda, he imagined that Anthony as head of the firm kept only his own private interests in mind and had no sense of responsibility toward the community in which he found himself: J.P. had convinced himself that his brother had no soul, no awareness of history, no human empathy. Anthony in his privilege had found a comfortable situation for himself and was never forced to look beyond his own narrow state of affairs. J.P. had learned a while back from correspondence with Thomas Gonzalez that Devaux Brothers had been talked into upgrading their information technology capabilities, and the idea occurred to him that Ariel might be planted in the firm to perform this task, while at the same time surreptitiously carrying out assignments that would further his own plans. He still hadn't informed Gonzalez directly about his return and therefore had gone to the public library to send an e-mail to his old friend to request that he recommend Ariel for the position. "I'm old," Gonzalez later responded, "and have very little contact with the firm anymore and even less with computers (except to e-mail my grandchildren, and, in this case, you), but even I know where things are headed and what will make businesses successful in the future, and I realized that Devaux's efforts in that regard were minimal. I told them I had learned from someone else about a person who had the skills they needed. Hope it helps."

J.P. had worried that Ariel had little chance at the job, since he knew how much importance Anthony placed on superficial appearance: he hoped "geek" and "nerd" (words he had only recently learned himself) would constitute the extent of the terms applied to the new assistant, rather than more derogatory epithets they might come up with to refer to other aspects of Ariel's person. But the recommendation he had made through Gonzalez ended up being followed, and things seemed to be working for the present, at least.

They met in a coffee place in a strip mall on Airport Boulevard. J.P. was already waiting in a booth when Ariel came in from work, wearing jeans and a loose-fitting shirt and sporting medium-length, blond hair the color of Billy's.

"How are things going?" asked J.P.

"Pretty well. Since they don't know that much about the type of work I do, and don't always know what they should say to me anyway, they pretty much leave me alone. There are plenty of hardware and software issues though. I have to justify pretty exactly any expensive upgrades, since they watch their pennies pretty closely. And modifications to the software are always opposed: people are used to doing things a certain way and don't like changes. But their existing system has been cobbled together in such a crazy way that I spend half my time fixing bugs and breakdowns that occur in it."

"How about getting into their files? Can you access their information and remain invisible in the process?"

"They have passwords for everything, and they want me to put in password protection for all the new stuff I set up. They're pretty lazy about changing their passwords themselves, however, and seem to think I can't get into all that or wouldn't have any need to, but of course I can bypass everything, in addition to looking over their shoulder when they're logging on."

"Atta . . ." J.P. started to blurt out an encouragement, but checked himself since he was not sure how he should complete the phrase. He continued instead with, "That's the spirit. Here's what I would like first: quarterly earnings reports for the last three years, lists of all their holdings, and current contracts that they have with people. Think you could do that? We can talk next time about getting into their e-mail. The help you provide me would be well worth the student loan money you insist you still owe."

"That's pretty generous. I really want to repay you since I don't like to be beholden to anyone, but the sooner I can get free of that debt the better. I like doing what I do, however, and don't want to jeopardize my future."

J.P. felt a pang of guilt, wondering whether or not he should even be holding an I.O.U. But he was not entirely free of a reluctance to part with his money, and he definitely needed a skillful assistant to help him carry out his plans.

"How legal, how risky is all this? And do you actually want to harm them?"

"Public corporations regularly publish their financial reports and lists of what all they own. Legal records can also be accessed at the courthouse. So I doubt that there could be much objection or danger if anyone found out. Besides, if we were to turn them in, we could point to things the authorities could corroborate on their own and not say how we were tipped off." He knew he was bluffing, even as he amazed himself with his sudden business acumen. "Anthony wouldn't like it, though, so it's best we keep it under wraps. I'm certainly not going to let him know where I got the information, or even let him know that I have it. It's not harm I'm after but help. I suppose you'll have to be careful when you print it all out."

Ariel looked at him in surprise. "Don't you have a computer and a printer?"

"I've been meaning to buy one. Maybe you could help me."

"I certainly will. That way I can download the information to a disk, and you can read it on your computer or make a hard copy at home."

J.P. marveled anew at all the ways information could be transmitted: wedge-shaped impressions in sun-baked clay tablets, ink traced with quill onto parchment, lead type pressing down on paper, bits of electronic 1's and 0's loaded onto hard drives, all to be eventually interpreted and stored by synapses in the brain. He somehow had the feeling that the clay tablets were the most permanent of the repositories and would be lying around long after the last human had disappeared from the earth and the computer circuits had all oxidized. But what of the data that are recorded? How do we know what is valid? Through trial by ordeal, trial by jury, trial by empiricism? And when does information become intelligence or wisdom, he wondered yet again. When is knowledge science, and a bringer of progress? Information technology is what people were beginning to call Ariel's field: was linking the second word in the term with the first going to cause a complete transformation in the way we perceive things and even think? J.P. became somewhat uncomfortable when he wondered whether he would simply be collecting facts or manipulating them. Wouldn't the latter run counter to what he had tried so scrupulously to avoid in his years of employment?

He interrupted his reveries by hurriedly picking up his mug and downing the remaining cool, brown remnant. Having finished their coffee, he and his companion headed down the street to Circuit City to look for new equipment for J.P.

π

"In this city," Umbricius said, "there is no place
for honest enterprise, there is no profit in such work. . .
So let us leave you, native land, let those of Artorius' and Catulus'
ilk live there, let them stay who turn black into gleaming white
and thereby land the fruitful contracts for building temples,
damming streams, clearing harbors, and burning corpses,
who even offer up their very heads for public sale."
—Juvenal, *Satire* III, 21–22, 29–33

IN ADDITION TO PROVIDING UNDERCOVER information gleaned from computers, Ariel was in a perfect position to keep J.P. informed of the daily goings-on around the office, which had open areas, doors left conveniently ajar, and cubicles. And moreover, he had even installed wiretaps.

"Is this young Anthony?" said the tinny voice coming over the telephone wires.

"Yes," replied 'young Anthony' impatiently, continually annoyed when his childhood moniker resurfaced, even among relatives who had used it for years. It had been applied to distinguish him from his father. "Junior" somehow seemed too common; "Tony" had been rejected by his mother as too Italian-sounding, as had "Little Anthony," because it had already been claimed by a bygone rock-and-roll singer, although the name of that performer's band, "The Imperials," would have been a fitting designation for this branch of the Devaux family. In any case, "young" was better than "little" for a man of his self-imagined stature, thought young Anthony, as he waited for the caller to continue.

"This is Herbert Anderson, I'm a friend of your father's. He's out of town at the moment, I understand."

"Yes, that's right," the scion replied curtly, but trying not to display annoyance: if his father had not been out of town, he would have had an easier time leaving early on this Friday to get away to the family hunting lodge. As it was, he had arrived at work late, slightly aching from a hangover that he had acquired the previous night hanging out with buddies at the Mariner on Old Shell Road. He and his friends, all with similar resumés from the private boys' school and the state's flagship university, topped off with MBA's from the local institution, maintained what they perceived as their youthful bad-boy attitude by avoiding when possible an association with their elders at the bar at the country club and slumming instead with lower-class types in shady dives. Many of them seemed never to outgrow the testosterone bursts of their youth, letting themselves instead be convinced that such behavior was what determined manhood. But unlike the carpet layers' assistants and Super Lube mechanics who came in to forget financial problems arising from having to pay for an asthmatic child's treatments with no health insurance or the fear of a layoff from a downturn in the economy, young Anthony's kind could go back to their gilded domesticity at any time, and in hobnobbing with the regulars they fooled only themselves into believing that some sort of social convergence had occurred. Their talking about last weekend's football scores, or bragging about cars, or joking about pussy was viewed with a wary eye by the men who did not have to work in offices.

"I called him earlier in the week about putting in a bid on a property in Washington County but never heard back. I wonder if you could check on the status of that."

"Sure thing, Mr. Anderson. Just give me your number, and I'll holler back at you."

Anthony plopped down the receiver and sat for a while. He had come to work for his father's firm, because, as the basis of the family's wealth and the likely source of his own future income, he was expected to take that path, both by his own parents and by himself, and also because he simply could not imagine any other possibilities. Pursuing the details of investing, or developing, or "venture," as the company had now restyled itself to keep in step with the times, was harder for him to carry out. The nineteenth-century designation "Lumber Factors" had given way to "Land Company" and then to "Development": the new name, "DeVauX-XVenture," complete with a pastel logo, had been implemented by a young go-getter executive-advisor that his father had later had to let go. All Anthony had to do at the moment to fulfill this particular request was to check with his father's secretary, though he preferred for the moment thinking about the missed opportunity to be cleaning his duck-hunting guns while drinking a beer. He pulled at the khaki fabric that was squeezing his crotch, yawned, and then walked over to Ms. Hieronymus's desk.

"Iris, did my daddy do anything about a land purchase for a Mr. Anderson in Washington County?" He gave a sidelong glance to Ariel, who was kneeling beside her printer.

"Yes, he submitted a bid, and we were waiting to hear back. Just a minute: I have the folder on my desk—yes, it was put in on Tuesday."

"Thanks." Anthony wondered if asking Iris to call Mr. Anderson back would be tantamount to giving him some sort of brush-off or would increase his perceived stature by making him appear busy. He decided, however, to call the man himself in order to stroke the personal bonds that kept the firm going to the extent that it still was.

But before he could pick up the phone, a second call came from his wife Tina: "Did you realize you left a folder on the table by the front door marked 'Rodgers Account'? I didn't know whether it might be important." In his mind's eye Anthony hit his forehead with the heel of his hand, since he didn't want to make the actual sound or visibly indicate some shortcoming to anyone else who might happen by the door. This same motivation extended to his hesitation to offer to come pick up the file himself, though a trip out would also have allowed him to stop at one of the what seemed like fifty or sixty new Starbucks locations that had opened recently in town.

"Honey, would you mind dropping it off? It's something I need to get to this morning, and I'm kind of in a pinch here." He again readjusted his pants.

"I was on my way out to the Junior League meeting, which is in the other direction, but I guess I could bring it by and be a little late."

"That'd be great, Sweetie. I must have just walked right past it without seeing it."

He refrained from concluding with "I'm sorry," since he didn't want to overdo the appreciation. He felt that it was important to maintain just the right balance between attachment and distance to keep the proper connection; he assumed that women who married guys like him aimed at a certain position in society, and they usually needed their husbands to assure it for them. But they couldn't be treated like dirt either, for various reasons. Besides, he liked his wife, except when she was bugging him about the time he spent out with his buddies. "I can tell he is actually fond of Tina," Ariel told J.P. in one of their frequent conversations about the firm, "despite his bluster around the guys. As far as his thoughts on other matters go—it's amazing how much he reveals to others."

Anthony checked his calendar and then his inbox; until Tina dropped off the Rodgers folder, there was not that much to work on. Land purchasing was slowing down at the moment, though there were still killings to be made, including one especially big one that was on the front burner. The city and state were actively seeking foreign investors, and if one owned prime sites or at least the options on them one could do well when the interested parties finally came in and decided to build a factory. But guessing where those sites might be was another matter: he didn't want to tie up any company money in swampland that turned out to be under some new environmental protection, as he had done once before and for which he had been royally blessed out by his father. Maybe he should do some scouting around out in the county, but perhaps that would also just be wasted time. Maybe the company needs to be a little more imaginative and handle something besides land and stocks. Buying and selling derivatives might be the answer, but first he would have to find out exactly what those were, or at the least learn how to convince clients that he knew what they were. He pulled out the glossy report from the Chamber of Commerce to see what some of the other businesses around town were getting into. It had been easier in his grandfather's day, he assumed, when things were not so spread out and diverse or encumbered with regulations. Or was he just losing the old enterprising spirit and more concerned with his own security than with the risks needed to expand?

He jolted up suddenly when he noticed a figure standing in his doorway.

"What do you want?" he blurted out, immediately worried that his impatient severity might have revealed insecurity.

Ariel, with characteristic tranquil expression, answered, "I heard you were having some computer problems."

"Oh, yeah, that's right. You wanna have a look at it?"

After enduring some confused explanations of what the machine was doing and failing to do, Ariel took young Anthony's place at the desk and told him he was free to go elsewhere, since an IT expert could best handle it alone—machines don't respect the hierarchy of employer and employee. Anthony, glad to have an excuse to step away, wandered off to get another cup of coffee and chat with coworkers.

Ariel immediately began investigating the directory and without any trouble located the important business files, including ones that 'old' Anthony had conveyed to his son. Ariel inserted a 3.5" floppy and began copying them, putting in a second disk when the first became full. Another task involved reading through e-mail, copying and pasting ones that appeared relevant to a notepad file which was then deleted after being saved to the diskette. When the voices of Anthony and his colleague Ted were heard approaching, the young technician switched over to a diagnostics program to clean up the clogged hard drive, a sign of sloppiness on almost everyone's computer that was a constant source of irritation.

"Won't be much longer."

"No rush, wouldn't want to have to work too hard."

When Ariel finally retreated back down the hall, the lowered voices of young Anthony and Ted were still audible.

"Sometimes it gives me the creeps—always hanging around, seeming to hear everything."

"Gives me the creeps in more ways than that. I never know which pronoun to use. Why does your father keep her? or him?"

"She knows her stuff. The systems are all running better now. Come on, she's cute, you ought to ask her out," giggled Anthony.

Ted, snickering, made some remark that Ariel couldn't hear.

"It's a tough job," Ariel later told J.P., "but you promised I'd soon be free."

• • •

One afternoon shortly thereafter, over glasses of unsweetened iced tea with sprigs of mint from the garden, Ariel opened the files on J.P.'s new home computer to see what they might contain. A very recent one labeled "\Benefite.doc" proved especially interesting: it involved detailed plans for a plot of land not far from the bay near Dog River and the ship channel that the firm hoped to sell to a Belgian chemical company to produce something called Benefite, perhaps a code name. The site had the advantage of good road and waterfront connections for shipping and was near other industries that had located in the area.

"And look at this," said J.P., zooming in on the site plan. "This section marked 'Waste Dump," which is also designated with the more benign label 'Holding Pond' in parentheses. No doubt that's the term their P.R. department will put out. It directly borders the bay: quite convenient if there's a leak, which there almost always is."

"They've done more background work than I would have expected," said Ariel. "Here's a file that deals with preempting objections which might arise because of the company's pollution at some of its other plants around the world. It's probably harder for them to get away with that sort of thing in Europe, and that's why they want to come here."

"Sounds like they're true descendants of King Leopold. It also looks like preparations for P.R. are at least as extensive as the economic and environmental planning, though the latter seems to get a mention. Ammonia, hydrochloric acid, isobutyraldehyde, methyl methacrylate. Some of these names sound downright scary. I doubt they intend to publicize them in a large, boldface font. But if they do have to release them, I'm sure they'll offer the argument which has been used for decades to defend the paper-mill stench we've been cloaked in: 'Smells like money.'"

They continued scrolling through the documents, and J.P. observed, "Miranda told me: 'Read your Humboldt.'"

"What did she mean by that?"

"Alexander von Humboldt realized how everything in Nature was connected, and we along with it. He also described the harm the Europeans were causing in their New World colonies: deforestation, monocultures, excessive irrigation, slavery. He knew all that at the beginning of the nineteenth century. Why does it take the rest of us so long to catch up?"

"Probably for the same reason it takes us so long to learn to treat our immediate neighbors right. Hey, here's what I was looking for: here's another problem they'll have to deal with first. A big portion of the lot is on public parkland. How are they going to get ownership?"

A little more searching revealed steps to be undertaken to solve that problem as well. Contending that people tended to shun the West Bay for the East Bay and the beaches at the Gulf, demonstrating that new road configurations and nearby industries had decreased attendance at the park, and pointing out that the baseball diamonds there were no longer used by the Little Leagues, they apparently intended to argue that the city would be better served by devoting the land to foreign investment which would provide jobs for locals.

"But will they win their argument? They will have to convince a majority of the council members who may be reluctant to give up their constituents' parks."

"Doesn't money always provide the loudest argument?" answered J.P.

He culled the pages that Ariel had printed out for him for information which might be useful to his own interests, with which the community's were beginning to overlap: it was drier even than some of the material he had disseminated during his employment at USIA, and certainly a lot less interesting to him than Pindar and Virgil. As Ariel scrolled through the e-mails J.P. noted that the left hand was jotting down notes with a pencil while the right operated the mouse.

"I didn't know you were left-handed," he remarked.

"I'm ambidextrous."

After a while his assistant said, "I think I've found it."

"Found what?"

"How they plan to get the votes. Your brother thought he was being careful about covering his tracks, not to mention his ass, but he wasn't careful enough. In forwarding an e-mail to his son from Sebastian Rapier he forgot that prior correspondence in the chain is included at the bottom. He was apparently planning to give a kickback to Sebastian's much older half-brother Alphonse, the mayor, after the land gets sold to the Belgians, but Alphonse seemed reluctant to take part in anything like that."

"I'm not surprised. Alphonse was put in a couple of years back as a sort of respectable elder statesman to preside over the various factions in the new governmental organization. He was always somewhat wishy-washy in spite of continually looking out for his own interests; right now he would mainly want to serve out his term in a non-controversial way, even though he has quite a bit of dirt on his hands from the past. Including of course his help in deciding my fate."

"Yes, because he's so eager to get the land, Anthony proposes replacing Alphonse in the party hierarchy with Sebastian by discrediting him somehow, leaking some hint of scandal, true or not, to the newspapers. Sebastian answered that he was reluctant to harm his older brother, but Anthony told him to get off his ass: he would never get anywhere being lazy. Look: here he even reminds him that he himself got where he was by replacing his own sibling. Sebastian should take note, and they could repeat what was successful once. Nor should he feel guilty, he says: what matters is the result. I guess years of getting what they want, because they have the power to take what they want, haven't taught them anything except to want more of what they think they want."

It occurred to J.P. why Anthony was successful in the business, and why he himself never could have been: when other people revealed their impotence, Anthony grinned and moved in to take advantage. J.P., on the other hand, was disappointed when he noticed any weakness in others: he felt pity, but soon moved to distance himself from them rather than taking any action to benefit either himself or them.

"You're right," he replied to Ariel. "Old habits never seem to die. I'm sort of surprised though that he has the gall to admit it. And at the lengths to which he would go to betray associates. There must be something more in it for Anthony, however."

"Yes, in addition to insuring the chemical deal, he hopes to be less beholden to Alphonse's bank."

"I wonder how successful he will be."

"Sebastian has apparently come around to the idea of selling the park land and is tasked with getting enough additional council members on board. I suppose the negotiating period will extend past the change in government. Maybe there'll be a change that will make things more difficult for them."

"Don't fool yourself. The mayor's race is officially nonpartisan, but everybody knows which label would be attached to a particular candidate if designations were allowed. Fifty years ago the current occupants would have called themselves by the other party's name, but the underlying effect would be the same: maintaining the status quo of the already powerful. And Sebastian under Anthony's thumb would certainly be worse than Alphonse."

J.P. fanned out the papers in front of him and shook his head slowly as he surveyed them.

"Whew! What names can you put on this: kickbacks, bribery, racketeering, extortion? They're following right along in the tradition. In my lifetime, and in the last couple of decades in particular from what I've read, there's been a whole raft of congressmen, district attorneys, city commissioners, county commissioners, school board presidents, city department heads, civic auditorium managers, mayors of nearby towns—you name it—who've been convicted or gone to jail. You may have found the smoking gun, as they say. And I'll bet you can find more: they'd also have to bribe various environmental and transportation officials to expedite the necessary permits. But who knows whether their influence would keep this from going anywhere if I took it to the D.A. However, I prefer to exert my own pressure first."

"You know, though, they are involved in a lot of other things as well, maybe not criminal but just as harmful in their effects."

"What do you mean?"

"Take for example their new developments on the Eastern Shore, their subdivisions and shopping centers. All those projects involve cutting down trees, eroding the soil, and creating structures that serve as sources for run-off of automobile pollutants, lawn-care poisons, household chemicals and lots of other junk. I read not long ago that what the chemical industry contributes is only 2% of what

these non-point sources add. And most of this will flow down into
the Delta."

"The Delta!" exclaimed J.P., thinking about his Eden.

"What do you think you'll be able to do?"

"Yes, what can we do? But do we must."

J.P. had recently received a letter from an old friend in Beirut, who
had stuck out the civil war and was now complaining about the new
developments in the urban center since the end of the fighting. A
large corporation had been formed by people of power and wealth in
both the private sector and in government to rebuild large swaths of
the city in an effort not so much to restore as to provide a money-
making venue for the investors. "They're destroying our old neighborhoods," wrote his friend, "to fill them in with modernistic high-rises
designed by foreign architects, to be occupied with high-end
boutiques and expensive restaurants for wealthy Arab and alcohol-
drinking European tourists. They're gobbling up land at artificially
low prices and driving out the little people. The old café where we
used to meet for tea is long gone. The little family-owned businesses
where everyone used to shop—forget it." Capitalism knows no
bounds thought J.P.: a global collusion between the authorities and
the affluent to take advantage of the less well-off in order to expand
their empires. Do they control property or does property control
them? The same chains filling the malls here will soon have stores
there in what they are calling *souks*. He thought that his current
plans would at least hobble this dynamic in its own way locally,
though he hadn't yet pursued his idea to its conclusion and considered to what extent its single-handed destructive force might precede
a better replacement or how it might be confusing nostalgia with a
forward-looking vision. Or whether his idea of deconstruction was
preferable to his brother's building up, whatever its flaws.

His anger again stirred up, J.P. dashed off a note about the new
revelations concerning Anthony in his book, and then went back to
poring over the print-outs in order to figure out some way to put his
plan into motion.

ρ

Long I pondered this long-standing feud.
I stand here now where I struck the blow
and thus fulfilled my plan.
I don't deny it—truly.
Around him I cast a net as if for fish,
a richly fatal robe from which he could not
escape nor flee his doom.
Then twice more I smote him.
         —Clytaemnestra, in Aeschylus, *Agamem-*
non

THE SUMMER CONTINUED WITH ITS QUICK succession of quotidian and seasonal activities of various kinds, yet it was also the period of the year when time itself often seemed stationary. At this new stage of his life, when he had returned to a fixed place and had no specified task or duty, J.P. began to notice two strands of temporal progression coming to the fore, sometimes alternately, sometimes simultaneously as they wove their way through his days: our existence is actually polychronic, he thought. One strand seemed to rush past in a manner he did not remember experiencing when younger, causing Friday to come hard on the heels of Monday and lunchtime intended for one o'clock to arrive at two, seemingly minutes after the breakfast dishes had been cleared with hardly anything accomplished during the morning. This phenomenon was most evident when he sat outside reading, and the sun's advancement behind the trees was visibly apparent as it suddenly made the white of the book blindingly bright and then too dark for the eyes to quickly adjust as it cast the pages into shadow in its unstoppable progression. The months since his return already seemed like mere hours in a day. The other strand, in which one day was like another in endless succession in a life of voluntary solitude devoid of particular obligations, opened doors onto corridors of opportunities for pursuing myriad lines of thought at leisure with no threat of being closed off at the other end of the passage and in whose expansiveness he could explore and develop as he wished. In this way J.P. devoted his usual attention to his own reading, but he also doggedly pursued his plans regarding Anthony, making things up as he went along.

He also started the volunteer work to which he had committed himself. When he drove out to the D'Iberville Apartments that first Thursday afternoon he was shown to an empty room with a number of folding tables and scuffed, aluminum-legged plastic chairs. The cinder-block walls were painted in a drab, institutional green, and the vinyl baseboard molding was peeling away in a number of spots. He took a seat and, while waiting for his assigned tutee, thumbed through the reading instruction books he had been given. The room was large, and the need for literacy great, yet there would be only the two of them he realized. Despite the books, he had for the moment largely been left to his own devices to determine how to proceed. He had some idea of what to do, since he had once performed similar functions during his time abroad, graciously bestowing on foreigners the benefits of his native language.

After a while the door opened and a figure limped in. To his shock J.P. realized that it was Caleb, the strange creature he had encountered in the Delta, and Caleb too was almost simultaneously taken aback. He halted in a sort of momentary retreat to ask accusingly, "D-d-did you plan this?"

Consternation registering on his face, J.P. stammered to put together a reply. "No, no, I merely signed up. I had no idea who would be coming. I didn't recognize who it was: the first name on the form they gave me was indicated only by the initial C, and I had never learned your last name." He couldn't repress an uncomfortable feeling, however, that this appearance somehow represented a further threat, asserting claims on what he had set out to do.

They continued sizing each other up before J.P. finally said, "So you don't know how to read."

"A little," answered Caleb with downcast eyes, not wanting to admit any sort of weakness in front of this particular adversary.

"Well, there's no reason you can't," said J.P. in an attempt to be encouraging, but also from his view that because he himself could read, everyone else should be able to as well. "Let's begin with these letters," he said, not knowing how else to continue the conversation. "Tell me which ones you can name," he continued, drawing the printed symbols one at a time in random order from a stack of cards. Pleased to see that Caleb recognized all of them, he was able to proceed in the first session to the sounds of words of one syllable, which contained a short vowel and consonants at each end: *sad, cat, lack, black, cash, class, bed, bled, grasp, fact, mud, man, dust, dam, limb, hunt, fish, clam, scum, drip, slam, slash, smack, smash, tent, camp, nest, trap, path, end.*

"The letters on the page correspond to the sounds of the words that you already know and speak." And both the written and spoken words correspond to the reality they represent, he was tempted to say, but didn't know whether he could claim that: maybe a correlation between shape and sound was as far as you could go. His mind began to wander, and he wondered how he might indeed explain the relation of Ovid's poems to current or past reality. Because they stuck to the phonemes and printed words and avoided discussions of other aspects of the actual world around them, the hour for the most part went well, despite a few stumbles that resulted in a number of patience-trying repetitions. At the end they both seemed to accept that the arrangement was one that now had its place, and they agreed to meet twice a week in the future.

"I assume you live here," asked J.P. as they walked out the door. "When you're not out in the swamp poaching," he added, unable to keep himself from throwing out a little barb.

"My cousin lives here. He tol' me 'bout the lessons."

"Your cousin? Where do you live?"

Caleb eyed him suspiciously, not knowing how much he should reveal. "I mostly stay at my mama's apartment in Plateau."

J.P. perked up at this. "Apartment? It wouldn't be the DelMar apartments by any chance?"

Caleb's eyes widened in astonishment, as though he were in the presence of some sorcerer or conjure man. Could this person see the unseen, as his mama could? "How'd you kn-kn-know?"

"Just a guess," said J.P., who had merely named what he seemed to recall was another piece of Anthony's empire. "But you apparently spend a lot of time in the Delta as well."

"I breathes better out there. No po-lice lookin' over your shoulder, stoppin' you on the street to aks questions when you ain't done nothin'."

"Do you have a job?"

"Sometimes I runs errands for Mr. Jenkins."

"Have you got time for more jobs?" J.P. seemed to recall a list of ethical rules regarding tutor-learner relationships that advised keeping a certain distance, but decided that he would know well enough how to keep things on a proper footing.

"I 'spose so."

"You're not scared of heights are you? Can you climb a ladder?"

"I reckon I can."

"I might ask you to clean out my gutters sometime. They seem to be pretty full of leaves and acorns. I'd pay you of course."

"Okay."

"I'll talk to you about it next time."

They parted, each having to take time to digest what had just gone on.

• • •

On the weekend he drove down to the island for a beach day with Miranda; since it was so hot she had decided that a picnic under the oaks and pines in the wooded park in the island's mid-section would be preferable to eating under the full sun on the burning sand. They could stroll down to the Gulf afterwards to cool off: even the bath-water temperature of the sea at that time of year would provide a relief. While Miranda was laying out the food and J.P. filling glasses with ice and tea from the jug he had brought, another car pulled up near theirs and a young man hopped out.

"Frederic, glad you could make it," cried Miranda with obvious delight in her voice.

"Wouldn't have missed it."

J.P. froze and stared intently at the newcomer to size him up as best he could: he seemed robust and good-looking enough, without much hint of the decadence that J.P. halfway expected from generations of inbreeding. Frederic hardly glanced in his direction, having only admiring eyes for the old man's daughter. After sharing a brief, extended-arm hug around the waist with her friend, Miranda said, "Frederic, this is my father."

"It's a pleasure to meet you, Mr. Williams," said Frederic, holding out his hand. At the unexpected address, J.P. looked past Frederic to his daughter, who merely gave a slight shrug of her shoulders and an enigmatic smile, which might have been conspiratorial, or an expression of exasperation at having to keep up the charade. "Any relative of Miranda's is bound to be all right."

"Would that one could say that of all relations," was all that J.P. offered in reply.

"How can I help out here?"

"Lots of ways, I'm sure," said J.P.

"You could slice some of these tomatoes," said Miranda quickly, to cut off any speculation about the intent of her father's reply.

Soon they were enjoying their lunch at the picnic table, despite the heat.

"Retreating to the shade apparently means abandoning the breeze. The dunes seem to shelter us here," observed Miranda.

"Too much shelter can lead to stagnation. I've perhaps sought too much of that in my time. You look fit though, Frederic. Do you do sports?"

"I run."

"Not from anything, I hope."

"No sir, only towards the goal."

J.P. was not sure whether he was annoyed at the "sir" because it gratuitously underscored his age, or because it was unnecessarily obsequious in the presence of a girlfriend's father, or perhaps mostly because it was an expression of the acquired, obligatory gentility of the local ruling class which was not always sincere. Or maybe he was just searching for any little thing to quibble about in his daughter's new relationship. Had she fallen for the outward appearance of this "hunk," as they now seemed to call them, and was he really so handsome, or simply clever enough to know how to project that quality? He decided not to mention any of these things but instead said, "Tell me about yourself, Frederic. Miranda says you're out to right the wrongs of the world."

His daughter gave him a sharp look as if to warn him not to be too harsh. He wondered why his young offspring should be the one telling him what to do, though he had on more than one occasion come to see that she was justified.

Frederic finished chewing a bite of his sandwich before replying, "Let's just say that so much is being done to take advantage of people who don't have the means to resist, and I'm just trying to contribute any effort I can to oppose the harm that's being done."

"Sounds noble."

Miranda rolled her eyes at what might have been perceived as sarcasm in her father's comment.

"What does it involve exactly?" continued J.P., beginning to show interest.

"The main thing we are concentrating on right now involves pollution from a trucking company that operated on a site just north of the city for ten years. What they dumped there got swept under the rug, or rather topsoil, and is now seeping to the surface, endangering the health of people living in apartments that were later built over it. It's been dragging on for a long time and we're trying to bring a class-action lawsuit on behalf of the residents, few of whom have the knowledge or resources to pursue the matter. Some are pretty savvy though: there's one woman that got the whole process started, and her energy is what keeps it going. In fact I have to pick up a lawyer from the Environmental Hazards Fund this afternoon. He's flying in from Washington to lend us some expertise."

"Apartments? Which apartments? Do you know who owns them?"

"The DelMar Apartments, run by Heron Bay Realty. But our real target is the trucking company that caused the mess in the first place. Besides, Heron Bay Realty wasn't the original owner, and the value of the property has plummeted since it became a superfund site."

J.P. was surprised to learn that the place in question was where Caleb lived and wondered whether the toxic chemicals might have affected him in some way.

"Do you know who built the apartments?"

"I believe it was Devaux Brothers, but they didn't own it for long."

J.P.'s surmise had been correct, and his interest was newly piqued. "But if they knew about the problem when they were building the complex, or at least knew about it when they sold it, wouldn't that make them complicit as well?"

"Maybe."

"Listen, there's something I've been working on that might line up with this. Do you think you could dig into it a little deeper and find out what their role might have been? It would be a big favor to me."

"I guess I could. But I'll be busy with this visiting lawyer and helping to prepare the materials for the upcoming court hearing: we still have a lot of evidence to put in place about the original polluters. It may take some time until I get to it, but I'll do what I can."

J.P. was pleased that Frederic was apparently devoted enough to Miranda to be willing to carry out a task for her father; in that respect he had passed a portion of the test already. Any information he handed over would be lagniappe.

"Great. I'd appreciate it," he said, before continuing the topic in a more general way. "Another thing. What about future pollution? Have you given any thought to trying to head that off?"

"We're concentrating on our more specific task first, but we're aware of it. The manufacturers, the Chamber, many politicians cite the EPA's latest Toxics Release Inventory to say that air and water pollution has dropped significantly in the last decade. The largest polluter, for example, has cut its emissions by half. But you also have to realize that that company still makes up 20% of the state's toxic emissions, and our county still ranks 15th in the nation for harmful industrial pollution."

"Boy, you know your statistics. So we may be going forward, but not fast enough?"

"You could certainly say that."

"Well, it might be a wise idea to keep your eyes open about anything involving the Belgian chemical company that wants to put in a plant here. If you run across anything along that line, I'd also be curious."

"We're definitely on a constant lookout. People see progress and get complacent. They fail to notice new problems sneaking up, especially when they don't concern them directly."

Frederic, who wondered what the interest of Miranda's father in these chemical matters might be, but, not wanting to appear nosy, asked a question of a different sort. "Miranda tells me you were in the foreign service. I'd like to hear more about it."

"I don't know how much service I provided, but it was foreign all right."

"Whatever it was, I'm sure it's worth relating."

They finished up their lunch with fresh peaches and chocolate which Frederic had bought at a downtown candy shop; while J.P. was carrying the cooler over to deposit in the trunk of his car, he overheard Miranda say, "My father's not as bad as he might seem. Don't take his orneriness too seriously: that's just the way he is."

"I don't mind—it's not that bad."

The conversation continued out of J.P.'s earshot: "And don't get too wrapped up in his projects. I know how much time it takes to go through all those documents. You've already told me how overburdened you feel with the trial preparations."

"It might not be that much—probably wouldn't require a lot of extra digging, and it relates to what we're doing. But actual proof of fraud might be extremely difficult to find, especially at a level that's once removed. But the main thing is, if it puts me in his good graces with respect to you, I'll do almost anything."

"I'll help. What if I come over Monday night and look through the papers with you?"

"Monday night? Not just Monday evening?" he teased. "If you put it that way, it's a deal."

She was about to kiss him when J.P. returned empty-handed. "How about that swim?" he proposed.

"I'm ready," said Miranda.

"Wish I could join you, but I have to get to the airport. Y'all enjoy the water though."

Father and daughter drove to the public beach next to the little schoolhouse and carried their lawn chairs, towels, and cooler over the dunes and down to the shore. As they were setting up not far from the fishing pier, J.P. was the first to speak.

"Williams?"

"I never told him that. I just always referred to you as 'my father.' I know you don't want your presence broadcast yet, and as you see,

I'm keeping true to your wishes. But aren't you going to have to address things at some point? And even if your brother's actions were as bad as you claim, hasn't a lot of time gone by? Shouldn't things be laid to rest at some point? The direction your life took wasn't so bad, except of course for those financial losses which were not your fault. But you have to admit, for other losses you have a lot to own up to. Rejection of kin seems to run in the family. I know you want a heart-warming conclusion for the two of us, and so do I, but we still have some things to work on. But to get back to you and Anthony, obsessive revenge can't be healthy for you, and that's what I'm most concerned about."

He was stung by the chastening, which he knew he had to address in a better way, and he was prompted to recall his discussions years earlier with Miranda's mother, in which he had argued that it was important for militants not to become so blinded with hatred that they ended up becoming what they opposed. Maybe he did need to heed this lesson for himself. He noted however with some satisfaction that it was Miranda's concern for his well-being which seemed to dominate, despite her criticisms.

He exhaled deeply and continued. "It's not just the wrongs to me. It's to you too, and to others: you heard what Frederic said about the chemicals at the apartment Anthony's firm built. And what about the principle of justice itself? Almost everything they've been engaged in is like a pervasive seep of toxins that won't go away if it's not confronted."

"Of course none of that should be ignored. But what is the best way to bring it to right? And how is Frederic involved? I get the suspicion that somehow you think he is."

"His father was allied with my brother in the whole takeover. His father still has power in the community, the connections still exist, and things won't improve until it all gets exposed and overturned."

"But Frederic didn't take part in any of it. He's far-removed: as I told you before, a late offspring of his father's second wife. You can't hold anything against him. By your logic, I would have to reject you as my father because of the family you come from. You claim to have overcome it—why don't you think he can? Besides, he's actually working hard to deal with one aspect of the 'toxic seep.' What do you think of him, by the way?"

J.P. had to pause. He was still trying to sort out his initial worry that the young man might be trying to carry off his daughter into a way of life he had struggled to avoid and thus remove her from him a second time. He realized, however, that he would have to let her make up her own mind and tried, at least for the moment, to take a more optimistic view of things. "He makes a good impression in a lot of ways. He seems to be on the right side and doing good things, but somehow this community organizing seems like a temporary occupation until he finds something better to do."

"Better? Do you know what it involves? How smart and persistent you have to be to sort through and tie together what all is involved? In my work, to understand the natural environment we live in I have to know a lot about a lot of different disciplines. And for me person-ally, in order to really understand and express it, art is essential. In Frederic's case he has to know the science, local and national politics, the economy, the legal system, plus he has to have the social skills to meet with people who have been affected and to listen to them and communicate what his group is doing. How well could either of us do that? Some of it may seem like boring grunt work, but it's what it takes to get the job done. And he's actually helping to make a change. Like changes we may make at the lab with new discoveries. Some-times I think it's awfully ironic, don't you? I live on an island, but that island is part of the world. I'm connected to all the seas, and my imagination interacts with everything in my art. You're living in a city, and always have, but sometimes I think you're enclosed within the island of yourself."

"Whew! You've obviously thought it all through." Despite feeling stung by her criticism, J.P. admired the similarity he observed to her mother's strong adherence to her convictions. "You certainly defend Frederic well, and I detect a strong affinity in addition. He also seems to like you, which would be essential for me to like him, but you can never be sure about a young man's intentions. I'll try to keep an open mind, but promise me you won't rush into anything."

"I'm hardly rushing. And besides, we'll soon be separated for a month when I go on that research voyage through the Gulf and the Caribbean I told you about. Our ship leaves in less than two weeks."

"That means I'll be separated from you too. What will I do with myself, and how will we keep in touch?"

"I'll have to check and see what the telephone and e-mail situation will be. We should have it from time to time, at least when we pull into port. And you can visit Aunt Clotilde: time with her is always well spent."

"You're right there. I'm glad you two hit it off so well. Will you have your same e-mail address?"

"Of course. Your address doesn't change with your physical location. Welcome to the new virtual cyberworld. Ariel can always help you if you run into difficulties."

"Yes, what would we do without Ariel?"

"Race you to the water," she said as she took off running.

After cooling off in the surf, they stretched out on their towels and beach chair. Miranda read while J.P. dozed off to the distant sounds of crying gulls and shouting children, muffled by the steady sea breeze and susurrus of waves. He awoke some time later to the remnant of a dream whose details he could not recall: all that remained was the intense feeling of submersion in a real situation. Maybe that's all that life or its recollection is composed of.

• • •

He sat at his desk, writing checks to pay the various bills, too numerous it seemed for a simple existence such as his own, more numerous in any case than what he had had to put up with during the years of his career. And then there were the other paperwork matters to be taken care of, and the time spent on hold on the telephone to resolve a problem with, of all things, his telephone service. Not to mention trying to figure out when he could make time to take his car in for an oil change or schedule a dental appointment or return the coffee maker that was not working properly. It seemed as though the routine affairs involved in the maintenance of life were crowding out life itself. How do people who are not retired manage it all?

He was disturbed by a knock at the door, an interruption that he initially cursed, but then greeted as a welcome break when he realized it would take him away from the annoying paperwork. It was Ariel, who had come to upload to his computer more of the files that had been collected and to print out relevant ones for his perusal. Since the computer was on his desk, he surrendered his seat and took his checkbook, bills, and postage stamps down to the kitchen table. As soon as he had seated himself again, there came another more tentative rapping at the front door. This time it was Caleb, who had come to clean the gutters. J.P. was momentarily satisfied that his directives, his plans on various fronts, were moving apace. They walked through the house, pausing only briefly so that J.P. could answer Caleb's questions about why he had so many books and who all the people were in the small selection of family photographs hanging in a bit of free wall space in the hallway. He obviously had a curiosity, which in this case was perhaps not merely nosiness but an admirable quality that showed he could do his own thinking. They proceeded out the backdoor to the ramshackle garage, hardly deep enough to park a car of the latest vintage, and sorted through various bits of detritus to extract a ladder, which J.P. had noticed had been left by some previous tenant. Hanging from a nail on the wall was a rusty mattock, which he recognized from his childhood. How many people use mattocks these days, or even know the word, he wondered. He scrounged up a plastic lawn-and-leaf bag, and walking back to the house, said, "It sure helps to have you do this. I don't know why somebody even put up gutters though. Most houses here don't bother with them, given our frequent monsoon downpours. I'll bet you didn't know we're the rainiest city in the country, with almost 70 inches a year."

"No sir, but I feel it."

After helping Caleb place the ladder against the side of the house and warning him to be careful, J.P. told him he could deposit the leaves on the compost pile in the back corner of the yard. With his employees dutifully occupied, he announced that he was going to get the oil changed in his car, and if he was not back by the time Caleb finished, he would pay him at the next tutoring session. It seemed to him that Caleb gave him a piercing look as if to determine whether or not he could count on that.

"How's that reading coming, by the way?" he added, referring to a children's book of Greek myths that he had lent him. "Have you finished that story about Herakles cleaning the stables?"

"I read it. But it didn't tell me much. "'Cep' that kings cheat people, make 'em do all the dirty work. But I already knew 'bout all that shit."

"Well, maybe it wasn't anything new, but the point up to now is just to get used to recognizing the words. Let me know what you'd rather read about, and maybe we can find something."

"Okay." Caleb began humming some slow melody, unascertainable to J.P., as he climbed the ladder.

As J.P. drove off, he considered hiring Caleb in some additional task, possibly as a kind of thug in his plans to get back at Anthony. But he knew that was just an absurd phantasy.

• • •

From his spot with a view out the dormer window Ariel could observe Caleb creeping along the roof line, scooping leaves from the gutters into the plastic bag. At one point he looked up quickly from the computer screen when he heard a cry of "God damn!" and saw Caleb frantically clutching at his hand.

"Damn wasps!" Caleb muttered to himself. "Shit! Flew right up out the gutter! Be just like him to know they there when he sent me up here." After sucking on the sting, he continued to mutter. "I wisht he'd get stung sometime, or bit by one of those snakes always crawlin' 'round his place in the Delta. Then he might find out what it's like. His place my ass! I had the rule o' the place, 'fore he show up."

Ariel unobtrusively opened the window a crack so that he could hear better.

"He probably put 'em there hisself just to sting me. Jes' like in the swamp—makin' things difficult. But he just wait—I learn his stuff and then I be ready."

Soon a third set of visitors arrived in an old car pulling a weaving trailer loaded with lawn equipment. They had begun rolling their riding mower down the ramp when Trick spotted the figure at the roof line. He pointed him out to Steve as he grinned and made some obviously disparaging remarks before yelling up to Caleb.

"Hey, is Boudreau here?"

"Who?"

"The owner."

"You mean Mr. Deveraux."

"Whatever."

"No, he gone, but he be back shortly he say."

"I see he's got you cleaning the gutters," said Steve.

"Um-hunh."

"Looks like he might have hired us for that," muttered Trick.

"How much he paying you?" probed Steve.

"He didn't say."

"I thought as much. He's quite an operator, lookin' to get by with as little as he can."

"Playin' us off against each other," said Trick. "He knew it was our day to come mow."

Ariel continued to observe the proceedings from his dormer window. Steve walked back to his car to retrieve a can of Pabst Blue Ribbon from the cooler and take a swig while contemplating the matter.

"Listen, we're lookin' to expand our business. We could take care of a lot more yards if we had a bigger crew. We could pay you top dollar if you're willing to work. You don't seem to mind gettin' your hands dirty."

"How much you pay?"

"Minimum wage, plus maybe five percent more later on if you're good at it. How about it?"

"I'm thinkin'."

"Well, you just keep on a-thinkin'. Say, you ever been in his house?"

"Once."

"We've peeked in the door ourselves. He's sure got a lot of books in there—spends most of his time reading 'em. Some of them must be valuable. You reckon he's got other valuables in the house?"

"I wouldn't know. What you aimin' at?"

"Well, since he's hirin' us, but not necessarily payin' us what we deserve, we might try to even things up just a little bit, know what I mean? Maybe borrow a little petty cash, or pawn something he might not notice was missing."

"Or take his books. He thinks that what make him powerful," observed Caleb.

"Yeah, we could check out a few books from his library and hold them hostage for ransom, since he'd hate to part with them. We wouldn't have to damage them or anything: I bet just threatening to burn them would do the trick. Wouldn't nobody have to know who was getting the payment. All easy and quite harmless to all concerned, wouldn't you say?"

"Maybe. He's got a daughter too. Mighty pretty—I seen her picture."

"You think the door's open now?"

"I'm sure I seen him lock it when he leave."

Ariel watched as Steve marched up the front steps to try the front knob and then walk around to the back for the same purpose, but to no avail.

"Remember what I said, and we can get to it eventually. Say, can I give you a beer?"

"I guess so."

From his vantage point, Ariel could see Caleb's arm reach out and down to retrieve the can.

"And here's my phone number: S & T Lawn Services," said Steve, handing over a card and pointing at the same time to the magnetic sign affixed to the passenger door.

All the outdoor laborers had gone by the time J.P. returned, and Ariel was just finishing up inside. Before leaving, however, he gave J.P. a report on what he had overheard.

"Those scoundrels," J.P. said. "And to think they would try to rope in Caleb! What do they have in common? After all they're big supporters of the closet racist "Dupe" Duplin, who hardly has the interests of people like Caleb at heart. Steve and Trick are only out to use him."

"Unlike us," said Ariel.

J.P. looked closely to see if his employee's facial expression betrayed any irony.

"You can't trust anybody these days. Including Caleb: you say he said Miranda was pretty? We will indeed have to watch out. I don't want any of them around when she's here. Maybe I should follow up on that ad for a home-security system that came in the mail yesterday. What do you think?"

"I could install a camera or two for you. Or even a fake camera. That might be enough, and it would be a heck of a lot cheaper."

"That's a good idea. We'll have to keep our eyes on them."

• • •

Later that evening, as J.P. was fretting about the possible wickedness of his employees, he was reminded of an event that had shocked him back in the early '80s when he was stationed in the Far East. The awful deed had not happened in that part of the world, however, but in his home town, as he was informed through a letter and newspaper clipping from Billy. Early one morning the body of a nineteen-year old Black man was found hanging from a tree on a city street, a 13-loop noose around his neck. But his death had occurred earlier from a severe beating and a slit throat before his body was hauled to the site and strung up. Although many signs pointed to the Klan, the police originally arrested some "junkie types," as though it were a drug deal gone bad. They were let go, but years later, one of the actual perpetrators confessed and the other was sentenced to electrocution. The young victim's mother, however, forgave the penitent witness and opposed the form of violence that would end the life of the unrepentant killer. And several years after that, when the Klan had been bankrupted in a civil suit, she used the money she received to help the sad people who didn't even have enough to eat. J.P. was pleased that some type of justice was eventually served, but he recoiled at the resurfacing of horrors that he assumed had been put to rest: just because most of us are insulated from the worst of it most of the time, doesn't mean that evil doesn't exist. He realized moreover that it was not only the actual perpetrators who maintained the climate of terror, but those who failed actively to pursue them. J.P. found inspiration in the nobility of the poor Black woman who had lost a son and who doggedly pursued truth and justice, while renouncing vengeance. At the same time, he wondered whether progress was really being made, and what his own obligation might be.

During their visits over those months, Clotilde sometimes asked what she should tell Anthony, who on rare occasions inquired whether she had heard any news from J.P., but for the moment, he did not know what to say to her.

σ

The name that really counts in this league or any other league from now on is the one you make for yourself and likewise the fathers that count are not necessarily the ones that begat us but the ones we choose for ourselves as we need them in certain situations and predicaments as we need and choose our own personal tools and weapons.

—Albert Murray, *The Seven League Boots*

J.P. WANDERED THROUGH HIS LIBRARY as he did periodically, looking for space to put newly acquired books, but the shelves were overflowing. He knew he should get rid of unnecessary volumes: he realized he would never read all of them for a first or second or third time anyway. But it was hard to tell at this point to which ones his attention might later be devoted; he thought he needed to retain all the proper ones to bring everything together in the end. Even those authors who wrote something worth considering often sit long forgotten on library shelves, only to be picked up on infrequent, intermittent occasions, like the early twentieth-century Swiss writer, so enigmatic but surprising, whom he had rediscovered just the week before. There were also a few items he had written himself, unpublished except for the pamphlets and position papers he had composed during his employment and a single translation of a poem that had appeared in a foreign journal. Included in that lot were his random jottings, scribbled over the years in notebooks or on scraps of paper saved in manila folders containing ideas, plans, memories, and other thoughts and observations that he hoped one day to assemble and employ in some project or other, and which he now hesitantly stroked with his fingertips. Yet any attempt to organize the collection would take on such dimensions that at some point, especially as his life grew shorter, he would never go through it all again, and he saw that the intention of preserving these ideas for future use was contradicted by their very nature and its vast scope—instead of forming lasting, prominent features in his life, their sheer number destined them to invisibility. Was he engaged in preservation or oblivion? He stared into the distance and wondered who would ever read those things. Perhaps someday, someone would run across them and find some value there. It was all one could hope, when even most daily conversations fail to hit their mark. Maybe he should save potential future readers the trouble, however, and dispose of them all now. Our nation has an archive to store all its documents; what is that motto on the statue of "Future" seated in front of its building? He tried to recall it. Doesn't it say that what has occurred in history is a foretaste of what is to come? Isn't it admonishing us not to forget? But why—so we'll realize we're doomed to repeat what came before, or so we'll take note and know how to avoid it? The latter course doesn't seem to be working very well, he thought. Or maybe, as Anthony would have it, so that one can use previous misdeeds as a rationalization for current crimes.

Perhaps he should continue his attempts to synthesize his knowledge and ideas in that nice leather-bound journal he had recently found and in which he had begun to formulate his plans for Anthony. Wasn't it all of a piece anyway? In digging through the old stuff in order to clear things out and make room, he could not shake the reluctance to throw away any book, pamphlet, map, photograph, poster, or notation, because it would be like abandoning a part of his life, never again to be retrieved. Finally bringing an end to his ruminations and rummaging, he managed to fill about three-quarters of a banana box with books he thought he could part with.

When he finished that task he turned to a large carton of materials which Aunt Clotilde had given to him and which had been waiting for some time in its temporary repository next to the bookcases: he decided it was finally the right opportunity to get to work on it and carried it to his desk. It contained original holographs and photocopies of letters, journals, and miscellaneous scraps of paper written and retained by various family members since the end of the century prior to the one preceding his own. Clotilde had begun organizing and transcribing a few of them and, thinking him the member of the family most capable and interested, had asked him to continue the task. Perhaps the utterances contained in these papers were where his true origins lay. For a moment, though, he wondered whether the connection by blood to these documents made such a difference:

maybe a collection of the state's newspapers from the last hundred and fifty years would describe his make-up equally well. In assembling his own family's correspondence he was not trying to establish a dynasty that validated him; he would simply be learning from what they had to say, for better or worse.

Was he dredging up ancient history? When he was a young boy the Civil War, or War Between the States as they called it back then, had seemed a very long time ago, but now that his life was approaching the span that separated his boyhood from that event he realized it was not so long ago at all.

As John Prosper clasped the oldest letters of his ancestors, they seemed at first touch so far away, yet those who penned them were linked to him by the ever-so-slight but very real connections of oral family lore and the printed register of genealogies. But as he read, their voices and those of their descendants started to come alive and speak to him more directly. Their children, and children's children, settling in to the new land and growing into the ways placed on them by necessity and the conventions of those who surrounded them, took on the optimistic, rational outlook of the Enlightenment and the vigorous initiative of the Age of Enterprise. They communicated by written epistle, went from place to place by horse and wagon, and began to assume comparatively comfortable life styles. The ownership of enslaved people, a practice whose contradiction of their ideals seemed to trouble them little; the acquisition of land; and the raising of crops and timber for trade formed the bulk of their wealth and the means of increasing it along with their privilege. The immediate descendants of that generation lived to see the advent of the telegraph, railroads, and urban sanitary systems: their young men went off to college and sometimes war to prepare themselves for the changing world. The letters of these later generations, though still imbued with a whiff of alterity for J.P., seemed somewhat less remote. As he proceeded through the correspondence he reached yellowing pages written by those who had died before his birth but whom his father had known as a child, and as he continued further among the documents, his grandparents began to be mentioned before emerging as writers of missives themselves. These people, with whom he had actually spoken, took visual shape behind the lines, for he had shared breakfasts and suppers with them, gone to the same church services, heard the same conversations at an earlier time which did not seem so long ago because it was a part of his own life. And their forebears, whom they had still known and engaged in dialogue, in turn now took on more of a reality, for the chain of generations is not broken by abrupt stops and starts, but rather is marked by overlaps, and his great-great-aunt Berthe, who for him as a child was known only through family anecdotes and seemed a relic from an ancient past of carriages and crinolines and acquaintance with those born into slavery, was to his grandfather loving kin who stroked his head and told him stories. And realizing this, J.P. felt that he could almost reach back and touch her, though his awareness did not yet reach the point of contact with those who made her early life possible but who remain silent, because they were denied the ability to write. It was a tangled skein of various connections in which he was inextricably involved.

In reading and editing this family correspondence, J.P. realized that he was plowing the same ground his aunt, father, grandfather, and grandmother had previously covered, and thus he too participated in the narrative and reacted to the lives and observations of those ancestors long dead who had once been fully alive on the earth with their human concerns, which they faced with their own particular combinations of strength and weakness, talents and foibles, somehow surviving, at times through minor triumphs and in spite of occasional humbling reverses, eventually succumbing to the mortality that faces us all. Their lives, so consequential as they were being lived, were now long gone, their only remnants these fortuitously preserved texts that in a faint but no less real way rekindled the spark of their existence. He had personally known his own now-deceased father, grandfather, and grandmother and occasionally conversed with them about these predecessors and their letters and diaries, though never in great detail. But in re-reading this older correspondence which linked the writers first to one another and then later to their more immediate descendants, he re-entered the conversation with them, and also engaged in the uncompleted one with his more recent relatives, who had spoken to their ancestors in their own minds as well, incorporating them, at times perhaps rebelling against them, but in any case weaving their peculiar concept of them into the fabric of their behavior and lives and their relations with their own contemporaries.

He also considered his distance, or perhaps his proximity, in space and time, to his mother's home town of Mytilene. Separated by 4 miles of city street, plus 14 of Interstate highway and 63 more of two-lane blacktop, he could if he wished reach it by late afternoon, park his car and stroll the half dozen blocks of uninspiring habitations, many in need of touch-up paint or serious repair, in that settlement that was long ago regarded as the site of a new Eden, where a rich agriculture in a prosperous outpost of civilization was supposed to be developed: such was the goal of that ancestor who strode across the land from the depleted fields of the Eastern seaboard and made his way through the forest wilds to the edge of the new frontier (as he no doubt would have described it, ignoring even as he brutally displaced the ones who had long lived there). But was J.P. closer to that physical place now than he was to what was recorded in the letters from long ago?

He paused to think about anachronisms—normally considered *faux pas*, out-of-place inclusions, or a technique of fantasy when they appear in novels or film. But present-day people live with the remnants of the past in their memories and outlooks, and inhabitants of past times also kept in view the future that they were trying to bring into being. Anachronisms must be a constant feature of everyone's life and make-up: maybe it's synchronicity instead. He pondered the irony of spending time with the documents of those people from the past, who in their day were looking mainly toward the future. But how to understand the past and the future that we must build? History as we know it exists as a result of our consciousness and the way we construct it. The past is dependent on the present view of it: we too easily distort it into a predecessor which existed only to create the outcome we see today. But our consciousness is formed as well by the history in which we live. J.P. repeatedly clenched his fists by turns in his struggle to sort out the apparent paradox and to find the proper way forward.

Despite his admiration for the struggles of his ancestors, J.P. knew that the past could not be viewed through a filtered, nostalgic lens: the actions of those predecessors had also all too frequently resulted in damaging consequences which persist in present-day institutions and outlooks. Those men knew what the order was and were convinced of their place at the top of it, although they most likely never considered that the "order" did not exist objectively in the external world other than to the extent that their own "realization" of it and their success in convincing or forcing others called it into being. Its fragility was a notion that they dared not face up to. Yet the legacy of slavery with which we still live is dogged in its persistence. Some of the more rebellious males or the old wives and aunts (that is, the ones who were not striving to secure their own place in the order by acceding to it), although they were equally cognizant of it and rarely confronted it directly, had a different concept of it altogether and were well aware that it itself was little more than an arbitrarily accepted construct: they could therefore regard the reigning men's view with a sense of irony. In the outlook of those observers, a servant of integrity was superior to a short-sighted, stuffed-shirt banker, and through their awareness of this, they could make it so, in an implicit and knowing way that chipped away at the overt status quo without immediately shifting it. This too was a lesson J.P. had learned as a child from the raised eyebrow, the wry smile, the understated cutting remark of Aunt Clotilde as she reacted to family conversations. But remnants of the outlook, the established order, have continued to survive with force. It is an ongoing dialogue, he realized, that should result in action.

At one side of his desk he spotted an oyster shell he had picked up on the island near Miranda's sea lab from a mound that had been formed by the area's earliest inhabitants: was it a natural artifact or a cultural artifact?

• • •

Taking a break, and a gin and tonic in his right hand, he headed in his usual hurried way out to the front yard, but stopped short at the sight of a couple of brittle, brown leaves on the floor of the hallway, their presence a seemingly inexplicable marker of intrusion and death. Had someone been there, unbeknownst to him? Or had they merely blown in from the water oak tree in the yard, itself no doubt hollowed out and decayed on the inside like they all get and liable to be knocked over by the next gust of wind? Only briefly wondering how the leaves had gotten there, he physically shook off the feeling and went out to take a seat in one of the synthetic wicker chairs that had replaced the less comfortable wrought-iron ones. From this vantage point he had a good view of the street and any passers-by through the trees and azalea bushes and could keep track of the local goings-on, to the extent that there were any. He had noticed that walkers rarely looked over or noticed him: either they had their eyes set firmly on the direction in which they thought they were headed, or they were too polite to intrude even ocularly, or they simply didn't suspect that anyone would be sitting there. At the moment no one at all could be seen, though he heard the delighted squeals of children playing in a neighbor's yard or riding their bicycles somewhere nearby. He marveled whenever he saw the faces of children glow in pure delight at encountering something for the first time: eyes widening in total absorption and spontaneous smiles of ecstatic innocence. He was glad that they could at least be granted such unimpeded enjoyment at one stage of their lives. At my age, he thought, that rarely happens any more—except when I see children, rapturous with delight.

He took a long, slow sip of his cooling drink and began to ponder his own life, starting with his childhood, but he was soon troubled that his memories were like the books in his library: an increasingly overwhelming quantity, too great to be stored, too numerous to recall or organize in a coherent way, or even to hold on to, since many slipped away on their own or transformed themselves in insidious ways. He wondered whether there was any way for Ariel to somehow fix them more permanently in the computer. J.P. had reached a stage in his life when he had begun to reminisce frequently, to try to draw connections between that earlier person that was himself and the later one that he was now, to see if there really was a coherence between those bundles of nature and nurture, will, dreams, character strengths and flaws, knowledge, judgment, and everything else that made up those constantly developing, contradictory integrities. But if he was having difficulty sorting it all out, how much harder it must be for someone like Ariel. He could sympathize, however, since there are probably very few who can be easily categorized. Things don't necessarily happen in life as the result of providence, or even as the result of an individual's preconceived plan. The connections are made as you go, it seemed to him, in both retrospect and prospect. The narrative is perhaps more a set of juxtaposed, seemingly disparate events, as opposed to a continuous development.

He raised his head quickly as just then a random memory from his younger days popped into his mind: an amateur film which he had scripted and acted out with friends, one of whom had acquired one of those little 8mm Brownie movie cameras that were just beginning to make their appearance. It was silly, he recalled, and he was glad it had apparently disappeared and that through no quirk of fate would he have to watch it again now. And yet—it contained something, an impulse, a spark that sought to express a dissatisfaction with the way things were and a response marked by creativity, which despite its immature irony, represented perhaps the only possible reaction, and one which was a product of the same person he was today. His feelings continually alternated: he often thought he still inwardly contained the fresh lively 18-year-old that he once was. But when he viewed the photograph of his younger self from without he thought he was looking at a completely different person. In maintaining through his aging years the perceptions, feelings, and outlook of his youthful days he was not attempting to fool himself or anyone else, but merely trying to remain open to the multitude of forms of human experience and ages within himself.

But would any new-found awareness that he might attain about his situation have any relevance beyond his own curiosity? Who, for example, would care if a random individual's life were published as a biography? And would such a pursuit, were he to undertake it for himself, remain merely solipsistic? But would denying the importance of summing up a life mean that the life had no validity at all? And could he not just as easily justify pursuing the life of a cousin, or leading citizen, or homeless vagrant, or neighbor down the street? Are their lives only for the moment, destined to be forgotten but for a name carved on a tombstone? He slowly shook his head in perplexity.

It was the kind of vexing problem that required engaging with his companion in conversation, his partner in dialogue, his debater in the dialectic. Taking another sip of his drink he said, "I sometimes look at myself from outside, that is, regard myself in the third person."

"Or sometimes even the second person?"

"That too. And on occasion it seems that language is what defines me, puts words in my mouth, does the talking for me. And there are even those times when I say, 'Words fail me.'"

"Isn't that a false attribution of blame? Isn't it you who fails to come up with the words?"

"I suppose so."

"Do you consider all this hyperanalysis normal?"

"No, I suppose rushing headlong through the world is normal. That is apparently what gets things done. Not this continual moping."

"Or maybe both are necessary?"

"Yes, maybe both."

"Could you be specific?"

"Well, for example, when I was on a trip to New York not so long ago, strolling through the Museum of Modern Art, I saw another gentleman already looking at the painting toward which I was headed."

The man he had noticed had thinning, sandy hair mixed with strands of grey and round, caramel-colored, tortoise-shell glasses, through which his liquid blue eyes stared intently ahead. He was wearing a well-cut tweed jacket and light-blue shirt of Oxford cloth, along with a classic burgundy tie decorated by diagonal rows of some tiny silver insignia. Grey wool trousers and cordovan shoes rounded out the wardrobe of this slender man of average height, who looked well for his age but a tad on the frail side of fit. To J.P. he had immediately stood out from the rest of the spectators who were milling through: the young city women in their clinging, little black dresses and high brown boots, their young men with somewhat shaggy hair and grey sweatshirts, the pudgy middle-aged women from nearby suburbs, olive-skinned tourists from some country far to the south or east, and the teachers with their throngs of school-children. He was able to determine at a single glance that the man had a family background, education, income level, regional origin, and set of manners similar to his own: they could have been brothers, blood or fraternity, and could doubtless have understood each other's standpoint right away, were they to come into conversation. Yet he realized that the man's politics were likely to be diametrically opposed to his own, his intellectual interests completely different or even barely existent, and his priorities set on another path. Maybe J.P. would in fact have had more in common with the scraggly young student gazing at the abstract on the side wall.

"I couldn't tell if the man had spotted me, or if he had, at what conclusions he might have arrived, nor could I tell if those glassy eyes were seeing the painting in front of them, or being held there in a perfunctory sense of obligation. Was he a doppelgänger, or a perfect stranger?"

"Both, I'm sure. To the extent that there can be either enough similarity to produce a doppelgänger or sufficient distance to result in total strangeness. And was he an evil antithesis, or merely a pale imitation, a bland philistine? Suppose you had engaged him—where might that have led?"

"Good question. I sometimes become frustrated at the futility of most conversations. At one of those inevitable parties, for instance. When one intends to convey some observation, fact, or argument, one is usually foiled by another participant's interruption that takes the train of the discourse on an entirely new path: it seems that almost everyone prefers injecting his or her own words to paying attention to those of others. People forget that at least half of a successful dialogue consists of listening. And often the fault lies with me: you would think that my immense curiosity, which voluminous readings have attempted to satisfy, might contribute in a meaningful way to the discussion, but I seem only able to stammer. In addition, there are the frequent non-sequiturs in the responses, time constraints, and external interruptions like ringing telephones or a hostess calling everyone to the table, not to mention that many are more interested in distraction and the mere act of being social than they are in the topic of conversation or the actual people with whom they are talking. It's a wonder that a genuine discourse can occur at all. But what is talk anyway? Talking often rubs salt into the wounds of the sensitive. What is perceived to be said is frequently what has already been said, and therefore useless, or even insulting. But not to talk is not to know, and even more useless still."

Often J.P. would leave a party early, with a sense of annoyance at the mostly desultory remarks, the mindless chatter, the futile attempts of those who did not know how to carry on a conversation, and the many chance and thoughtless disruptions of the words of the few who actually appeared to have something to say. Was it his fault that he seemed to be condemned to that sensibility that made sense of the world in ways that few others understood, and that he had difficulty putting into words which they would comprehend? The clinking of glasses and the snatches of the barely audible background music tended to provide an appropriate accompaniment to the mishmash of utterances that attempted to pass for meaningful communication in the contemporary world. But did all of this absolve him of the duty of trying to make contact with other people nonetheless?

He let out a sigh of resignation before continuing. "The atrophy of conversation seems to have extended even to profanity."

"What do you mean?"

"Haven't you been listening to people, or gone to any movies lately? All cursing has been reduced to variations on the single word *fuck*."

"Which in itself is ironic."

"How so?"

"Because all sex seems sometimes to have been reduced to the blow job."

But J.P. closed his eyes as he recalled what adequate intercourse might be. After a gathering on the previous evening, for example, he returned home and, settling into his comfortable, plush chair beneath the solitary reading lamp, found his place in Eckermann's *Conversations with Goethe in the Last Years of his Life*: He quickly immersed himself in his book and found the discourse more real and stimulating than what he had encountered all day. He had the feeling that he was a third partner, silent except for his thoughts that were inspired by the remarks of the long-dead pair.

"Just last night," J.P. told his interlocutor, "Goethe commented to his amanuensis Eckermann on a remarkable letter he had recently received, in which Alexander von Humboldt reported on the last days of Goethe's recently deceased employer, the Grand Duke Carl August of Sachsen-Weimar. Goethe did not find it strange at all that the two men should have been lifelong friends, since, as he put it, 'the richly laid out, deep nature of the prince was always in need of new knowledge, and Humboldt was precisely the man, who with his great universality, always had ready the best and most thorough answer.' Humboldt related that even on his deathbed, the Grand Duke 'pressed me with questions about physics, astronomy, meteorology, and geognosy, about the transparency of the head of a comet, about the atmosphere of the moon, and about colored double stars, the influence of sunspots on temperature, the appearance of organic forms in the primeval world, the inner temperature of the earth.'

"I had to agree with them, that this wide-ranging pursuit of knowledge was admirable and something I myself had always tried to engage in. And I could also agree with Carl August's comments to Humboldt on religion: 'He complained about Pietism, which was rapidly gaining ground, and the relationship between this fanaticism and political tendencies toward absolutism and the suppression of all free expressions of the intellect.' And I noted that those tendencies still exist today and also observed that it was remarkable that a prince like Carl August, whom one might assume to be an absolutist, would have such views. Goethe regretted the early departure of such a man, saying, 'Only a measly century more, and how much he in such a lofty position would have advanced his time! But you know what? The world doesn't reach its goal as quickly as we think and wish. The retarding demons are always there, which interfere and oppose everywhere, so that on the whole things go forward, but very slowly. Just keep living, and you'll see that I'm right.' Eckermann replied, 'The development of mankind appears to be laid out in millennia.' 'Or in millions of years,' answered Goethe. And I agreed with them that the inevitable slowness is frustrating. Since Goethe was in a good mood, he called for a bottle of wine. I found that to be a splendid idea and joined the two in a glass. Although I shared their admiration for Carl August, I wondered how frequently such enlightened and knowledgeable rulers appeared. 'Very seldom,' replied Goethe. 'There are in fact many who are able to talk intelligently about everything, but they don't have it inside themselves and only crawl about on the surface.' I doubted that there were even many who could talk intelligently. Eckermann interjected that he admired the fact that he had only seen the Grand Duke ride in a carriage pulled by two horses, rather than the more customary, princely coach-and-six. Goethe said that Carl August didn't pursue such vanities but achieved fame nonetheless. 'A piece of wood burns because it's composed of the right stuff, and a man becomes famous if the right stuff is present in him. Fame can't be sought, and all hunting after it is in vain. The same is true concerning the favor of the people. He didn't look for it, but the people loved him, because they felt he had a heart for them.' Here I had to disagree, thinking that people could indeed be deceived. I thought of the increasing number of those following 'Dupe' Duplin, who pursued vanities and had not the well-being of the populace in his heart, but only his own interests. He was one of those retarding demons who interfere all too frequently, I opined."

But on the whole these nineteenth-century observations made mostly perfect sense to J.P.: although he avoided succumbing to the fallacy of believing in the immutability of all human thought, endeavor, and behavior, he was impressed by how much someone of that era such as Goethe could speak to him today and spark interest through his views on art, science, politics, and human interaction, even when he was pigheadedly wrong, as, for example, with aspects of his color theory. In his mental assents and disagreements, J.P. had considered, reacted, and expanded, to take the dialogue in new directions.

"'Talking with the book' is what enslaved people called it when they saw the white folks reading. But is that form of dialogue enough? Does sitting alone and occupying oneself with books have any value?"

J.P. pondered for a moment those authors who wrote years or centuries or millennia ago, or even quite recently: if he provided an audience through his readership, wasn't he doing his part in the intended dialogue, keeping the faith that would otherwise be lost if the books were ignored?

"Does it matter whether I have a discussion with anyone else about it or not?"

An insightful thought provided a response. "But don't you at some point have to interact with those in the world around you? You hold on to Diana as a fond memory, but wouldn't she have acted?"

J.P. deeply considered the remarks of his alter ego. Even if he made the attempt, who exactly would it be who was engaging with others? Would he be able to have it both ways? If he interjected his notion of his own great intelligence, knowledge, experience, and awareness in his conversations and remarks, he would run the risk of intimidating the others and projecting himself as arrogant, but if he acted according to his simultaneous cognizance of his own shortcomings that placed him in many respects behind even them and withheld his commentary, he might be perceived as uninteresting and irrelevant. But then he realized that there was no other course but to have it both ways, since both were who he was: not just the two in fact, but many others as well, and he was under no obligation to convey the clarity of consistency to others, nor should he be overwhelmed by what they thought of him. He sensed that the only proper stance for giving utterance to his views was the seemingly impossible combination of walking the narrow line between two contradictory attitudes: his own justified pride in holding what he considered the proper insights, and the honest humility required in realizing how difficult the achievement of an adequate expression can be. He paused and held up his hands a foot apart as if to use them to help him locate the words he had not yet found. It was difficult to discover the right way: he admitted he was often explaining, preaching, as if he were the only one who knew how things were. Wasn't he sick of those insufferable people who repeated their same prescriptions all the time? As if filling the air would prevent opposing views from emerging. He rattled the ice cubes in his almost empty glass, and considered refilling it.

"And," his bosom friend continued, "I don't just mean talking. What about real action? You think a lot about your plans for Anthony, but how far along are you in that regard? And do you really know Anthony?"

"I know his main motivation is looking out for his own ass, his own bottom line, as it were."

"Is that all? Does he have a sense of humor, for example?"

"Well, I remember one time when we were children and some adult asked, 'Where's John Prosper?', he piped up with 'Just around the corner.'"

"Maybe you are always just around the corner. Might not that sign of wit indicate that more is possible with him?"

"That single sign?" His face displayed a look of exasperation. "Maybe."

"He's your brother. Do you love him? Did you ever love him?"

J.P. frowned in concentration as he struggled to come up with an answer.

"Despite the difference in age, and my going off to college during his high school years, there was perhaps a certain affection once. But the main thing is, I know what he did to me. The memories of that meeting when I was railroaded out in a *coup d'état* and of the envelopes conveying worthless shares continue to live vividly at the front of my mind."

"His seizing of power was hardly a revolution. He basically insured instead that the status quo would continue."

"But progress must come about. His prevention of the inevitable is indeed usurpation."

"But didn't you inwardly consent, because you knew it freed you? Or perhaps because you were afraid of taking on the responsibility? Didn't you contribute through inaction? Was it usurpation or abdication?"

"Perhaps. But that doesn't take away from the fact that his deeds were done, that they were unjust. I know his schemes." In waving his arm, J.P. knocked his glass on the little side table, but caught it at the last minute to keep the remnant from spilling.

"His schemes are real, but doesn't he also accomplish things in the world?"

"His world consists of his cronies on his board of directors, at the country club, and in the hunting lodge, whatever their names are. He probably can't distinguish between friends and toadies. He lives in an echo chamber, a limited corner of the world that doesn't extend beyond his own preconceptions."

"What about your own echo chamber, inside your own skull?"

"You may have a point. Are you part of that? But I don't think I'm so completely full of illusions as Anthony. Ariel caught him scolding his son for his laziness. He claimed that he had built up the firm single-handedly and asked where it would end up if young Anthony failed to take the proper action. He fails to realize how many people's efforts are required to bring something to fruition and forgets what he inherited from our father. Sounds, however, exactly like what our father would have claimed."

"Isn't there perhaps more to Anthony than you think?"

"There's more to everything than meets the eye."

"Maybe you should find out. Didn't you read in the paper recently that he had donated money for the new branch library in the western suburbs? You've assembled a remarkable library for yourself, but the one he's building will be used to spread books among thousands of people."

J.P. squirmed. "The one 'he's building' is right: he donates money, but he also profits from the construction, and the tax breaks. Besides, if he creates a home for the books he won't have to read them himself."

"Cynicism is easy. People will be able to read his name above the door of the Anthony Devaux Branch of the Public Library long after you're forgotten."

"I failed to mention indulgence of vanity as another benefit of philanthropy for some people—they don't want so much to do good as to appear to do good. Let the mighty look on their works and despair. Or perhaps they'll endure the fate of the emperor Vespasian, whose name is still immortalized in the *pissoirs* of Paris and Rome. In any case, I don't need laudation myself."

"Are you sure? Don't you brood at times over the value of what you have accomplished? Hasn't Anthony gone a step beyond whatever your father may have done to benefit the community? And doesn't it get under your skin that it's a library that he's endowing?"

Again, J.P. had to admit that it did, especially when he viewed his own achievements. Although he could tell himself that he had indeed accomplished a lot during his working years, most of those tasks had left no artifact or record to be associated with his name, unless one pored through dusty files that may or may not have been preserved in government archives. His academic studies had borne fruit mainly in his own head and had not led to any publications, except on a single occasion. Once, when traveling to Rome as a graduate student, he had looked up a fellow from his hometown whom Clotilde had recommended that he meet. J.P. was not sure how to regard this exuberant raconteur, poet, and bon vivant a few years older than himself who seemed so certain of his own creative gifts and was continually punctuating his never-ending anecdotes, so filled with colorful exaggerations, with "Tum-te-tum," or giving a slight, repeated throat cough to indicate to a hostess that he needed a refill of his wine. It did turn out that this man knew quite a few writers, composers, and singers of various nationalities and also worked at times with famous Italian cinema directors, translating scripts and even playing bit parts in their films: J.P. actually met a few of those people at one of the wild dinner parties hosted by this expatriate, who was also known for his culinary skills. He frequently regaled his Italian, German, and British guests with imaginative variations on down-home Southern delicacies, while telling stories which one could never be sure corresponded exactly to the truth.

"When I was a teenager," the hometown poet once related, "the exiled Thomas Mann was on a speaking tour throughout the U.S. and gave a public reading in the auditorium of the big public high school I attended. I later read that his seven-year-old daughter had given him the nickname '*der Zauberer,*' and indeed I too was charmed by the magic of his words. So much so, in fact, that I got up early the next morning to buy some freshly baked rolls at Pollman's and hurry to the terminal, where I knew he was scheduled to take the first train to New Orleans. When he arrived at the platform, I was there waiting, holding out my package and saying, "*Ihre Brötchen, Herr Mann!*"

This fellow was in addition the principal editor for a multilingual literary journal in Rome, which had been established by a princess and which published the works of the latest authors in several languages, as well as older texts. Hearing of J.P.'s familiarity with the classics, he talked him into translating one of Horace's odes into English, and after a period of agonizing efforts and multiple re-workings J.P. was finally able to mail off his attempt and be later gratified at seeing his work in print:

> *Be wise, strain the wine, rein in your long-term hopes*
> *to the briefest of spans. While we are speaking, invidious time*
> *takes flight: pluck the day, trusting posterity not even a second.*
> —Horace, *Odes* I, 11

J.P. still had his rich, cream-colored copy of the journal, embossed in burnt umber with the name it had borrowed from its location on a street of shaded shops; probably the journal itself has remained obscure to most, he thought. Like himself—had he unconsciously followed Goethe's advice, as stated to Eckermann? "Had I, however, known as clearly as I do now, how much excellent writing has existed for centuries and millennia, I would not have written a single line, but would have done something else." He realized however, that even though he was too imaginative and dreamy to be a businessman, he was too practical and routinely competent to be an artist; his overriding trait seemed to be his awareness.

In truth J.P. held a suppressed longing to be recognized for who he was, for his essence: but although he was too aware to think that meant some proper dynastic place, he could not altogether expunge every trace of that feeling. He realized, however, that such concepts were irrelevant, and any recognition or acknowledgment would only be deserved on the basis of what he did during his existence here. Was Anthony admired in the community for his heritage or for his financial skills? If he were to lose all his money, would he still occupy the same place in the public's opinion? Aristocrats are not born but made: it was up to him to create himself, to choose his own fathers, to look to the future rather than to the past, heeding all the while

Horace's advice to live fully in the present. Thinking about the task ahead, however, was accompanied by the queasy feeling at the pit of his stomach, the sense of uncertainty, which he so often felt and which never seemed to go away completely: he thought he shouldn't have to endure such doubt at his age, when his goals should have been accomplished and he was winding down. But of course his goals weren't fully accomplished, and besides, life never ceases. Its demands, fair or not, continue to impinge upon one's existence. But perhaps the disquiet was not the result of attacks on his short-comings, threats to him directly, or his own self-doubt. Perhaps it was the weight of the world, the plight of others in direr straits, which was subconsciously eating away at him. There was much to ponder.

He would have to have another talk with Ariel: to find out more, and to put more precise plans in place. Why was it taking so long? Because his typically endless research involved ferreting out every detail in advance, or because he questioned the validity of his purpose?

For the moment, he would have to have another gin and tonic. And to stop talking for now: sometimes there were just too many words sent out into the void, verging on meaningless glossolalia.

τ
Mesologue

Straightway Jove shuts up the North Wind in the cave of Aeolus,
together with those others who chase the clouds away.
He turns the South Wind loose: the Wind flies out with dripping wings,
his countenance veiled in pitch-black fog, his beard weighed down
by pouring rain, his hoary locks in flowing billows. Across his forehead
gather clouds; his folds and feathers scatter the watery drops.
His broad hands squeeze low-hanging clouds and cause
a dreadful crash; from the firmament a mighty storm pours down.
—Ovid, "The Flood," *Metamorphoses*, I, 262–69

THE AWARENESS THAT THERE'S ONE OUT THERE—listening to the radio, catching the hourly weather reports on TV, tuning in more often as the announcements increase in frequency: first a tropical wave off the Cape Verde Islands, later a tropical depression with increasing organization, then a tropical storm with attendant christening, and the forlorn hope of affected observers thousands of miles to the west that it will take its inevitable northern path sooner rather than later, steering up into the mid-Atlantic and presenting a danger "to shipping lanes only"—the real but somewhat shallow sympathy for those poor souls in the Caribbean who endure the wrath of the fledgling hurricane in their tin-roofed shacks as its churning path takes it across the Leeward Islands—the brief suspense as to whether it will cross Hispaniola and Cuba or follow the Yucatan Channel into the Gulf—rare television footage of those islands as savage rains cause mudslides near Cape Haitien and winds whip the palm trees along Havana's Malecon and newscasters report with uncharacteristic concern for the populace of those island nations—the dreaded sound of the name Dry Tortugas to announce a more northerly entrance into the Gulf of Mexico as it appears to take direct aim at the central coast—ominous intensification into Category 3 over the unseasonably warm waters, and still three days out—the silent prayers, almost immediately regretted but never rescinded, that it strike somewhere to the east or far away to the west—the perverse sense of relief on the part of some that the danger provides a thrilling respite from responsibility and the opportunity for Dionysiac abandon in a hurricane party—the queasy feeling in the pit of one's stomach resulting from the awareness that it just might indeed hit close to home, coupled with the gnawing sense of obligation to carry out the necessary tasks of preparing for this moveable but unpredictable feast by clearing all loose items from the yard, stocking up on water and non-perishables, filling the car with gasoline, withdrawing cash from the machine, and trying to postpone the decision of whether or not to evacuate—sitting continuously in front of the television, as if the periodic announcements of slightly changed coordinates marked ritualistically on the charts might somehow portend salvation—the seemingly inexorable path that appears to bring it toward a direct hit, and the awareness that hurricanes inevitably change course and could at the last minute veer away—Category 4—the hunkering down and waiting—awaiting the arrival of the widening gyre—wondering when the suspense will ever end, as a blessing or a curse. . . .

υ

For fifty days, following the summer solstice,
when the hot and wearisome season has reached its end,
then is the proper time for mortal men to start a sailing
voyage.
Then you will not smash your ship, nor will the sea
cause the crew to perish,
unless the earth-shaker Poseidon, or Zeus,
king of the immortals, wishes their destruction. . . .
—Hesiod, *The Works and Days*

MIRANDA'S SHIP PLIED THE WAVES, even as back home her father was ploughing through his books, hoping eventually to reap some value from them and trying to piece together how his own voyage would yet go, settling in the meantime for the pleasure of the flow of words:

But make haste swiftly to get back home:
Do not wait for the season of new wine and autumn thunderstorms
and the approach of winter and the fearsome gales of the south
wind Notus,
who comes along with the heavy autumn rains of Zeus and roils
the seas
and makes the waters dangerous.

The rhythm—regular, almost musical—seemed almost predetermined. As she leaned on the railing and looked out beyond the bow of the *Cosmos,* the captain, a leather-skinned old salt who had been a shrimper in his younger days, came and stood beside her holding his binoculars against his chest.

"We can expect some squalls this afternoon, but it shouldn't be too serious. I'm keeping my eye out though: at this time of year you never know what might develop."

She recalled the first of the "Shipboard Rules and Regulations," handed out at departure and posted in prominent places: "The Captain has the total responsibility for the safety and well-being of all persons aboard this vessel. Therefore, **do exactly as the Captain says**." Though she bristled at the authoritarian tone, the man himself was reasonable, as were the rest of the printed rules, which she had little trouble obeying. She didn't smoke, and found it made perfect sense to wear "closed rubber-soled shoes at all times on the vessel." She had been known, however, to ignore the one that stated "Never go on deck at night without a companion," when she sometimes ventured out to marvel at the starry sky.

She stared a while longer before taking a seat on a capstan, pulling out her sketchbook and tracing an abstract of the precise, pelagic pattern of the waves in graphite. Did this form a better record of their quest than the words and figures of their scientific reports or the lyric of poets? As she drew, she heard, amidst the deep thwunk-thwunk-thwunk of the engine noise and the whir of the constant breeze, scraps of voices from her colleagues, working amidships with samples they had collected. The light began to weaken imperceptibly, and the water and sky started to take on a uniform shade of darkening gray.

After a while she went below deck to her computer to write an e-mail to her father. When she was finished she found that there was no reception so far out in the Gulf, so she saved it to her drafts folder to send after they had reached the next port.

```
Date: Thur, 5 Aug 1999 18:23:59 -0400 (EDT)
From: Miranda Williams <mwilliam@isllab.org>
To: "John P. Devaux" <jpdevaux29@aol2.com>
Subject: my trip

[The following text is in the "ISO-8859-1" character
set.]
[Your display is set for the "US-ASCII" character
set.]
[Some characters may be displayed incorrectly.]

Dear Dad,

We've been out for several days now and are about 350
miles south of where you are. We're well into our
routine: sending down probes of various types to
```

measure the extent of deoxygenation and ocean acidification. These will help form a baseline for making comparisons to past and future studies and establish time scales for changes in the ecosystem. We took quite a few samples over the shallow continental shelf right after we left port and then a lot more in the Central Gulf. Some of the other experiments involve chemosynthesis, which is sort of like photosynthesis, only with chemicals instead of light, but I guess you could parse that etymologically. Some of my colleagues are examining cyanobacteria, and others are looking at benthic invertebrates. The deeper waters are where I have been concentrating on my task of documenting the range, population and habits of the *hydrolagus alberti* and *hydrolagus mirabilis*, if you prefer the Latin names to the English(!)one of Gulf Chimaera. It's a medium-sized fish with an ugly face that prefers the depths and it's living up to its name: it's so hard to find that it sometimes really does seem to be a fabulous illusion. We doubt that it's been affected by over-fishing, since fleets don't usually come out this far, but we're trying to determine to what extent the changing climate is having an effect. Soon we'll be heading through the strait between Yucatan and Cuba and do some work in the Caribbean, including along the barrier reef of Belize to see how much difference there is in those waters and their coastal ecosystems.

The weather is good so far: temperatures hot but the breezes are pleasant. Looks like the decade is about to close out on track, with every year warmer than in the 1980s, which was by far the warmest decade up till then. Don't worry about me though: I'm using plenty of sunscreen and wearing my big floppy hat, but I'll probably be a lot browner next time you see me. Most of my shipmates are fun, and the food is not bad either.

Do you ever see Frederic? Give my love to Aunt Clotilde.

Love,
Miranda

It was several days before J.P. received her e-mail: although he eagerly grasped at every scrap of communication from his daughter, he tended to run on a different clock from most people and consoled himself with the realization that an old-fashioned letter conveyed through the various post offices between there and here would have taken much longer. Not knowing when she would receive it, he dashed off a reply, trying to emphasize his admiration for her accomplishments more than his worries about her precarious position on the surface of the deep. Premonitions seemed to rear their heads these days more frequently than he thought fair: the blessing of having a daughter was increasingly accompanied by anxieties.

• • •

In the meantime he decided it was time for him to advance his own pursuits and made a note to himself to speak with Ariel more specifically about the next steps. When he returned home one afternoon he was happy to see that the satsuma tree in the side yard was already beginning to bear fruit; someone had planted it long ago and left him a legacy to appreciate. He couldn't wait until the satsumas were ripe and he would be able to peel off the loose, green skin and bite into the juicy citrus. Such bounty is indeed available: if only he knew how to cultivate it better. He wondered whether he should try planting a scuppernong vine.

　　As he stepped into the front hall, he paused with one hand on the newel post when he heard faint singing coming from an upstairs room:

> And you give me a penny and think you're really swell
> And you gape at my rags and this rundown old hotel
> And you don't know to who you're talkin'.

Who was in his house? And what was that song—it sounded familiar. Yes, it was the Pirate-Jenny song by Brecht and Weill, but he had only heard it in German during his time abroad, or so he thought at first. But then he recalled he had also once listened to and liked the version by Nina Simone, which might be the one he was hearing now. This was no recording of Nina's voice, however, but an actual person. He stepped to the foot of the stairs to be able to hear better:

> *At noon a hundred men leave the ship and come ashore*
> *And round up all they see from every single door*
> *And lay them all in chains and bring them up to me*
> *And ask me which should die—and hear me answer: All of them!*

It was Ariel, who had come early to do some work on J.P.'s computer. But what did it mean? Just a random tune being hummed? His assistant, he knew, was in the habit of bursting into song at odd times. Was Ariel in effect in the position of handmaiden like the singer of the song, abused by employers, J.P. perhaps included, and dreaming of retaliation? Or was J.P. himself Pirate Jenny, feeling abused and planning to exact revenge on Anthony? He tried to convince himself that it was justice he wanted, not vengeance. He certainly did not have a black freighter with fifty cannon at his disposal. Who indeed is entitled to carry out the wrath of God?

He was reminded, however, of his experience of the previous night: very late, when it was darkest, unable to sleep he had turned on a light and wandered through the upstairs rooms. In the other houses that he could see from his vantage point he noted that all the windows were dark. The feeling that he was a solitary and misunderstood genius welled up again within him, and he tried to focus on what his special calling could produce. But the other current within him returned almost immediately, reminding him that it was a mistake to separate himself from humanity, to think that he could offer something lasting apart from them. For didn't crackpots and despots and evil-spirited egoists think of themselves in a similar way? J.P. had struggled with his feelings, tossing and turning as he tried to find a way to properly relate to others and find the appropriate course.

When J.P. entered the study, Ariel said without looking around, "Just what do you propose to do with all this information I've been gathering?"

J.P. had no ready answer, but replied, "Unsettle him. Stir things up, blow everything around so maybe he'll come to see. That's the first thing. Probably a combination of things, however. We can use the inside information about the backdoor land deals and payoffs to make them think they're under threat of indictment, or actually move things in that direction if we want to take it that far. We need to put the fear of God into them, don't you think? And what about this Y2K problem I've been hearing about? Aren't all computers supposed to freeze up on January 1, 2000? Won't they fail to recognize the new year, and think that time stops? And if the machines stop, then won't we all, because we have become dependent on them?"

"The media like to hype things up, the way they do when a new disease appears on the horizon. Everyone thinks the apocalypse is around the corner. Y2K is a problem, but not as big as the public thinks. To save storage space, programs often record the year as two digits rather than four, such as 97 instead of 1997. The year after 99 would be 00, but some computers and operators would think that meant 1900 or 19100 instead of 2000. It would mess up calculations, but probably only a few machines would actually shut down, depending on what the program was supposed to be doing. Also, there's the problem that 2000 is actually a leap year."

"Of course it is. It's divisible by 4."

"But years divisible by 100 normally aren't. However, years divisible by 400 are."

"The facts you have to know. Well, even if the firm's computers don't shut down, couldn't you scare them into thinking they will, or actually introduce some sort of, *glitch* I believe you call it, to cause a temporary malfunction?"

"I suppose so."

"And finally, we need to have an actual confrontation, I just have to decide where and when and how. I had thought maybe out in the Delta or one of the little offshore islands, but I don't know how they could be lured out there. Don't you know a lot about drugs of various kinds? Maybe we could enhance the performance in that way as well. What do you think?"

Ariel continued to stare at the screen dispassionately: so unlike Jenny, thought J.P. Ariel seemed reluctant, although J.P. doubted that there could have been a sudden change in attitude toward the employers at Devaux: Ariel repeatedly told tales exemplifying disrespect and ill-treatment at work. Perhaps it was now a matter of cold feet, a fear of stepping outside the bounds of the legal, and, if caught, becoming trapped in a new way.

"It'll be okay, we'll get it all wrapped up shortly," J.P. said in an attempt to add a tone of reassurance. "And soon, since you so responsibly insist on keeping tab, all your debts will be paid in full."

"At least that. I don't want to keep being beholden to you. Anything else for now?"

"Well, on a different subject. Something else that I've been wondering about, especially now that I've got a daughter again. From your experience, who has it rougher, men or women?"

With lips pursed in concentration, Ariel paused a long time before replying, "None of us has it easy. People don't seem to be able to respect others for who they really are. First, though, you just have to find out yourself who you really are."

Impressed, J.P. paused to ponder the reply a few moments before they got back to work.

After Ariel summarized the new information for him and they agreed to start working on a system to tamper with the computers, J.P.'s odd familiar departed, and he began sorting through his things. But just as when he had returned home a short time earlier and been confronted with unfamiliar strains of music, his senses were again touched in an unexpected way, though this time through his nostrils. He became aware of the faint, sickly odor of rotting flesh, which dissipated or intensified depending on the direction he turned his head. When he went downstairs it became stronger, and despite his repulsion he traced it to the half bathroom off the hall. He spotted nothing behind the toilet or anywhere else on the floor, but kneeling down he sensed it most acutely coming from the point where the lavatory drain pipe entered the floor. It must be beneath the house, he thought. He wondered if he could have asked Ariel to crawl under there and check it out, but that would probably be more of a task for Caleb. However, he wouldn't see Caleb until the following Tuesday, and by then, if it was emanating from something as large as a possum or raccoon, the smell would be enough to drive him from the house altogether. He briefly considered calling Steve and Trick, but thought better of it. When no one else came to mind, he decided to step outside to investigate the opening to the crawl-space in order to see whether or not it was something he could tackle himself. I knew there was something rotten in this godforsaken state of ours, but why did it have to manifest itself in my home? he wondered.

At the back of the house he knelt down beside a rectangular opening no larger than 12x18 inches. He removed the grate and peered inside with a flashlight. Then he changed into his yard clothes and scrounged up some rubber gloves and a plastic bag; finally he tied a bandana around his face in an attempt to ward off the smell before taking the plunge. At least he was slender enough to make it through the hole, though the narrow space between the floor of the house and its underlying layer of dirt did not allow for any type of movement other than a slithering belly crawl. He was careful to keep his head down to avoid coming into contact with the nails that protruded from the flooring, and he tried to stir up as little dust as he could, though it was impossible not to get it all over himself. I'm too old to have to do something like this, he thought, as he inched closer to the drainpipe and its offending companion. When he finally arrived at his goal and saw nothing on the ground, he directed his flashlight upward to reveal a naked pink tail hanging limply from a mass of gray fur squeezed in between the pipe and the floorboards. A rat had become lodged in the narrow space and been unable to escape. J.P. opened his bag and began pulling on the tail, but the flesh had become so decomposed that it no longer held together, falling off in squishy, putrescent clumps instead. He wondered whether he would have to crawl back a second time with a screw-driver to scrape out all the pieces, but mercifully found a large nail lying in the dirt with which he could accomplish the task. A horde of flies swarmed around the carcass, and rather than admiring the iridescent metallic blue of their abdomens he felt the disgust stemming from the object of their attraction. As he repeatedly waved them away, one kept landing at the same spot on his own cheek: an obscene kiss that made him wonder if he had somehow taken on the quality of carrion. Gagging, he tied up the plastic bag and made his way back as quickly as he could, knocking his head only once on the boards above. Once outside, he hurled the sack and its sickening contents as far as he could, and, ripping off his bandana, collapsed onto his back, frantically inhaling in deep gulps. Although the appalling, rotting flesh had been cast aside, the odor continued to cling to his palate like a putrid slime from which he could not escape: Death, the corporeal, in the midst of life.

It was an oppressively hot afternoon, and the humidity was sinking down like a damp blanket, causing beads of sweat to form on the back of his neck, forearms, and belly, making his filthy shirt cling. There was not a breath of air, not a leaf stirring anywhere in the trees; no movement, or hint of relief—he felt a longing for a storm to come and clear the atmosphere.

• • •

While Miranda was off on her voyage, J.P. took her advice to drive over to Ocean Springs to visit the museum there that was dedicated to the eccentric, reclusive painter who was so closely tied to his native locale, despite having made numerous journeys of thousands of miles on foot and by bicycle and by boat to absorb all he could of the nature and the art that the many regions and cultures of the world had to offer. Only vaguely aware of him previously, J.P. wondered how he could have missed his work before now: but then, he was away during the years that the artist was becoming known, to the extent that he was. In the museum, J.P. was immediately struck by the vibrancy and hues of the watercolors, oil paintings, block prints, and drawings and amazed by the range of mediums in which he worked, including ceramics and wood carvings. Also on display were his illustrated journals with extensive writing: he was constantly immersing himself, observing, reacting, and creating—*realizing*, he called it. Purple gallinules, blue crabs, ducks, alligators, magnolias, tortoises, live oaks, rabbits—all the elements of the natural environment that surrounded him. But what really bowled J.P. over were the murals. One covered the four board walls and ceiling of the little room that had been discovered in his cottage after his death and transported to the museum. Luminous hues of lemon, orchid, peach, teal, and coral covered every inch of space, including the window frames through which the sunlight streamed: they formed flowing abstract patterns composed of the mingling shapes of zinnias, egrets, butterflies, and deer. It reminded him of the painted walls in the *Kabinett* in the palace on the Pfaueninsel near Berlin, but instead of being a longing for a faraway Tahiti, this was a celebration of a day in its own Gulf Coast setting, proceeding from sunrise on the eastern wall around to sunset and night. A narrative taking place all at once as it surrounds; a visual paean created by the artist to echo the 104th Psalm: *"Thou art clothed with honor and majesty, covering thyself with light as with a robe, and stretching out the skies like a tent."* Words or pictures: which expressed it better? Or each in its own time? The longer murals painted for the Community Center displayed similar styles and colors, but with different overall motifs: in one, Native Americans played their flutes within the natural background as French explorers arrived to plant the flag in 1699. Another depicted the seven climates of the coastal areas, watched over by the pelican. After standing, staring, taking in as much as he could, he left at closing time, first buying a few books in the gift shop to take home and add to his library.

After a crabmeat supper in a restaurant on Highway 90 that was painted in a loud hot-pink, he decided not to take the main road home, but to follow smaller paths which hugged the sound, if that indeed should turn out to be possible. He drove back through town and followed Shearwater Drive, with its views of Biloxi Bay and the nearby Deer Island, until it ended and looped back inland. He found another street that took him across a section of the National Seashore and wound its way through more neighborhoods. After encountering several dead-ends and switchbacks he came across a road called Beach Street, whose name sounded promising, though it at first passed only through piney woods before finally taking a turn to the right toward the water. As so often in his life, J.P. was groping for the proper path. He drove until the road ended in a stretch of sand, where he parked the car. No one else was around, and he began walking along the shore, listening to the lapping of the waves and observing the lone sanderling that ran furiously before him in search of sustenance. When he approached too closely, the bird would fly up and light again a little farther along. He sat down on a driftwood log and peered out across the five miles of sound to see what he could of Horn Island, vainly hoping to glimpse in the fading light at least a scintilla of what Walter Anderson had observed during his frequent, solitary stays on the deserted isle. The mad painter had never been able to find his way as a husband or father, though he had found his island, the wellspring of his appreciation of the majesty of nature before returning to the mainland and community to share the phantasmagoria of what he had created there. Was it possible to have it all? Would J.P. ever find his island? After a while, he headed back to his car, discovering that he had walked much farther than he realized.

When he turned the key in the ignition, however, there was only a weak, sickening ungh-ungh-ungh: no confident, strong sound of an engine turning over. He frantically repeated his action, not knowing what else to do, ceasing only when he realized he might be running the battery down further. Had he stupidly left the lights on? He looked around in panic, but there was nothing in his field of vision that might provide a solution: no other cars or people. He did not even have jumper cables, nor Triple A, though he had no idea how he would call them from there if he did. He locked the car and began walking back toward town, but it seemed as if he had come miles since the last home or business. He began to feel sorry for himself and wondered why he had to be at the mercy of unreliable machines and singled out for such a catastrophe. He hated the feeling of helplessness, the lack of control, of being totally alone in the world. The initial sense of uncertainty led to a nagging dread, whose constant gnawing seemed almost worse than outright fear. As he walked, his sense of panic grew and he began to wonder what sort of rural deviate he might encounter on the lonely stretch of road: each day's newspaper had at least one horror story about a victim of senseless crime. He too could become a statistic: brains blown out by the side of the road by an unnecessarily powerful semi-automatic pistol in this gun-loving, Bible-thumping region in return for the few dollars scrounged from his wallet. It was almost completely dark

when a pair of headlights came his way. He wondered whether a
Black man or a white man would be more likely to be dangerous,
before condemning himself for even entertaining such a thought. He
was trying to decide whether to remain unobtrusive or to flag them
down when the driver made the decision for him, bringing the car to
a stop a few feet beyond and then backing up. Before the tires had
ceased their crunching on the shells covering the shoulder, the man
yelled out through the side window, which his passenger had rolled
down, "Need some help?"

"I've got a dead battery."

"Where's your car?"

"Down where the road ends."

"Hop in. I've got cables. Let's see what we can do."

Reluctant, but seeming to have no choice, J.P. climbed into the
back seat.

The driver, a white man of about forty with a dark beard and
ponytail, said, "Don't worry, it happens all the time."

J.P. tried not to imagine what happens all the time. The driver's
girlfriend, somewhat younger, turned and gave a sort of smile, but
didn't say anything. She looked down toward the front seat as she
turned back, just as the man took his right hand off the wheel and
reached down there as well. Is he grabbing a gun, thought J.P., or
her hand? But nothing happened until they reached his car.

Fortunately, the man not only had cables but knew how to use
them, a skill that was beyond J.P.'s ken.

"Don't turn off the engine until you've driven a ways so it gets
charged up and won't die on you again."

Finally relaxed, J.P. thanked them profusely and asked what he
might owe them.

"Nothin' atall. We was coming out here anyway to enjoy the
beach, if you know what I mean. If you run across somebody else in
dire straits, you can help them."

The man gave a sideways wave over his head as he drove off. J.P.'s
heart rate began to slow back down to normal on the drive home as
he considered his groundless fears and suspicions and the plight of
people with real problems. The next day he took the car into Sears at
the mall, where the mechanic confirmed that he was indeed in need

of a new battery. Although the situation involved uncertainty, the inconvenience of a boring wait, and an unanticipated expense, it was a problem that could be solved with a little time and money. Humanity, after all, had developed institutions for that purpose, thought J.P.—things seem okay, but does that mean everything is as it should be?

While he was waiting he looked out through the smudged window across the wearisome asphalt with its litter of plastic shopping bags and tire-smashed fast-food cups oozing rancid chocolate milkshakes, but what he pictured in his mind's eye were the radiant wood lilies and Stokes asters in an ordinary ditch that had been depicted in a watercolor he had seen the day before; he desperately tried to grasp the connection.

• • •

```
Date: Tues, 17 Aug 1999 16:17:53 -0400 (EDT)
From: Miranda Williams <mwilliam@isllab.org>
To: "John P. Devaux" <jpdevaux29@aol2.com>
Subject: my trip

[The following text is in the "ISO-8859-1" character
set.]
[Your display is set for the "US-ASCII" character
set.]
[Some characters may be displayed incorrectly.]

Dear Dad,
We've been docked at Progreso, Yucatan, to take on
some supplies and give us a chance to stretch our legs
on shore. We'll be leaving soon to head out to the
Sigsbee Deep, the deepest abyss on our trip, so I
thought I would dash this off while we still have
reception.

The coral reefs of Belize were fantastic! We anchored
just out from them and took the smaller boats in since
the water is so shallow--less than 5 fathoms in most
places. I got to snorkel in the bright, clear water
and swim among the fish and turtles. Had to dodge
```

```
jellyfish and rays a few times but no real danger.
I'll show you my sketches when I get back.

From here most people went down to spend the day in
Mérida, but a few of us took the opportunity to make
an excursion to the Mayan ruins of Mayapán, about 25
mi. south of there. It would have been nice to go to
the more impressive ones at Chichen Itza, but we
didn't have enough time to go that far. You should
make an effort to see them sometime--I think you'd be
surprised at how well they compare with your ancient
Mediterranean architecture. Your studies won't be
complete until you consider what people in this hemi-
sphere created. The main pyramid is impressive, and
there are fortifying walls, temples, observatories,
and lots of other buildings. The murals inside some of
them were especially interesting to me.

This will be the last leg of our trip-- we'll be home
in a little over a week. I look forward to seeing you
then.

Love,
Miranda
```

J.P. was happily reading this latest e-mail when he heard a whispered voice hiss "Quiet!", to which there was a low reply of "But you don't think he's here, do you? I don't see his car."

Looking out the window J.P. didn't see anyone else's car either; whoever it was must have approached on foot. He had let Ariel borrow his old Toyota to run some errands while Ariel's car was in the shop. He could hear light footsteps on the front porch stair and remained motionless to listen for more. The morning was still cool enough to have the window cracked and the air conditioner off.

"How do you propose to get in?"

"I can jimmy the lock with my Visa card."

"You know how to do that? I wouldn't have given you that much credit."

"What a damn joker. Quit your lame-ass puns and look sharp."

By now J.P. had recognized the voices: it was Steve and Trick, apparently in the process of carrying out the scheme that Ariel had previously apprised him of. He and Ariel had set an alarm for such an event, but J.P. couldn't remember whether or not it had been turned on. He heard some scratching sounds, and then someone said, "Is books all we're gonna take? I could use a little cash, not to mention some new clothes."

"He's hardly a fashion plate, not to mention your size. But I'll tell you what: I'll let you take five as soon as we get out of here."

"Ha ha."

"A dose of your own medicine. This fucking lock's giving me more trouble than I would have expected. Might have to try the back."

At that moment, however, there was a creaking sound as the door opened, accompanied by a simultaneous blast from a screaming bass voice: *"A murrain on your monster, and the devil take your fingers!"*

"What was that?" asked Steve in a worried voice.

"I didn't say nothin', I swear, that wasn't me," replied Trick.

But the voice, familiar to J.P., continued its imprecations. *"I will deal in poison with thee, or in bastinado, or in steel. I will bandy with thee in faction; I will o'er-run thee with policy; I will kill thee a hundred and fifty ways; therefore tremble and depart. . . . Pistol's cock is up, and flashing fire will follow. . . . By this hand, I will supplant some of your teeth. . . ."*

At this point there was a clatter of feet on the floorboards, and soon J.P. could see two frantic figures as they emerged from beneath the porch roof to beat a path to the corner of the yard. Instead of an alarm siren or camera, Ariel's warning device was attached to a tape recorder with quotations from Elizabethan drama, which continued to blare from the loudspeakers long after the scoundrels had disappeared: *"Your hearts I'll stamp out with my horse's heels and make a quagmire of your mingled brains. . . . Would thou wert clean enough to spit upon! I'll beat thee, but I should infect my hands. . . . You whoreson cur. . . . Get you gone, you dwarf! You minimus, of hindering knotgrass made! You bead, you acorn! . . . Direct thy feet where thou and I henceforth may never meet. . . . Go thou, and fill another room in hell!"*

Ariel had doubted that such archaic language could be effective, but J.P. assured him it was valid for all time, and indeed, it had seemed to work. His only decision now was whether to call the

authorities or to confront Steve and Trick about their escapade when
next they came to mow the yard. Or perhaps it would make more
sense to sit down and try to reason with them in an attempt to bring
them around. This led him to thoughts on their general outlook on
life. This latest scheme of theirs was hardly different from their
support of the political firebrand Bud "Dupe" Duplin, neither of
which would, in his opinion, provide them with the better situation
that they dreamed of. Maybe he should explain how such actions
were actually working against their own best interests. But who was
he to say that he knew better what their interests were? He was well
aware, however, that the history of the state and country was rife
with populist demagogues who stirred up their supporters' fears and
resentments, giving them a displaced feeling of satisfaction instead
of offering means for a real improvement in their situation. Folding
and unfolding his hands on his desktop, J.P. decided it would
probably do little good to talk to them: it wasn't a matter of providing accurate facts and rational arguments to change their political
positions, but altering their entire mode of perception. The problem
was epistemological, rather than ideological. Perhaps this was also
at the heart of his confrontation with Anthony. In the meantime he
tried to console himself with the hope that in the approaching
millennium we might all be free of such. Somehow gratified that
Caleb must have declined getting involved with the yard crew on this
misadventure, he went downstairs to turn off the alarm and stepped
out onto the porch. A kicked-over can of Blue Ribbon was still slowly
dribbling its contents across the floor and over the edge.

• • •

After he had seated himself the next morning with a cup of dark-
roast coffee at his breakfast table, he began his day as usual by
turning on the little plastic weather radio which he had bought at the
beginning of the summer to keep himself apprised of tropical
developments, hoping each time that there would be no announcements that would necessitate clearing his yard of unmoored items
that might become missiles in the face of driving winds, or hoarding
food and water and boarding up windows. The tinny voice, full of

static at 162.550 megahertz, droned in with its thick, Deep South accent, monotone cadence, and relentless recitation of facts: "Tides at the mouth of the Pascagoula River high tide 11:13 pm low tide 6:37 am. Tropical weather outlook: a tropical wave located over the Bay of Campeche developed into Tropical Depression Three in the late hours of August 18. Further intensification not expected at this time. Conditions for the central Gulf Coast region high temperatures today in the low 90s. . . ."

Bay of Campeche! repeated J.P. with impatience, shutting off the radio and rushing to check immediately the exact location on the nautical chart of the Gulf of Mexico that had been spread out on his desk for a couple of weeks now. Where exactly is Miranda? A tropical depression—what about my depression at hearing such news? He would have to carry the radio with him during the day to keep tabs. Far to the west and south of where he was, the storm posed little danger to him at the moment, but the queasy feeling that arose in local residents intermittently throughout hurricane season now manifested itself in him because of his distress for his daughter.

And sure enough, the storm (or was it only a disturbance?) was located in the area where her e-mail had said her ship was headed. He tried to distract himself with his other reading projects until it came time to head out for his tutoring. As usual, his punctiliousness put him in the room ahead of his pupil, and he leafed through a children's book on the Founding Fathers, which he had brought to see if it might inspire more interest. After a few minutes Caleb strode surefooted into the room, humming a tune, and also carrying a book. J.P. wondered if Caleb had lost his limp, or if it had been the result of a temporary injury, or if he had ever had one to begin with. Perhaps monstrosity, as well as beauty, is in the eye of the beholder. Maybe he himself was the one who was hindered.

"What have you got there?" he asked.

"'Prominate Native Americans'," replied Caleb. "Found it at a yard sale in my neighborhood."

"I believe that's 'prominent'," said J.P. as he thumbed through the book, heavy on text, but also illustrated with colorful pictures of Indian warriors. He had a momentary feeling of resentment that his pupil was attempting to supplant him by providing his own text. Was this perception of a threat of insubordination a mirror, a projection of his own personality? Was he facing an otherness within himself?

"You think you can read this?" he asked abruptly.

"Yes," replied Caleb. To demonstrate he opened it and began speaking slowly and with many pauses and occasional mispronunciations, stumbling, but not stuttering, as he proceeded. Had he overcome that impediment as well, or again, was it J.P.'s imagination? Maybe race itself was a figment. Had he been unknowingly taking on the view of his own subculture toward the Calebs of the world through a product of its own creation, rather than from an accurate and sympathetic observation of who they actually are? Through constant repetition such views gain widespread acceptance, he realized, even among those of us who should know better, as well as among many of the very ones who had been stereotyped.

"'You want by your dis–tinc–tions of Indian tribes — in al–lotting to each a par–tic–lar, to make them war with each other. You never see a Indian en–deavor — to make the white people do this.'"

"Very good. You've made a lot of progress. But do you understand what you just read?"

"Course I do. You teach me to recanize the letters, but I don' got to understand 'em the way your authors try to put 'em together, I understand what happened back then, and what white people still doin' now. Dividing. Even among yourselves. Do you understand it? And what about all them slaves and slaughtered Indians, who gonna redeem them now?"

Just as the Shawnee chief Tecumseh had confronted the Ohio governor in the passage, Caleb was now confronting him. J.P. reflected and wondered if he should counter with examples of the violence the Shawnees had employed in their wars against the encroaching Europeans, or that the Red Stick Creeks had directed against American settlers and those branches of their own tribe who sought accommodation with them. He, after all, had done some reading too. But he was forced to admit that the preponderant response of the Indigenous was to seek, albeit under duress, reconciliation through treaties, most of which were later broken. And more recently, the civil rights movement had held the moral high ground with non-violent resistance to the terror of the Bull Connors and Klansmen. He began to wonder who was teaching whom.

"Come, let's read on," he said, letting Caleb continue in the book he had brought. J.P. had begun to give Caleb the tools for literacy, he realized; Caleb was now employing the literature to help find his identity and place in the world. And the language to confront me, ironically, in the way I confront him. He wondered if they couldn't somehow work together better to pursue the proper ends. His initial indignation when finding that his pupil was not adhering to his curricular plans began to subside as he recalled Tecumseh's words:

> *Brothers, we all belong to one family; we are all children of the Great Spirit; we walk in the same path; slake our thirst at the same spring; and now affairs of the greatest concern lead us to smoke the pipe around the same council fire! Brothers, we are friends; we must assist each other to bear our burdens.*

• • •

J.P. walked back to his car, but before putting the key in the ignition, he turned on the weather radio to learn that the depression had become a tropical storm with the name Bret, heading northward and showing signs of additional strengthening. When he got home, he checked his e-mail to see whether there was any word from Miranda, but his inbox contained no new messages. He turned on the television and rotated the dial in search of a report, but it was not the hour when news programs were usually broadcast. He wished now that he had subscribed to cable so that he might view the Weather Channel; when he had bought the TV, however, he thought that most of the programs were junk and that it would be a waste to proliferate nonsense in his household. He rarely even looked at the news programs to which he had access: it seemed as though the dumbing down was increasing exponentially. Since there was little he could do at the moment, he warmed up some leftovers before trying to distract himself with a novel until ten o'clock. But the text lay before him not as an open, colorful panorama of landscapes and street scenes, or as a stage of human passion, intrigue, and development, but as a random pattern of inky black marks on white paper. When the news finally came on it was reported that Bret continued to gain strength, information that only served to fuel a restless night.

As he lay in bed images whirled through his head, tossed together in confusion. Was it fate that was dooming his progeny and him as well? He recalled a trip that he and Diana had made to the Kunstmuseum in Basel at the time when their courtship was turning into something more lasting. He had caught up with her standing rapt before an enormous blue canvas of two figures linked in a peaceful embrace while their bedclothes swirled in waves around them, as though tossed on a stormy sea. "Bride of the Wind" was the painting's title, though "Tempest" and "Tristan and Isolde" were apparently alternatives that the artist, Kokoschka, had considered. The eyes of the bride were closed in satisfied repose, while those of the man were open, as though restlessly searching.

"Is that who we are?" asked Diana at the time.

Superimposed on his memory of the image were the opening lines of the poem Georg Trakl had written on this very painting, shortly before his own early death from depression and a cocaine overdose while serving as a medic in the carnage of the First World War: "*You I sing wild cleaving, in the storm of the night.*" A cruel blow had split J.P. from the bride to whom he had clung; was a new fissure about to separate him from his child as well?

Neither of his alarms, not the mechanical clock nor his own sense of dread, was able to wake him the next morning. When he finally roused from a restless night, he found he had missed the early TV news, and the *Press-Register*'s report in print was outdated at that point. Not surprising, he thought: everyone continued to call the paper itself by its old name (when they weren't using the more pejorative monikers 'mullet wrapper' or 'Cash-Register'), even though its owners had christened it with a new one a few years earlier. As he drank his coffee it occurred to him that the Sea Lab might be able to provide information, and after frantically searching in vain in the telephone book and calling the marine sciences department at the university to get the number, he dialed them up. Additional frustrating delays occurred as he was transferred from person to person, until someone was eventually able to inform him that the ship had radioed that thoey were heading northwest to avoid the storm's expected path and the strongest winds on the leading edge. He tried to console himself with this information: surely an experienced sea captain would know how to handle the situation. But doubts remained: do storms always take the expected path, and would the ship's new course keep its passengers at a sufficient distance from damaging blasts?

The ensuing hours turned into days, and the days stretched out as endless minutes as he remained glued to the weather radio to catch every update. On Saturday Bret (a name he found stupid and cursed at every opportunity) became a hurricane, ratcheting up his worry to a new level. To put his mind on something else he tried reading a few poems in an anthology of African American literature.

At some point the next day the telephone rang: it was Clotilde, who, with concern in her voice, was calling to see whether or not there was any word from Miranda.

"Have you been following it?" asked J.P.

"Of course I'm following it. My whole life has been punctuated by storms. Did I tell you that I lived through the Great Hurricane of 1906 right after I started first grade? We couldn't go back to school for weeks, it seemed like. And those poor people in Coden and Bayou La Batre who earned their living renting rooms to tourists in waterfront hotels. Completely wiped out."

"You've told me that many times."

"I suppose I have. We seem to mark our lives by those storms. And retell our stories often, as if attempting to outdo one another. I suppose I should try to avoid that temptation. Then there were two major cyclones in 1916, a big one that hit just west of town in the summer, and another that came in over Pensacola a few months later. And, as if on a pre-determined ten-year schedule, the hurricane of 1926—they didn't have names back then. That one brought an awful lot of flooding to some parts of the county, but we hunkered down at home and entertained ourselves. We weren't even concerned about a lack of electricity: we just lit the coal-oil lamps and put another Toscanini record on the hand-cranked Victrola. I could go on."

"I'd rather you didn't."

"I expect you don't. You were lucky to avoid all of that, living overseas like you did. You even missed Georges last year. Not a particularly strong storm—it sure flooded the downtown streets though."

"But I read about them, in the newspapers and in letters from you and Billy. I felt it along with you, as well as I could, which was probably little in comparison. But I really feel it this time."

"I can well imagine that you do. Have you heard any news? Poor thing, out in that boat on the water."

J.P. related what little he had learned, telling her that he was hoping for the best and would let her know as soon as he became aware of anything new. During the conversation the spark of life which was always so evident in her eyes was conveyed through the phone by the concern in her voice.

To calm his mind, and in an attempt to restore normalcy, he drove to Delchamps to buy bread and milk, but it did little good. By Sunday the winds had reached 145 miles per hour, bestowing on the hurricane a Category 4 status. Impressive to those eager to be thrilled from their safe distance, it was like a dagger to J.P.'s heart. The barometric pressure had inversely and accordingly sunk to 944 millibars or 27.9 inHg, an abstract statistic that took on concrete menace.

At some point in all this there was a frantic knocking on his front door: it was Frederic, who was trying to appear calm, despite his tired, haggard look and two-day beard. He was accompanied by a well-dressed, handsome young Black man of about his same size and build.

"I tried to call, but couldn't find your number in the phonebook, and information didn't have it either."

J.P. realized that this may have been due to the false assumption that his name was Williams, but merely replied, "I guess I haven't been here long enough to have made it into the book. I'll have to give it to you." He realized though that he would have to copy it off the label in the center of the rotary dial, since he had not been able to memorize it as of yet.

"Have you heard anything? I haven't been in touch with Miranda for days."

J.P. replied that he had had no luck either, only the report from the Sea Lab that the captain was planning to head the ship out of harm's way. "But let's call them again. I just heard from the latest report that the hurricane is heading northwest instead of northeast, which might mean it's now aiming at them."

"By the way, this is Malcolm, the lawyer from Washington I've told you about before. We're on our way up to Prichard to check on some things before he has to fly back."

"Pleased to make your acquaintance," said J.P., extending his hand to Malcolm, whose face bore a serious but friendly expression and who also offered a firm hand in greeting. "Come on back, we'll try to reach the Sea Lab."

J.P. dialed the number he had left on a scrap of paper by the phone, but he could get no answer. The switchboard was apparently left unattended on a Sunday. Frederic suggested going to the website to get the names of some of their employees and try and call them at home. After some impatient searching they compiled a list of numbers: they were unable to reach the director, and a couple of professors that they tried lived in town and had heard either no news at all or nothing since Friday. They finally reached a staff member who said she knew whom to call and would get back with them.

J.P. and Frederic sat back in their chairs and stared at each other and the floor, not knowing how to make small talk in the meantime. Malcolm was a patient observer. Finally the staff member called back, but she could offer nothing more recent than what J.P. had last heard. Her assumption that the radio had somehow been damaged offered little consolation.

"I guess there's nothing we can do but wait it out. And drink. Can I pour you a bourbon?"

"That would be great," replied Frederic.

"Little early for me," said Malcolm. "But a glass of water would be fine."

Each took a few sips before any words were spoken.

Finally, J.P. began by asking, "Miranda tells me you don't get along so well with your father."

Surprised at this turn in the conversation, Frederic paused before answering, "No, I don't. But that's a long, complicated story."

"It would have to be. I'm sure he thinks you should look at the world exactly as he does, but you have a different vision."

"How did you know?"

"You're not the only one. *'Deep in the festering hold thy father lies, the corpse of mercy rots with him, rats eat love's rotten gelid eyes.'*"

"I beg your pardon?"

"It's a poem I was reading last night. I took it as referring to me. My father died when I was young, so I didn't have to face him after that, nor even his memory, except on rare occasions. But the poem deals with a burden more widely shared. Especially by people whose sufferings we can't imagine."

J.P. thought he caught a gleam of recognition in Malcolm's eye, who had perhaps read Hayden, though Frederic looked somewhat confused.

"I spend my time with the law, politics, environmental science, and social services. For you, poetry provides the answer."

"Not the answer—it opens up new directions. I'm like Lessing: when given the choice of receiving the truth or searching for the truth, he chose the latter."

"Well, I hope the lines you quoted refer only to fathers and not to daughters."

"Somehow, I can't believe that they would refer to daughters. Despite my fears, my hope is stronger. There's another quotation, this one from Walter Inglis Anderson, which I ran across last week on my trip to Ocean Springs: *'The first poetry is always written against the wind by sailors and farmers who sing with the wind in their teeth. The second poetry is written by scholars and students, wine drinkers who know a good thing when they see it. The third poetry is sometimes never written; but when it is, it is written by those who have brought nature and art together into one thing.'* I think we still need that."

"Thanks," said Frederic, with a sincerity that J.P. noticed, as the young man finished his bourbon and carried his and Malcolm's glasses back to the kitchen.

At the front door he and J.P. promised to inform each other at the arrival of any news.

On Monday the first report was via the weather radio, which announced that Bret had weakened to Category 3 and made landfall on Padre Island. Shortly afterward, the Sea Lab called to inform J.P. that the crew of the *Cosmos* had restored the damaged radio and reported that they had successfully circumvented the storm to the south and would arrive home late the next afternoon. He called Frederic, and they were at the dock when the ship arrived to much jubilation and lengthy embraces. Miranda acted as though it had been nothing, and although she found their concern touchingly sweet, she teased them about unnecessarily suffering more than she did.

"Bobbing up and down in the swells, it was sort of like dancing."

Despite the relief, it took a few days for J.P. to fully calm down again. From habit he kept listening to the weather radio: Bret continued to weaken as it moved inland over Mexico, though it still brought extensive damage. Fourteen inches of rain caused heavy flooding in Coahuila, Nuevo Leon, and Tamaulipas, which destroyed numerous buildings and left many homeless. There were four deaths in Texas and three in Mexico, and $15 million in damage. J.P. noted how storms do not affect all equally: it was usually the most vulnerable to begin with who suffered most and had the least chance at restoration. He wondered as well whether more listeners were attuned to the number 15 million rather than to 7 as the cost of the devastation. His own price had been sleepless nights, and he resolved to concentrate now on what was most important. His thoughts soon returned to his own evolving plans, which involved a coming storm of a different sort.

φ

Dies iræ, dies illa
Solvet sæclum in favilla,
Teste David cum Sibylla.
. . .
Lacrimosa dies illa
Qua resurget ex favilla
Judicandus homo reus.

Huic ergo parce Deus:
Pie Jesu Domine
Dona eis requiem.
—Mozart, Requiem (K 626)

HE HAD MEANT TO CALL CLOTILDE, but hadn't, to arrange a time when they might meet and chat again. Instead, the telephone call came to him, not from his aunt, but from her caretaker Bertha, bearing the melancholy news that Clotilde had passed away peacefully in her sleep the night before. Hearing the unexpected tidings, he could do nothing but collapse into his chair in anguish. Was he unhappy for her sake that she was no longer able to partake of this life, or did the gloom revolve around the loss to his own life, which now caused him suffering? He recalled her fondly: a constant presence, a steady anchor, a moral beacon, one of his few reliable conversation partners, was now gone. He felt angry that there had been no warning, and he regretted not having had the opportunity to utter some final words to her: one's life story seemed to him an ongoing series of sins of omission. But what would those words have been, and are words ever final?

Ninety-nine, he thought, realizing that if she had lived until her next birthday in the coming year, the first of the new millennium, she would have completed a hundred. At least she did not have to suffer, and perhaps it's better not to have to face the new century, if the next go-round doesn't turn out any better than the last long and bloody one. Will it repeat the cycle of wars, genocide, racial and ethnic hatred, environmental destruction, starvation, brutal dictatorships, deadly pandemics, and threat of nuclear annihilation? Will it contrive other evils not yet imagined, or will it just muddle along on its own course? Maybe Clotilde looks at what's happened in the same way as Walter Benjamin's angel of history, which was in turn inspired by an image in a monoprint by Paul Klee:

> *He has turned his face toward the past. What appears to us as a chain of events, he sees as a single catastrophe that piles rubble upon rubble and hurls the broken fragments before his feet. This storm drives him unceasingly into the future, to which he turns his back, while the pile of debris grows in front of him to the heavens. What we call progress: that's the tempest.*

But she lived her life through all of that with integrity, and what significance do those rounded numbers have anyway? Lives, events, begin and end when they do. Hers was long in any case, unlike those cut short by an early death that seems so unfair. But on a geological scale, any human life is extremely short and unfairly cut off before it has had a chance to reach full development. Can't it nonetheless have worth, beauty, meaning within the brief span of its existence? Clotilde's life had a significance that he understood and cherished for itself. Like Diana's, which had an even more abrupt and tragic conclusion. He gazed out the window into the distance. And what of his own? He reflected on his biography and wondered how the many parts fit together: was it just a pile of rubble, a random collage, a void? It certainly did not seem like a book, which has a table of contents and chapters that follow one in another in a logical, timely order, along with an index to retrieve and comprehend the myriad details. How can books, however, come close to giving us a clue as to what it's all about, and isn't even their arrangement an arbitrary contrivance? He tried to imagine an alternate development for his life: what if he had come home to run the business but had taken it in a new direction, one which did not involve exploitation or corruption of individuals, the social fabric, and the environment? But that would have perhaps required a certain foreknowledge, which he lacked even now.

He imagined what he might have told his daughter had he been around at the age when she perhaps would have asked, "Father, what will be the trajectory of my life?" What could he have said, other than, "You'll finish the grades of school in numerical order, then go off to college from which you'll graduate in 4 to 5 years. Maybe you'll take a break of a year or two and then attend graduate school, which you'll also complete according to the prescribed guidelines. This will prepare you for a career, which you will enter and in which you'll advance. In the meantime you'll get married and have children, or not, depending on what you want. Your career will level off at a comfortable plateau, and at the appropriate time, you'll enter retirement, which you will enjoy, having prepared for it in the proper way. And at the end you'll die." And might she then say, "In other words, not the stuff of novels, or of dreams?" He realized, however, that what matters is not the skeleton of the framework, but how the life is fleshed out on a daily basis.

J.P. had begun to become increasingly aware of the diminution of his abilities in a number of areas: physically, he no longer had the stamina to continue tasks that failed to convince him of their importance, even though he could labor for hours on a project with hardly a break, as long as the work provided enjoyment; he could no longer turn his head as far backwards to the right or left, making driving more difficult and even causing pain as he sat in his chair or laid his head on the propped-up pillow at night to read. Mentally, he occasionally forgot names or no longer felt able or willing to think a problem through to its conclusion, even though he could recall with acuity events from his childhood that he had not thought about in years. Socially, he was less and less interested in others or being patient with them, frequently avoiding small talk or the kind word. He knew that much of this was normal and inevitable, but he wondered to what extent he should or could arrest the development.

Maybe he would someday simply disappear from the world like a bit of flotsam, eventually sinking beneath the waves after a storm. He began once again to think about his legacy and significance. He recalled how he had once found himself on a stage, amidst a group of dignitaries who were about to receive awards: in his case, however, he was only a substitute, filling in for a boss who couldn't be present. He was feted, but not for any accomplishments of his own. He felt that an obituary listing actual facts from his life would in some ways be a similar counterfeit adulation: the imposter phenomenon codified in the last words. He lightly stroked the arms of his chair as he tried to process the grief for Clotilde, while attempting to recall as many fond thoughts as he could.

When he called Miranda to give her the news, she said, "That's so sad. I wish I had had more time to get to know her better. When is the funeral?"

"Next Friday, I think. They don't have all the details yet. I'll let you know when they do."

"Are you planning to go?"

"I don't know that either. Depends how large it is, and how well I could blend into the background."

"You mean so that your brother doesn't see you. Don't you think this is getting kind of silly? Hasn't it gone on long enough?"

"I'm beginning to believe you're right. I just don't know if I'm ready quite yet. In any case, it'll be soon. What about Frederic? Are you going to tell him?"

"Will his father be there?"

"I'm sure he will be. He was one of the directors, along with Clotilde and just a few others, when my father ran the firm. I'm sure he'll wish to continue showing solidarity with Anthony."

"Frederic would probably prefer not to encounter him. I think each considers the other a lost soul. Besides, I'm still trying to avoid mentioning my own family connections on your account, awkward as that is. That's another reason I wish it could all get resolved. I'll try to get off work and slip in on my own."

When he later heard that the service would be held in the cathedral with the archbishop conducting the ceremony, he realized that he could probably attend unobtrusively, though he still had mixed feelings about being there: the eulogies of others would be mere words revealing more about the speakers than about Clotilde—he preferred to cherish his own expression. Besides, the pomp itself was a bit much: although she had never abandoned her childhood faith, he was sure that her wishes for a funeral, if she had written them down, would have been more modest. He suspected Anthony of concocting these plans to draw attention to the family and the firm. He decided finally to skip the ceremony and attend only the burial that would immediately follow it. Actually seeing the coffin lowered into the ground might give a sense of closure, as they call it, and enable him to come to terms with this death. He could ask Miranda later to report on the service, if she made it.

• • •

Autumn was drawing to a close, and the sky descended in a cadmium yellow wash from an overcast of charcoal grey: the low sun was hardly able to force its way through the clouds, lending the ones closest to it the palest of faded light, as though life were being washed out as well in the waning season; filaments of rain fell to earth in the far distance. There was intermittent drizzle in the cemetery as well, which made it seem even colder than it was. Gazing out at the threatening sky, he was determined to avoid succumbing to the pathetic fallacy, but he found he could hardly avoid it, sensing what he did of the impending situation in the world.

The trees and grass retained their green in the ever-verdant landscape, though the intensity was starkly muted by the darkness of the lowering clouds. J.P., having avoided an early arrival, parked his car on the grass behind the last of the vehicles that had gotten there before him. He adjusted his tie and his hair in the mirror before stepping out into the still air and walking in the general direction of the canopy that had been erected amidst a plot of graves on the right. Several mourners had already taken seats beneath the tiny bit of shelter that the canvas provided; others were standing in small groups, chatting with what he could tell were restrained but embarrassed attempts to find remarks that hit the proper degree of reverence. He was taken aback by a somewhat out-of-place, garish figure who approached him with extended left arm, as if to serve as his guide to the grave. Oiled hair of an unearthly orange color was plastered in place atop his scalp and draped across his brow, and artificially white teeth gleamed from an immobile, grinning rictus. Single beads of inexplicable sweat rolled slowly down his cheeks, smearing what seemed to be a patina of makeup: it looked almost as though he had tried to embalm himself but been able to achieve only a waxen approximation. My God, realized J.P. It's Mr. McPherson! Is he still alive? He was the director of the funeral home when I was young. It can't be—he would have to be older than the people he's burying.

Mr. McPherson placed his extended palm on J.P.'s right shoulder, giving a little push as he directed him to the place set for the ceremony. His polyester jacket, though dark in color, displayed an inappropriate plaid that he had no doubt found stylish at one time. "It's about to begin," he said. "Everyone should take their place."

"Thanks," said J.P. tearing himself away. "I think I'll just stand over there." Why was the man hurrying things? Didn't life go by fast enough, without having to rush death as well?

Unnerved, J.P. hastened to a small grove of cypress trees that kept him sufficiently far from the thirty or so mourners, yet still close enough to hear. He placed himself behind most of the spectators and out of Anthony's line of sight; he hoped that his beard would also hinder recognition. He tried to redirect his thoughts to his late aunt, though he was distracted by the sight of other relatives and former acquaintances. Anthony and his wife Susu (did they still call her that?) sat in the front row, along with "young" Anthony and his wife Tina. Also present were his ancient aunt Helen and her daughter Louise. Thomas Gonzalez, who now walked haltingly with a cane, would probably not spot him with his weak eyes: he must be well over ninety himself, thought J.P. He was surprised at how much they had all aged, though he shouldn't have been: after all, the clock had been working on him in the meantime as well, difficult as it was for him to admit the discrepancy between his outer appearance and his inner image of himself. What remained of Anthony's hair was grey, and his paunch had expanded considerably. Instead of the face of the satisfied, self-made man, his visage appeared careworn, though his lips with their seeming perpetual sneer indicated he did not lack the resolve to lash out when necessary. J.P. realized that his brother was intelligent enough to get ahead according to his own way of looking at things, though it seemed he made money in order to spite life in an attempt to convince himself and others that it provided pleasure; it was obvious, however, that it didn't make him happy. Anthony's wife was also grey, both her hair and the drawn expression of her face. Her dress matched as well: J.P. noted that the uniform black of the funerals of his childhood seemed to have fallen out of fashion. Louise had on a dress of a dark but brilliant blue, and Tina's was even a shade of deep red. He pulled the collar of his overcoat up around his ears and kept his tweed cap pulled low: the scattered raindrops gave him an excuse to keep it on, and when it came time to remove it, all the mourners would have their heads bowed anyway.

He turned when he heard someone coming up behind him: it was Clotilde's caretaker Bertha (he hesitated to use the word "maid") escorting Mary Merritt Hollinger, who was now her only ward. They had just arrived and were apparently forced to park in the next lane over. J.P. put a finger to his lips in a sign to Bertha not to say anything or acknowledge his presence: since she was well aware of his situation and wishes, she merely gave a dignified, barely perceptible nod and kept moving. How much we owe her, thought J.P. Why don't we let her speak, or more important, take the trouble to listen to her. Mary Merritt, however, whose memory was none too reliable, drew up and addressed him.

"John P., you here by yourself? Where's your wife?"

"My wife?" he asked, perplexed and speaking as softly as possible, hoping that his tone would cause her to lower her voice as well.

"Yes, I expected to see Elizabeth here."

She thinks I'm my father! thought J.P. I guess there's no escape. He realized that his parents had indeed been absent a long time, both on this earth and in his thoughts.

"I'm all alone," he muttered, before Bertha managed to pull Mary Merritt away and escort her to a seat that had been saved behind Anthony. His brother, who had noticed their approach, turned to ask Bertha something, but she only shrugged her shoulders.

As soon as they were settled, a single violin began playing a piece he recognized as the "Lacrimosa" from Mozart's "Requiem": the initial series of longer, single notes followed by two shorter ones seemed like footsteps leading to. . . where? *Dies irae*—day of wrath? he wondered. The music fell into a smoother, more flowing passage until it got louder near the middle and the bowing became more frantic: he could hear in his mind the chorus announcing that guilty man would arise from the ashes to be judged (*judicandus*). He immediately protested to himself, however, thinking that the guilty one was not lying in the coffin before them, but sitting in the front row: and shouldn't that one meet his judgment already in this life? The brief piece ended with its harmonious plea for mercy and eternal rest (*Dona eis requiem*). J.P. was sure that Clotilde had achieved her peace before she died. Whether Anthony or he himself would, remained to be seen. The book, which contains everything that exists and out of which the world will be judged, is yet to be written, he supposed.

It was at this moment that he spotted Miranda, wedged into the last row between some people he didn't recognize. More chairs than usual had been squeezed under the canopy because of the rain. She saw him too and gave a brief upward nod of the head in recognition. She at least was decently dressed, he thought. The priest then stepped next to the burnished mahogany coffin and began reading the appropriate lines from the prayer book. The liturgy has the benefit, thought J.P., of providing us with a formula for dealing with the situation so that we don't have to embarrass ourselves with the nonsense we might otherwise come up with. Since the service had just been held, there were no eulogies here, and the observance was briefer. When the lines had been read, attendants stepped over to lower the coffin into the grave with ropes. The priest cast the first handful of earth, followed by members of the family. J.P. wanted to pay his aunt this respect as well, but decided it would be just as valid if he waited until the others had cleared out of the area and he could do so unobtrusively. After exchanging brief comments with one another, and glancing nervously at the sky, most then strode rapidly to their cars.

As Bertha and Mary Merritt passed him on their way back to theirs, J.P. asked without looking directly at them, "Did my aunt see that you and Mary Merritt would be taken care of?"

"Mr. Anthony said we would be."

"I'm relieved, but you let me know if there are any problems."

Bertha nodded in recognition as they continued their slow pace.

J.P. was about to make his way to the grave when he was approached by a woman who had arrived just as the ceremony was almost over and been standing nearby. She was about fifty years of age, slightly plump, and wearing a light raincoat. Her somewhat disheveled, ash-blond hair was given a hint of order by a dark-blue scrunchie. She carried a small umbrella, which had been raised earlier, but was now collapsed.

"Excuse me, you are here viss ze Devaux funeral, no?"

Startled by this voice with a German accent, J.P. stared at her a brief moment before replying, "Yes, that's right."

"Perhaps you can tell me if John Prosper Devaux iss here?"

Cautious, J.P. inquired, "Who's asking?"

"I am Sabine Eberhardt. I was a friend of his wife."

"Sabine," he repeated in astonishment—the coincidence couldn't be real. "I am John Prosper Devaux. Were you. . . were you the one, with that other German, Hans-Ulrich, who picked up my wife in Beirut?"

"Yes," she replied meekly.

He churned inside with mixed emotions: he was suddenly eager to hear from a witness, but distressed to have this bitter experience, with which he had never fully come to terms, brought up once again in such an unexpected way and from one who was in some way responsible for putting Diana in the path of danger. He wanted on the one hand to make the woman disappear, but on the other, to learn from her everything he could.

"How did you come to be here?" he asked, not knowing how else to begin.

"It iss my first trip to the United States. I am traveling from Florida to New Orleans and then to California. I stayed last night in a hotel here and I happened to see the death notice in the newspaper this morning with the name Devaux. Then I remembered that Diana's husband was from here and saw his—your—name in the list of survivors. It said you lived in Washington, but I thought maybe you might be here."

"You thought correctly. What can you tell me? What happened after you left Beirut? What do you know?" Once he had started with his questions it was hard to stop. "You can't imagine how I've agonized all these years not knowing."

"I am sure. I am sorry. I always thought I should write you, but I didn't know how. Also, for many years it was better for me to remain, if not in hiding, at least not obvious. For a long time I was scared. And confused myself."

Miranda, who had been lingering at the grave, was now coming nearer, but she hesitated to interrupt the conversation.

"Miranda," said J.P., waving her over. "Here's someone you need to meet. This is Sabine. She knew your mother."

"Diana's baby? She would be so happy." Sabine smiled and looked her over from head to toe. "You are so alive, so like your mother."

J.P. noticed that the gravediggers were about to begin with the actual shoveling, so he first stepped over to throw in his handful of earth and to meditate on what his aunt had meant to him. He resented that he, the one closest to and most understanding of Clotilde, had been marginalized at the ceremony, and he wondered when he would have the chance to properly grieve. Those thoughts, however, were crowded out by the excitement concerning what of Diana might now be restored. Coming to terms with his grief for Clotilde would have to come later.

He, Miranda, and Sabine pulled three of the folding chairs into a tight circle so that the visitor might recite her tale. He had thought about inviting them to his house or to a café to get them out of the drizzle, but decided he did not want to put up with any delay in hearing the tidings.

"So you and Hans-Ulrich picked up Diana in Beirut? And then?"

"That's right, and first she took us to the children's clinic where she volunteered in the refugee camp. She was so excited about it, and you could tell how she had found something that she thought was a worthwhile outlet for her energy. And for the world."

"Yes, she communicated the same intense excitement to me. She was sometimes exhausted, and frustrated at the toll the situation was taking on people who had the fewest resources for dealing with it. I tended to stick to the more pleasant parts of Beirut, but she was not afraid to confront the reality of the squalor and hardships that so many faced. She reminded me that there was always someone worse off than we were, and therefore always something to be done. She was somehow fulfilled by this work."

"Yes, she was. And that was a difference we noticed when we now saw her again in that new place. Hans-Ulrich and I were still spouting our slogans and viewed everything through a narrow lens. We didn't see how it affected people. And we paid for it."

"And we have to conclude she was killed in the explosion?" J.P. said more somberly, eager for certainty despite his great reluctance to visit the painful moment again. He noticed that Miranda sat rapt and wide-eyed, wanting only to hear everything.

"Yes, I'm positive she was, along with Hans-Ulrich." Sabine continued her tale, first relating that rather than visiting the ruins at Baalbek, which had been merely a diversionary story for Diana and anyone else, they drove to a PLO camp in the desert and then to the Beddawi settlement in Tripoli. Chafing at the pace of Sabine's narrative, but nonetheless wanting to know every detail, J.P. asked her about their association with the Red Army Faction. She said that she herself had never been a member, and though she couldn't say for sure, she didn't think Hans-Ulrich had been either, though he seemed to be moving in that direction. But they both had been sympathizers at the time, and on one occasion had even housed RAF fugitives for a night in Hans-Ulrich's apartment in Munich. Diana, who had never been especially close to them, had never gone as far as they had and wasn't aware of the extent of their involvement; the pair realized when they got to Lebanon that she opposed violence altogether, despite her continuing, vehement opposition to those forces that were perpetuating injustice in the world. Hans-Ulrich argued with her the whole time: Diana didn't disagree that something needed to be done, she just felt the first task was to find the proper course of action and not settle for what she called the easy cop-out of guns and bombs. Sabine admitted that many people in the groups they hung out with were rather loose in their affiliations and secretly rejoiced when radical bands struck a decisive blow; she said that she herself later came to realize that many followed these groups for the wrong reasons: a romantic sense of glory, the wish to be accepted in certain circles, petty revenge. Hans-Ulrich's desire to pursue things further was what led them to visit Lebanon and see how different organizations were working together and learning from each other. He apparently also had some courier mission whose details he kept from her. Sabine was now sure he knew that their PLO guide would be showing them a bomb-making plant at the end of their visit, though the topic had never come up in her or Diana's presence, and she had had no idea herself at the time. Hans-Ulrich was probably willing to take Diana along to the facility in the hope it would impress her. Sabine came down with a severe stomach virus the last night they were in Tripoli and begged off the next day's excursion, desiring only to remain in bed. Diana wanted to stay and nurse her, but Sabine, to her sincere regret, urged her to go along, since she had no idea what they were going to visit; besides, feeling miserable, she wanted only to be alone and did not wish Diana to be in any danger of catching her bug.

"And then it happened. I learned of it soon afterward, and, when the shock and numbness wore off, I panicked. Diana's things were still in the room, and I disposed of anything that could identify her. I knew I would be in trouble and held for questioning, and the scrutiny would continue back in Germany. The government considered anyone guilty who had any association whatsoever, or at least we thought that's what they thought. And the boulevard press! They could ruin one's life. I left the country as quickly as I could, by way of Turkey, hoping no one would think I was involved in any way. It seems like weak excuses now. I was only thinking of myself. I should have notified you but thought even that was too risky, and I rationalized by telling myself you would figure out what happened."

J.P. had been listening in silence, and did not know if he could, or should, offer any words of forgiveness at that point, managing only to make a rather general comment: "I know how easy it is, simply to let time pass without attempting to set things right."

Miranda, hearing this account of a mother of whom she had almost no memory, had tears in her eyes.

"I know I should have tried harder to let you know what I knew. Especially since I could tell how much you meant to her. On the last night she said she was eager to get back home, as she called it. She said you taught her curiosity, the pursuit of knowledge, the breaking free of ideologies that claim to have the entire truth but often keep

us chained. Her remarks later made me start to look at things in a
new way. What the RAF did—just individual attempts. A desire for
power, or maybe personal fame, and no means of establishing a
better basis. Maybe we just need now to let it be."

Upon hearing of her mother's sentiments, Miranda glanced with
admiration at her father, who felt a great part of his burden had been
lifted.

"Needless to say, I admired Diana greatly and learned a lot from
her as well. Through her I was finally able to take a risk and participate more fully in life, and to integrate the pursuit of knowledge with
experience. Together, we created a new life. Why can't we say those
things to each other at the time?"

"I guess we have only ourselves to blame. Sorry. . . I did not mean
for that to sound so harsh."

"Can the truth ever be harsh?" he asked before continuing. "By the
way, did she happen to mention finding a name tag?"

"Name tag?"

"Yes, I had made a presentation shortly before that and whoever
printed the name tag linked me with an organization that I had no
affiliation with—at least not that I knew of. If she had seen it, it
might have upset her. Opposition groups tended to view it as a
source of evil at the time."

"No, she never mentioned anything like that."

Because she hadn't seen it, he wondered, or because she had and
it didn't matter? Either way, he supposed, it was somewhat of a
relief. But that was not important now. What was, was to be true to
her. He thought of Pericles' Thaisa, presumed to have died in
childbirth at sea and thrown overboard by superstitious sailors in
order to quiet a storm: years later, however, following a revelation in
a dream, Pericles finds her alive as a priestess in the temple of
Artemis. Unfortunately, J.P.'s mate could not be returned to life: but
had there not been a restitution of a sort? He realized that he had
learned to grow up through Diana by learning how to grow young: it
was as though he had been born as an adult and seemed to remain
the same age throughout his life—a precocious child, who had been
more interested in the conversations of grown-ups than the prattle
of his contemporaries. Similarly, but from the opposite direction, he

now knew for certain that Diana had embraced him as someone who could guide her in the wider wisdom of the world, even though she never stated this directly to him. What about the world, however? Would Diana be disappointed, disillusioned about what had become of the hopes of her active years? Had they dissipated like the ripples of the receding tide?

The goings and comings of life still seemed at times inscrutable. He wondered what his own course should be from that point on: was his life winding down or ready to start anew? He still saw plainly the viciousness with which the greedy constantly seek power and kick the powerless in the teeth with enjoyment and spite. When is rage justified, or even obligatory? When is it appropriate to refrain from rage? Are there only two extremes, putting up with injustice, or destroying the system in which it thrives by forcefully taking matters into one's own hands and dictating a new course? In the arc of history, he decided, justice doesn't simply arrive on its own. And even if the path is an asymptote that does not become tangent until infinity, shouldn't we do our best to approach it as closely as we can? He shifted edgily on the uncomfortable metal chair.

When Sabine had concluded her story, they sat in exhausted silence, punctuated only by the slow thud-thud-thud of falling clods of earth. J.P. asked their messenger what her plans were, and learning that she had to catch the one daily westbound Sunset Limited later in the afternoon, he suggested that they have a late lunch in a downtown oyster house before taking her to the station. Settling in to partake of their seafood, they noticed that every inch of the walls of the place was plastered with cards printed with the corniest of jokes:

> "*Diner: 'Say, waiter, this steak is awfully small.' Waiter: 'Yes it is, sir.' Diner: 'And it's tough.' Waiter: 'Then you're lucky it's small.'*"
>
> "*Politician: 'Did you hear my last speech?' Voter: 'I certainly hope so.'*"
>
> "*Experience is what you get when you're looking for something else.*"
>
> "*When it comes to giving, some people stop at nothing.*"

"Nervous cruise line passenger: 'Do ships like this sink often?'
        Captain: 'No, just once.'"
"No matter what happens, there's always someone who
        knew it would."
"Life is a game, the object of which is to discover the object
        of the game."

Was the atmosphere surrounding their meal incongruous or fitting? He tried to picture Diana in their midst, and decided she would have laughed.

X

*Here are the ones, who while they tarried in life, cast an evil eye
upon their own brothers, or pushed back against parents, and
entangled a client
in fraudulent schemes, those who rested alone on the riches
they'd won,
not setting any aside for their own kin—this crowd is the greatest in number.*

—Virgil, *The Aeneid*, VI, 608–611

RETURNING HOME ONE DAY, as the year was drawing toward its close, he found Ariel waiting on the front porch, leaning against the rail and singing softly, as was so often the case.

There will be no mourning over wayward loved ones
There will be no lonely nights of pleading prayer
All our burdens and our anguish will be lifted
At that meeting in the air.

"Ariel, glad to see you. What are you singing this time?"

"I think it's an old Carter Family song. My father left a ton of LP's of all kinds, and I've been playing my way through them. He had an amazing collection—glad it's been preserved and his old record player still works. Anyway, I've brought some more files for you to download, including some e-mails that might be interesting."

"Did you find anything more about possible bribes from my brother to various people regarding dealings with the Belgian company?"

"Yes, that's what I was referring to. Of course it depends on the interpretation. But within the context, it certainly appears that way."

"This is great," said J.P., who was tempted to rub his hands. "We can really go after them now. But listen, I've got another idea for putting a scare into them. The more we outflank them the better. Didn't you say you created running spreadsheets that you've tied into market reports so that they can keep daily track of their assets? "

"Yes, I've got that in place. It really pleased your brother to get a clear, up-to-the-minute read-out. He also likes the feeling that he's up on the latest technology, and that he doesn't have to make his own calculations from the listings in the morning paper. I think that might have solidified my job if nothing else did. So I want to be careful not to jeopardize it. I hope we can move cautiously."

"Are you planning to make a permanent career there?" asked J.P., his brow furrowed in skepticism.

"Not at all. In many ways, I can't wait to get out. But it's giving me experience for now and could provide a good recommendation for later. I can fly away to something else when the time is right. For now I've still got my debts to pay off."

J.P. guessed that meant he was the one keeping Ariel trapped in the job and tried to offer an assurance. "You don't need to remind me. If you didn't have such a strong sense of responsibility I might have forgiven them long ago. At any rate you won't owe much longer. Your help in this matter more than pays it off."

Going back to the topic of Anthony's vulnerability, he asked, "Anyway, do they happen to own stock in any of those technology companies, or dot-coms as they call them?"

"Quite a bit, actually. They said that when tech and internet stocks started climbing earlier in the decade, their broker informed them that it would be a good idea to get in on the deal."

"They tell you things like that?"

"I overheard them."

"Anyway, now a lot of people seem to think the dot-coms have climbed higher than they deserve, and the bubble will soon burst."

"That's what they say. I didn't realize you kept up with it."

"Well, couldn't you tamper with the financial reports to have them show fictitious losses that are rapidly increasing and make them believe that the implosion has already begun? You could insert values into the spreadsheet that indicate a sharp decline to make them think that the worth of their company is taking a serious hit. Or even adjust the formula to indicate that those stocks make up a greater share of their holdings than is actually the case? That would really put a panic in them."

"I could, but if they found out what had happened, I could be in big trouble. I don't know how long the false information could be kept under wraps. After all, they read the newspapers."

"But don't they believe your spreadsheet? Isn't that their new window on knowledge? Do they check quotes independently?"

"Anthony's pretty lazy in some respects. I don't know exactly what he does, but I suppose it's easier for him just to look at that one report. If he panicked and wanted to sell, however, he would find out. At least he's without a regular stockbroker at the moment: he had some sort of falling out with the old one, and they just recently parted ways."

"Not surprising, knowing Anthony. But if worse came to worst, couldn't you blame it on a minor bug in the program?"

"That wouldn't make me look so good either, would it? Tell me, is this what you did in the USIA? Spread misinformation? Was it in fact really the USMA?"

J.P. was abruptly taken aback. His enjoyment at spinning plans was suddenly confronted with a doubt about the means he was employing. Perhaps his project was indeed getting out of hand.

"No, I didn't spread misinformation. At worst, I glossed over negative aspects of our country's behavior." Though he didn't say it, he also recalled those instances when he suspected that some of his research activities were being put to shady purposes, or when his reports bordered on psy-ops. "Well, we can think about it for now," he continued. "Keep an eye on the dot-coms and how the software might be altered. In any case it would make more sense to wait and do it just before we act in order to keep them from finding out too soon that it was a hoax."

"Just what do you hope to accomplish anyway?"

J.P. had avoided articulating even to himself the precise results he hoped for and paused before answering, "I'm not sure. Maybe by indulging in greed, violence, fraud, and treachery, he is already in the lowest circles of the inferno without realizing it. Maybe he's a slave, entangled in the system that regulates his actions. Would you be happy if you were in that state? If Anthony comes to catch the slightest glimpse of the flaws in his view of the world and the wrongs he has caused, wouldn't that constitute at least a small victory, perhaps the most that can be hoped for?"

Still not altogether sure what they were doing, Ariel asked, "When do you plan to act, and what constitutes an act?"

"We should really get moving and not drag this out. You know that Global Millennial Carnival Ball they're planning for the 31st of December? I think that would be the perfect opportunity. It may provide the only instance for exercising the little power and art that I have. In any event, it would somehow bring it all full circle."

"Funny you should mention that. Young Anthony's wife is on the committee, and he asked me if I could help her out with the technical stuff for the opening *tableau vivant* that some of the other committee members are scripting. I already said I would, since I think it would be fun to take part in a show like that—you know: lights, music, smoke and mirrors."

"Sound and fury. Yes, that's excellent! Instead of a tale told by idiots, we could devise something cleverer that would really bring them to their senses. I didn't know that you knew how to do that sort of thing. I thought you were only into computers."

"Audiovisuals, media interest me too. It's all related in a way."

"I suppose I should keep up. I have to keep reminding myself that knowledge isn't communicated solely in print anymore. What have they got planned so far?"

"They want to highlight three hundred years of progress, anticipating the city's upcoming tricentennial. Costumed figures representing different groups from the area's history arranged on the stage, with multiple slide projections and videos and appropriately corresponding music."

"Above all, tasteful, no doubt. Indians welcoming the colonists, happy slaves helping their masters build up the new Eden, King Commerce contributing to the welfare of all—I get it. How hard would it be to create alternative slides and change the sound track?"

"Not hard. Since I would be coordinating all that on the computer, it would be easy to switch it to a different routine. They're mainly giving general guidelines anyway and leaving some details about specific images and soundtracks up to me." Ariel paused, then asked, "Are you *sure* your experience isn't in providing *mis*information?"

"You think what the city fathers and society matrons will come up with will be information? Self-serving fluff! This will just be our part in putting things back on an even keel. What do you know about music?"

"Ms. Young Anthony even asked me about that as well. They're going to have different bands playing music aimed at different age groups. She asked me if I could recommend a rock 'n' roll band, as she called it. I have some friends in a punk band that could use a gig, so I suggested them. Only I called them an alternative rock band to make them sound more palatable. The only problem was their name: 'The Gadarene Swine.' She didn't like that, so I said I would keep looking."

"Pity. They might have freed us of our demons. But I think I know how to solve the problem."

"How?"

"You renamed their genre: simply rename the band as well. How about 'Reap the Whirlwind'?"

"That might work. As long as she doesn't think it's some sort of satanic heavy metal group."

"This time be sure to tell her it's a Biblical name. Not inappropriate, I might add. It's what will result if the powers that be keep the lid clamped tight on injustice. We can be thinking about songs the band could work in. Ariel, you've made my day."

"Well, it gives me new energy as well. What the committee was talking about was kind of boring."

"Clichés. All they know how to do is to keep repeating the same. Inbreeding of ideas, an end to the dialectic. They sustain a ritual, which creates the illusion of logic and common sense. For our part though, we'll need to get to work and move fast."

"I'm up for it. Long as we're careful."

The enticements of the new project seemed to have overcome the earlier hesitancy concerning the appropriateness of their undertaking, even though this course would make it clear who was behind the changes. J.P. was already having magnificent visions of what they might create and imagining ideas to jot down in his book as he accompanied Ariel to the door.

Walking out to the car, his assistant began softly humming a spiritual:

> God gave Noah the rainbow sign,
> No more water but the fire next time.

• • •

But J.P. didn't remain alone for long: soon a familiar, dented car hauling a hulking, rattling trailer pulled up in front of his house. This time they're showing their faces, he thought, watching as Steve casually exited the vehicle with a graceful, two-fingered slamming of the door before sauntering up the walk and pausing only to spit off sideways into the grass. Either he doesn't suspect I know what they tried when they were last here, or he cockily doesn't care. Should I fire them on the spot, or try to bring them around somehow?

Trick walked back to the trailer to extract a rake.

"Thought it might be time to have your yard cleaned up for the winter."

"Might be, though it doesn't look too bad. What do you propose?"

"Rake up all this pine straw and carry it off. And all the leaves and sticks that are layin' around. Get rid of any scraggly weeds and trim out the deadwood."

"If you could do the same for society it would help."

"Beg pardon?"

"The pine straw—I suppose you'll sell it to some nursery and get paid twice for the same work."

"What good does it do you spread all over the grass?

"You could rake it under the azalea bushes for mulch. The cover, and the acidity, are good for their protection and growth. Think you could do that?"

"Might could. Whatever you say."

"How much?"

"Oh, say one-ten for everything."

"Come on, the yard's not that big. And I'm on a fixed income," replied J.P., using a phrase he had recently heard.

"But we got to put food on the table ourselves. We can't do it for less than one hundred."

"Ninety. But that's my final offer."

When an agreement was reached on the task and price, the pair set to work. J.P. watched them a while from the window and noted they were in no particular hurry: they probably had no other jobs lined up and didn't want to overexert themselves. He settled back into his comfortable chair and picked up his reading. Despite the lateness of the season, the weather was warm enough to leave the windows open. From time to time he caught snatches of Trick's laments to Steve about his sister's struggles with her son, who had become addicted to pain killers after an automobile accident. He had sought replacement drugs on the street and lost his job as a result, resulting in increased depression and a further downward spiral. Steve followed with his own complaints about still having to pay court costs despite having been acquitted of a minor traffic violation and how the government always had you coming and going. J.P. guessed their lives were full of problems he was completely unaware of, and he wondered whether either they or he would ever see a clear path out.

Sometime later, when the workers had finished and J.P. had halfway extracted the bills from his wallet but not yet handed them over, he couldn't help but remark, "Say, fellows, I was wondering. I notice you have a bumper sticker for 'Dupe' Duplin. Tell me how you think he's going to improve your situation."

"He's not like other politicians. He identifies with people like us."

"Because his slogan says 'He's one of us'? You believe him just because he says so?"

"No, he really is. He'll look out for us, instead of for people who don't deserve it."

"But he's a multimillionaire. Do you really think he has your interests at heart?"

"He made his own way. He came out of a simple background and figured out a way to make money. He came up with a product and got rich in the free market. Enterprisin', I call it."

"With a diet supplement, if that's not an oxymoron. He appeals to people's vanities and they think they've become enlightened and are shedding weight because of *Luz-Mor*, but they're actually dropping pounds because they're not eating other things. And they could do that on their own. Reputable, scientific studies have discounted the effects of his product, but people somehow ignore the facts because they wish to."

"But they do lose, and that's what they want."

"They convince themselves. Maybe that's all they want. Duplin makes money by promising a loss, and hopes to acquire political power by promising a gain—either way it seems like chicanery to me. Just exactly what sort of gain do you hope to see if he gets elected?"

"We won't have to take anybody's shit anymore, pardon my French. Isn't that what democracy is? We get enough votes, and then we rule. We'll come into our own."

"Your own? Can you even imagine what that would be?" J.P.'s voice took on an increasingly impatient edge.

"We'll have lower taxes, more money in our pockets, less tax dollars wasted on freeloaders. It'll help you too, believe me," replied Steve with the assurance of one who was certain of what he believed in.

"One thing I can believe is that his tax policies will help him and others in his income bracket who donate huge sums to his campaign. Crumbs will be thrown to those less well-off: enough to make them think they're getting something, without further busting the budget. They'll be happy as long as they think someone below them is getting the shaft. Are you sure you're not settling for the feeling of vindication you get when he mouths off about somebody else, rather than actually delivering anything? It sounds like the kind of scam you would invent, not the kind you'd fall for."

Steve gave him a hard look as if to ponder what he might be implying.

"Anyway, think about it. I just don't like to see anyone taken advantage of. And speaking of which, here's a little extra. Christmas is coming up before too long. Don't know that there'll be any need for more yard work before then."

Trick, obviously pleased, tipped his cap; Steve and J.P., each trying to decide whether true generosity was involved or some ulterior motive, merely gave one another a half smile and a nod.

As Steve zipped up his quilted, olive-drab parka and began walking back to the car, J.P. wondered whether the world can ever renew itself as long as so many people remain in fear, and because of their fears continue to hate and exploit others. Is it Duplin's fault or that of his supporters? Do people fall for the very worst, because they're acting on their own worst impulses? Without such adherents, the Duplins, who know how to take advantage of those impulses, would never get anywhere. Or was it the fault of the ones who really held the power, like Anthony and Alphonse and Sebastian, who stay in the background and let the Duplins do their dirty work for them, knowing they themselves will never be threatened? The Anthonys of the world can remain at a safe arm's length from overt violence, while enjoying the fruits of the inherent violence in the system. Or is it also the fault of people like himself, who fail to speak out and just let things ride along? Maybe it's the quiescent ones who allow the strong to take over.

Snapping up his head with a jolt, he suddenly realized that it was Thursday, and he would have to hurry to make his tutoring appointment.

• • •

Seated in the instructional room, he pondered whether he and Caleb might not find somewhere else to meet. Somehow the whole atmosphere bothered him more that day than usual: the color of the walls resembled dog puke; the shoddy construction merely deteriorated with age while failing to show the least sign of grace; and the greasy dust which coated the baseboards seemed to encroach on everything around, including his own skin. Are those who have the resources to build these things doing the disadvantaged a favor by erecting such structures to enclose them? What about his own tutoring endeavors? What good did they do? Reporting his hours provided a statistical illusion that something was being accomplished and even a reassurance to himself that he was performing a valid function: but did reducing his task to those cold facts really mean anything?

He glanced over the newspaper he had brought to see which article might be the most appropriate for reading. It was not unusual for Caleb to be somewhat late, since the buses were not always reliable, but today the minutes dragged on, and J.P. repeatedly looked at his watch. He wondered how long his current feeling of Yuletide magnanimity would compel him to wait. The carols that had been piping for weeks from the Muzak in the stores had not fully succeeded in penetrating his spirit. Finally his pupil ambled in and headed directly for a seat at the table. He was wearing an old maroon T-shirt with a slogan that J.P. couldn't read because the black vinyl jacket was zipped more than halfway up. One sleeve was smeared with dirt—he had probably been doing some sort of yard work, though probably not with Steve and Trick, whom J.P. had just left. Or maybe he had been back out to the Delta, competing for his place in that realm.

"What you got lined up for me today?" began Caleb.

J.P. grasped from the words and tone of voice of his only subject an acknowledgment of the existing power structure with a simultaneous questioning of its validity. "I thought we'd read something from today's paper," he said, handing over the main section of the *Press-Register*.

When he glanced down at it, Caleb immediately settled his eyes on the small, black-and-white photo of an African American youth enclosed in an article with the headline, "Tyriq Chatom Sentencing Scheduled for Today," a phrase he slowly sounded out.

"Well, we sure don't have to read tomorrow's paper."

"What do you mean?"

"We know what they gonna do to him. Still in his teens, got roped in by some bad dudes in his neighborhood, just happened to be in the wrong car at the wrong time when one of their stray bullets hit that bystander. They'll give him the electric chair, or maybe life in prison, which is about the same thing. It's really death in prison, since he'll never get out."

"We don't know for sure. Let's wait and see. The judge or jury might consider mitigating circumstances."

"How long you been livin' 'roun' here? Do you have any i-dea how many innocent people they are, sweatin' on death row with nothin' to do but wait 'til somebody tell 'em the exact time o' they date with Yellow Mama? Ever' now and then a lucky one gets let off, but most don't even have no way to get out the prison. Or, like Tyriq, these kids, guilty or not. You know what their real crime is?"

"No."

"Livin' while Black. You aks me sometimes why I go out to the Delta. When the po-lice gets a little too active and starts rounding up too many suspects, I find it best to hightail it a while and go out where I can ease my min'.'"

"Do you consider yourself Black? I thought you were mainly Choctaw."

"It don' matter what I think—it's what you people, like you put it, think. The ones that got the power defines who we is. You even call yellow black—how much sense that make? You consider yourself white? What is white? I can tell you what the ones who call themselves white always be doin' to us. Dependin' on who they got in they sights, they decide how to signify, dignify, stigmatize. Which one you gonna do next? You even know you'self? You may think you not doin' anything, but what you doin' to stop it?"

J.P., caught off guard, was aware of a tenseness in the muscles of his own face: he pursed his lips and squinted his eyes, as if to object to what had just been said, but actually just to make time to consider it for a while and realizing how closely it actually lined up with his own thoughts. He pondered Caleb's language, which despite or perhaps because of the emotion seemed to flow naturally, swing rhythmically, and express effectively through its color and tempo. It was locally idiomatic and natural and full of life, in contrast to his own stiffer, more grammatically correct, epigonisms. He found himself studying the language and locution of the pupil he was supposed to be instructing: who was the tutor here?

Realizing in any case that there was little more he could say to Caleb's observations, he turned back to the task at hand. Since Caleb's experience provided him more information on Tyriq Chatom than the sentences in the article would, they decided to read a more innocuous feature on the construction of a new playground in a poor neighborhood. A small but positive chipping away, or an excuse to avoid the basic conflicts and exploitation? It would actually provide

something for children, thought J.P., but how far it would go in
changing either side's feelings about the other? Sides? Why are there
sides? he asked himself. When would the illusion of race, still so real
today, disappear?

Caleb was reading more fluently now, and J.P. tried to praise him
profusely, hoping to allay some of the anger that the poor soul must
feel at the general situation. He wished, however, the indignation
toward society did not sometimes seem to be directed at him—after
all, wasn't he giving his time to Caleb and helping him acquire a
needed skill to allow him to gain a better foothold in the world? And
didn't he help him financially too, with small payments for odd jobs?
But when did paternalism end and generosity between equals begin?
He was once more annoyed that his lesson hadn't proceeded as
planned, but who was he to determine such things? And was he
really more afraid of an outright rebellion? He still hadn't gotten rid
of a slight nervousness concerning Caleb, a lingering suspicion that
the fellow could possibly become violent; he wasn't altogether free,
for example, of his fear with regard to Miranda. What right though
did he have to decide whether Caleb could rebel or not? It's not just
up to Caleb to change to fit into society, decided J.P., it's up to
society to change to admit Caleb.

● ● ●

Since there was still some time left in the afternoon, he decided to
swing downtown and straighten out some snafu that had arisen with
regard to his Social Security payments. He felt lucky to find a parking
space not too far away on Conti Street and, in his pockets, some
quarters for the meter. After conducting his business, he strolled
down Government Street to take in anew and at a leisurely pace the
sight of the old buildings and the changes that had occurred in the
streetscape over the years. He was still trying to figure out his home,
if that was even the right word. Would he really come to know it, or
anything else for that matter, to arrive at *anagnorisis?* He allowed
himself to be temporarily comforted by the continuing presence of
the Greek Revival Barton Academy, now the headquarters of the
school board, which had been standing on the spot for 160 years. His

father had attended classes there, though by the time he himself had come along his parents had decided to send him and his brother to the private boys' prep academy, rather than the new public high school several blocks to the west that had been built in 1926. He admired the balanced proportions of the imposing three-story building before him with its central portico and domed cupola surmounted by a lantern, which he recognized as a copy of the Choragic Monument on the Acropolis. He was pleased that at one time, at least, citizens had an appreciation for the classical and beautiful, and that they would devote such abundant resources to promoting education. He was less than thrilled, however, by the peeling paint on the stuccoed walls and the signs of water damage that indicated a deteriorating structure. Was it ever possible to keep what we have? But these thoughts were pushed aside by the doubts that he had come increasingly to experience. Was it purely a monument to aesthetic proportion and to the ideal of learning, or did its gleaming whiteness stand testimony to the social and racial hierarchy that it meant to impose and preserve by enlisting a limited interpretation of a heritage that it arbitrarily chose? In that case, perhaps the peeling paint was a healthy sign that we need to rethink and reform our sights and values.

Walking on, he encountered quite a concoction: century-old mansions, more recent arrays of nondescript small businesses, extensive parking lots and garages, and the inviting green of the plaza across the way, whose benches and statuary had been donated by the sister city of Malaga. In some spots along the street the live oaks were still there to provide welcome shade in the heat of the summer; in others they had disappeared, leaving nothing but asphalt. Across from the handsome Presbyterian Church, built in the same year and by the same architect as Barton, was a tall, cylindrical hotel that had been erected during his years away. J.P. sat down on a bench and tried to assimilate in his mind the jumble of the coexisting. Warmed from his walk and the anything-is-possible-in-December weather of the Gulf Coast, he unfastened yet another button of his jacket. He had to crane his neck to gaze upward at Government Plaza across the street, which was only five years old. Towering façades of windows and stone on the two ten-story halves were connected by a lofty, glass interior atrium. Curved, barrel-vault roof structures, which suggested sails, steel spars rising from the apex, which resembled masts, and cylindrical forms that looked like funnel stacks gave the edifice a nautical feel. J.P. chuckled at the locals who were still fussing about the building, either because they considered it an out-of-place monstrosity or because they hated the expenditure of any public money and regarded downtown as a crime-ridden site to be avoided at all costs. He wondered why architecture could not just as rightfully appeal to the town's maritime traditions as to any Greco-Roman heritage it might claim to have. It was certainly more interesting than the merely functional structures of the preceding decades, though he himself had mixed feelings about it. Maybe it was just a random pastiche of styles, an unfortunate postmodern combination resulting from a lack of certainty about what it should be: the manifestation of a deficit of knowledge and inability to forge its own expression. But in that case it perhaps echoed the overall street scene, itself an evolving mixture, sometimes displaying a graceful harmony of architecture and landscape and sometimes a disturbing clash. Some people can't stand any change, he thought; why not give them something new to think about? Each age had to come up with its own view of what was valid: unfortunately, many of the recent ones seemed to have settled too frequently on the unconvincing. Would society as a whole ever get it right? In any case he enjoyed just sitting and letting his thoughts delve into the place, its manifestations, its history, its sparkle, its filth.

He closed his eyes and pondered the manner of his sensation of his surroundings, how extended experiences permeate one's body and imperceptibly influence one's perceptions over the succeeding moments before giving way again to one's habitual outlook. These feelings are in some respects like those of a dream: the unvoiced awareness, for example, that a character is a known friend, even though she looks nothing like any friend in real life. Or how the particular route one takes in returning home after a long absence imprints itself on the way one views one's home. If he drove back on country back roads to approach his abode over the minimum number of city streets, he often had the feeling that the house was set at the edge of a vast rural landscape of fields, forests, shacks, and farmhouses. Or if he spent time at the beach and came back by the long bayside road, he would feel that he lived in an almost tropical setting close to palms, water, and warm breezes. But if he took the longest path through the town itself, through gritty urban neighborhoods filled with litter and abandoned storefronts, he tended to have the impression that he dwelt in the midst of a sprawling, stagnating city. The optical view of the house is the same upon each arrival, but each felt perception of its place within its environment is different and no less real, though the effect fades over time.

He opened his eyes and noticed from a sign on the lamppost that he was sitting at a bus stop; he was soon joined by a white man in his twenties chatting away on a cell phone.

"It'll take me a while. I got to ride the bus. My car's in the shop. . . . Yeah, didn't I tell you? Some nigger wasn't payin' attention and rear-ended me. . . . Yeah, you're right. No tellin' what people like that might be on."

After listening to several similar comments J.P. tried to give the man a disapproving look, disheartened that this generation did not seem to be aware of the struggles of the outgoing century and the reasons behind them. The man, however, gazed straight ahead and seemed to see only in his mind's eye the person he was talking to. Just as the fellow was snapping his phone shut, J.P. heard a new voice.

"Jeff, my man, what's happ'nin'?"

A Black man of the same age had just strolled up, and the two greeted each other with a slap of the palms and an interlocking thumb movement with which J.P. was unfamiliar.

"Not much, dude. How 'bout with you?"

"Same old same old."

"I hear ya."

"Say, they want us to be at work at the same time tomorrow?"

"That's what the man said."

"Never ends, does it?"

"Doesn't seem to."

J.P. realized he would never have been able to duplicate the relaxed idiom of these workmates and tried to reconcile the current conversation with the first man's previous dialogue on his phone. Are we making progress or not? he asked himself, as he did periodically, looking back on the century's history: was it in a spiral or a straight line, proceeding by fits and starts, with a step forward followed by a step or two back? Slavery was followed by emancipation, but after that came Jim Crow and the regressive constitution of 1901; segregation had officially ended more recently, but the old state constitution was still in force. He had even read that the anti-miscegenation laws were still on the books. But civil rights had come along with affirmative action, while many were still waving the Confederate flag. There's so much asynchronicity that it's hard to sort it all out. Things are better, but are they good enough? Surely the coming century will get it right. Or will it?

A bus pulled up with a loud whooshing noise and a piercing squeal of brakes. The two young men entered, and the driver kept the door open while looking at J.P., apparently expecting him to ascend the steps as well. After the situation registered with J.P., he indicated with a wave of his hand that he was not going anywhere. But the smell of exhaust from the departing bus prompted him to stand up and proceed on down beneath the wrought-iron galleries of an old federal-style building that had been one of the city's more venerable hotels in his youth; now it apparently housed law offices. Before rounding the corner of St. Emanuel Street he stopped himself from giving a perfunctory salute to the statue of Admiral Semmes, who had long ago been put on a pedestal but, rather than the waterfront, he now guarded the entrance to the tunnel which had been constructed some time later. Frozen in bronze, what did the old navigator see, and who saw him anymore, or more precisely, what did people see in him? Had the idea that had put him there become frozen in people's minds as well, was society itself in stasis? Erected in 1900, the same year as Clotilde's birth, the statue had stood for 99 years. He had been a fixture of J.P.'s youth, taken for granted by him back then as a hero, but a hero for what? What did he represent? The Confederate cause of 1861, the white supremacy reemerging with its new racist constitution at the time of the erection of his statue, bravery on the open seas, or simply the aesthetic ideals of the eminent Bohemian-born sculptor of monuments who had designed the work? He tried to sort through the over-determined multiplicity of meaning. One might admire the derring-do of the bygone blockade runner but shouldn't deny that he had considered Blacks inferior and cast his lot with a state contrived in order to preserve slavery. A purported memorial, not a memory: rather, a fabricated substitute for memory, foisted off on an unsuspecting (or even fully aware) public. It's a good thing the cause he fought for lost, thought J.P., believing his Aunt Clotilde had endured the test of time a lot better. The statue merely preserved the attitudes of its era in cold stone and frozen metal, whereas she had remained open to change and was not afraid to embrace it. Like the anole chameleons that run around our porches and can shift from the drabbest, most unobtrusive of grey-browns to a vibrant, electric chartreuse. Although the brazen navy man once stood as a solid part of a seemingly stable background attesting to the way things once were and therefore were still assumed to be by those who unquestionably accepted what had been passed down to them, the world had shifted in the meantime, calling for a reconfiguring of that background. We shouldn't forget him, but we shouldn't continue to revere him. Besides, what the erectors wanted to memorialize was not the naval hero himself, but their own white dominance. An unchanging, reified statue cannot by itself embody the situation we find ourselves in; only a narrative can begin to do that, mused J.P. The true iconoclasts will not sweep history away, but will regard it with a keener eye and offer a better interpretation. The old warrior will not disappear, but will form part of a different constellation. Not just the statue, but the underlying outlooks will have to be changed. I think we're ready to put the admiral to rest and find a new role model: someone who struggled for inclusiveness, for resisting oppression rather than abetting in its preservation. Diana would have been able to provide a few ideas. With determined resolve, he converted his unthinking, incipient salute to a dismissive wave of the hand.

He crossed Dauphin Street to Bienville Square, glancing back over his shoulder at the Van Leyden Building, where he had spent many summers working in the family firm. That's all past, he thought, water under the bridge. Anthony had moved operations out of the newer building his father had erected to an even larger tower nearby, though J.P. doubted that bigger was necessarily better. Since he was in no hurry, he took a seat on a bench by the multi-tiered iron fountain and, to the trickling sounds of the watery bounty, watched the handful of pedestrians passing through: businessmen on the way back to their offices, a couple of homeless men, some tourists, and a few who simply seemed to have leisure time. He noticed a couple taking photographs, close-ups and long shots, of themselves and the surroundings, and he wondered why they felt a compelling need to seize those things and what they would later do with the captured images. Why not just look and remember? Wouldn't one then be more likely to notice and appreciate the crystalline glints of the specks of quartz in the rock, the raw umber of the dirt caught in its fissures that glowed warmly in the light of the sinking sun, and the velvety fuzz of moss that shone fluorescent and dusky green in the flickering chiaroscuro, rather than view the object as a "beautiful motif" that required a fixing possession, a possessive fix, that one would file away for later recall when one sought it in an album, if one ever bothered to do so? Unlike the days when the clock of his professional life dictated the pace of his activities, he now realized that on occasion he could exert enough control over time to take in the seasonal, brilliant yellow of hickory leaves amidst the green of the surrounding foliage or the seemingly impossible combination of various notes and patterns supplied by all the different instruments of the orchestra, arranged in such dissimilar ways by Boccherini and Stravinsky.

A woman in a long, orchid dress and elegant, sable jacket entered the square at the opposite corner and came striding toward the center. As she approached, he was struck by her beauty, but when she came nearer he observed that her face was marked by several apparent flaws: an asymmetry in her mouth that raised one side of her upper lip in an enigmatic expression, and a lack of parallelism in her eyes that caused the left one to seem to view him acutely from the side. But instead of detracting from her beauty, these intriguing features made her all the more appealing. He regarded her for what she was instead of what he wished to impose. Aware of his perceptions, he was happy to note that certain feelings were still there. He followed her with his eyes as she disappeared onto Conception

Street; he then lifted his gaze to the statue of Cupid, cocking his bow atop the fountain. Love or covetousness, he wondered, before chastising himself for the ridiculous need to seek symbolic meaning in everything—things should be taken for what they are at the moment, even as they are making a transition to the unknown.

Five o'clock, the time usually assigned by the world as the point to wrap things up for the day, was approaching; he considered wandering over to De Tonti Square to see what might have changed there during his absence. But he decided it was getting late and he could do that on another occasion. Instead, he headed back toward his car. Proceeding up the street and noting the new shops, restaurants and overall development that was beginning to occur amidst the historical structures and dilapidated buildings, he suddenly stopped short in panic: a dozen yards ahead of him on the sidewalk stood Anthony, talking to a man with a pencil behind his ear and a drooping set of plans between his extended arms. Anthony was pointing alternately at the blueprint and at the abandoned building before them. The crumbling structure and its lot were filled with rubble, but few would discern the footprints of those who had once walked there. J.P. averted his face as if to stare at the pottery and paintings behind the glass of an artists' coop gallery, but in fact he continued to study his brother out of the corner of his eye. He realized Anthony had spotted him at the funeral, but doubted that any sort of recognition had occurred. Why not confront him now and get it over with? It might end with a certain finality in fisticuffs, a wrestling match with hands around each other's throats until one relented or the other took his last gasp. No doubt the former football player would triumph, but even if the odds unexpectedly ended up in J.P.'s favor, would that solve anything?

To avoid an actual encounter, he decided to keep his distance while continuing to evaluate the situation. Always scheming, or was it "planning"? Was Anthony going to demolish and rebuild with cheap materials, replacing old blight with new, or was he going to renovate and restore? He watched as Anthony, with an impatient nervous nodding of the head, listened to what the other man was saying. His brother then pointed demonstratively to the building and lowered his extended index finger firmly to the outstretched blueprint, tapping it decisively while saying something in no uncertain terms. The other man shrugged his shoulders briefly, then nodded in assent. The architect may be the expert, thought J.P., but it's obvious who's in charge. He briefly considered that Anthony's deeds were perhaps not all bad, that it took a certain amount of action to get things moving; he was forced to admit that the historical buildings in the city were new at the time they were built. When people imagine they are longing for the past they tend to deny what the past really was in its day. Nostalgia is in fact often yearning for the oldness that exists only in the present. If we are true to the intent of the original builders, he asked himself, wouldn't we be erecting new structures of our own, in keeping with the spirit of our times, rather than in continuously preserving the old? Or mix the two in the right way? Was Anthony actually more like those pioneers than he himself, who was so concentrated on preserving their memory, their remnants, their ideas? Edifices of stone and brick might provide more lasting monuments than most of the print that is churned out. But he remembered that he had other fish to fry with regard to Anthony and reminded himself that on balance, he believed that what his brother had done in the past was more detrimental than beneficial. Turning his back on them, J.P. crossed Dauphin before reversing his direction one more time and heading over to Conti, resolved more than ever to carry out the plans he had begun to put in motion. Or were they schemes?

• • •

Back at his house he went to the kitchen to check whether the refrigerator contained something he might warm up for supper, or whether he would have to drive down to Mack's Wheelhouse and order a mixed seafood platter with hush puppies and cole slaw. Preparing food for himself was no problem: although he had never spent a lot of time developing his culinary skills, he had managed to keep himself fed during all the years of his wandering, working life. On the top shelf were plastic containers of leftovers, one of okra and one with the crowder peas he had prepared a few nights before. The pale, grey-brown liquid in which they were submerged did not look particularly appetizing, but the rich aroma he sensed when he subsequently warmed them up in the saucepan brought on immediate pangs of hunger. He found a slab of ham wrapped in a piece of tinfoil: he wished he had a microwave to warm it up quickly, but an empty space on the wall with holes where screws had been only advertised the absence of that appliance. He did not know whether the previous occupants had ripped him off, or whether it had been theirs to begin with. He told himself that the toaster oven would be almost as fast, and began setting the table. He also warmed a slice of cornbread that Bertha had given him and served the peas in a bowl, enjoying the salty, spicy taste of the pot likker more than the peas themselves. I suppose a Bordeaux goes as well with this as with *boeuf bourguignon*, he said to himself.

At about that time there came a knock at the front door, and he was delighted to see that it was Miranda and Frederic.

"Can we come in?"

"Of course you can come in. You don't need to ask," he said with a smile.

"What are you doing?" asked Miranda, as she removed her scarf and lightweight, pale-blue jacket, which was stylishly cut short in the waist. Frederic unzipped his fleece, but kept it on. Both were comfortably dressed in blue jeans.

"Finishing up my supper. Can I offer you something?"

"Thanks, we already ate. But don't let us disturb you."

"You aren't. How about a glass of wine?"

"We won't say no to that."

"Let me shove some of these books aside to make room. Frederic, grab a couple of glasses out of that cupboard if you don't mind."

"Don't mind at all."

"I've got to use your bathroom first—'Little girls' room': isn't that what your generation so endearingly called it? I had a beer with dinner and I'm about to burst."

When Miranda returned, she put her hands on her father's shoulders, giving his clavicle a squeeze on either side. "You know, Dad, you really should get your bathroom redone. I had to jiggle the handle several times just to get the toilet to stop. And that aqua tile with the cracking grout! Is that your way of hanging onto the glorious past? Old times here are not forgotten?"

"Look away. I'll get around to it one of these days, I suppose."

His daughter gave a knowing smile and asked, "Are you by yourself?"

"Ariel was here earlier."

"And? What were you two plotting?"

"The way we'll finally confront my brother. It'll be accomplished by the end of the month."

"Your brother? Plotting? Miranda never mentioned an uncle."

"Yes, I'll explain it later."

"It's about time, for various reasons," chided Miranda, her face taking on a serious look.

Trying to change the subject, although he was actually staying on the same topic, J.P. turned to Frederic and asked, "Did you ever find out anything more about whether Devaux Brothers had any prior knowledge of pollution when they built the DelMar Apartments?"

"As a matter of fact, I finally ran across something, or I should say 'we.' Where would I be without your wonderful daughter? There's a report made by an inspector after the Devaux firm expressed interest in the property, which I photocopied. The inspector documented the pollution on the site and recommended against construction there. But I'm sure they got the property more cheaply as a result and apparently covered it up. I'll have to do some more digging, however."

"Warts on the ass of progress is what Ariel's father Billy would have called them."

"Dad!"

"The words are nothing compared with their deeds. But what you've come up with is excellent! Just as I suspected. It's all coming together."

"As long as it comes out all right," said Miranda.

"Your brother? Your suspicions? Is there some connection here?"

"You're obviously as smart as Miranda thinks you are. In any case, you've passed the test in my book. As I said, it will all soon be clear. I hope everyone will understand it better by and by."

"We can't wait till then. In any case, I'd like to see your book sometime. I'll bet there are a lot of people that don't come off too well."

J.P. quickly realized his daughter was referring to the metaphor contained in his last remark, not to any knowledge of the ledger he was keeping. He quickly shifted to another topic.

"By the way, I was wondering if the two of you are planning to go to the Global Millennial Carnival Ball at the end of the month."

"I read about it," said Miranda. "Why?"

"I'm sure all my relatives will be there," said Frederic. "It's the sort of thing I used to have to go to but have recently tried to keep as far away from as possible."

"It might be interesting, bringing a lot of things together. Not just this locality with its sister cities—Worms, Malaga, Pau, Rostov-on-Don, Ichihara, Košice, Havana, Veracruz, and whatever they all are—but the Black and white carnival societies, civic and business organizations, old and young. And who knows—there could be even more expressions of unity that develop."

"You seem like an unlikely civic booster. Now you've got me intrigued."

"I'm sure you won't be disappointed. I can get you tickets."

"As long as I don't have to sit with my father and uncle," said Frederic.

"No, you can sit with me. I've reserved a table on the periphery. In the shadows."

"But I declai-yuh, I don't have a *thang* to wai-yuh," said Miranda in the thickest of local accents that she had learned to imitate.

"And I don't know if my tails will still fit."

"Don't worry. Formal attire is fine, but for this ball, not just members of the mystic societies but anyone attending can dress in a costume of your choice, Mardi Gras or international. That way no one will recognize you. That's what I'm going to do. Mystify in my own way."

"Well, I suppose," said Miranda. "It could be fun."

"And perhaps instructive as well: as Horace put it, not just *delectare*, but also *prodesse*."

"Always the Latin teacher. But we came here for another reason, Dad. Our own 'expression of unity,' as you put it."

J.P. looked at her with an expectant glance, not knowing whether her tidings would be good or bad news for him.

She reached over and took Frederic's hand in hers. "Frederic and I have decided to get married."

He inhaled deeply before replying. "Well, that is big news. Somehow, I can't say I didn't expect it."

"That's two negatives in one sentence: I hope you view it positively."

"Of course, of course. It just takes a moment for it to sink in. You've thought about it seriously?"

"No, Dad, it was the result of a sudden whim." She paused with a sparkle in her eyes before adding, "Yes, of course we have."

"I realize that. I've seen how well you consider things. Tell me, who proposed to whom?"

The young couple immediately looked at each other and paused a split second before bursting into laughter. "We both did," they said.

"Well then, it's all right. Frederic, you may think I have been harsh with you at times, but you cannot imagine how dear this daughter has become to me, how much I love and respect her. If you were ever to mistreat her, you would be sure to incur my never-ending wrath."

"I have no fear of that, sir, and you shouldn't either. I've also come to see what you have seen. Be assured, we're both in it for the long haul. We have only each other's interests at heart."

"Then you have my blessing," J.P. said as he placed his hand on theirs. "Let's raise a glass to celebrate."

He worried that his remarks might have sounded like sesquipedalian platitudes, archaic phrases, though he completely meant what he had said; he just hoped that the others found them convincing.

And he trusted that the union was not the restoration of an old order, but the beginning of something new.

Ψ

Imagination! who can sing thy force?
Or who describe the swiftness of thy course?
Soaring though air to find the bright abode,
Th' empyreal palace of the thund'ring God,
We on thy pinions can surpass the wind,
And leave the rolling universe behind;
From star to star the mental optics rove,
Measure the skies, and range the realms above.
There in one view we grasp the mighty whole,
Or with new worlds amaze th'unbounded soul.
                    —Phillis Wheatley, "On Imagination"
                              (1773)

HE HAD PARKED HIS CAR IN THE PUBLIC GARAGE and was crossing the pedestrian bridge that spanned the six busy lanes of Water Street. The traffic was lighter than on a business day but still somewhat nervously hectic as drivers hurried to accomplish whatever it was they had to do on this New Year's Eve. He had never understood the significance of the date himself, or why it represented a reason to celebrate. Every day, every moment was the start of something new. This was even recognized in a cliché, though he was annoyed by the saccharine bromide exhorting one to heed the first day of the rest of one's life. Why was December 31st, especially this particular year, endowed with symbolic significance? Because of what was ending, or what was beginning? Hope for the future, he supposed, though he had lived long enough to know that forward motion in time does not always bring improvement. He paused to stare out toward the riverfront and the public park, which had replaced the old corrugated sheds of the banana docks where he had watched stevedores unloading ships from Central America in his boyhood days. Directly before him was the modern convention center, barely six years old, in glass and gleaming white with its graduated spire pointing upward: to greater things no doubt—*per aspera ad astra*. The supports looked like the fins of a rocket which was yet to take off, illustrating the epithet of local wags for the city as a site of 'perpetual potential.' He wondered when the repressed energy might become kinetic. For the moment, there were only a few wisps of clouds in the pale grey sky, motionless, as if there were no weather at all.

Inside, in the lofty-ceilinged lobby area, attendants in black trousers and maroon vests were busily stacking programs on tables for the evening's carnival ball. J.P. grabbed one of the bright purple brochures with its golden images of folly and diverse masks and read over the list of hosts, advisors, reception committee members, Chamber of Commerce participants, Mystic Society and Sister Cities representatives, and all the others that were not to be excluded. Prominent on the list were Alphonse Rapier, designated by his position as mayor as host for the occasion (the king of the ball, thought J.P.), Alphonse's brother Sebastian, and his own brother Anthony, as well as many others whose last names read like a local version of Burke's Peerage. Also listed were African American citizens of the city, including those who held elected office, and the royal courts of both the white and Black carnival associations. Progress perhaps, but had well-meaning appeals to right moral behavior been sufficient to bring this event about, or was economic self-interest the factor that enabled it to be staged? Or did that matter? And was this pageant sufficient for convincing the public that segregation had been overcome, when in so many ways it hadn't? He had realized for some time that Anthony did not have to feel troubled by the presence of Black office-holders, police chiefs, and teachers in the formerly all-white schools. Successful business-men like his brother knew how to take advantage of capitalism's chameleon-like adaptability which enables it to survive and even expand. But will it at some point inevitably crumble, and will they then be left behind? They are not outright racists, acting from ignorance or primitive fear and hatred, but willing to overlook and even exploit existing racism to maintain power in a system in which not all share, but which continues to rock along nonetheless. No need to be a racist when the structure does that for you. Also singled out for attention this evening, he noted, was a delegation from Brussels: not a sister city, but as J.P. surmised, not coincidentally chosen, since it was the headquarters of the chemical company with which Anthony and Sebastian hoped to cut some sort of under-handed deal. The contributions of business concerns were duly listed, stressing the economic basis for the cultural overlay. As usual, things were storming in his own mind.

After some searching he finally located Ariel in a cubicle overlooking the two large ballrooms whose dividing accordion wall had been pulled back to provide a larger venue for the festivities. Ariel was bending over a computer and rapidly punching keys in response to bright images that appeared on the screen.

"Everything going okay?"

"Technology always comes up with snags to slow you down, but yes, I think I've got it under control. The backdrop projections and canned music that the committee envisioned will begin the program, but we can segue pretty seamlessly to the changes you wanted. I even told Tina and the group about some of the ones that appear convincing enough, though I didn't reveal everything. They seem content to leave matters they don't understand to somebody else. Besides, there's been a rush to put it all together, and different members of the committee have been supplying things piecemeal. I told them I was collating all their suggestions; no one's seen a finished product. The 'actors' don't really act: they just pose, so it's easy enough to get them to follow the instructions. Most didn't even need to rehearse."

"'Actors' is indeed the wrong word. In German they would be called '*Statisten*,' extras who just stand there. Maybe that's what most of us do anyway, just stand around waiting for things to happen, rather than act."

"Here let me show you how it looks so far."

J.P. was thrilled to observe the visuals and music that Ariel had put together and was gratified that the few weeks they had spent in frantic researching of facts, ideas, prescriptions, images, and sounds might actually pay off.

"I tried to make the transitions subtle—some might not even notice it at first. But if the higher-ups get pissed and I get fired at Devaux, which is not at all unlikely given my role in this event, I've resigned myself to the thought that at least my freedom from financial obligation to you will let me make a fresh start. Assuming you carry through on your part. Working on this project is like a whole 'nother job. And unpaid at that."

"Unpaid is not exactly accurate. Anthony's crowd is paying you for the part they roped you into. And as you just indicated, what I contributed to your education and medical expenses, helping you become what you are, is not nothing. Starting tomorrow though, you will indeed be free. And, I hope, the rest of us as well, if we dare. How can I help you out now?"

"There's not much you can do. Most of it's on the computer. But you could go down to the main floor and let me know about the acoustics and volume when the sound's turned on."

J.P. complied, indicating from below with his thumbs whether the audio was okay or whether it needed to be turned up or down. Everything appeared to be proceeding as he had directed it. When he returned to the projection booth he mentioned that he had not had lunch and was thinking of going out to get some, but Ariel had brought a sandwich and still had too much to do testing the lighting to be able to join him. Besides, a member of the program committee was scheduled to check in and get an update, and it would be better if J.P. were not there.

Outside, J.P. buttoned his jacket against the chill as he crossed Water St. again and headed up to Royal; looking down the street he did not spot many possibilities and entered the first open café, a dirty dive that probably did most of its business in the evening and nighttime hours with sailors or people from the outskirts looking for a cheap good time. The darkness of the interior, broken only by a few dim lights and neon beer ads, seemed to him an affront to even the cloudy, winter daylight outside; the floor felt grimy under his feet, and a stale, beery odor permeated the place. He took a seat at the counter, and from the laminated menu, which was covered with the greasy fingerprints of numerous customers, he chose a hamburger and fries, along with a glass of iced tea, which he hardly ever drank out of season. It occurred to him that in the long span of his life he had rarely or never hung out in honky-tonks, road houses, drink houses, or juke joints: there was a lot he had missed and large parts of the populace that were outside his accustomed realm. For the moment, he tried to make some sort of contact by biting into the dripping burger and exchanging a few words with the middle-aged bartender, who had pasty-white skin and tattoos snaking up his arms. The man was friendly enough, though he seemed generally bored with life.

"Who's that singing on the jukebox?" J.P. asked.

"I believe it's Etta James," came the reply.

"Isn't she a Black R&B singer?"

"Yeah, that's right."

"Singing a Hank Williams tune?" he asked, surprising himself with a certain degree of pride that he could identify the songwriter, whom he had snootily looked down upon back when he was in college and the troubadour still alive; his tastes and outlook had matured and broadened in the meantime.

"Yeah, why not?"

The powerful, husky voice, accompanied by a piano, chorus, and clapping hands, along with the lyrics themselves, gave an uplift to the surroundings that J.P. had found lacking to that point. It was country and not, all at the same time.

> Just like a blind man I wandered alone
> Worries and fears I claimed for my own
> Then like the blind man that God gave back his sight
> Praise the Lord I saw the light.

He had to squint at first when he returned to the street. Back in the convention center, he cleared up a few loose ends with Ariel, discussing the chemicals that would enhance the proceedings and the ringers whom Ariel had recruited to join the performers in the *tableaux vivants*; they also examined the meeting room around the corner where those helpers would be preparing themselves. He then returned home to rest up and get dressed for the evening's happening.

• • •

He entered the hall long before the nine o'clock opening ceremony in order to take his place at his table on the mezzanine from which he could survey what was occurring on the main floor below. He was wearing a long black sorcerer's robe and pointed cap, decorated with moons and stars in various constellations: Orion, the hunter, had his back. In his right hand he carried a wand, with which he already seemed to be conducting the proceedings. He pulled out his opera glasses and, reading the numbers on the tables below, noted that the one reserved for Anthony and Sebastian, although in the first row directly in front of the stage, was at the far right edge: not exactly front and center, but somewhat displaced, he observed with satisfaction. Are they already being supplanted from their position in the hierarchy? But even if the specific personalities become uprooted, is the underlying, controlling order significantly changed? Maybe they were fungible, like everything else. And maybe what he was undertaking would make little difference. Packing his binoculars away, he pulled down the black mask to cover his upper face. People had begun entering and milling about, dressed in their formal *costumes de rigueur* or various types of Mardi Gras apparel and international dress: harlequins, Renaissance courtiers, flamenco dancers, Alpine maidens in dirndls. Ladies in elegant, floor-length ball gowns bared their shoulders, letting fashion take precedence over the calendar, while their escorts chortled with one another as best they could, given the tightness with which their white ties grasped their necks. As more and more people entered and began circulating, the background noise grew into a hubbub of indistinct, undistinguishable voices, a mixture of all present, a cacophony that resolved itself into a unified hum. As the mixture of costumes became more colorful and varied, however, the whole prospect resembled a kaleidoscope of diverse, glittering crystals. As multifarious as the flora and fauna in the Delta?

Alphonse Rapier and his party, including the elderly and slow-moving Thomas Gonzalez, took their seats at the center table, along with some people that J.P. assumed were visiting dignitaries from Brussels and the chemical company that was hoping to grasp a foothold in the area. When the lights began dimming shortly before nine, however, Anthony and his cohorts still had not arrived. Worried, J.P. made his way to the projection booth to see if Ariel had any information on his brother's plans.

"They're spending the holiday weekend at their villa on Pleasure Island and planned to come up here by boat. I heard Anthony complaining that this wasn't a 'real' Mardi Gras ball, but he knows he has to put in an appearance to keep the wheels rolling. He was pretty upset on Friday when he discovered my planted figures indicating that his dot-com holdings had tanked. It'll probably be Tuesday before he becomes disabused, but I don't know if the scare's enough to keep him away. Tina and Young Anthony are already here, and I'm sure the others don't plan to miss it. Maybe they got delayed."

J.P. went back out to the lobby and made his way to a window overlooking the outdoor terrace along the river, and sure enough, a luxury motor yacht with the firm's logo emblazoned in gold was pulling up alongside: a crew member had just leapt ashore and was securing a rope to one of the cleats as the vessel bobbed on the water. Heavy rain was predicted for later in the evening and the lowering clouds were beginning to thicken, but the downpour had not yet begun. He continued watching as Anthony, a glass in one hand, staggered onto the dock, followed by Sebastian and others in their entourage. He wondered if it would still be necessary for Ariel to spike the beverages. Just outside the ballroom his eye was caught by two figures in waiters' costumes bearing aluminum trays: with a start, he realized it was his yard men, Steve and Trick. In addition to their trays they had water bottles, which he overheard Steve explaining could be filled with more potent stuff by a bartender with whom he had made friends, though the flunkies' job, J.P. assumed, would be more to remove empty glasses and pick up trash from the floor than to deliver refreshment to the waiting party-goers. He started to address them before realizing that they had not recognized him in his costume; he relished the fact that he could enjoy the evening in anonymity.

Returning to his spot to continue his watch over the proceedings, he now began to wonder what was keeping Miranda and Frederic. At that moment two masked figures approached his table, one in a white lab coat with microscope and artist's palette dangling from the belt, and the other carrying a clipboard and wearing khaki pants, white shirt, tie, and a baseball cap bearing the scarlet inscription

Forward! He quickly recognized them as his daughter and future son-in-law, though each was wearing the clothing more appropriate to the other.

"Well, we made it," said Miranda, giving him a hug.

"I'm glad you did. Realistic costumes?"

"We originally thought of going as Antony and Cleopatra to show the renunciation of power for love."

J.P. gave an understanding smile, with a pang of reminiscence.

"But we changed our minds and went for this. Kind of fantastic in its own way."

"Well, make yourselves comfortable, and get ready to enjoy the show. I have to go check on something with Ariel. Let me bring you a drink when I come back. What are you having?"

"Is Ariel here? What is going on? I have a feeling it's more than meets the eye."

"It will indeed meet the eye, and more. Tina's committee hired Ariel to handle the special effects."

"I'm certainly curious," said Frederic. "But to answer your question: I noticed the Port City Brewery is serving draft lager—can you bring me one of those?"

"I'll have a glass of Pinot Grigio."

J.P. found Ariel flipping switches in the projection booth and clicking menus on the computer screen, all in the aura of its glow.

"Glad you're here. I printed out your instructions for the role players in the tableaux. Can you take them down to the dressing room? The names are at the top to indicate what goes to whom."

Glancing at them on the way down, J.P. reread the lines indicating that the person portraying Bienville was supposed to handcuff the Indian when the music switched from an 18th-century minuet to a trumpet march. He quickly located the character who looked as though he had just been transported from the court of Louis XIV, gave him the sheet, and then distributed the rest of the scripts as well. It took longer than expected to fetch drinks from the bar, which had quickly become the most popular spot in the place. Perhaps they're all eager to drown memories of the horrors of the outgoing century, he surmised. But are things here really that bad? Despite the poverty, no one here is being rounded up to be put in camps at the moment, or forced to flee their homes before a rain of bombs. The demagogues stir up the resentments of real and perceived problems, but we are hardly approaching the apocalypse they predict. Neither are things as perfect at the moment as the comfortably well-off in their sheltered environments take them to be. A slight rocking of the boat is no great tragedy: we're not on perilously high seas, but it's not completely smooth sailing either. We've weathered extremes before and will undoubtedly get through this patch, but is that reason enough to be complacent? I have to admit I can't really complain. And yet. . . .

He carefully cradled the two glasses and started making his way back up to the mezzanine. The big-band orchestra was playing a medley of those peppy, repetitive Mardi Gras tunes, and he heard some young thing screech, "Party like it's 1999!" Simile becomes reality, thought J.P., whatever that means. Was this maybe more like a hurricane party, one last excuse for self-indulgent debauchery before the onslaught of the deluge? Meanwhile, on the center stage, the figures of Folly and Death chased each other around the broken column of life. Incessantly, just like last year, and the year before that. And probably in the coming years as well. Folly obviously enjoyed thumbing his nose at a stuffy status quo, and, despite his macabre expression, Death appeared to relish happily the prospect of putting an end to it all. We're supposed to wonder who will win, thought J.P., but whose victory is preferable, and what if they're both the same?

He delivered the drinks and took his seat as well as a sip from his own glass, which he had been nursing earlier at the table. The lights dimmed, and the music switched to something slower, with more pomp, as appropriate to the occasion. The old mayor rose from his chair and cautiously climbed the few steps leading to the illuminated podium; he nodded gravely to the applause that filled the hall. He then extended both his arms and motioned for the royalty seated at the two adjoining tables to join him on stage, and to the piped-in strains of Handel's "Water Music" the two regal pairs, white and Black, slowly ascended from either side, followed by young equerries and flower girls who held up the flowing ermine and jewel-studded trains. It was a sign of progress that the courts of both races were included, but though they were now displayed as equal, they were separate nonetheless: division was still a marker of the times. When the costumed royalty, stand-ins for the truly powerful, had assumed their places, beaming along with their scepters, the mayor began his welcoming remarks. J.P. glanced over at Frederic to observe his reaction to his elderly father's presence, but the young man's face did not give anything away. The monotone voice recited the predictable: a platitude-filled speech belonged as much to the occasion as did dancing and drinking. Reading from the paper held tightly in his quivering hands, Alphonse duly recognized all the appropriate individuals and organizations before he began describing the bright future that awaited everyone in the new millennium. He motioned for the Brussels delegation to come forward and receive a beribboned proclamation of official welcome. Selling our birthright? thought J.P., his cynicism kicking into high gear. Those who once colonized are trying to stay on top by throwing in their lot with new colonizers. The initial remarks concluded to polite applause, and as the various dignitaries took their seats, Ariel started the show by following the committee's plan and switching the soundtrack to some anodyne film score, which could provide accompaniment for any type of scene.

J.P. looked over at Frederic again, who simply stared ahead and muttered with a sigh, "'*Between the acting of a dreadful thing/And the first motion, all the interim is/Like a phantasm or a hideous dream.*' As you see, performing in school plays can be useful in later life."

To which the future father-in-law replied, "'*Between the idea and the reality. . . falls the shadow.*' Is that what the present is: a nightmare?"

Against the backdrop on the stage below was now projected a colorful image from early 18th-century cartography, a map of the bay showing the islands and rivers labeled with their French names in a decorative, archaic font. Off the tip of the Isle Dauphine one could spot Pelican Island, which had long since disappeared but which, in the swirling changes of wind and waves, J.P. had heard, was actually beginning to make a comeback as the new century arrived. Geology moves at its own pace, he thought, as he pondered how hurricanes are a natural feature of the coastal environment, destroying and rebuilding barrier islands and the marshes necessary for the regeneration of aquatic life. Our lives are a process: for our own renewal, do we need tempests in human affairs from time to time? Out in the Golfe du Mexique was an imaginary island sporting palm trees, noble savages, and fanciful creatures from the animal kingdom. The music switched to a Couperin *sonade* as the curtain opened and the golden glow of the spotlight fell on the brothers Bienville and Iberville standing tall amidst a triangular arrangement with kneeling, half-clothed Indigenous figures. The audience oohed and clapped politely at the artistic spectacle whose frozen figures looked as though they might be taking part in a cordial *fête champêtre*. But a sudden, discordant blare of trumpets accompanied a swift movement by Bienville to shackle one of the Indians. Although the historical Frenchman had in his admiration of the native custom decorated his own body in snake tattoos, the eventual actions of colonizers hardly incorporated the earlier inhabitants as equal sharers. The last gesture of the scene altered the mood entirely, as the curtain closed to allow the next tableau to assemble. The new map that was projected came from several decades later to accompany the changes brought by the powers that ruled over the region in succession. Figures bearing French, British, Spanish, and American flags crossed slowly, meeting their replacements and surrendering their banners in turn, one after the other, to the strains of music indicating their various nationalities. Fife and drum suggested the American revolution, which initially waited behind the Spanish occupiers. A figure with a tousled grey mane and long rifle then entered from the right and took aim at one of the natives still on the scene: a sudden explosive sound and a puff of smoke preceded the victim's fall as the music grew more strident and disturbing. Old Hickory the Indian-killer had done his deed, and Spain disappeared from the scene as well.

The sorcerer aimed his opera glasses at one of the tables in the second row and observed that young Anthony was leaning over toward his wife and speaking heatedly; she was merely shaking her head and raising her hands, palms up, as if to say she had no explanation. At his own table, the faces of Miranda and Frederic displayed amused surprise and anticipation. Turning in a different direction, J.P. saw that the waiter hired by Ariel was standing on cue with a tray of drinks beside his brother's table. J.P. aimed his wand, equipped at the end with a laser light, and darted the illumination around the table in the mad dance of a will o' the wisp or St. Elmo's fire. The waiter nodded and began distributing the glasses to the assembled party.

"What are you going to give them?" J.P. had asked Ariel while they were making their plans several weeks earlier.

"Enchanter's nightshade: it causes mild disorientation and forgetfulness, along with occasional slurred speech, silly behavior, and slight confusion between visions and reality. I know you don't want to harm them or put them out altogether. They'll still be coherent. I chose something that would calm them somewhat and perhaps enable them to look at things differently. If they're lucky, maybe even a touch of euphoria, though I know that may not be what you're aiming for."

"Nightshade? Isn't that poisonous? I don't want to go that far."

"Deadly nightshade is a different plant that has no relation to this one."

"I guess there's not always something behind a name."

"This one's scientific designation is *Circaea lutetiana*, named for the enchantress who bewitched Odysseus. People in the 16th century thought this was the plant she used."

"I like that much better. If the result on them is as effective as the etymology is on me, I will be satisfied."

"I didn't buy any of the prescription drugs that imitate its chemical qualities; I just gathered this in the wetlands, and its effects should be mild yet effective."

"Well, you should know. It's somehow fitting that the charmed herbs of earth can point the way."

If the waiter didn't get the glasses mixed up, this is what Anthony and Sebastian would now receive, as well as Alphonse Rapier, while their wives got only a mild sedative and Thomas Gonzalez nothing at all. And of course selected participants at Young Anthony's table would not be forgotten, in order to forestall any mad, premature rushes toward the control booth. The thought that he might be engaging in his own form of chemical pollution crossed J.P.'s mind only briefly.

Meanwhile the antebellum tableau was being staged: a standing plantation owner was overseeing the production of wealth in the form of a kneeling field hand, bent under the weight of an overloaded sack, and including additional enslaved people in the process of toting a bale aboard a barge, which a waiting boatman was ready to set in motion. Even the pageant's original planners had not been so tasteless or unaware as to include happily singing slaves, but J.P. had also struggled with choosing the right music for this scene. He knew from reading Frederick Douglass how astounded the abolitionist was to hear people say that the singing of enslaved people was evidence of their contentment, since he well knew they *"sing most when they are most unhappy. The songs of the slave represent the sorrows of his heart. . . . The singing of a man cast away upon a desolate island might be as appropriately considered as evidence of contentment and happiness, as the singing of a slave."* The blues are something they create themselves, to help them get through it. Though J.P. had experienced some of the feelings of the castaway, he had no knowledge of the agonies of those in involuntary servitude. The superimposed banners "Agriculture" and "Commerce" lent to this scene an abstract significance to the labor that was literally embodied beneath. The banners faded, to be replaced by the projection of an animated cotton boll wearing a kingly crown and prominently displaying a dollar sign, to whom all beneath were apparently subject. J.P., who hated the simplistic, reified quality of symbols, which tend to confine rather than point outward in new directions, almost regretted employing them so blatantly, but then, wasn't he merely reworking something the ball's organizers had initiated? Besides, that was perhaps what they understood best. And anyway, the music and the art, which in his view were the best way of conveying anything, should be strong enough to give adequate expression. The initially cheerful, recorded strains of "Dixie" started to become more and more dissonant and raucous through the overlapping intrusion of the punk band, while roving red spotlights created a chaotic effect and the lash came down on the field hand's back.

At this point gasps could now be heard from several quarters, and an enraged Anthony stood up to scream, "Stop this nonsense!" The drug had hardly had time to produce any effect, but Susu put a hand on his shoulder to urge him back into his seat and be quiet. Worse than anything portrayed on stage, to her mind, was a breach of manners. The unrest was drowned out by the return of the pleasant, recorded film music, which along with softer colors in the lighting, temporarily provided the spectacle with a more relaxing interlude. These musical notes gave way to happy, martial tunes from the Civil War, as proud soldiers in grey and blue stood heroically in a circle, before firing on each other and drawing the blood inevitably resulting from the refusal to reconcile the conflict of brother against brother. The melody of "When Johnny Comes Marching Home" in a dirge-like minor key was increasingly amplified as the needle scratched and the turntable revolved more and more slowly, plunging the music ever deeper to a final end.

The audience was again given a brief reprieve before the setting changed to Reconstruction. An African American man in a handsome black suit, raising his hand in an oratorical gesture, was delivering a speech beneath the image of a capitol dome; the new situation, and the accompanying excerpts from Dvořák's symphony "From the New World" that were influenced by Negro spirituals and Native American music underscored the dignity of the living picture. J.P. grabbed his binoculars to look more closely at the central figure in the suit who struck him as somehow familiar, and sure enough, determined that it was Caleb: Ariel had not pulled any punches, and J.P. wondered whether any of this was being directed at him. He tried to recollect whether Caleb had perhaps played an Indian in the earlier scene as well. The harmonious tableau before him quickly changed when some white men in linen suits carrying large tablets marked "1901 Constitution" ran onto the stage and chased the Black man away as the hopeful, conciliatory tones of the "Goin' Home" section of the largo again gave way to discordant strains from the band Reap the Whirlwind. It'll still be a while before Dvořák's longed-for destination is reached, thought J.P. He scanned the various tables below with his glasses: the mayor merely smiled uncomfortably and nodded at the Belgian visitors. Anthony, who had already downed most of the second glass that had been provided him, was attempting to move his head in time to the music as he followed the darting spotlights with the drink in his outstretched hand. Sebastian appeared mainly bewildered, as did young Anthony, and J.P. decided it would soon be time to go down and have a talk with them.

Many of the young in the audience probably thought that the swirling, flashing lights gave a disco quality to the evening, since a few had gotten up to dance, even though the actual ball portion of the festivities had not yet begun. Older spectators on the other hand resignedly wondered what the world was coming to. Frederic said he never would have thought the community could have staged such a spectacle, and Miranda looked at her father with a quizzical look as if to ask, "It's you and Ariel isn't it?" J.P. nodded with a smile, pleased that everything was going according to plan so far: Ariel's skills and imagination amounted to genius. J.P. was glad that the big band orchestra was prepared to do as they were instructed, and that the Gadarene Swine were versatile enough to adapt to the kind of music needed when called upon to supplant the recordings. Their accompaniment to the scenes of industrial growth and two world wars had enough of a melodic hook to carry the audience along, even as the sights of patriotic gore, imprisoned chain gangs echoing the earlier scenes of slavery, and grotesquely fulsome expressions of self-congratulation might have repelled.

J.P. excused himself from his immediate companions and made his way down to his brother's table. By the time he approached it, he discovered that Alphonse Rapier and Thomas Gonzalez had arrived there as well. Apparently all still had most of their wits about them and hoped to learn from the others what was going on. He stood off to the side at first to observe Anthony's reaction to the penultimate tableau, which began with brief videos of gently waving marsh grasses in the wetlands along the bay. At first there was palpable relief at the prospect of a restored, wholesome world, or at least the image of it. But as with the earlier scenes, this one faded in a lap dissolve to something completely different: a shot of dead, broken trees in the bizarre landscape of a garishly colored chemical dump. Glimpses of signs posted along its edges revealed it to be a gold-

mining site in the Congo maintained by the very company that was
seeking to locate in their vicinity. J.P. thought he detected a glimmer
of uncertainty and discomfort in the face of Anthony, who started to
squirm. The music, if it could still be called that, was shrieking like
banshees in the wind, and vapors from blocks of dry ice rose in
disconsolate clouds.

Ariel, who was masked and clothed in a swirling, diaphanous
gown, had come down to play the role assigned by J.P. for initiating
the confrontation. Meanwhile the computer was taking care of the
rest on autopilot. The spotlights on the posed figures began slowly
fading, and in front of the scenes of environmental ruin appeared
hebraicized Roman letters, which came into view faintly one at a
time before increasing in intensity and seeming to float in the air:
MENE MENE TEKEL UPHARSIN.

A panicked and disoriented Anthony called out, "What does it all
mean?"

Dancing around the table, Ariel looked directly into Anthony's
face and asked in a disguised voice, "What are the limits of greed?
You have accumulated much, but at what price? Only repentance can
provide solace in this place made desolate by your grasping."

Anthony, groggily slammed his fist down on the table and yelled
uncertainly, "Get out of here! Whoever you are, you've no business
here."

"In some quarters you might be able to command, but here you
have no sway. You and your co-conspirators will get your due. Deeds
have consequences: prepare to face them."

Sweat now covered Sebastian's face as well, and the mayor looked
at them quizzically, as if seeking an answer.

The gentle old Gonzalez merely smiled calmly and said, "Foul
weather seems to have set in: everyone looks so gloomy." Turning to
Anthony, he asked, "Why are you so upset?"

"I seem to be accused of everything that's wrong in the world, my
stocks are tanking, and things are spinning out of control."

"But think of what all you have: family, sufficient wealth, your
health. Contemplate the sorrows of all those who have suffered so
much more. You have all the means you need to live."

"But not the means to get ahead."

Gonzalez paused before continuing, "The time is out of joint, or whack, as they say these days, but looking back on this cursed century, when wasn't it? If I were king here, do you know what I would do?"

Anthony laughed bitterly and replied, "Make everyone be nice to one another."

"Indeed, but it would occur naturally. If you would only pay attention you might see that those whom we claim to be our inferiors often show a superior grace. There would be no hierarchies, no ranks, no exploitation, no rich nor poor, no divisions at all."

"Your paradise is defined by what it doesn't have. Meanwhile, we're the ones who produce needed things and make this desert bloom."

Sebastian chimed in as well, "People are naturally selfish. How would you keep that in check? By ruling over everybody to make people do things your way? You think your prohibitions would bring freedom? An interfering, over-regulating government, that's what you'd institute! Utopias turn into their opposite when enforced to the letter, or haven't you noticed that?"

"But would we be better off if we failed to imagine?" asked the old counselor.

And Anthony said, "Who would saw the timber, and who would turn it into furniture, and who would supply the tools and take it to market if everyone was the same?"

"Work would not seem like work. We would all do what we wished, saw logs in the morning for the satisfaction it gave, and make tables in the afternoon. You could go fishing when you wanted to, and write poetry after supper. No need for money: each would contribute what he could and be provided with what he needed. There would be no necessity for wanting more."

"I already hunt and fish when I want to, and as for poetry, who needs that?"

"Because you have people working for you, who enable you to have the time," interjected Ariel.

"You're getting fuzzy-headed in your old age, Gonzalez, but that's okay," said Anthony. "Go ahead and live in your realm of idealistic dreams. You deserve a rest: no need to know any more how things work in the real world."

Observing the interaction, J.P. realized that neither the drug nor the lesson of the pageant seemed to have had much effect on Anthony, who was firmly locked into his old way of looking at things.

"And the real world is working so well, is it?" asked J.P., feeling the need to intervene for the first time. Ariel swept over them with arms waving in the wing-like sleeves of the gown before darting back up to the projection booth to continue monitoring the spectacle. J.P. whispered as his assistant passed, "Well done! Now I've got them where I want them. It's almost over."

To which Ariel replied, "Justice, yes. But retribution? Is vengeance really ours to bestow?"

"Ariel, my friend, you have more empathy than I do. I hope I'll be able to emulate you soon."

"Maybe so. You have to remember, I've walked in more shoes than you have," the sprite-like figure said while flying off. "If being human means mistreating others, then maybe I'm not human."

Taken aback by everything, and still slightly inhibited by the *circaea*, Anthony stared at the strange wizard before him, whom he was now noticing for the first time and who addressed him again. J.P. observed in Anthony the sagging of pale, fallen cheeks, which pulled the corners of his mouth down as well.

"Maybe it's not the world who owes you, but you who owe the world. Those who accuse others of having a sense of entitlement are usually the ones who feel entitled themselves." Despite himself, he realized his didactic tendencies were again making their way to the fore as he tried to salvage what the tableaux had thus far failed to bring about.

Trying to make sense of what was going on, Anthony stammered out, "And you? Who are you? Do you think I owe you something?"

J.P. moved in closer and, ripping off his mask, stared his brother in the face.

Seeing through the beard and wrinkles of age, Anthony was struck with the force of recognition, and his face went paler.

"John Prosper," he whispered. "Where the *hell* do you come from? What do you want?"

"Restoration is what I used to think I wanted. But what would be restored? The grand order we all grew up with? Heaven forbid. That would only be postponing the inevitable. Your whole being, your behavior, your hold on power are all tied to property. How could I gain from a restoration of property or power? It would just put me in your place. I don't want your position, your job, your money. But things have to change."

"Change? What kind of change?"

"Want me to draw you a diagram? Look at the picture," J.P. said, waving his wand at the screen on stage and letting the laser light dance. "Is that what you want to create for all of us? For your children and grandchildren? For your legacy, if there's nothing else that matters to you? You have to learn how to see things in a new way."

His tongue thick in his mouth, Anthony groped for words. "But you, you, you don't know squat about how things function in the world. If it was up to you, the economy would grind to a halt. No fuel, no production, no jobs. Stop this charade, this puppet show! It has no substance. It's merely the illusion of power."

"One can't deny history. Does what you see have less substance than the realm which you inhabit, which too will one day disappear? But not without first keeping others enslaved to your pursuit of Mammon. You would like to have the show changed, but you would have to change history first. Did you ever think that you just might be in a position to do that?"

"You liberal hypocrite, and moralizing curmudgeon to boot!" Anthony snarled. "You criticize us for the problems that come with progress, but you're all too happy to benefit from its products in your comfortable life. You condemn us for not bending over backwards to the illegal aliens, but what do you do for the situation? You're mighty free with your holier-than-thou attitude, but your type is all too happy to eat the abundant produce that's been grown with the help of pesticides and harvested with cheap labor. So don't come talking to me about pollution and amnesty and such rot. You're as fuzzy-headed as Gonzalez. Making and using money is what works wonders. Without that, we'd all still be living in caves. Your head has gotten too big from all the stuff you've been reading in your books! Go back to your cloud-cuckoo land!"

"We can't escape, any of us. But you can refrain from inflicting the worst."

"The worst? Look around outside, it's not so bad. The year you were born three shipyards, an aluminum plant, two paper mills, and the city itself poured all their unfiltered waste and sewage directly into the bay. But that doesn't happen anymore and I can go out there and fish and safely eat the fish I catch. And I hunt too. I suppose you have something against that as well. But let me tell you: there are now more turkeys than ever, and there are fewer limits on deer. All because of changes brought about by the free market."

"A regulated market you should say. And you're conveniently forgetting the chemicals in your storm-water run-off and the ticking time bombs of the coal ash pits. How come we can still list so many ways the degradation still occurs, and why do so many of us think that the invisible hand is about to reach up and grab us by the short hairs?"

"We'll see, we'll see," said Anthony, putting his head down on the table on his crossed arms.

"And another thing," whispered J.P., leaning down closer to Anthony's upraised ear, " I could, if I wanted, blurt out the nefarious plans that you and Sebastian are planning for Alphonse."

With a bolt, Anthony sat upright and stared agape at J.P., his wide eyes silently asking, "How the hell did you know that?"

J.P. was surprised that Anthony wasn't even more enraged, or why he himself wasn't, though he doubted that a furious approach would have been any more successful with his brother. Would things just end up rocking along in the same way?

"I had a notion you might be back," said Thomas Gonzalez to J.P. "Clotilde let something slip at one point, but I didn't pursue it, knowing that she was keeping counsel. I'm delighted to see you: welcome."

J.P. went around the table to give the old man a hug. "I apologize for not coming to see you right away, but, as you might have noticed, there were other things I had to take care of first. I owe you so much for helping me get through those years, especially at first."

"John Prosper, I'm not surprised your name is linked with this indictment," said a groggy Alphonse. "I realize I did you wrong and I hope you find it in your heart to forgive me. You spoke of change: change is what *I* need. My life can't go on the way it has. Ever since I lost my son, I've felt alienated, without purpose, rudderless. Maybe what I helped do to you was the first act in the drama I ended up carrying out with respect to my own son."

"What do you mean lost?" asked Sebastian. "Frederic's here in town."

"But he took a different path, one I didn't understand or accept, and my harsh words led to our estrangement. We never see each other: I can't seem to keep from doing the wrong thing. It appears I have no one: ever since my daughter refused to marry the man I picked out for her and ran off with that South African paleontologist, she hardly sees fit to come home anymore. How wonderful it would have been, for example, if Frederic could have been here with me tonight. But gradually I've come to see that maybe I was the one who became lost. Helping Anthony do what he did to you way back then, John Prosper, that's just one example, and I beg your forgiveness."

"And I'll grant it, since what you just said indicates a real turn-around, a step in the direction of the change I'm talking about."

"This change—will it be some idealistic touchy-feely place that exists only in your mind?" asked the ever-skeptical Anthony, tugging at the collar behind his white bow tie.

All he needs is a top hat and a cigar—always playing the role— thought J.P. *But maybe I've been acting too with my lofty words and preaching.*

"Don't worry: you don't have to restore me to my place in the firm. I don't need that anymore, nor its accompanying seducers, power and money. What's rightfully mine is nothing other than what's rightfully anyone's: to be respected and be given the chance to succeed on the rising tide." *Maybe I'll end up forgiving him alto-gether,* thought J.P. *If change occurs, I suppose it must involve me as well.*

The music dropped its ominous tones in favor of something softer, contemporary, and more inspiring: J.P. had wanted to end on this different note, with a vision that was aimed more at Miranda and Frederic than at the villains in front of him. His children, he hoped, would eventually supplant the latter. The images of the manmade dystopia, with which he had replaced the self-satisfied culminating picture of the committee's pre-planned tableau, morphed dialectically into a pristine, riparian landscape by the bay, clearly a local scene but labeled in the supertitles as Tír na nÓg, the mythological Celtic island of youth, and Ogygia, the Homeric island of Calypso. Goddesses in Attic tunics bearing overflowing horns of plenty took their place on either side; Justice, with her blindfold and scales equally balanced, stood at the center. As a wedding march played, smiling mixed-race couples promenaded in: at the banquet table there was a place for everyone. Many of the background images from the committee's original slide show had been retained, since it was a hopeful vision that they presumably all shared, though it was now set in the future and not assumed to reflect the reality of the present.

"Looks very nice," said Alphonse, "but it doesn't do me any good."

"I understand. I lost my daughter, but have had the good fortune to learn what it means to find her again. But that doesn't mean possess or dominate: they have to make their own way, you know. The common notion that I'm about to lose her again through marriage is a ridiculous one. As the old cliché would have it, I'm gaining a son. Maybe you can too. Come, let me show you."

Not sure what would be accomplished, Alphonse slowly stood and tottered behind J.P. to the mezzanine. At their table Miranda and Frederic were holding hands and smiling as they gazed into each other's eyes as if lost in their own game, but one in which there were no winners and losers, just enjoyment for all in the playing.

"Kind of cheesy, don't you think?" asked Miranda, glancing over to the visions on the stage.

"Oh, I don't know. It's actually got some merit to it."

"Sort of like our Constitution," said J.P., breaking into their intimate realm. "Not perfect, but better than our practices at the moment, and changeable, in a way that suggests the achievable. We first have to know what we should become. I think I'm forced to admit no one person can do it alone."

"We know, Dad," said Miranda, affectionately impatient with his moralizing. "Maybe though, even if your drama didn't convey *the* truth, it managed to present some truths others don't want to see."

"It seems everybody knows what's wrong with the world, but if you listen to their stories, no two are ever the same. When will we ever learn?"

Frederic froze when he saw who was behind his future father-in-law.

"Frederic, my boy, you're here!" cried Alphonse, extending his arms in an embrace. Slowly taking in the fact that his father's long-standing rejection had somehow changed to an acceptance whose origins he couldn't fully fathom, Frederic loosened his stiffened arms and reached them around his father's back.

"Well, don't you work wonders," Miranda said to her own father.

"I wish I could. Everything takes time: transformation in the system, and changes in the attitudes of others. I am beginning to break free of the illusion that I can control things."

"But shouldn't we also break free of the illusion that nothing we do makes a difference?" she asked. "This evening, I was somehow preparing myself to expect revenge, but I'm glad it appears to be reconciliation."

"I'm not sure I would go that far. It's a two-way street. Knowledge is what I've been pursuing my entire life, but didn't Einstein say that knowledge is less important than imagination? I'm not sure Anthony has either one of those. He's apparently satisfied to be contained in his own little realm. Maybe if he eventually comes around we'll notice a difference."

"And who is this divine creature?" Alphonse asked, noticing his son's companion for the first time.

"Let me introduce Miranda, my fiancée, the daughter of this gentleman here, who I had no idea was acquainted with you. I would have introduced you before now, but . . . ."

"I'm probably the one that should apologize for that state of affairs, but I'm certainly delighted to meet you now, Miranda."

On the stage below, the pageant was reaching its conclusion: at the feet of the figures seated at the banquet crabs, flounder, and shrimp crowded ashore in a wondrous bounty, and bells rang out to announce the jubilee. At the forefront, Artemis appeared and drew her bow, letting the arrow fly: but which way the arc would bend, toward destruction and harm, or toward healing and fair-mindedness, was not immediately visible. Would justice and righteousness run down as a mighty stream, or would injustice roar through like a tornado?

As the scene faded through Ariel's machinations of the various devices, Frederic said that he regretted its disappearance, but Miranda assured him they could create their own vision.

"I would hope at least that the magic of love and art will remain," said J.P. "They are the only things that count. As my wise daughter indicates, there is still much for us to do ourselves, before we all disappear."

The lights in the hall brightened a bit, the big band struck up a tune, and couples surged onto the dance floor.

Ariel reappeared at their table and asked J.P., "Time for the moly?"

"The what?" asked Frederic.

"Moly," explained J.P., who had been previously schooled by Ariel. "Homer's name for the snowdrop flower, a plant sacred to the gods. Hermes gave its root to Odysseus to ward off the spell of Circe. It's an anticholinesterase, which acts as an antidote to the—never mind."

"Holy moly?"

"That's right—exclamation or divine counterpoison. Go ahead, Ariel. Who knows what good either medicine does. Do you think there might be any antidote to the human condition?"

● ● ●

When one band took a break, the other started in, and the music alternated among swing, waltzes, rock, and rhythm and blues to play to the variety of individuals in attendance. People danced and partied, as carefree as they were able, though some were troubled more than others by the spectacle they had just seen, or by the memories of the era that was disappearing behind them. At the countdown just before midnight, there was anticipation about what would happen next. J.P. ignored the hoopla for the moment to go get himself another drink. On the way back he was startled by a looming figure who suddenly crossed his path. He recoiled, before recognizing who it was and stuttering, "Ah, C-caleb, I th-thought I spotted you."

Surprised at his vacillation, he recalled his dream of the previous night of an encounter between himself and Caleb at some unfamiliar location.

"I thought I seen you here," he had said to Caleb in an unaccustomed vernacular.

To which Caleb had responded, "Your instructional skit is quite amusing. In fact, I liked your pointing out the perversion of appropriating the bounty of nature, which has been given to us all and which resounds in my ears like the notes of a beautiful song, as private property for the benefit of a few. But really, my man: abstract images to represent whole races? I'm a flesh-and-blood human. I'll never disappear, any more than will my people, or those whom you project as my people. Am I your worst nightmare, a thing of darkness?"

"Hey, don't mess wid me, man."

"If didacticism can be dismissed as such. What's good for the goose, heh? Just because you schooled me in your knowledge, though, doesn't mean I'll turn out just like you."

"What's happnin' here, man? Like, I hardly know what's goin' on. Know what I'm sayin'?"

In his dream J.P. had wiped a hand across his brow as if to clear his confusion about what he was hearing and his inexplicable choice of words. Was this happening now in real life? He stared at the drink in his hand and wondered if he had accidentally grabbed the glass with the potion intended for Anthony. But maybe he was only imagining it.

Caleb, who seemed to have assumed J.P.'s full stature, replied to his actual remark, "Course you did. I've been here, and I've been there. And I now know where to go."

J.P. stared at him, allowing his comprehension slowly to return, realizing that, like Ariel, Caleb had more empathy, and despite indicating repeatedly his awareness of the wrongs that he and his had suffered in the long years of the nation's troubled history, never transformed any presumptive feelings of resentment into actual malice toward J.P. or others. Caleb understood more than his brother and nephew did and had grasped the nature of power even before he himself had. Had he been attempting to consolidate his own power by turning Caleb and Anthony into threatening others, just as Anthony had done? Maybe it was time for him to include rather than exclude and acknowledge them both as brothers. But in Anthony's case, there is perhaps only so much one can do with people who exclude themselves. He reached out to give Caleb a hug and said, "And now you can go where you wish."

"Thanks. Can you?"

A little later, as Alphonse noticed Anthony and his party getting ready to leave, he grabbed his son by the arm, and asked him and Miranda to join him for the rest of the weekend at his beach house, which was just down the road from Anthony's holiday villa. He also linked arms with J.P., who was still trying to sort things out; the group then made its way down to the main floor. Ariel and Caleb also fell in behind the departing cluster of people who were heading toward the boat. What a huge craft, thought J.P.; it seems almost too big to maneuver in the bay. Was it purchased for the actual comfort it provides its owner, or for a supposed increase in esteem through the image it projects, for providing a mask that would make others believe he had "made it"? If Anthony was pursuing happiness, he surely hadn't found it yet; he hadn't even found the sign pointing to the proper path. At least the craft was big enough to accommodate all those seeking passage at the moment, who found places scattered around the deck or down below.

ω

Watch the water push and pull
In and out, in and out again
From the shores of this barrier island
What a hasty farewell
It's ok, I even wrote out how it'd be
But I never dreamed
The words would lift so gracefully
From the pages
And come pouring out of your mouth
So hurtfully
But I'll let it go, love. I'll let it go.
I'll let it go, love. I'll let it go.
                    —Jessica Jones, "The Flight,"
                    Every Barren Branch

J.P. LEANED ON THE RAILING, STARING OUT into the distance that was reduced to a nearness because of darkness and fog. The towering clouds must have dissipated, and the rain that had been predicted was merely an intermittent, soft drizzle, hardly enough to seek shelter from, falling simultaneously on the just and the unjust. The waves of the bay stretched out before him: an abstract landscape, but nonetheless quite real. Had the sea changed along with the weather? Had the worst been averted? Or did the mildness merely lull one into thinking that everything was all right when it really wasn't? Was it a slow death by a thousand chops? Should the little patches of rough water encountered from time to time be taken just as seriously as the raging storm, and a concerted effort made to navigate them in the appropriate way as well? Is it perhaps a prologue to a dire turn in an inevitable cycle?

What had he accomplished today, he wondered, or in life? Maybe the goal can never be to complete the change, but to take a few steps to prepare those who come after. He had completed his enchantment, but would the spell continually cast upon the world by the likes of Anthony be similarly soon overcome? If there had been a change in his brother, it was hard to measure. Maybe what he had done was all a phantasy, a cloud formation that would disappear in the next little puff of wind. Somehow he felt that it had not been in vain though, and that he would do it again if given the choice. But perhaps with a greater realization that he was contributing one voice to the dialogue, rather than attempting to monopolize it. Throughout his life he had often been the one who thought he had everything figured out and who felt it his duty to explain it to others; only lately had he come to recognize that there was more to it, and that it was as important to listen as to speak. Maybe only now, like Socrates, he had embarked on his second sailing. Or was it the third? In any event, aware of what he hadn't previously known, he was now in a position to start again, to reformulate, to find himself within the world of others. It's no good simply to declare it's all okay just because you don't have the patience, insight, or ability to make it okay. We can't quit.

He smelled the salt in the air: the salt of the sea, the salt of the earth. With the boat rocking gently beneath his feet, he began to hear snatches of voices, which he could not always identify, blown in and out by the wind, issuing out of the mist and intermingling with the words of his own thoughts that bubbled up within him.

"Are we still going to pursue the plan of ousting my brother?"

But the reply he failed to catch.

And from another area of the deck, "When should we set a date?"

"Anytime now. I would just as soon it be before too long."

"How about right now? Can't the captain of a ship perform the ceremony?"

From an indeterminate spot came some muffled groans, which J.P. realized were emanating from beneath the tarp of a lifeboat hanging at the stern. The emerging head he recognized as that of Steve, who was drunkenly complaining about the emptiness of the bottle in his extended hand. "More, Trick, there's gotta be more around here! A boat this size has gotta have a well-stocked bar!"

That's one way of getting through the situation, thought J.P., wondering whether the two were stowaways or, unbeknownst to him, employees of Anthony's as well. They, like my brother, seek escape in demons, either the liquid kind or in abusing those others they imagine to be inferiors posing a threat. How easy it is to create a visible, superficial aristocracy based on blood or race or class! To find the real demons, they should look in the mirror, thought J.P. But to be honest, maybe I should do likewise. Am I wrong to assume that they will remain what they are, unable to evolve? Will they be able to become themselves, that is, who they should be? I hope one day I'll be able to clink glasses with them, or clank cans. Strange bedfellows, isn't that the phrase that someone came up with? When will we ever not be strange to one another? Maybe that's when true nobility is achieved: when a person can understand another's plight and no longer look down at anyone with arrogance. A world in which all are on an equal footing without pre-defined power structures is perhaps more difficult to navigate, but no one can be free until all are. Or was he merely pontificating to himself again? He clenched the railing more tightly with his left hand and sighed.

"Tell me, what am I going to say to the Belgians? I feel as though I'm being pushed in more ways than one."

"Follow your conscience."

In the last remark J.P. recognized the voice of his wise old friend, and he supposed he should listen to his own inner light as well. In opposing hierarchies, he had set himself above them; in attempting to free others from their illusions, he had not entirely succeeded in extricating himself from his own. He thought he had rejected the notion of primogeniture at the outset, but had he somehow subconsciously held onto its claims? Was his banishment really Anthony's fault, or in large part his own? Usurpation or abdication? And what about his own treatment of Caleb and Ariel? Had he acted to benefit them or confirm his own sense of himself?

Carried on the breeze was a scrap of song, one of Ariel's old ones, no doubt:

> *Troublesome waters much blacker than night*
> *Are hiding from view the harbor's bright light.*

I promised to free Ariel, thought J.P., but Ariel is probably already freer than we know. Neither to be pitied nor scorned, Ariel should be esteemed for the imagination, courage, and self-knowledge it took for him to free himself from the body, the social conventions in which he had been trapped, but it is up to all of us to create the environment where she can now enjoy the freedom they and everyone else deserve.

And again, from somewhere farther toward the bow, a voice he recognized as fraternal: "It amazes me how all those people tonight were talking as though there would be some big change when the calendar rolls over to double zeros. Don't they know things will keep percolating along as usual?"

"I'm sure as hell not going to give up my comforts."

"That would be hard, wouldn't it? And yet, son. . . ."

"And yet? I don't quite understand what you mean."

That 'and yet': a first timid step out of his self-enclosure towards a new start, or just another lap on the treadmill? It seemed to J.P. that they were not entering the future that he had envisioned in the past; perhaps his recurring faith in progress was just that: faith, not reason. But which course would history eventually take? The present was not necessarily a better version of what had come before, but neither must it be an exact repetition: how we respond is crucial. What is the third stage? What comes after tragedy and farce? Had he himself advanced at all, or had he come full circle, cast out in a boat to make his way in the world anew with everyone else? Head bowed, he began pacing back and forth along the railing as fresh droplets of spray wafted across his face.

With a pang, he thought about Diana again and how much he missed her, wondering what she would have done. And the lyrics of a different song (from within? without?) surrounded him:

> We may never meet again
> I have struggled to forget
> But the struggle was in vain
> For her voice lives on the breeze
> And her spirit comes at will
> In the midnight on the seas
> Her bright smile haunts me still.

He wondered whether he was finally coming to terms with his loss. Looking back, he realized again how much he had gained in loving Diana. Together they had created a new life, for themselves and through their daughter. He did not idealize or encapsulate her though: he was aware of her shortcomings but also her drive and the feelings they had for each other.

"Do you think we'll end up staying here?"

"Hard to say, it's fine for now. No place is less or more important than another—every place has its strengths, its shortcomings, its needs, its beauty."

"You're right, but somehow I get the feeling we'll have to stay mobile and not get stuck inside one place."

"Yes, it's not really the end."

Was this pair the calm center around which everything revolved, or were they simply naive and inexperienced, not yet fully aware of the temptations and obstacles they would be facing? They would certainly have to keep up their courage to enter that new world which they were approaching. If anything, he was sure of their love: *"It is an ever-fixed mark, that looks on tempests, and is never shaken."* He was confident that they could come up with something better, even though they would suffer inevitable failures in the process.

"You free me, you'll free yourself." He wondered from whom this voice might have come: it could have been anyone, except perhaps Anthony. Ariel? Caleb? Although many would not admit it, emancipation and the end of legal segregation had freed the whites too, though the process was still not complete. Had he himself, however, doggedly refused to let go altogether of the master-servant relationship with respect to his erstwhile employees? Was he now beginning to find the superior knowledge which they had already been able to attain by actually doing something? He had an inkling that now being able to see Caleb somewhat more clearly, he had a more honest vision of himself.

"Somehow all these disparate voices will have to come together."

Who said that? Or had he been talking out loud to himself? Maybe the recognition he had sought from the beginning was slowly taking shape: maybe the discovery was starting to come about through his finding the proper relationship to others, to himself, to this earth.

The next words addressed him directly: they came from Miranda, who was standing right beside him.

"Still waving your wand?"

"Oh," he said, distractedly looking down at his hand. "I guess it'll do no good here." With a sudden, determined movement he clasped both ends and broke the stick across his knee before casting it over the railing into the waves: he had planned to cast a healing fairy spell, but perhaps his clumsy magic had been malevolent, or maybe as ambiguous as the pursuits in which he had engaged in his career. His costume had been just as much an illusion as the arbitrary robes and titles of the Mardi Gras royalty. His current gesture was more truly noble. Power itself was not the goal: overcoming its seductive, corrupting allure and that of its henchman, violence, was the genuine crowning achievement.

"The scepter that I hope I am leaving you is something different. Not an instrument to grasp for power or riches, but the means to pursue knowledge, to unite that knowledge with the heart and proper humility to achieve wisdom, and in gratitude and reciprocity relate it to the world so that you can make your own proper way. What good is a purebred lineage if you can't do that?" He still had not quite found his own language, however, and was not sure if his words were freeing him or hemming him in.

"You know you caused quite a commotion tonight. After you left the table I picked up your opera glasses and looked down at your brother and Frederic's father. They really seemed to be suffering."

"Don't worry. I doubt that they were harmed. And if nothing else, it was all for you. I wish I could say though that the loose ends have been tied, that everything has been resolved, but I can't, it's never that simple. I get the feeling it doesn't amount to anything more than a storm in a water glass, as the Germans say. It'll blow over. The pageant has already melted into thin air; everything flows, changes: *panta rhei*."

"But don't we have some responsibility for the direction the stream takes? Weren't you hoping at least for the first hint of change? How do you know that didn't happen?"

"I guess I don't yet. But in any case, what will take the place of the status quo of this moment? Something must."

She grasped his arm and looked intently into his face. "Yes, I agree. Family dynasties and hereditary classes may have become outmoded, but the unjust economic order morphs into new forms and endures, and those that rule it know how to divide the rest of us to keep it going. They go with the flow and always bob to the top as long as they control the means to stay on top. But how long can that last if they destroy everything beneath them?"

He stared down at the sea, hoping to spot evidence of a change. "You've obviously learned a lot already. But maybe they're not so sure as they once were. The way they do things has already taken a toll on their happiness: just look at their eternally shriveled prune faces and their painful grins. How satisfying is their wealth and power? Greed and over-consumption are gnawing at them from within and have them trapped, even if they don't know it. And of course there are the exploited ones who really suffer. What my brother did to me is minuscule compared with the ongoing theft of life, liberty, and the pursuit of happiness from the rest of us. It's up to you and Frederic. Everyone for that matter has to confront the real conditions of life. I'm afraid our generation hasn't provided yours with a very good place to start."

"But is it ever any different for any generation? What about your brother though? Is your business with him finished? I guess you'll finally have to introduce me now. Does he even know you're on board?"

J.P. was reminded of the book deep in the inside pocket of his gown. He withdrew the leather-bound volume and thumbed through it, not able to read in the dark but remembering full well the ledger entries of debits and credits.

"It's not just about me, and my supposed rightful place: everyone should have the chance to belong." He paused, then wondered aloud: "Can one forgive if the one to be forgiven refuses to ask for forgiveness, or is even so unaware that he does not know he has anything to atone for?"

"It does seem that the powerful, those who seemingly have suffered least, are the ones least able to realize it," said Frederic, who had walked over by then.

"And are maybe the most in need of it," said Miranda.

"You are indeed a marvel," said her father, who, clasping the book as one would a frisbee, hurled it far out to sea. "No, it's not over:

reconciliation is not a one-way street. We'll have to figure out the best way to proceed, for all of us."

"So you still have work to do?"

"Of course. I haven't ordered my cemetery plot yet. Though when it does come time for that I have a notion I'll be ready. But by then, I want my epitaph to say something more than 'He got by.' Should we accept our fate or master it?" He wondered whether he would really be able to start now.

His daughter answered, "You're right. It's never too late."

Hadn't Diana once said something similar?

Perhaps the desire for vengeance was a trap from which he was beginning to free himself as well. Had he wanted to make Anthony suffer or induce him to see? The answer was important, because Anthony's power was not illusory or harmless—but had he learned enough to begin to advance? If not now, perhaps later. The spectators and reporters at the ball would wonder about what they had seen and might dig deeper. Would the truth eventually form itself and supplant the organizers' deceptive, self-congratulatory platitudes?

The foam arrayed itself atop the ripples in little lines of letters, which dissipated with each passing wave. He was reminded of something he had read: *And all the host of heaven shall be dissolved, and the heavens shall be rolled together as a scroll.* It would be up to Miranda to tell the story and relate not just those things that had been already overcome, but also the ones that were still to come on the restless seas of time. He was confident that she could handle it and not fool herself into reductively drawing simplistic meanings. The last word was yet to be written.

"What was in that book?"

Her remark caused him almost to regret his act, because in addition to his list of reckonings, the journal had contained his attempts to distill his previous learning to the essentials. But perhaps that didn't matter, since all that he had read and met with in his life was now a part of him. He wasn't rejecting knowledge, merely his inadequate summation to that point. Knowledge can't be hidden between book covers anyway, and what he had assembled up to then would be the basis for something new. His ongoing formulations would take shape as a palimpsest. He often felt frustration, however, because he seemed as ignorant as the day he left for college. That realization, which only comes with age, is nonetheless more knowledge than most have, he thought. And what about his vast library, his archive at home? Will Miranda ever have room to store the physical volumes? Perhaps he should rewrite his testament and bequeath the collection to the Anthony Devaux Branch Library so that the public at large might benefit. Anonymously, of course, to avoid all implications of hubris. Books, learning will not disappear. But will willful ignorance and the desire for wealth and power, along with the violence that maintains them?

"Where do you think we are now?" Miranda asked.

"We must have cleared the point, and should be turning into Bon Secour Bay pretty soon."

"Seeking a safe harbor? Where are we going, exactly?"

"I assume to your uncle's beach house, and my father's, which is just down the road from it."

J.P. mumbled something about the island where the villas of the wealthy were located, which Miranda understood as "Oh no!"

At that moment, the regular vibrations of the engine, which had provided an almost imperceptible undertone to the voyage thus far, gave a momentary sputter, and the red and green running lights, along with the dim illumination in the helmsman's cabin, went out altogether. The door opened, and someone called out, "Mr. Devaux!"

"Yes, what is it?" came Anthony's voice from somewhere down the deck. "What's the matter?"

"We've lost electrical power, so the steering doesn't respond."

"But the engine's still going. Shouldn't that be operating a generator?"

"It should, but some of this complicated computer stuff on board must have shut down a connection. I can run a boat, but I can't handle all the electronics. Unfortunately, you can't navigate today without them. There's not even any sonar, or radar, or radio."

Instead of falling victim to wind and wave, they seemed to have been impeded by human industry and technology, which besides creating their wonderful means of transportation, sustained imperfections that brought on its eventual breakdown. Knowledge appeared to be having a hard time keeping up with itself. And in the future, as Miranda warns us, if the climate ends up destroying us all, that too will be largely the result of human shortcoming, mused J.P.

"Didn't I see Ariel on board?" yelled Anthony. "Maybe that clown knows something about ship's computers as well. Ariel!"

But there was no answer, merely a faint humming, heard only by a few.

> *Take me in your lifeboat*
> *Oh, take me in your lifeboat*
> *It will stand the raging storm.*

"You mean you can't steer at all?" Anthony was becoming more frantic.

"No. The boat just keeps on its previous course."

"You mean we're locked into a path? Aren't we supposed to be turning into the intracoastal waterway?"

"Yes, but if we get the power back on by the time we head out into the Gulf, we could turn and follow the peninsula down to Perdido Pass and cut in there."

"If we don't get lost first. Wouldn't it be better just to turn off the engine and drift?"

"We'll give it a couple of minutes more."

"Ariel!"

This time there was a faint shuffle of feet and a slight figure entered the cabin.

"Just don't fuck everything up! If you can get the electricity working again, I might even forgive you for ruining the pageant."

Soon the dark, low mass of Fort Morgan passed on the port side; since there was no evidence of restored power, Anthony called out, "Cut the engines! We can't just head out to sea indefinitely!"

Damn the computers! Reduced speed ahead—where will that get us? wondered J.P.

With another splutter, the engine noise ceased, soon replaced by the lapping of waves against the hull. But the inertia of the ship's motion continued to carry it slowly forward.

"Doesn't look like your brother's in control either. What'll happen now?" asked Miranda.

"Whatever happens, we're all in the same boat," said Caleb, who had joined them by then. "As my wise old mama always say, '*In a moment, in the twinkling of an eye, at the last trumpet: we shall be changed.*'"

"And freed, I hope," said J.P. As far he was concerned, his wards were now liberated from any constraints he might have placed on them. For him to feel completely free, however, he needed to hear that they in turn forgave him his faults. "I hope your mercy will extend to me," he said to his daughter and the others. "As well as everyone else," he added, knowing it was not something he could compel. "And if perchance, someone in the future should read about our deeds, would they be able to forgive us as well?"

In response to Miranda's earlier question, Frederic replied, "The Coast Guard will find us. There's a human network at work in the world to rescue people who are in need or go astray."

"I can almost share your optimism," said J.P.

At that moment a flare went up from the bow to send the alarm to anyone who might spot the scarlet arc.

The little group continued to stand at the rail, staring out, and wondering. A few others had come up from down below, puzzled by what was going on. The motion of the boat gradually slowed, and they could no longer feel a breeze. Utter calm—as in the eye of a storm, or was it more like the situation after the worst had passed? The craft continued its course on the outgoing tide; the fog began to dissipate, and the clouds to dissolve. After a mile or two, someone called out, "What's that ahead?"

Before them, the dark form of a tower rose a hundred or so feet out of the water.

"Sand Island Lighthouse," said J.P. "We're headed right toward it."

The ancient brick structure, its beacon long dormant and Fresnel lamp relegated to a museum, nonetheless provided a focal point for the moment. They knew they would have to wait a long time for the light they had lost, however. Soon a slow, sliding, crunching sound indicated that they had hit the shoals, and presently the ship came to rest altogether in the sand.

Ariel, who had failed to restore the power, reappeared on deck, continuing to sing:

> Take me in your lifeboat,
> Oh, take me in your lifeboat
> It will bear my spirit home.

Home? What is that? wondered J.P. Hadn't he left it long ago? He recalled how in the previous spring the empty house to which he had returned had seemed strange to him, and that it was something he himself had to make livable. How had the philosopher of hope once described *Heimat*, the homeland? "*Something that will appear in the world when humans comprehend themselves without estrangement in true democracy, something that shines into everyone's childhood, but where no one has actually ever been.*" It's in the future then: nostalgia that seeks a homecoming in restoration would be false and reactionary. We should reflect on the path needed to get there, which will have given us what we need when we finally arrive. So says that recent poet, a descendant of Greek predecessors, who maintains it's where we're destined to arrive, though there's no hurry and it's better if the voyage lasts for years and you're older and wiser by the time you get there: Ithaka granted you the marvelous journey, but now has nothing more to give.

J.P. heard the voice of Thomas Gonzalez asking if it wouldn't be better to disembark, since the boat continued to rock somewhat precariously and might drift out to sea again. Were they to be stranded on a tiny desert isle like figures in a cartoon? Was this the necessary comedy that would allow them "*to cheerfully depart from their past,*" as humanity had long ago done with respect to the Greek gods? A rope ladder was thrown overboard, and one by one they descended to the island, making their way ashore as their prehistoric, piscine ancestors once had. Thomas Gonzalez tried to reassure the ones among them that seemed distressed: "Don't worry, we're not lost. People have found children, parents, spouses, life partners.

And ourselves, our way in life." J.P. could not determine whether Anthony rolled his eyes, but he himself felt at peace.

Arrayed along the beach, they looked toward the east. For a brief moment at least, they stood together as equals—but as a random conglomeration or a unified family? The shifting sand at their feet was connected by the water to those other shores on the far side of the globe which J.P. had visited in his lifetime and where other humans had dwelled and left their legacy. The sky had a pearly, abalone iridescence, a shade somewhere between lemon and rose. What did the color portend, they wondered, storm ahead, or a radiant day? The sun, bright shining, would soon be rising. And then? If they looked west, toward the future, would they perceive themselves only as moving shadows? A line of pelicans flew low across the water, in solemn awareness of their destination. The passengers from the boat gazed out on the restless wavelets and knew without turning on a radio what the prognosis would be: A light chop in protected waters. But although they didn't need a weatherman's forecast to know that their situation, unlike that of so many people in other places and times, was not immediately dire and that their individual petty problems were relatively minor in the greater scheme of things, their task was no less urgent. Would the deceptive sense of calm continue to lull them into complacency, or would they be challenged to take on the needed changes by storm? As another poet wrote, not just fare well, but fare forward. They still had to determine what their own next course should be to keep themselves and the lands on which they stood and dwelt from being inundated.

The solar disc appeared above the horizon, transforming the ocean into a glitter of myriad suns, a string of pearls as varied as those who surveyed it. Miranda, looking as if in wonder at the people gathered together around her, and intrepid as ever, stated, "I can tell it's the beginning of something new. Maybe we'll all have a chance now, if we can find the strength to dare."

α₂
Epilogue

What came next, I did not see nor can I tell.
The arts of Calchas remain not unfulfilled.
Justice tilts her scales toward those who suffer
    as they learn,
and we will know the future when it comes.
Welcome it not beforehand, nor mourn it all
    too soon:
We will discern it clearly in the light of dawn.
          —Aeschylus, *Agamemnon*, 458-53

*T*HE GRADUAL WANING OF THE HOWLING *of the winds to intermittent squalls, and the subsiding of seas from their furious churning to a quavering expanse of little wavelets—the strange disconnects after the passage of a storm that has seemed to demolish even syntax, as people grope to explain what happened, and to destroy even time, which cannot be recovered, leaving only the necessity of going forward, without the precise knowledge how—the pictures of the stark devastation from wind and water which bring the awareness that a catastrophe has occurred, though not the ability to comprehend it—the widespread, and seemingly incongruous feeling of gratitude in one's own neighborhood that one has not suffered worse, even when the damage is painfully severe—the gathering up of the handful of objects that are still salvageable, such as a few precious family photos that have escaped the deluge—the immediate sharing of a bounty of food to prevent its spoilage in the now useless freezers—the recognition that others have suffered more, and a sympathy for their plight, which leads to the writing of checks and gathering of necessary goods, accompanied by a general numbness and paralysis that imposes a sort of distance to the victims and an inability to do more—the simultaneous greed in even these circumstances that leads some individuals to cheat the sufferers or to loot, and institutions to fail to provide what is needed—the anger that more was not done sooner to aid those stranded in rising water, an anger that all too often finds its* *only outlet in assigning blame—a realization of the need to take preventive steps and to shore up the infrastructure against threats that only a few seem to know are real, even though this storm will never be the last—a vague cognizance of the need to ward off those other storms of our own making by building a human infrastructure that guarantees liberty and justice, and the general welfare, of all—the call for a harmony between our lives and nature, knowing that we ourselves could demolish our own grand world with engines of our own devising in war or with instruments of imagined progress and temporary comfort which heat the climate to the breaking point and unleash hurricanes like we've never seen before—the gradual lull in this awareness, as the memory of the storm recedes, bringing an inability to fully draw the consequences and finally complete the task at hand because the winds have ceased blowing and the motion of the waters has moderated to short, broken movements. . . Yet: a determination to begin the renewal forced by the destruction, to pick up the pieces and start again after the big bang, as the twenty-four hours end and the diurnal cycle starts anew, when the dawn follows the darkest hour—*

• • •

"It's not me that has the last word, but you."
"We're on our way."

Acknowledgments

This book could not have been created alone: thanks are due to many, starting with the Bard whose *Tempest* provided an impetus to the plot and configuration of characters and proceeding to those many authors and singers over the centuries whose words are quoted and alluded to in the text and who make up so much of the life of the characters and of all of us. Those volumes could not have been acquired without the independent booksellers who stock them and the many libraries which serve as valuable repositories for this essential human knowledge: the libraries of the University of South Alabama and Wake Forest University are two that I consulted frequently. All translations from the German, Greek, and Latin are my own. In addition to the authors directly quoted, books and articles by the following were helpful in providing background information: foreign service officers Henry E. Catto, Jr., Nicholas Cull, Wilson P. Dizard, Jr., and Julius W. Walker, Jr. on the USIA; Bill Finch, Sam Hodges, William Rabb, and Daniel Cusick on the Mobile-Tensaw Delta and pollution in that area; and Silviane Diouf on the *Clotilda* and those it brought over (the publication of Zora Neale Hurston's *Barracoon* and the discovery of the slave ship's remains occurred after I completed my fourth chapter and long after the book's initial genesis around the turn of the century).

And I greatly appreciate the help of the many friends, family, and others who took the time to read drafts and responded with encouragement, criticism, comments, helpful suggestions, or combinations of all these: Kurt Corriher, Warren Dunn, Paul Gallis, Sally Jones Heinz, Miller Jones, Sam Jones, Christin Loehr, Pat Oglesby. Maya Pindyck, Phil Ray, Harry Roddy, David Sauer, Jan Sauer, Charles Skinner, and Tom Skinner, as well as to those whom I have perhaps failed to mention and to whom I apologize. Many of their suggestions helped make this a better book.

And of course to my immediate family, who also provided help, made it all possible, and without whom it would not have been worth it: to my daughters Sara, Miriam, and Jess and their spouses Rory

O'Dea, Brian Indre, and Jules Ohman, to my granddaughter Isabel, and especially Christa, who has had faith in the project from the start.

www.ingramcontent.com/pod-product-compliance
Lightning Source LLC
Chambersburg PA
CBHW030632020726
47493CB00006B/1678